THE MONSTERS OF SAINT MARK'S BOOK THREE

ST MARK

ROYAL BEASTS

NEW YORK TIMES BESTSELLING AUTHOR JA HUSS WRITING AS

KC CROSS

Edited by RJ Locksley
Cover Design by JA Huss

ABOUT THE BOOK

*W*hen a two-thousand-year-old curse is the only thing keeping you safe, you should probably just leave it alone.

Here's the problem—the curse is now breaking itself. The sanctuary is crumbling, Pell's anger issues come with a new destructive voice, Pie has no control over her spellings, and Tomas is trying to convince himself that, one day, Madeline is going to love being a dragon.

Add in an old friend (minus her couch and plus a big blue bus filled with orphan kids), a new version of Granite Springs where the devil lives in a bar, a hundred monsters reliving the teenage-years they never had, and a date to a prom in 1982 and we're getting close to the chaos that's coming.

Other worlds are calling, the new doors act like hallways, and nothing that mattered before matters now. The world is quickly changing and when the curse finally breaks for good —will there be anything left?

Royal Beasts is the third rompy paranormal, shifter, dragon, monster, ancient-Roman-gods rom-com in the Monsters of Saint Mark's series. You can't skip - so it must be read in order. KC Cross is the paranormal/sci-fi romance pen name of New York Times bestselling author, JA Huss.

PART ONE

The fairy tale can go awry
Just ask Tomas, Pell, and Pie
Happy endings are the goal
But they can also steal your soul.

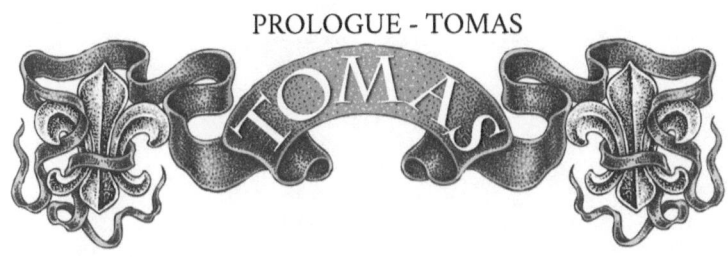

Once upon a time—in the land of damaged gods, savage saints, and royal beasts—there lived a dragon called Tomas.

That's how they all start, isn't it?

The fairy tale. The quest. The hero's journey.

And I have made myself the hero, haven't I?

Because I am. I truly am.

I'm the one who burned the sanctuary down to save Pie and Pell.

I'm the one who burned the town of Granite Springs to save Madeline.

I'm the savior, aren't I?

And, if history is reliable—and it always is, my darling—I will do it again to… well. Save someone else, of course.

And then we will all have our happy ending, won't we?

Of course we will. It's the rules. It has been written, as they say.

The ending will be glorious, I cross my heart and hope to die.

But first, before we get there, a little bit of filler…

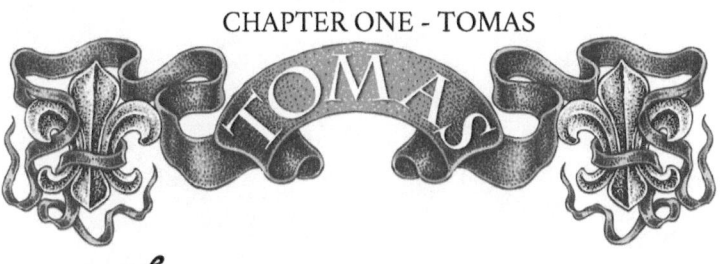

I am no longer Tomas.

I might never be Tomas again.

I'm not sure how I know that who and what I am is variable—like the hallways upstairs—and I don't know the mechanisms, of course, but I do fully understand that I am no longer Tomas.

Perhaps I shall give myself a new name to celebrate this change?

"What should we call me?" I walk over to Madeline and kneel down. She cowers away from me, the fear wild in her eyes. "Hmm?" I push a piece of sweaty hair away from her face with the tip of my sharp claw so I can see those eyes. They are changing.

"I don't... what?" She's breathing hard, eyes darting, trying to see everything. It's very dark in here but like her body being covered with scales—and me, becoming new me —her eyes are changing. So I'm mostly certain that she can see.

"I need a new name, Madeline. I'm no longer Tomas."

"Tomas?" She squints at me. Like, if she just narrows those eyes a teeny bit more, it might all make sense.

I smile at her, then pet her head. "Dear, sweet Madeline. You don't need to be afraid."

"A-a-afraid?" She mewls the word out.

"Not of me, beloved girl."

"I d-d-don't understand. What's happening? Where am I? Why am I here?"

She has asked me these questions a dozen times already. Her memory isn't so good.

But then again, neither is mine.

And it *is* a confusing time. I think we can all agree on that.

"You died, my love."

"Died?"

"That's right. That Russ Roth." His name comes out as a low, throaty growl. "He shot Big Jim, too."

"Oh, my God. What's happening?" She's becoming hysterical. But this is normal. She's mostly been hysterical since she woke up from her death.

I gently take her arm and hold it up. "Look, darling." It takes a moment for her to focus on the ammolite scales that now cover her entire arm up to her neck, but then there it is. The recognition.

"Oh, my God!" She's wailing. Kicking at me. Trying to scoot herself back deeper into the corner. "Oh, my God!"

I put a finger up to my lips. "Shhhhhhhh. You're just fine, my love."

"Who *are* you?"

"I'm the dragon who is no longer Tomas."

"Dragon!" And then her face becomes a mixture of disgust and horror. "What the—Oh, my—You're so... horrible! What is this?" She looks around like a cornered, feral animal.

I snap my clawed fingers in front of her eyes. "That's enough. It's fine if my true self horrifies you, but you don't need to be rude about it. A little self-control goes a long way."

She turns inward then, covering her face, and shaking her head, and sobbing loudly.

I sigh and lean back against the wall, absently holding her hand, still petting her. "It's going to be fine. You'll see. It's all going to be fine. There's a happy ending in our future, Madeline. There truly is. It might take a few thousand years to get there, but it's the journey, right? Not the destination."

I have never really bought into this whole journey thing. I mean, what is the point of struggle and pain? To build character? Absurd.

If I had my way, we'd all skip to the end and just live the happily ever after. It's the goal, after all. Why bother with the journey?

Anyway, where were we?

Right. My new name.

It's a big deal. Such a big deal I take a nap while I think. But when I wake, I'm still not sure what I should be called. Something... with purpose.

Well, I shall have to think on that.

But for now, I just look around my home and try to appreciate it. Because like it or not, this is the only home I've ever had. I have been here for several thousand years with only Pell, and the occasional slave, to keep me company.

But things have changed considerably over the last few months. Especially the last few weeks.

And it all started with a girl called Pie.

Pie is the catalyst.

You see, this is how magic works. It's just like... like a chemical reaction, except it's magical. You start with a snippet of this and that, add something spectacular to the mixture, and *wooobam*! You get something brand-new.

Pie is our something spectacular.

Her presence in the magical reaction affects Pell and I both. Which is curious, but not something I want to think about now.

Right now, I just want to think about Pie.

I remember seeing her outside on the lawn, just standing in the front of the sanctuary looking down at herself. I might even have startled her when I called out.

I think she was going to leave.

I think I was the one who stopped her from doing that.

She blames Grant or that flier she saw for her change of fortune, but it was me. I was the one who really sealed her fate. Because if I had not been on the terrace that morning there would never have been a slave caretaker of Saint Mark's Sanctuary called Pie.

She went to the door and I went back inside fully intending on meeting her down there. But I got lost in the hallways. They took me on a trip. The time is fuzzy, but all I know is that when I finally did make it downstairs, I was new again.

It doesn't happen often, so it's quite a big deal.

I could touch things. And feel things. And I didn't have to wear the dragon body or the ghost one, either. I wasn't human, of course. Have never been human. But it was very nice to have legs and arms and a face a woman could appreciate.

My eyes dart to Madeline. She is covered in scales now. Even her face. Which, I have to admit, surprised me. Because my current face is not covered in scales. Only my lower body is. She is a gorgeous dragon, though. And maternal, too. The eggs are huge underneath her human-sized body. Massive, like boulders. But she sleeps on top of them, draping herself all over them, doing her best to keep them warm.

They are in no danger of getting cold now. Two dragons in the nest is more than enough heat. Our radiant bodies alone are enough to incubate them to the end. Neither of us needs to actually sit on them.

I reach over and slide my fingers down Madeline's red-scaled cheek.

She is a blood dragon, like me.

What are the chances?

One in a trillion, maybe?

"How are we feeling, darling?"

Madeline growls at me, snarling and snapping her sharp teeth, forcing me to pull my hand away.

I chuckle. "That's marvelous, my love."

She is… well, I would not call her a disappointment. Not at all. She is my new best friend. She is my new lover, though we're taking our time in that respect. She is my *partner*. We are in this together now and that feels wonderful.

But she is not as sweet as she used to be.

In fact, she is rather mean now.

I do not hold this against her. Waking up a dragon is a confusing time. In fact, everything about being a dragon is confusing.

I think I've mentioned this.

It makes one do… punishable things. Imprisonable things.

Which is part of how I got here, of course. Dragons will be dragons.

But she has me to help her along. I had no one when I was born, because I hatched out of the egg and wasn't transformed by a magical bat-person. But Madeline has me to guide her through this.

She is not a prisoner.

Yet.

And she will never be one, if I can help it.

Though, if the eggs hatch, there's not much chance we will be welcome anywhere.

But that's OK. There will be five of us then. Five dragons are enough to change the course of a universe and all we really want to do is escape this prison and be free to find our happy endings.

When I brought Madeline in here she was, for all intents and purposes, dead. But Batty owed me and he paid off his debt in magic, bringing her soul back to her body for a second chance.

Of course, his magic would not have worked if Madeline

JA HUSS

wasn't already who she is. Deep inside, she was always a dragon. Though on the outside, for the most part, she was just a lowly eros.

The dragon gene is recessive, popping up every seventh generation. I wish I had her whole family history. I would love to know her ancestors.

The eggs, though, are not hers. She will not reach reproductive age for centuries.

No. These eggs have been here in the dungeon with me for thousands of years. I had hundreds of them when I was banished to my prison, but most of them disintegrated from rot.

Only these three are left now. And until recently, they were nothing but petrified shells. There must be two dragons in close proximity for eggs to incubate. These three looked just like rocks before Madeline moved in. Like a bit of crumbling wall or foundation stones. But within minutes of her arrival they began to change, and glow, and undulate with the waking of the dragon hearts within.

Their blue-and-black mottled shells are transparent in places. And sometimes, when the heart light inside throbs just the right way, and the little buggers are in a particularly wriggly mood, I can see the outline of a tiny muzzle or a bit of wing.

How soon they will hatch depends on many factors. Heat, humidity, and, of course, desire.

For it is desire that drives a dragon.

"Hel-looooo?"

I perk up at the sound of a distant voice drifting down from the upper floors.

"Tomas?"

"Pie?" I get up and cross the dungeon until I am standing at the bottom of the stairs. "I'm here. Are you coming down?"

"Um... am I allowed to come down?"

"Your home is my home, so my home must be your home. Isn't that how it works?"

"Mmmm... is it?"

I chuckle. "You're so adorable. Now, stop being silly and come down the stairs."

She hesitates. "Well, I've been down there before and you tried to burn us alive."

"When?"

"When Pell was stealing scales for that banishing spell."

"Oh." I chuckle again. "Well, I was a dragon, Pie. Now I'm a... something else. I will not burn you. That's ridiculous. I barely breathe any fire at all these days."

"Barely?" Her voice is still distant. "You burned Granite Springs to the ground."

"Pshaw." I wave a hand in the air. "That was but a burp. A bit of indigestion."

"Indigestion? Did you... eat something I don't know about?"

"Stop being silly. Get down here."

The faint sound of footsteps echoes down the stairwell until finally she peeks her sweet face around a corner and brightens when she sees me. "Well, you still have arms and legs. That's a good sign."

I throw my arms up with flair. "May I present to you my extremities!"

"And you still look like Tomas."

"The same face you have known and loved."

She comes all the way around the corner and plants her hands on her hips. "Huh."

"What?"

"You look the same."

"Why would I change?"

She shoots me a look. "Because you're a dragon. I've seen it." She points at me. "You burned the crap out of me with

13

your hellfire. Pell had to rub magic gel all over my back to soothe it."

"I bet you liked that."

"Hmm." She considers this. "It did feel pretty nice. But it was a super-stressful time, so I didn't really get to enjoy that part. Are you busy?"

"Not at all. And even if I was, I would not turn you away. You're my first visitor since Madeline came to live here."

"Speaking of…" Pie's eyes dart around the dungeon. "How is she?"

"Oh, don't worry about her. She's adapting wonderfully and resting comfortably."

"Ooookay. Anyway. Batty just had a long conversation with Pell and me, but we can't understand him, of course." She continues her descent, holding up a piece of paper. "I need a favor. If you're up for it."

"A translation?"

"Yeah. Batty has been going on and on about all kinds of things and we have no clue what he's talking about. So I figured I'd come down—to check on you, of course, but also to get you to translate this convo we just had. If that's OK, that is. I don't want to interrupt you and Madeline." Pie's eyes dart over my shoulder, then squint a little in the darkness, trying to see Madeline in the shadows. "Are you sure she's OK?"

"She's quite well. But not the same, of course."

This makes Pie cringe. "Not the same… how?"

"Would you like to see her?"

"Will she burn me?"

"She can't breathe fire yet. So you're good."

"Yet?" Pie continues her descent. "But she will one day?"

"Most certainly. She's dragon through and through. Come look. Even her face is covered. This is unexpected, but quite delightful."

Pie stops when she reaches the bottom of the stairs, then looks over her shoulder nervously.

"Pell doesn't know you're here, does he?"

"No. He wants me to stay away from you."

I grin, suddenly flooded with warmth, and extend my hand to her. "But you can't, can you?"

She takes my hand and shrugs her shoulders in that cute way she does. "I can't. You're just... one of us, Tomas. We're a team now, ya know? And that means I need to make sure you're OK." A pause here. "You *are* OK, right?"

"Darling, I am better than OK. I am marvelous. We're starting a family."

Her smile wavers, and then I get a gulp and the brave face. "A... *family?*"

"Indeed."

"I don't understand. How—"

"Eggs, my dear. Eggs."

"Yeah, but... she laid eggs? Already?"

"Oh, my, no. Madeline won't be fertile for hundreds of years. These were leftover eggs. From that time before."

Pie's brow furrows. "OK. I need all the information on the eggs, of course. And con... grat... ulations? And while I do adore you"—she brightens, smiling bigger now—"I have questions, Tomas."

"I am happy to answer them to the best of my ability. So ask all the questions you want, Pie."

"OK, well, before I get to that, how about you just translate this for me?"

I take the offered piece of paper and read it, handing it back just a few seconds later. "They're out of food."

"What? How can that be? They ate a feast for breakfast."

"It's magic food, Pie. A talented magical cook, like Cookie, for instance, could whip a few blades of grass into a delightful bacon and egg quiche. But he has run out and needs more."

"Oh. OK. I guess that's fine."

"Assuming the feed store in Granite Springs will still sell it to you. I mean, they know you now."

"Assuming the feed store has feed, is more like it. The town is *gone*."

"What? But I heard it rebuilt itself."

"It did. Kind of. But not really."

"You're not making sense."

"Well, in my defense"—she huffs out a long breath of air and her hair puffs up around her face—"none of this really makes much sense. The town did rebuild itself. It's still there. Just… all the people have disappeared."

"Fascinating."

"I guess. I haven't been there yet, only Pell and Batty have. But if we have to go get hay, I'm getting in on that trip. So I'll report back."

"That's very considerate of you."

"It's no problem." She smiles, tight-lipped, and rocks on her heels a little.

"What?" I ask. "You have more questions?"

"I do." She sucks in a deep breath and exhales it out, like she's steeling herself for what comes next. "I found a new… level. To the sanctuary."

"Did you?"

"Mmm-hmm. I did. It's, um…"

"A prison?"

She points at me. "It is. It's a prison. And there are…"

"Many, many monsters down there?"

"Yep. So my question is…"

"Am I a prisoner?"

"Yes." She exhales this word out. "That's my question. Are you one of them?" She has a pained expression on her face.

"I am."

"Oh. But you're not in a tomb."

"No. I'm not. I'm in a dungeon. I am rather big in my

16

dragon state, so I suppose this whole place is my tomb." I spread my arms wide to encompass the entirety of the cathedral. "And this dungeon is my private quarters."

"Smells better now." Pie looks around with a little more interest. "The last time I was down here, it smelled like rotten eggs."

This makes me remember my new lot in life and so I smile. "Yes. Well, many things have changed over the past few weeks."

"New eggs, I guess."

"Not new. Old, but still viable. All they needed was my dear Madeline to complete the circuit, so to speak."

"Yeah. About her." Pie blinks a few times, like she's trying to process things. "I have many, many, many, many, *many* more questions about all of this. But first—and I don't mean to make this all about me, OK? I'm sympathetic to your situation and happy about your new..." Her eyes dart over to the dark corner where Madeline is hidden in the shadows. Madeline is beginning to growl. "Your new... family status. But Tomas, what is that Bottoms place?"

"Well, you got it in one, didn't you? It's a prison."

"But... who runs it?"

"Who? My dear, you are the slave caretaker, are you not?"

"Yeah. I am, but..."

"They are slaves and you take care of them."

She makes a face of pure confusion, her brow furrowed and her eyes narrowed. "What? Wait." She puts up a hand. "I thought *I* was the slave?"

"Well." I shrug. "I guess there are many ways to interpret the words 'slave caretaker.'"

"And... the Book of Debt? Remember that?"

"Oh, who could forget. I hear you have a new one."

Pie blows out a breath of air. Once again, her hair flies up around her eyes. "Yeah. But it's not my book. Well, I guess it is my book, since I'm the one in charge of it. But it's for my frickin' sister."

I point at her, beaming. "Congratulations on your new family member as well!"

She presses a palm at me. "Don't. I don't want to talk about it. But this slave thing, those prisoners... why are they here?"

"They are... criminals? Isn't that why prisons have people in them?"

"What did they do?"

"Aren't there books down there? Each of them should have one. I have one."

"You do?" Pie's eyebrows go up.

"Of course. We all have a Book of Debt, don't we? And we pay those debts off by making ourselves happy."

"Um. Yeah. No. That's not how it works."

"Of course it is. Don't you see, Pie? Your debt goes down when you get happy."

"No."

"Yes. Happy people make pheromones. Pheromones are the giddy-drug of the universe. When you make people unhappy, you create debt for yourself. When you make yourself happy, you clear your debt."

"Yeah. That's definitely *not* how this works, Tomas. I bought crap I didn't need from overpriced stores. That's how I got debt. Though I really did need those tires. And the food."

"Hmm."

"You were there. Remember?"

"Of course. I was thinking about the word 'debt.' It's a lot like the word 'slave.'"

"It's... really not. But I'm open to anything at this point, so keep going."

"You thought you were the 'slave caretaker.' Two words to

describe one thing. But what if you were the 'slave-caretak-er?' One hyphenated word that means something different."

"Well, I like the idea that I take care of slaves better than the idea that I am a slave taking care of something."

"Could you be both?"

She sighs, frustrated. "I don't know. But assuming I am the caretaker of the prisoners in the prison, what the hell do I do with them?"

"You could set them free."

"Why would I do that?"

"Why wouldn't you do that?"

My question appears to stump her and she frowns, but then rallies again. "Speaking of freedom, how come you're free?"

I pan my hands wide to encompass my dungeon. "Do I look free to you?"

"Well, you're not locked inside a tomb. And don't tell me you're locked in here. You go upstairs. You went into town. It's definitely not the same living conditions as the prisoners of Saint Mark's."

"Part of that was an illusion. Part of that was magic. Part of that is still a mystery. But I wasn't a real person until you came. I was more ghostly. Non-corporeal, if you will. Then you showed up and presto. I was whole."

"*Why* though?"

"How should I know? None of the titles at the end of my name include the word 'caretaker.'"

She blows out another breath of frustration.

"Is there anything else?"

She tilts her head at me. "You know, that's twice now."

"Twice what?"

"Two times that you saved the sanctuary from outsiders."

"Hmm." I smile. "I did, didn't I? First time I burned the whole place down, second time I burned the town. But it's not gone. Only the people are. That's so interesting, don't you think?"

"Not sure I'd choose that word specifically. No. Pell has been there and he says there's a devil waiting in the bar."

"Oooooh. Sounds volatile."

"Yeah. I guess it does. We're gonna have to figure that out." She nods her head to the corner. "And her, Tomas. What if they come looking for her?"

"Madeline's kin are not coming to look for her, Pie."

"Why wouldn't they?"

"They don't want her. That's why she's here. The sanctuary doesn't let any old monster in. There's a selection process."

Far away, coming from high up in the main floor, a name floats through the air.

"Pell is calling for you."

Pie's eyes dart upward, then over to the corner again. "Is she OK?"

"She's lovely. Gorgeous. Beautiful. Perfect. And she will be the mother of my dragons."

"So. Many. Questions." But Pie's eyes once again drift upward.

"Later. Come back another time when you're not so busy."

She sighs. "OK. But you don't have to stay down here, right?"

"You tell me, dear Pie. You're the slave caretaker."

"Right. I'm gonna need that book of yours."

"I'm sure it's in the Bottoms library with all the rest. When you're done with it, bring it down. I'd love to reminisce."

"Well, OK, I guess I need to go see what's got Pell all grumbly. And you two..." Pie stops. Blinks. And then blurts out, "'A girl, a boy, a brand-new home. Eggs forged out of stone and bone. The dragon blood lifts you higher and the dungeon walls flow red with fire.'"

Neither of us moves. Or speaks. Or breathes.

Then the walls of the dungeon begin to sparkle with red bursts of light. It flashes so bright, I have to cover my eyes for a moment. But once the flash is over, I squint at them, trying to see what happened. "Rubies? Are those rubies sparkling in the walls?"

Pie blinks, then laughs. "I totally meant to do that. Congrats to... both of you. Just a little housewarming gift from us to you. And... well, yeah. I gotta go. See you soon, Tomas!"

She turns on her heel and trots away before I can even process what just happened.

I watch her disappear up the winding, stone stairs, then look around at the walls. There must be hundreds of gemstones embedded in the rock. Maybe thousands. And they emit a soft, and quite nice, light.

"Thank you!" I belatedly call in the direction of the stairs. "We love it!"

Then I turn back to my Madeline.

I walk over her and bend down. The eggs are placed in a massive dish-shaped dent in the stone ground. Our nest. Madeline's body is draped over two of the eggs, looking very maternal. When I push the hair away from her scaly face, she opens her eyes.

She looks terrified.

CHAPTER TWO - PELL

I come out of my tomb alone.

Which is not how it's supposed to be. When a man has a woman, as I have a woman, should a man not have that woman by his side when he leaves his tomb?

Is this caveman thinking?

Because I think it's reasonable that Pie should not wander alone around a fucking frat-house sanctuary filled with horny satyrs and half-naked wood nymphs.

All these monsters have been doing since the girls arrived is drinking, and smoking, and having sex.

And now Pie, *my* Pie, is out here among them after I specifically told her that I would like to accompany her around the grounds from now on.

Of course, she didn't agree to that. She just smiled at me, and patted my chest, and then gave me a kiss and called me 'cute.'

Cute? I am not cute. I am the Monster of Saint Mark's. She can call me 'formidable.' She can call me 'grumpy.' She can call me 'mercurial.' 'Dynamic' is a great describer of the monster that is me. She can even call me 'beautiful,' if she wants, though 'cut and handsome' is preferred.

But cute? No. I am not cute.

And I am not joking about her wandering the sanctuary alone these days. It's... too much. And when I complained to Batty about it, he called me a name in a language I don't even speak. But I got the gist of it. And while 'crotchety' isn't a word I would typically use to describe myself—'cut,' 'hand-some,' and 'dynamic' really are the winners here—it's a helluva lot better than 'cute'.

I'm just turning a corner in the maze of tombs when a monster carrying a squealing, naked nymph on his back goes racing past, clipping me in the shoulder. I spin, almost fall—thank God for cloven hooves—and then it almost happens again when two more monsters go by, their nymphs also shrieking with delight as their tits and asses bounce all over the place.

I sigh and look to the sky, asking for patience. "Do they ever grow up?"

"What's wrong, handsome? Feeling left out?"

I turn towards the sultry voice coming from behind me and find Nysta—Tarq's beloved woman—coming around the side of a tomb.

She isn't walking though. She's... like... slithering. It's weird. Everything about her is slow, and seductive, and scorching. Like she's trying to seduce the entire world. Even the tomb she's backed up against.

The wood nymphs used to be my go-to girls. I really liked them when I was young and new. They were so exciting. Always naked up top. And the breasts on these girls? Nice. All of them. Don't even get me started on their asses. Even when they're clothed, they are sexy as fuck. They wear flowy skirts or harem pants made of translucent, pastel fabrics. And their long, waterfall hair bounces when they walk. The little bejeweled silk slippers on their feet really pull the whole thing together.

But they have legs. And by legs, I mean humanish legs. Not monster legs, like my Pie. And no horns, or antlers, or fur either. They are pure wood nymphs. A rare breed, actually, unlike the chimera. In fact, I think every wood nymph in the known universe currently resides here at Saint Mark's.

They walk around here like they're high on lust, batting

their eyelashes, and swinging their hips, and puckering their lips. Practically begging any monster who walks by to bed them.

And Nysta is the most seductive of them all.

Everything about her is sex.

Which is fine, I guess. It's just her nature. Wood nymphs are famous for their sex appeal the same way satyrs are known for their big dicks.

But come on. Turn it off once in a while, ya know?

"Good morning, Nysta." Despite her constant cajolery, I am polite to her. She *is* Tarq's woman, which means she is practically family. "Not feeling left out, but thank you for asking how I am. I'm looking for Pie. Have you seen her?"

"Pie." Nysta taps her chin with a manicured fingernail. "Pie. Hmm. I don't think I know a Pie."

My eyes go lazy and low, so bored. "My woman. Pie? Remember her? She runs the magic in this place?"

"Oh, her. She was flirting with that bat-winged monster. I forget his name."

"Batty?" I deadpan this, even though Nysta deserves to be mocked.

"Yes! That's it. Batty. I saw her flirting with Batty over there." Nysta waggles her finger in a random direction. "You better go break that up, big boy. That bat-man is sexy, isn't he?"

"Um." Yeah, that's a big no. There isn't a chance in hell that Pie is flirting with Batty. But Nysta is a pot-stirrer. She's more than a troublemaker, she's a provocateur. And more times than not, the people she's prodding into action are willing to do her bidding.

I'm starting to think she's using some sort of magic to make this happen. Like a spell to compel.

I decide this conversation is over. "Thank you." Then I bow a little out of respect for Tarq. "Have a nice day, Nysta."

"Hold on there!" Nysta slithers over to me and places a

hand on my shoulder. It's a light hand, very delicate. "I have been asking all over the sanctuary, but no one can seem to tell me how one gets to town."

"What?"

"Town, monster. I would like to go to town. I have needs."

"What are these needs?"

"Never mind my needs, they're private. Apparently, you have the keys I need to secure transport. Can I have them?" She stares at me, straight in the eyes, and her eyes... flicker a little.

"No."

"What? What do you mean no? The answer is yes, big man. Yes. Give me the keys to the transport." She holds out her hand, palm up, and wiggles her fingers in anticipation.

"Nysta. You're not getting the keys and you're not going to town."

"Says who?"

"Says me. You know, the master of this place?"

She looks confused for a moment and yep, I was right. She is using magic cajolery to influence people. And for some reason, it does not work on me.

I smile at her. "I am the master of Saint Mark's. Whatever magic you're using on the others? Not gonna work on me. Now if you'll excuse me, I have matters to attend to."

I push past her and turn the corner of a tomb as she huffs, and sputters, and cusses me in low whispers behind me.

Immediately, I come upon a gathering of drunk satyrs with wood nymphs in their laps. They are kissing, and writhing, and generally doing things that satyrs and wood nymphs do when left to their own devices.

But, my God, enough already.

I just keep going. Even though I hate all these people here mucking up my privacy, and peacefulness, and solitude, I do not want to become the buzzkill guy.

I'm not their mother. I should not care what they do, as

long as they're not hurting anyone. And from what I can tell, everyone is pretty happy with the way things shook out.

So whatever. I let it go.

I turn the final corner of a tomb, heading towards the cathedral, when I notice there is a mob of monsters down in the little back patio area. They are arguing about something.

I lower my head, do not look them in the eye, and mutter, "Please, please, please," in a praying way as I walk past.

But it doesn't work. They start calling for me. They don't say the name Pell—they call me something else—but I know, in their tongue or whatever, this is my name. It comes out as a bunch of syllables mushed together. I can't even spell it, but if I had to try, I would say the name they're calling me is Mulfeffur.

Pie has shortened it to Muffler, so of course now they all call me Muffler. "It's cute," she said, patting my chest.

That word again.

I look up at the sky just as the mob of monsters approaches me and yell, "I am not cute!"

Everything vibrates and there's a commotion off to my left as plaster slides down the wall of a tomb.

This voice. That's another thing. Every time I put emotion into it, it causes something like that to happen. My words shake things.

Just then, Eyebrows appears with his stupid tape measure. He starts measuring my legs. Inner thigh first, like I need another pair of fucking pants. I have an entire closet full already. His hand bumps my dick, and I flash him teeth. In this same moment, Cookie is in my face going on, and on, and on about things I don't understand, waving a butcher knife around in the air.

Then they're all there. Complaining about... whatever. And I'm not in the mood, so I growl at them, bare my teeth at them, then say with way too much emotion, "Get out of my way!"

27

A tomb collapses, and I just sigh.

It's a good thing this place can repair itself. Because my voice is starting to make a mess of things.

The monsters gasp. Then whisper. Then disperse.

Well, at least that voice is good for something.

But I'm unsettled now. Wood nymphs, and satyrs, and dragons.

Speaking of dragons, this whole thing with Tomas has me worried. And I'm starting to get a sneaking suspicion that this is where Pie is right now. She told me last night—all casual and shit—that she was going to go visit him today.

I, of course, forbade her. Which made her giggle, and pat my chest, and call me cute.

I raise my fist in the air. "I am not cute!"

Another tomb crumbles. Poof. It is dust.

More gasping and whispering occurs all around me. But now the monsters have the good sense to hide behind tombs as they talk their shit.

I go into the cathedral and take the stairs up to the main level seven at a time. This used to be the great hall, and it's still a pretty great hall, but now it's a full-time dining room. There are a few monsters lingering by the tables and when I approach, they start pointing to the tables.

"What?" I'm so annoyed now.

They point to the tables again.

"I don't know what you're talking about. Have you seen Pie?"

They argue for a moment, but then one of them points to the hallway that leads to the real dining room, but also leads to the dungeon.

"I knew it." I grumble my words out. Then I head in that direction, calling Pie's name.

The hallways rearrange, as they tend to do on this side of the cathedral, but they spill me out into a hallway that I know leads to Tomas's dungeon.

And who do I find there, just kicking back against the stone wall?

"Batty." This word vibrates the air and the torches around me flicker when I say his name. "Where's Pie?"

I don't really need to ask. I know she's down there. "Pie!" I call out, trying not to put too much emotion in it. Still, it comes out a little frustrated.

The torches flicker again, but no walls crumble.

Hmm. Interesting. I wonder if the moving hallways are immune to my new power?

"Stop bellowing, Pell! I'm coming!"

And sure enough, a moment later, Pie appears in a stair-well that was not there a moment before.

"Did I or did I not forbid you from going down there to see Tomas?"

Pie just grins as she walks over to me. Then she pats my chest. "You're so cute with all your caveman stuff, Pell."

"I am not cute!" And once again, no walls shake from my annoyance.

"Oh, of course you are. You're not allowed to boss me, Pell. Well"—she tilts her head, like she's thinking about this— "you can boss me all you want because I think it's cute, but don't expect me to listen."

I'm about ready to argue with her, but then she bats those long eyelashes of hers—flashing eyes as blue as the sky—and I momentarily get lost in them. Before I know it, I'm smiling.

She leans up on her tiptoes and kisses my cheek, then takes her mouth to my ear and whispers, "Cute."

Even this makes me smile. And a whole slew of happy feelings floods my body.

Batty clears his throat, trying to break up our moment. And immediately, I'm annoyed again. I miss my peaceful sanctuary. I just want time alone with Pie. Time where she is not worried about everyone, or trying to make the monsters happy, or thinking about the future.

"Oh," Pie says. "Yep. I got the translation—"

"What translation?"

"That's why I had to go see Tomas. Who, by the way, is… scary. And there is an egg situation down there that we really need to talk about. But later. First—" She holds up a piece of paper and turns to Batty. "I get it. You guys need more food. We'll get that today, all right?"

Batty spends the next minute and a half talking to himself, and Pie lets him do this. "It makes them feel listened to," she told me the other day. "This is a sanctuary, Pell. A place of refuge for monsters. I feel like it's our mission to make them comfortable."

But this is not my mission. My mission is to get rid of them so Pie and I can have the whole place to ourselves. Tomas can stay, but eggs? I don't know. Kids? I'm not good with kids. I can't even remember the last time I talked to a child, let alone cared about one.

"Pell?"

I snap out of my introspection and look down at Pie. "What?"

"Town, right?" She waves a hand at Batty. "I think he's waiting for you to agree." But then she shoots Batty a sharp look. "Though he's not the boss of me, so… if I tell you I will get you hay, I will get you hay."

Batty smiles at Pie. But he's humoring her, I can tell.

And so can she. Because she tilts her head as she looks at Batty, like she wants to say more about how 'in charge' she is.

I point at her. "Cute."

She slaps my hand away. "Don't placate me."

"I'm not. And he's not. I'll get the hay. Happy?"

"Not you, Pell. *We*." She points to herself and me.

But then Batty is pointing at himself as well, wanting to be included.

I don't want Pie to come, but it's either take her with me

or leave her behind with all these sex addicts. "Fine, you can come."

"I can?" She brightens, pressing her palms together like she's praying, and then claps using only the tips of her fingers.

"You can. And so can you." I point to Batty. "I don't understand what's going on with the town. It could get dangerous."

"How dangerous?"

"Well... the devil is waiting for me in that bar."

"Hmm." Pie seems to be changing her mind. "Maybe I shouldn't go?"

"No. You have to go. You can't stay here with all these degenerates." Batty takes offense to this, but I growl at him, "Everywhere I turn, people are fucking. I'm tired of it. I'm tired of the parties, and the sex, and laughter."

Both Batty and Pie just stare at me, like I'm being unreasonable.

"What? I like my peace and quiet."

"It's a sanctuary, Pell." And here she goes again. "It's our job to protect them."

"Protect them? The walls protect them. I feel that it is my job to maintain order."

Batty snaps at me. And once again, I don't need to speak his language to get the gist of it. He's telling me to do that, if that's my job.

"I will," I retort back. "You watch."

"OK, boss man." Pie chuckles and pats my chest.

I point at her. "Do not call me cute."

"Fine. I'll call you Grumpy from now on. Grumps. Let it be known"—Pie raises her voice—"that the monster formally called Pell is now called Grumps!"

Batty says, "Muffler." Then he and Pie both break down in a fit of snickers. I sigh, so annoyed with this day and the sun just barely came up.

Batty flies while Pie and I drive the truck. The weather is cold and there's a little bit of snow coming down. But it's the fog a few miles outside of town that really gets my attention.

"Is this normal?" Pie asks, leaning forward and squinting as we crawl through the thick haze.

"It is now. I'm pretty sure it means the entire town has been glamoured."

"But the fog? I don't get it. It's like that same fog before I put the ring on."

"Hmm."

"Do you think it means we're in some kind of in-between stage?"

"It's possible. But I can't say for sure. I've only ever seen the fog around Saint Mark's."

"But you said that Grant glamoured the town, right?"

"I assumed he did. To make them forget about us. But there was never any fog involved."

"Well, this has to mean something. We need to figure it out."

"Yeah," I agree. But it comes out as a long, tired sigh.

"You really have been grumpy, Pell. What's up?"

"What's up?" I just look at her for a moment. "Really?"

"You hate the monsters."

"I don't hate them. I just don't want them around. I miss the old days when it was just me, and you, and Tomas." I shrug. "Is that evil?"

"No." She giggles a little. "Not evil at all. But don't you think that the whole point of the sanctuary is to... you know... provide sanctuary to wayward monsters?"

"I would think that. Maybe. If there wasn't a door inside my tomb that leads to a monster prison in an alternate, upside-down parallel universe. Maybe we're keeping the world safe from those monsters and that's why it's a sanctuary? Maybe you're assuming too much when it comes to the new residents?"

"Maybe," Pie agrees. "But either way, these monsters need our help. And the wood nymphs were your idea. I wash my hands of Tarq. I know he's your friend, but I don't trust him."

I sigh again. We have had this conversation about Tarq a dozen times, at least.

"I'm not complaining about the nymphs, Pell. Or Tarq. I'm not the boss of you, either. So you can be friends with anyone you want. But I would like to register my hesitation with this whole 'king' thing. And I'm not going back to Vinca. Ever. I don't like it. I don't even care if I'm from there, I live here now. I'm staying here."

"What about Callistina?"

"What about her?"

I shoot her a look. This look comes with one eyebrow raised. "You haven't been back down to the Bottoms since the day you put her there."

"So?"

"Don't you think you should check up on her?"

"Not particularly."

I raise that eyebrow again, side-eyeing her as we crawl through the fog.

"What?"

"You put your sister, the Queen of Vinca—who is kind of a spectacular lioness chimera, I might add—"

"What's that got to do with anything?"

"Nothing."

"You think she's pretty."

"She's not my type. You're my type."

Pie makes a face. It's a wrinkled one and comes with narrowed eyes. "I'm gonna let this go, but I'm taking notes."

I stop the truck, take her hand, and place it against my

chest, my heart thumping under the pressure of her hand. "Pie Vita?"

"What?"

"This heart belongs to you. And while Callistina is a striking specimen, a woman..." I shake my head. "A woman she is not. Because women, even strong women such as yourself, are soft. They are not made of sharp edges. They are made of curves, and whispers, and long quiet moments." I remove her hand from my heart and bring it up to my lips, kissing her knuckles. Pie smiles. Maybe even melts a little. "So to be clear, Callistina is not, and never will be, a threat to my love for you. No matter what she looks like. And this is all beside the point because the point is... you need to go down there and—"

"No." Pie narrows her eyes and pulls her hand away. "I'm not ready for that."

"But that's where all the answers are, Pie. Don't you think we need those answers?"

"You just want to get rid of the monsters."

I can't deny this, so I don't bother trying.

"And besides, you haven't been back to Vinca, either."

"That's because Tarq needs time."

"Time to do what?"

"Learn to rule. I can't be there, cramping his style."

Pie snorts, then points at me. "I think you know I'm right."

"Right about what?"

"That making Tarq king was a very bad idea. You know this, you just won't admit it. And when you go back there, you're gonna see that."

I don't answer her. Not because this matter has been settled, but because even though we have been idling in the road for a couple of minutes now, the fog has parted around the truck.

Suddenly, a large wooden sign comes into view on the

side of the road. At one time it was painted white, but that paint has crackled with age and flaked off in several spots. The lettering is elaborate and large, done by hand, the way it used to be done a hundred years ago.

Pie leans forward, squinting at it. "Wow. That's new, right?"

"It is."

"It doesn't say 'Granite Springs' though. What's that about?"

She's right. The sign does not say 'Granite Springs.' It says 'Welcome to Savage Falls.' "I'm not sure."

"Hmm. Should we go somewhere else, Pell?"

"Where?"

"I don't know. But this is rural PA. There has to be another place to buy hay."

Just then, Batty lands in front of us, apparently intrigued by the new sign as well. He walks over to it, then looks at us. Pie cranks her window down. "What's up?"

Batty chatters on and on about something, which does us no good since we can't understand him. "You really need to come up with a potion so we can understand them, Pie."

She looks over at me. Blinks. Then, "'A tooth, a tongue, a mouth and lips.'"

I narrow my eyes at her. "What?"

"'A whispered call in a hall of quips.'"

"What are you talking about?"

"'A monster's words carved from stone. Listen now. They are known.'"

"Pie?"

She blinks again, then laughs. "I totally meant to do that."

"Meant to do what?"

Batty is still talking, but now he makes sense. "I'm telling you two assholes, this is not safe. Do you see this sign? He's warning us. We should go back. Like... right now."

"B-b-batty?" Pie stutters.

"Why do you people never listen?"

"We're listening," I growl. "You just called us assholes."

"What?" Batty looks surprised.

"I totally meant to do that," Pie blurts.

But she didn't. The spell just came out of her mouth and now we can understand Batty.

"Well," Batty says. He tugs on an imaginary coat, like he's trying to straighten it, even though he's only wearing fur. "Finally. You fucking people. I'm so sick of talking to myself. And by the way, my name is *Darrel*."

I look at Pie.

"I totally meant to do that."

"You didn't."

"I—" But she stops. "OK, fine. I'm having a little trouble controlling my spellings. But it's OK, right? I mean, we understand him now. That's convenient, isn't it?"

She's scared, I realize. Not that I will get mad about her not being able to control the magic, but scared because she doesn't understand what's happening. "Right," I say. "It's totally fine."

It's not. It's very bad. But I want to think about this before I panic her more.

"Can we just get on with this, then?" Batty says. "If you're going to insist that we shop here, let's do it quickly."

I can hear Pie's heartbeat and smell her fear. So I reach over, place my hand on her leg, and say in the most calm voice I can manage, "It's great. That language spell was exactly what we needed."

Immediately, her heartbeat slows and her fear recedes. Like my gentle words have just as much power as my menacing ones.

Everything is changing. And even though change is not only inevitable, but welcome—I have been stuck in a curse for thousands of years, after all—it's scary for me too. I want things to change. I do. I want to be rid of these duties, and this curse, and all the boundaries that have been drawn around my life.

But at the same time, the sanctuary is my home. Even more so now that Pie is here. When she said we can't break the curse or we will no longer be safe, I got a weird feeling inside my chest. It took me a moment to identify this feeling as relief. And then another moment to feel guilty about that relief.

One day this will end. That's for sure. All things end. It's the way of the world.

But I'm not ready for that end. Not yet. I just want a quiet life with Pie. And maybe Tomas. I'm kind of used to him. I want to explore the hallways, and dance our way through exciting moments in history, and then come home and sleep next to Pie in our magical forest inside my tomb. I want us to take our time with the doorways and the rings. I want it to be an adventure of a lifetime.

"Well?" Batty is barking at us. "Are we going to buy hay, or what?"

I ease the truck forward, crawling up Main Street. Batty flies in front of us, leading the way, his enormous leathery wings flapping the fog away.

Pie's window is still open so the cold winter air is filling the cab of the truck. But she keeps it down, leaning her head out a little to get a better look. "Wow. It really is abandoned."

"Not all of it." I point to my right. "See? That sign in the bar window is lit up."

"Savage Saints." Pie whispers the words as she reads the red neon.

Music leaks out of the building as we pass, that same song —the ball and chain one—playing on the jukebox inside. And then I speed up a little because Batty is already at the feed store waiting for us.

I pull up to the barn where they store the hay and then

37

back up to the large garage door. Then Pie and I get out and meet Batty in the parking lot.

He growls, "Who's going in?"

I volunteer. "I'll go in. You two—"

"No." Pie puts up a hand. "I'm going too."

"Fine." I'd rather have Pie with me anyway. "You stand guard, Batty. If anyone comes—"

"If anyone comes, I'm flying away."

"Nice," I say. "Why are you here if you're not gonna help?"

"I'm not here to help you. I'm here to make sure you do as you're told."

I grab Pie's hand and pull her away from him, heading for the front doors of the feed store. "Wow. He's a dick."

"Yeah." Pie wilts a little. "I'm disappointed. I kinda liked him too."

So many things run through my mind as I process her words. Mostly about her impromptu spelling, then the consequences of it. But there's no time to think about these things because we're here. And we need to think about this right now. Hay, and the town, and getting out of here as quick as we can before the devil inside that bar comes out to greet me.

I open the door, then look at Pie. "Maybe we can undo the spell. Shut them all up, huh?"

She smiles at me. "You'd like that, wouldn't you?"

I just grin back and we go inside.

There's no one there, of course. I didn't come in here, or check every building in town a couple weeks ago, so I guess there was a possibility that someone was still living here before we came inside. But it's clear by the dust that covers everything that no one has been in here in... well, a lot longer than two weeks, that's for sure.

"Wow." Pie drags her finger through a significant layer of dust on the wooden countertop. An antique cash register sits on one end, and on the other end is a line of glass jars filled with contents unknown, since they are so dusty it's impossible to tell what's inside. "This is... not the feed store that used to be here, is it?"

"I don't think so."

"What happened? Did the whole place go back in time?"

"I'm not sure. Maybe we just... skipped over into another realm, or something."

"It's funny. A couple months ago that would sound crazy. But now that we control doors that lead to new worlds, it's actually a pretty reasonable assumption. So what should we do?"

"Look for hay, I guess."

"Won't it be old and moldy?"

Pie and I look at each other. I just shrug. "What else can we do?"

"We should look, since we're here. But I'm not hopeful. We're probably gonna have to venture out to another town to get hay."

I point to a sliding barn door. "When I was here with Tomas, that door led to the barn where they kept the hay."

"Let's check it out." We walk over to the door and she slides it open. There's a room on the other side. It does not have hay. It has a cot, and a little stove, and a chair. Like someone lives here. But it's all pretty dusty, so not recently.

But there is another door. And when we go through that one, we find the barn and the hay.

Pie plants her hands on her hips. "Huh."

"It looks... fresh."

"Yeah." She cocks her head a little, sniffs the air. "It even smells fresh."

We look at each other again. "That's good, right?"

Pie nods her head. "It is. It's just..."

"Concerning?"

She points at me. "That."

"Because it shouldn't be fresh? It should be old and moldy?"

"And that too."

"So it's… some kind of magic? And we should get the hell out of here and tell the monsters they're out of luck?"

"Well…" She cringes. "I feel like maybe this hay is meant for us?"

"In a good way? Or a bad way? Because I didn't even like Granite Springs. And now I'm thinking Savage Falls is a big fucking no."

"Yeah." She sighs.

But then, just as this breathy admission of defeat passes her lips, the garage door opens at the far end of the barn and Batty is there, waving his arms and carrying on like an asshole. "Can we get this show on the road? Fuck's sake. What are you people doing in here, sightseeing?"

And then, like just the sound of his voice was enough to set things right, the sound of his voice actually sets things right.

The age and dust of the place disappears and it's just… the feed store barn from a few weeks ago.

I blink. Look over at Pie, who is also blinking. Then we look at each other. "Did we imagine that?"

She shakes her head. "Unless it was some kind of mutual delusion, that's a no. We saw it."

"Saw what?" Batty snaps.

I point at him. "Shut up. I liked you much better when I couldn't understand you. Don't speak to us again. Just… fly home. We don't need you."

He presses his monster lips together, like he's holding his tongue, then lets out a breath. "Ya know what? Fine. You're on your own." And then he flings himself up into the air and disappears.

"Wow." Pie looks up at me. "I hate to say this, but—"

"He needs to go?"

"He might."

I just grin. "Come on. I don't know what's going on. But this is good hay. The town is… just the town. And whatever we saw inside the feed store was a vision that can be sorted out later."

Pie backs the truck into the barn and I toss bales into the bed. We secure it all with ratchet ties, and then head out of town, neither of us looking at the red neon light in the bar window.

We're pretty quiet on the way back, so my thoughts wander to the spell that Pie did. She didn't plan that spelling. She didn't even know it was going to happen. And it scared her, so I can only assume that this is not the first time it's happened.

I'm just about to open this topic up for conversation when Pie says, "What the hell is that?"

She's pointing to a large blue school bus pulled over on the side of the road up ahead. There seems to be a problem with the tire and there is a teenage kid pumping up a jack and a woman pacing back and forth on the road next to him.

"Should we stop and help?"

I shoot Pie a look.

"What? That woman might need help."

"Looks like she's got it covered."

Pie wants to protest, but I press on the gas to speed up. We're not stopping.

She looks out her window as we pass, then she gasps. "Holy shit! Pull over! Right now!"

"What? Why?"

"That's… *Jacqueline*!"

I *first met Jacqueline Larue* when I was fourteen and we were staying in the same foster home back in Philly. I liked her immediately, mostly because no one else did. Everything about Jacqueline is way too much for most people. She's too tall, she's too buxom, she's too loud, she's too pretty, she's too smart, and she's too determined.

If Jacqueline Larue wants something, she just goes out and gets it. And just like that, she will change her life in an instant.

She's always been that way.

She is a natural redhead. And that hair of hers is something a goddess dreamed up, that's how gorgeous it is. Not orange or auburn—but cinnamon. Naturally wavy, never a hint of frizz, and it falls all the way down to her butt like a waterfall flowing over a mountainside. I have never seen her in anything else but a pair of soft denim jeans and cotton t-shirts or thermals. And that's exactly what she's wearing underneath her black leather biker jacket covered in zippers and band buttons as I stand here, on the side of a rural PA road, and take her in.

"Pie." She practically moans my name, and it comes out *Pahhhh*, in that little-bit-hick accent she's got.

"Jacqueline? What the hell are you doing out here? And... where's your couch?"

I don't know why, but I can't speak, or even think,

Jacqueline's name without seeing a made-up version of her couch in my head at the same time. It was my last hope for a while there. And even though a couple months have gone by since I really needed to hold on to that bit of hope where sleeping on her couch and not being homeless was the best I could expect in life, I still, for some reason, keep that couch in close association with Jacqueline's name.

My weird question does not faze Jacqueline Larue in the least. She just puts her arms out wide and comes at me like a bull. The next thing I know, I'm gettin' a bear hug. She squeezes me tight, and it lasts a long time as far as hugs go.

I let out a long breath during this hug. And I kinda let myself relax into her giant boobs. When we break apart, I'm almost sad this greeting is over.

She pushes me out to arm's length, then looks me up and down. Jacqueline's scrutiny makes me squirm. Whenever I leave the sanctuary these days, no matter what I'm wearing before I walk through that gate, I'm always wearing the slutty schoolgirl outfit. I don't get a say in this. And I'm not sure what it means, but I'm also pretty sure some god or goddess is fucking with me and using this outfit to do it.

"Girl, have you joined a cult or something?"

"What?" I laugh.

"What are you wearing?"

I don't have a good explanation for this because I haven't been in contact with anyone human in many weeks, so I didn't even bother coming up with a lie. "Um." I decide to just go for the truth. "Leftover Halloween costume?"

This makes Jacqueline giggle. "You're so cute. Well, I love the new look." And that's when Pell comes up behind me. Jacqueline gives him the same scrutiny, but this time, her eyebrows shoot up to the top of her head.

When Pell leaves the sanctuary, he looks like some kind of rogue movie star currently filming a bad-boy action movie. Like Brad Pitt in *Ocean's Eleven*. He's wearing jeans, boots, an army-green bomber jacket, and a pair of mirrored shades. Add all this to his already tall, muscular body, blond beard, and too-long hair and he kinda morphs into Jax from *Sons of Anarchy*.

How is this fair? When I leave the sanctuary, I look like a hot slutty mess who just fell out of a frat house. When Pell leaves, he looks like he's about to save the world and look good doing it.

"Well, who do we have here?" Jacqueline is enamored. As she should be, because Pell is enamoring.

Pell is not enamored back. He frowns, crosses his arms, and looks at me for an explanation.

"Pell... remember I told you about my friend in Toledo?"

He grunts.

"Well." I wave my hand at Jacqueline to present her. "Here she is!"

He grunts again.

Jacqueline tsks her tongue and looks at me. "The handsome ones are always moody, aren't they?"

I don't answer that. Pell is totally that stereotype, but we have pressing matters at the moment. And this is when the situation finally hits me. She's here, in my part of rural PA, on the side of the road, and a teenage boy is changing a tire on a pale-blue school bus. "What are you doing here? And what the hell is happening with this bus?"

The boy stands up. He's tall, lean, and frowny. "It's fixed." His voice is kinda deep for a kid. He opens some compartment in the side of the bus and throws his tire iron in there with a clang.

I look back at Jacqueline.

Jacqueline looks at me.

There is a moment here. A moment when we have a silent conversation with our eyes, just like we used to back when we were kids. Jacqueline is saying, *Just give me a moment to explain*. And I'm saying, *What the hell have you done now?*

Because this is how Jacqueline Larue changes her life on a dime. She does something crazy and unexpected. "This," she used to tell me, "is how one changes their fate in the world. You commit to opposite day and become someone else. And then, after a few weeks of this total-immersion therapy, you *are* someone else."

Our internal convo suddenly plays out in real life.

"Just give me a moment to explain."

"What have you done now?"

"I had to, Pie. They were gonna send them to awful places."

"*Them?*" My eyes dart up to the windows of the bus and there I find several little faces peering out at me behind floral-patterned curtains.

"I couldn't let them do that. I mean, that's why I went to school in the first place, right? If one is going to be a social worker, then one must commit to being a... a... a *force*, if you will. A force for good in this evil world where children are just discarded like yesterday's trash. I got a master's and everything, Pie. I'm committed, ya know. *Committed.*" She stomps a combat boot.

I get a really bad feeling in my stomach. "When you said you had kids..."

"They *are* my kids. Aren't you, Cecil?" She smiles and pulls the teenage boy close. He wriggles a little, but when Jacqueline Larue gets committed to you, no amount of wriggling will get you out of an embrace. He gives in, then smiles.

OK. I get this, obviously. We both grew up in foster care, so I understand. But... "What—" I wave my finger at this bus. "What is happening with the bus, Jacqueline?"

"Have you ever heard of van life?"

"Of course. You sell everything you own, buy a van, and live in it."

"Well." She pauses. This pause means she's about to stretch the truth. "We're doin' bus life."

I grab her by the leather jacket, pull her away from the kid, and Pell, and the bus, and drag her across the street. "Jacqueline. Who do these kids belong to?"

"Someone needs to explain what's going on here." Pell's voice is loud and rumbly. Not the kind of rumbly that shakes down tombs inside the sanctuary, but it still has a presence on the outside too. It makes Jacqueline jump a little, which isn't easy to do.

"Never mind him. What are you doing? Did you take these kids out of foster care and leave the fucking state?"

Jacqueline's face goes serious now and her eyes narrow down a little. "I rescued them, Pie. You were in the system. You know how bad it is. You know there are very bad people taking in kids just for the paycheck."

"I get that. But you can't just acquire kids, Jacqueline."

"Why not? They disappear all the time. Do you have any idea how many children I've seen disappear from foster care in the past three years, Pie?" Her eyes are locked with mine. They dart back and forth a little as we stare at each other. "Twenty-seven."

"What?"

"Twenty-seven kids. Gone. With no explanation. Just... gone. One of them was only two years old."

"What?"

"You heard me. *Two* years old. And no one batted an eyelash over it."

"How is that possible?"

"How is that possible? Let me tell you how. That little girl's mother was a drug addict. No family came to claim the baby when she was born and tested positive for opioids. So they sent her to foster care. Everyone wants a baby. So it started out great. Nice middle-class family. Everyone was happy. Until the little girl became a problem. Now, if you give birth to a problem baby, the majority of parents will hang in there. They will commit to that child. And maybe some foster parents will too. But that's not how it happened for this little girl. She was sent from home to home and finally, she got to her last stop."

"Did she die?"

"She's probably dead by now, but no, Pie. She did not die. She was *sold*."

"That's... ridiculous."

"Is it? Human trafficking is a hundred-and-fifty-billion-dollar business. And don't ask me any more about that. I know things. I've seen things." Her eyes go a little crazy. "And all the kids on that bus are little monsters. They got to their last stop and it was either send them to the black hole of who-knows-what or take them with me." She stands up straight, raises her chin, and stares me straight in the eyes. "So I took them. Because the system isn't gonna save them. Because the system is fuckin' broke, Pie. The system fuckin' sucks. So someone has to stand up and say, 'Enough!' And that someone is me. I'm gonna save them. And I'm here, looking for you, because I know you will want to save them too."

There is a pause here. A moment where everyone has to make a decision.

Finally, I let out a breath. "OK. Let me talk to Pell."

Jacqueline smiles.

She is way too determined.

I walk over to Pell, tug on the sleeve of his leather jacket, and pull him back to our truck. We both get in and close the doors.

"What the hell is happening?"

"OK. This is gonna sound crazy—"

"No."

"Pell! Just listen!"

"No!"

"You can't say no until I ask you something."

"You want to bring those people to the sanctuary."

"Well…"

"And the answer is no. Saint Mark's is not a sanctuary for humans. It's a sanctuary for monsters."

"Yeah, but… they *are* monsters."

He blinks at me. "No."

"Yes! She used that word. She called them 'little monsters.' They're gonna get caught, Pell. I mean…" I glance over my shoulder. "The bus is blue. How she even got this far is a total miracle. The state police must not know yet." I look back at Pell. "The point is, these kids are about to be thrown into the abyss of something really bad."

Pell scoffs and shakes his head.

"They're problem kids, Pell. With no parents. And in the outside world that means they get thrown away. They're monsters and they need sanctuary."

He looks out his window. It's beginning to snow. "It's a nice idea. But Pie…" He looks at me. "What are you going to tell your friend when we walk through that gate and we suddenly have horns, and hooves, and fur? Hmm? What are you gonna tell them about Tomas? There are monsters and nymphs having sex in the open, Pie. The sanctuary is not a place for children. And even if it was, these people are not part of our world. You know this."

"Well…" I sigh. "They're not part of this world either. And would it be so bad if we made rules for the monsters and nymphs? Shouldn't we just tell them they need to keep their clothes on and have sex in private?"

"It won't work."

He's right. They're satyrs. Most of them don't even wear clothes. They hate pants. And the nymphs are pretty much all bitches. I don't like any of them.

"And even if we could tamp down the sexual urges, there's the whole problem of magic doors, and rings, and prisoners, and the fucking Queen of Vinca."

"Well, I can't leave Jacqueline here on the side of the road with a bus filled with kids. We need a solution."

"Maybe we could… hide them."

"Hide them how? And where?"

"There is a whole town hidden from the outside world by magic fog just fifteen minutes behind us."

"Granite Springs? Pell, it's like… haunted. And you said the devil is living in the bar."

"I didn't say it was a *good* idea. But it's all I can think of. They cannot come to the sanctuary. You understand this, right? It's not a place for kids."

He's right. Maybe, with some work and due diligence, and a lot of bribing, it's possible that we could get these monsters under some kind of control. They were much better before the nymphs came. But I think that was because of Tomas. I think those monsters knew that Tomas wasn't what he appeared and they were kind of afraid of him. Hell, I think I'm the only one who didn't get it.

But I do now. "I do, Pell. I get it. We can't bring them there yet."

"Yet?"

"Or… maybe ever. But for sure, not yet. Granite Springs might be our only option, but how are we going to explain what's going on there?"

"Tell them it's a ghost town."

"Where do you think we are? Wyoming?"

"Just tell her it's an old company town. From… railroad days. And the sanctuary owns it now so it's all perfectly fine and legit."

"You do realize there's this thing called the internet? She can look this shit up."

Pell gets growly. "Well, it's either this or send her on her way. She's not coming to the sanctuary."

I sigh. I love my new life. I really do. I like the monster side of me. And I love Pell. I have daydreams about having his monster babies. But this world I'm now part of comes with so many... problems. It's continuous. But this is it. This is his final offer. "And the devil? How am I gonna explain the devil in the bar?"

"Tell her to stay out of the bar."

"I doubt that will be enough."

He shrugs. "That's all I have."

I lean back in my seat, thinking. "What if I... did a little spelling?"

"What kind of spelling?"

"Something to make them stay out of the bar, obviously."

He narrows his eyes at me. "Will it work?"

I shrug. "My spells seem to be pretty powerful these days."

"Right." He eyeballs me and I know what he's thinking. They *are* very powerful these days. But he knows I'm not really in control of it. "It's up to you."

"OK. That's our best solution. Take them to Granite Springs and spell them into staying out of the bar. Wait here. I'll go explain."

JACQUELINE IS SURPRISINGLY **receptive** to the idea of living in our privately-owned, former-company ghost town. In fact, she tells me that she was looking for the town—because I told her where I was when I made that phone call after my disastrous date with Russ Roth—and there was no such town on the map. She was just driving the backroads looking for it when they got a flat tire and had to pull over.

So this narrative—that it's all private and left over from railroad days, or whatever—kind of fits.

Here's the part that bothers me. She was *looking* for me. And if she had traveled five more minutes up the road, she would've gone right by Saint Mark's. All she had to do was look to her left and she would've seen the sanctuary. Because she was *looking* for me. And I'm a hundred percent positive this matters in the whole 'no one can see us' magic happening there.

What if she had pulled over at the gate? Would the gate be locked?

I don't know. I don't understand all the rules of Saint Mark's.

Back when I first got there it felt really safe. There were those big walls, and the magic, and it was just us. Russ Roth put a little dent into my safety rating, but still. He's one guy.

Now, though? Now we've got a hundred new magical beings living there with us. And Batty can leave whenever he wants. He just flies up over the walls. And he's not the only monster with wings.

This is the moment when I realize something important. I don't feel safe at Saint Mark's since the monsters and nymphs came. And it's not really them, it's all of it. It doesn't feel like a sanctuary anymore. It feels like a... like a trap. I'm constantly thinking about doors. And that's another thing. Pell and I can't be the only ones able to work magic portal doors. There have to be others.

The doors are only locked if you don't have the rings.

Isn't it possible that there are more rings out there?

Isn't it possible that these ringbearers could come right through their doors into our world, the same way Pell and I walk through our doors into someone else's world?

This is what I'm thinking about as Jacqueline's blue bus follows our hay truck back into Granite Springs. But this time, when we pass over the city limits, there is no old-timey sign declaring this place to be Savage Falls. It's just the same

'Welcome to Granite Springs' sign that's always been there, so that's hopeful.

Maybe what Pell and I saw earlier wasn't real? Maybe it was just some kind of mutual hallucination?

But that's not it. Because if it were, there would be people here.

And there are no people here.

Which presents its own problem.

"I don't understand." Jacqueline has pulled her bus over in front of the Honey Bean Diner and we are standing at the front window, looking in at a perfectly functional diner, minus the people. "What is happening here?"

It would've been better, I think, if the place *had* looked like a ghost town. At least then it would make sense.

"Jacqueline." I sigh her name out. Because this day has been super-stressful and it's starting to get to me. "Can you just trust me? Can you just… not ask any questions?"

She and I stare at each other and have another private conversation with our eyes.

She's saying, *You're up to something here. I don't understand it, or know what it is, but I'm on the run with stolen orphans, so who am I to judge?*

And I'm saying, *Thank you.*

"OK." She gives in. But it's one of those tired give-ins. Like she's tired and ready to believe anything just so she can relax for a moment. "I trust you, Pie. Where should we stay?"

"Up there." I point to the second floor of the diner building. "There are apartments up there. They're furnished." I'm assuming they're furnished, because up until a couple weeks ago, townspeople lived up there. "Just help yourself to anything you want and I'll check on you later. We have a load of hay to drop off at home and I have to do a few other things, but I promise, I'll be back."

I don't bother telling her to stay out of the bar. That

53

would just pique her curiosity. I will just do a spell once I'm back in the truck with Pell.

Jacqueline exhales again, this time louder. Even though she is the most confident person I have ever met, she's stressed out too. She wants this to be real. She wants to let all her suspicions go and relax. She wants to believe me.

She doesn't believe me, but she wants to.

So that's what she does.

"Thank you, Pie." She takes both my hands and gives them a squeeze. "You saved us today."

We hug again. Then I leave her, and her blue bus filled with stolen children, and get back in the truck with Pell.

"Done?"

"Yep. I just need a spelling. Drive home and I'll—" But before I can finish my sentence, the words are already spilling out of my mouth.

"'A woman and kids with monster scars

'Stay away from the devil's bar

'Live your life, be free and roam

'Never go into the haunted home.'"

I blink and look out the front window, the final words coming out of my mouth just as we pass over the city limits. Pell reaches over and takes my hand, gives it a squeeze, just like Jacqueline did. "You're a good girl, ya know that?"

"And you like the bad ones."

He grins, looking over at me. "It's opposite day."

We both laugh and some of the stress melts away. But his last words linger in my brain as we make the quiet drive back to Saint Mark's.

It's opposite day.

These exact words popped up in my thoughts when I saw Jacqueline. This is how she changes her life. Do the opposite for long enough, and it changes you both inside and out.

That's the theme of my recent life, I guess.

Nothing is the same.

WE'RE DRIVING *along the country* road that leads to the lake and the back of the sanctuary, enjoying the beauty of the woods as the season changes from snowy winter to midsummer, when—

"Do you hear something?"

I'm cranking down my window when Pell says this. And sure enough, yes. Yes, I do hear something.

"Is that… music?" My question is rhetorical. It is music. It is loud, it is thumping, it is obnoxious music.

Pell groans. "Now what the fuck is happening?"

But as we come around a corner and the lake appears, it is very clear what is happening. The monsters of Saint Mark's are throwing a rager.

Pell stomps on the brakes as a naked nymph goes running by, laughing and squealing as she leaps into the air. A moment later, there's a pursuing satyr. We watch as he tackles her and they both fall into the lake, disappearing under the water.

"Um…" I'm holding up a finger. "Should we break that up?"

We watch, waiting for the two monsters to reappear, the seconds ticking off, my heart thumping a little in my chest. And I'm just about to get out and go in after them when two heads bob up in the middle of the lake. They are kissing.

"I think they'll make it," Pell deadpans, once again easing the truck forward.

My jaw drops open as Pell turns into the gravel parking lot behind my cottage. There are monsters on the roof. Like dozens of them. I don't even know how the roof is still there.

They have to weigh an actual ton. I squint and blink a few times to make sure I'm seeing this correctly. "Are they holding Solo cups?"

Another rhetorical question. Because the monsters on my roof are indeed holding red cups. Which are presumably filled with alcohol because there's a keg on the roof.

"Holy shit." I look at Pell. "How the fuck did this happen? We've been gone like thirty minutes!"

"It's actually been four hours."

"What?" I pull out my phone, and sure enough, it's already after two in the afternoon.

"But this ends now." Pell parks the truck and he's just reaching for his door handle when I put a hand on his shoulder.

"You don't want to be a dick about this."

"Me?" He points to himself. "I'm the dick?" He points to the rager. "They're about to crash through your roof, Pie."

"Be nice about it, that's all I'm saying. Because the way I see it, these monsters are like teenagers. They do things to make you react. They want this anger, Pell. And if you give it to them, it's gonna divide us into groups. Us and them. Do we really want that kind of division when there is already so much going on?"

He sighs and looks out his window. "So I'm supposed to ignore this?"

"Not ignore it. But you need to play it smart. Go in there, turn off the music, and... I don't know. Give them all jobs to do."

"Jobs? You think that's the answer?"

"It'll keep them busy."

"They're drunk, Pie. And they're satyrs. They want to fuck, and drink, and smoke."

"But they were fine for weeks."

"That's because there were no women. Now we've got bad girls coming out our asses. I need to go in there, scare the shit out of them, threaten them, and then probably maim two or three. Otherwise they'll just keep doing this."

"Maim? You're not going to fight them, are you?"

"Why not?"

"It's kinda childish, don't you think?"

"Childish?" He raises an eyebrow at me. "They've got a keg on your roof, Pie. They need to be put back in their places. And that includes Nysta. She's the ringleader of all this. We need to send all the wood nymphs back to Vinca."

"What if Tarq's not ready? Didn't he tell you to wait for his signal?"

"He's not the king of me. And Saint Mark's is mine. I'm the king here and I'm over it."

I expect him to just get out of the truck and go do all this, but he waits.

This makes me smile.

"Why are you smiling?"

"Because you want my approval."

"I don't require your approval."

"I didn't say 'require.' I said 'want.'" I smile bigger. "Because you care about my opinion."

"Well? Do you agree I should do this?"

"Not really. But... maybe you're right. Maybe a heavy hand is necessary." We both look at the party. "Maybe it's just a few of them? Maybe we should go inside and look before we get all fired up?"

"Fine. I'm not really inclined to give monsters the benefit of the doubt—unless they are Tarq, of course—but I will do it this one time. Just in case it's not what it appears to be."

"Why do you give Tarq the benefit of the doubt?"

"What do you mean? He's my best friend."

"Best friend?"

"Well, you're my best friend." This makes me smile. Because he's so serious. "But Tarq is my oldest friend. He has earned the benefit of the doubt."

"Has he, though? Has he really? I mean, you guys haven't even seen each other in thousands of years. Isn't it possible that he's a dick and you just don't realize it yet?"

"What are you saying?"

I sigh. Did I or did I not just spell out what I mean? It's like Pell has some kind of block about Tarq. None of what Tarq's been doing seems suspicious to Pell.

"Never mind." I drop it because if there's one thing I know about Pell, it's that he's loyal. And even if, in my opinion, his loyalty to Tarq isn't deserved, Pell needs to see it for himself. "Let's go."

I get out of the truck and meet up with Pell on his side.

A bottle crashes down onto the gravel not even ten feet away, glass flying everywhere. A little bit of it sprays into my arm, stinging me. And when I look down at it, there's blood.

I look up at Pell. "Don't overreact. It's a tiny cut."

But he's about to explode.

"Pell."

He takes a deep breath. "I've got it covered."

Then he takes my hand and we walk through the gate.

Inside, it's every bit as bad as it is outside.

Actually, it's worse.

There are naked monsters having sex everywhere I look. Big, giant dicks all over the place. Nymph tits, and asses, and... yeah. This is gross. I'm so glad that Pell didn't let me bring Jacqueline and the kids here.

Aside from the sex, the air is thick with smoke. And I don't think it's pot. It smells totally different. When I look up the hill, I spy a hookah on top of a tomb and about a half a dozen satyrs and nymphs dancing around it as they toke.

We walk up to the top of the hill and just look around. There are kegs everywhere. I'm talking like... thirty or forty of them. "Where did they get all this shit?"

I say this to myself, so I'm not really expecting an answer. But Pell does answer me. "They got it from him."

He's pointing to the black tomb. Well, he's pointing to the gold dome on the top of the black tomb. And on the top of that gold dome sits Batty, black bat wings lazily spread out and drooping. Like he's wasted and can't be bothered to tuck them up along his body at the moment.

There is a ledge along the edge of the dome and that ledge is lined with crates. I don't know what, exactly, is inside those crates, but there's definitely bottles of alcohol in there because he's tossing them to waiting satyrs and nymphs below.

"What the fuck is going on here?"

Despite Pell's promise to be reasonable, these words come out with the power of his new magic. He shakes the world. In fact, he shakes the world so hard, Batty loses his balance on the gold dome and goes sliding down the side of it, laughing and cackling like he's a fourteen-year-old boy who just got drunk for the very first time.

When I look around, I realize that quite a few of our new roommates have fallen to the ground from this rumble.

But they aren't taking Pell seriously. They are all laughing and hysterical with happiness. I'm just turning to Pell, just about to tell him that he should not take this personally, that they are just wasted, but he's already rumbling again.

"I said! What the fuck! Is happening here!"

This time, tombs crumble. I'm not talking walls either, I'm talking entire tombs. And the earth beneath my feet cracks open a little. Pell has to grab my arm and tug me into him so I don't accidentally fall in.

The music stops and as the rumble recedes, the place goes quiet. The monsters near us pick themselves up. A silence comes over the sanctuary. But it's not one of reverence, like you might find in a church. It's something else. An air of... I dunno. Disdain, maybe. Someone coughs and another snickers.

"Someone had better answer me right now."

Pell is not fucking around. He is mad. His voice is making the whole place rumble and his horns are lit up with fire.

It's not the first time I've seen that, of course. I've used that fire to make magic and he often gets a little glow-y when he's turned on during sex or having a nice sleep. But this is the first time I've seen it appear in anger. And it is different. There are flames coming from his horns.

But not *just* his horns. There are flames coming from *him*. They flicker off the tips of his fingers, like all he has to do is wave those fingers a little and the flames might fly out in all directions.

He's either really fucking pissed and I've never seen him this way, or... this is new.

I wish I had time to think harder about this but I don't. Because Batty is right in front of us. "What the hell are you doing? You can't just throw that voice around like an animal."

"Animal?" Pell scoffs. Then he takes a step towards Batty and before I even know what's happening, Pell has pressed his flat palm into Batty's chest, making him fly backwards. Batty crashes into the remains of a tomb wall, stunned, blinking, as the plaster crumbles down into piles of rubble on top of his head.

The monsters gasp. A few nymphs shriek. Like Pell is the unreasonable one here, and he's scaring them.

I sigh. Give me a fuckin' break. They are not scared. They are... aghast. But not in an astonished way. An appalled way.

This is not going to go well. Even though Pell has every right to be pissed, and Batty deserved that push, especially after what happened in town, Pell is coming off like an *authority*.

And I mean that in the most oppressive way possible.

They are going to turn on us. And I don't think we can stop it at this point. Somehow, since the nymphs came, the whole vibe of Saint Mark's has changed. The vibe used to be one of peace and whimsy mixed in with a healthy dose of confusion. But now it's just... disdain.

"Well?" Pell demands.

Cookie appears and I'm in the middle of a sigh of relief—because he's so reasonable—when he spits on Pell. "You don't run this place, Pell. Saint Mark's belongs to all monsters."

Holy shit, my language spelling works on him too. I'm excited to hear him talk. After all these weeks of him pampering me with amazing food and mothering me like I'm his personal responsibility, it's kind of amazing to be able to understand him.

Except... he just spat on my man. So... what the fuck?

Cookie and Pell are eye to eye now. And I think the whole sanctuary is holding their collective breath, waiting to see what happens next. "You're nothing but the stand-in."

"I am the master!" Pell roars this, making already-crumbled tombs crumble even more. "Saint Mark's is my domain. You are here as my guests. And I want to know just what the fuck you all think you're doing."

That's when Eyebrows appears. And again I have this sudden feeling of relief. That he might set things right. That he might be the reasonable monster. He has been making me pretty tailored clothes all these weeks, right? We're friends, aren't we?

But he roars back at Pell too. "You're no longer necessary here, monster. Be gone now." But he just dismissed Pell with a flick of his finger.

"Be *gone* now?" Pell and I both say this at the same time. Then we look at each other and laugh. After the laugh is over, we look back at Eyebrows. "We live here." And once again, we say this together.

"I am the master," Pell says.

"And I'm the slave caretaker," I add. "You people are literally *guests*. And I think you should start acting like it."

"Should we?"

Everyone turns to find Nysta slithering her way along a tomb wall that didn't actually fall down during Pell's rumble. I don't know why she has to walk like that. I think, in her head, she feels like this is some kind of seductive, sexy thing. But it's not. It's... reptilian. And gross.

Pell is just about to answer her, but I put a hand on his shoulder. It's an 'I got this' gesture. He looks at me, kinda shrugs, and then makes a little wave of his hand to indicate Nysta.

I step out in front. "Nysta. I'm only gonna say this once." And then... then... then the fucking words come spilling out of my mouth! It happens so fast, I'm already on the second verse before I realize what I'm doing!

"'A wood, a nymph, a space alone.

'A woman now without a home.

'Once a power, now a shell

'Go away, live in your cell.'"

And then... poof!

She's gone.

CHAPTER FOUR - PELL

It's a bad idea. I know it's a bad idea. But the words come spilling out of Pie's mouth so fast, no one even has time to think. And this is interesting. Because it's kind of a lot of words. And it's not like people can't hear it coming. I mean, she has to spit out a whole poem. So one might assume that one has time to counteract these spellings my Pie does.

But that's not how it happens. It's like once the spell is in motion, it's already working. It kinda stuns people.

And after it's done, there's another moment of stunned silence. A moment where all the monsters process the empty space where Nysta used to be, but now isn't. They can't move. They just stand there, mouths open.

But then there's always that other moment. The one that comes after the moment of stunned silence. The moment of pandemonium. The moment when their confusion turns into outrage.

I take control now. Because there will be no outrage in my sanctuary. So I use my new voice to stop them. "Do you see now?" My words roar across the grounds, weaving their way around tombs and along gravel pathways. They burst up into the air, like a mist, and cover everything and everyone. "You. Are. Guests. You have no idea what this place really is."

I don't either, but they don't need to know that.

"It's a debt prison," Pie says. "And you are all in debt to us.

And now Nysta is in a gloomy cell, hidden from all of you. And I can do that to anyone I want."

Well, that escalated quickly. It's probably true that Pie can banish any and all of them to the Bottoms and she does appear to be in charge of handing out Books of Debt, but it's a threat too far, I think.

And all the other monsters think that too. They do go silent and they do not argue. But they've got that look on their faces. It's a defiant look. It's a look that says, *You might be in charge now, but you won't be forever.*

And because Tomas is not here to smooth things over, I decide I need to smooth this over. "You are guests here." I'm still using my voice, but it's a low rumble, a soothing one instead of a threatening one. "And all we ask is that you respect our home. Because this *is* our home."

"We get it." Eyebrows steps forward, like he's the leader of this little band of misfit assholes.

And wow, did I ever get that guy wrong. All of them, actually. How did I ever think they were so… harmless?

"You're the boss. Fine." Eyebrows looks over his shoulder, then looks back at me. "Be the boss. But you will not use that voice on us like we are children who need admonishment."

"Well, you're acting like children." I cringe when these words come out of Pie's mouth. She's not usually so confrontational and this is not really the time to start. "You're running around here like"—*Don't say it, Pie. Do not*—"like animals."

There is a collective gasp across the sanctuary. It's kind of the ultimate insult in monster world. But Pie's not from monster world, so I don't think she means it that way.

"What she means is"—if I don't interrupt here, we're gonna have another scene—"you're disrespectful. And we take offense to that. You will be considerate of the sanctity of Saint Mark's. You will not run around fucking, and shrieking, and partying."

"What are we supposed to do then?" The question comes from a petite naked wood nymph, still riding the back of a large bull-like monster I've never interacted with. "If we're stuck here and we can't have fun, what are we supposed to do?"

And this one comment opens the door to all the complaints.

"Yeah."

"She's right."

"We didn't ask to come here."

"We're bored."

"This place is stupid."

"We want to go to town."

I raise a hand to shut them up. "If you want to party, do it down by the lake."

"Outside the walls, then?" I turn to find Batty back on his feet. There are still bits of plaster in his hair and lining the bones and webbing of his wings, but he's mostly pulled himself together.

"Down by the *lake*." I say it again, just so I'm clear. "Do not leave here without permission."

I know how this sounds, and I know how they will react. The same way Pie reacted when I told her she needed to ask permission to leave. But when you start a negotiation, you have to be unreasonably heavy-handed or you'll lose too much ground.

"Permission?" Batty says this, but he's not the only one. There's a lot of whispering now as the monsters get all riled up over my command. "Again, you seem to think we're children who need minding. We're not."

"You're not. I agree. But you are in my world, living under my protection. You are eating our food. Pie goes into debt with every bite you take. And she does that willingly. Following a few simple rules is the least you can do to pay us back."

"What if we don't want to stay here?"

I turn to the small wood nymph again. "You cannot leave the boundary of Saint Mark's."

"Why not?" she asks.

I don't really know the answer to this, I just know it's true. To a point.

I redirect my gaze over to Batty. Because he *can* leave the boundary of Saint Mark's. All he has to do is fly upwards until the magic dissipates, and he's quite literally free. And he's not the only one. There are half a dozen winged monsters here. So far, none of them have left the sanctuary's sphere of influence. But that doesn't mean they *can't* leave. It only means they haven't.

I decide this question needs to be answered, so I make something up. "You cannot leave because you have debt. And if you leave with debt, you have to pay the price with years off your life."

This is mostly true. Well, for Pie, anyway.

But it could apply to them. Maybe. It sounds good, anyway.

"Debt? We have debt?" This comes from another wood nymph. Average height, long dark hair, and big, wide, green eyes. She's actually wearing clothes—translucent pink harem pants and a matching halter top. It's unusual for a wood nymph to wear a top, so this is interesting. Plus, she's not hysterical. She's actually quite calm and reasonable. "How do we get rid of this debt?"

"You pay us back, of course."

This one steps forward now. In front of Batty, even. Like she just decided to take command of the Saint Mark's monster army. "And how do we do that?"

"I'm sorry, what is your name?"

"Isla."

"Isla, you get rid of your debt by making me happy."

She snickers. "Is that so?"

"That's right." Pie steps up next to me. "I have all your Books of Debt down in the Bottoms prison."

"Bottoms prison?" This question reverberates through the crowd as a whisper.

"It's where all these monsters you see in front of the tombs are kept behind bars." Pie waves her hand at the hundreds—thousands, probably—of tombs. "I have a library down there where all the Books of Debt are kept. If you'd like to see your book so you can understand your debt, you can make an appointment with me, and we'll go over how you can make Pell happy and erase your debt."

I'm not actually sure this is a lie. Pie told me about the Bottoms, of course. And I know all the tomb monsters really are down there behind bars, as well as Callistina. But a library of debt books?

Maybe it's true.

Ultimately, it doesn't matter. These monsters think it is. Their expressions of mocking disbelief slowly change to unsettled understanding.

"That's not fair!"

"This is bullshit."

"We never agreed to this."

They kinda sound like Pie the day I explained how her curse works. Which gives me an idea. "It's a curse." I use the voice again. "Saint Mark's Sanctuary is cursed, you fools. And if you come in, you become part of that curse."

Isla plants her hands on her hips. "No one told us about this."

Pie snickers. "Well, no one gets a warning. Duh. If you had a warning, you'd get a choice. And who the hell in their right mind chooses a curse?"

Isla scowls at Pie. "It feels... sneaky."

Pie just shrugs. "I don't make the curse rules, Isla. And Pell doesn't either. The gods control the curses. And neither of us were given a choice when we got stuck here, either. So suck it up. It's not asking too much that you take your partying to the lake and leave the main grounds a peaceful place."

There is a collective exhale from the crowd. Which is a good sign, because it means they've accepted what we just told them. They don't like it, but they've accepted it.

"Go on." I use the voice again. "Take your party to the lake."

Both Batty and Eyebrows shoot me a look. They don't like the voice. They find it insulting, I think. But it works. Quite well, actually. Because all the other monsters turn and start making their way down the hill towards the lake. And by the time they hit Pie's cottage, they're laughing, and joking, and squealing again.

Batty and Eyebrows are still here though. I rumble at them, "You have something to say to me?"

Batty points to me. "We're not children."

"I'm not treating you like children. I'm asking you to act like adults."

They exchange a look with each other, have some internal conversation, then turn away and walk down the hill without further comment.

Pie lets out a breath. "Holy fuck. That was kind of intense."

"Yeah." I take her hand. "Come on. Let's go to my tomb." I lead Pie through the maze of tombs, noticing that there are a lot of crumbled ones now, thanks to my new power. And then I have a sudden moment of panic as I envision my own tomb crumbling like that. What would I do without my tomb? Before the monsters and nymphs came, I didn't think much about it. I didn't even think I liked it. It was just... where I went to be moody and sleep. But now, it's my only privacy. There are way too many monsters at Saint Mark's for my comfort level.

When we get to the tomb my eyes automatically scan up

to the words that Pie wrote over the top in Sharpie. Her first real act of power that kinda started everything. The beginning of magic, and doors, and whole new worlds.

When I look back down at Pie, she's smiling at me. Remembering that day, I think. But then, as we walk into the first entrance of the tomb, both of us look at the statue of me.

I never liked that thing. It doesn't even look like me. I'm in some kind of Egyptian get-up. It's all very... I dunno. Spooky. And it makes me think about the past.

I've been doing that a lot lately. Ever since I found the blacksmith shop and started remembering a few of the things I've done over the centuries, lost memories come quicker now. Just random little things about who I am will suddenly pop into my head. And I think maybe I'm afraid that one day, some random little memory about how I'm really an Egyptian god will pop up too.

I don't like the looks of that guy on the throne in my portico. He looks like he's up to something and whatever that something is, I don't think I'll agree with it.

Pie doesn't like him either. At first, she was keenly interested in him. She would stand in front of the statue and just stare at it. But even she could tell that guy's not really me.

I mean, he looks like me. Same face, same horns, same build. But his eyes are empty. Literally. There's just plain stone there. In fact, my body is all just plain gray stone. Only the horns, which are made of black marble, and the clothes—the Egyptian skirt and armbands—are brightly colored. Cobalt blues, and red derived from insects, and gold, of course. Though not a lot of it. It's just an embellishment for the jewelry that statue me is wearing.

We pass by quickly and go into the woods. Immediately, I am more relaxed. I like the humidity in here. I like the pressing leaves of giant trees and the low boughs that occasionally meander across the pathway. I even like the smell of it these days, something I hadn't really noticed before Pie started sleeping in here with me.

It smells like dirt, but the good kind. The wet kind. And flowers, of course. There are a lot of flowers blooming these days. Again, I hadn't noticed them before Pie came. I didn't really look around much. I certainly didn't go exploring. I just... came in, walked to my favorite tree, and settled down on the grass underneath for sleep.

But Pie and I often go for walks in here. And we have discovered that the woods are like the hallways upstairs in the cathedral. They change all the time. But the paths in here don't really lead anywhere except right back to my favorite tree.

That's where the doors are too. It's kind of a home base, I guess.

They are all lined up—closed, thank God—and ready for... something.

The bag of rings is kind of hopeless at this point. I never did get Tomas to seal it up properly, so they stay in there sometimes. But other times they just float in front of the door they open.

Pie and I do not open the doors.

We will have to go back to Vinca and check on Tarq and his people and we should really do that sooner rather than later. Pie's not entirely wrong about why I haven't gone back to Vinca. Was making Tarq king a great idea? Probably not. But I don't think it was a horrible one, either. He needs time to assert his authority. Maybe wage a war or two in the process.

I'm perfectly happy giving him all the time he needs to do that without my input.

What do I care about Vinca? I'm not from there. And even if my best friend is the king, I don't see any reason to go back. Especially when I will be pushing all these satyrs and wood nymphs through that door the first chance I get.

"What are you smiling about?"

We've reached my tree and Pie and I are just lying down when she asks this.

"I'm thinking about how pretty soon we can push all these annoying monsters through that door over there and be done with them."

She giggles a little, settling her head onto my chest. "I hate to say this, but I'm with you. I don't like them here."

"Me either."

She props herself up on one elbow so she can look me in the eyes. "I don't think they belong here."

"Agreed."

"And…" She sighs. "Are you disappointed that Batty and Eyebrows turned out to be total dicks? Because I am." She lies back down, sighs heavily again. "Were they always like that? Because I never got the impression that they hated me when Batty was giving me grains of sand and Eyebrows was making me racks and racks of custom clothes. Even Cookie looked pissed off."

I mull this over for a moment and have to agree. "It is kinda weird. They didn't pay much attention to me, but they were all pretty enamored with you."

"Maybe it was Tomas? Maybe he was the one kinda keeping them in line. He didn't much act like a leader, but now that I think back, they did treat him like one."

"Speaking of Tomas—"

"Don't start, Pell. He's not dangerous."

She says this almost convincingly. But when I turn my head to look at her, she's biting her lip, which means she's lying. Or, because Pie's really not a liar, she's maybe holding something back.

"What?" I ask.

"What do you mean, what?"

"What aren't you telling me?"

She sighs. "I know you don't want me to see Tomas, but I'm not gonna stop doing that."

I didn't figure she would. But this is not the point she's trying to make. "OK."

She turns again, resting her chin on my chest so we're face to face. "It's kinda creepy down there. There are eggs, Pell. Not rotten ones, either."

"What?"

"He's hatching eggs. And Madeline?" Pie cringes. "She's got red scales all over her face. And she's not some dragon chimera, either. I think she's slowly turning into an actual real dragon."

"Well, that's wonderful. That's all I need. Crazy Tomas and his pet dragon raising babies in my basement."

Pie giggles. "That's not nice."

I let out a long sigh. "Where do you think this is all going?"

"Going?"

"You understand that this is... you know, a plot, right?"

She sits up a little, breaking contact with me. "What kind of plot?"

I'm immediately sorry I started this conversation. I just want to forget about the outside world now. In fact, ever since Pie spelled her way into my tomb, this is really the only place I want to be.

But only if she's here.

And she is here. So I push her back down. "Never mind. I have something better for us to think about." I roll over on top of her, propping myself up on my elbows, and stroke her cheeks with my thumbs. She opens her legs a little and my hips fit between them like they are meant to be there.

"You're changing the subject, Pell."

My smile is big. "You're so smart, Pie."

"If I recall, you used to think I was slow."

"Slow to love me, that's all."

This answer makes Pie huff out a laugh. "Well, you certainly didn't love me those first few days."

"I would beg to differ. I was insanely jealous when you went on that date with Russ Roth."

"You were?"

"In-*sane* with jealousy. I was playing it cool though, so..." I stop talking because her blue eyes are twinkling with delight and I just want to get lost in them for a moment.

"You played it *so* cool. But about this plot."

I lean down and touch my mouth to hers. Her lips are soft and she tastes like honey from the lip balm she made last week in the apothecary. I shiver a little when her fingertips make contact with my back. They dance their way up my spine as we kiss, our tongues slowly twisting together.

And as we kiss, our short history begins flashing through my mind. Scenes flicker. That first day when she arrived and I scared her. The moment when she realized she was trapped here with me and could only pay off her debt by making me happy. Her long, sad face after her date with Russ Roth. And then the happier one after she called her friend, Jacqueline, and realized she was still real.

She was vulnerable back then. And even though she's so much stronger now—her spelling is quite impressive, even Tarq thought so—she's still vulnerable.

There's a part of me that wants to take her away now. A part that wants to leave this place. But there's that other part of me that wants us to stay here forever. Just... get rid of these monsters and go back to the way it was those first few days.

Everything was so exciting when Pie showed up. And even though I complained about it, it was the thrilling sort of exciting. The kind that comes with confusion, and opportunities, and all kinds of feelings.

Then everything got complicated. And now Pie thinks

that the curse is protecting us. And we're both questioning the goal.

Should we even *try* to break the curse?

Because if we do, then we open ourselves up to all the bad shit that hasn't been able to touch me over the centuries.

But if we stay here, we're just... master and caretaker. That's all we'll ever be.

There is a part of me that wants to let the monsters have it. Let Tomas hatch baby dragons in the dungeon. Let Batty and the rest of them terrorize humanity in whatever way they want. Maybe even free the prisoners in the Bottoms.

Just... let it all decay the way it should've a thousand years ago.

But I'm afraid that this is taking it too far.

Because I am a monster out of time.

I don't belong here in this age any more than Saint Mark's does.

And if it goes, maybe I go with it?

Pie pulls out of our kiss, her breath a little bit heavy and those sparkling blue eyes of hers half-closed. "What are you thinking about?"

"You."

"Liar."

I chuckle. "Later, Pie." And when I kiss her again, her hand slides between us and grabs my growing hard-on.

She whispers into my mouth, "You were much easier to seduce when you didn't wear pants."

More flashes of memories come with this statement. Her demands that I cover myself up. Her blushing face whenever she accidentally saw my 'package.' That whole conversation in the Pleasure Cave when she thought she had accidentally put a love spell on herself.

There is no way to stop my smile.

And that's how I kiss her as I spread her legs open wider,

pull my pants down out of the way, slip her panties aside, and push myself inside her.

I kiss and love her—smiling.

She gasps when I go a little too fast and I always slow down when she does this. I want to ask her if she's OK. I want to make sure I'm not hurting her. But she always reassures me before I can get the questions out.

This time is no different. She places her hands on my face and just keeps kissing me, urging me to continue.

But I keep the pace slow and easy after that. We're not in a rush. We have all the time in the world for this. And she just makes me feel so good, I want to prolong the experience.

But eventually, she does something that just turns me on so bad, I can't hold back. She leans in to my shoulder, tipping her mouth up to my ear, and she says, "'I love you more than you can know. I see us now, and as we grow. I'll be there for you 'till the end—your wife, your lover, and your friend.'"

It's an offer, a proposal, and the ultimate promise all wrapped up in one Pie spelling.

A pledge with a twist of magic.

And then my mind flashes with—not a memory, but a possibility.

A wedding.

She comes underneath me, moaning into my ear, clawing at my shoulders, her legs wrapping tightly around me.

And then I come too. And in this moment of pure ecstasy, I understand what I need to do next.

We're gonna need another ring.

CHAPTER FIVE - PIE

ell and I stay together in his tomb for a while. I'm practically lying across his chest, dreamily replaying that last spelling in my head. I didn't plan it. I haven't planned any of them all day. And maybe the first couple sorta freaked me out, but this one... I actually sigh out loud. This one was perfect.

"What are you thinking about?" Pell is stroking my hair, lazily dragging his fingers through it.

"I just love you." I can't see his smile, but I can feel it. "And I don't know what's coming, but I meant that spelling." I lift my head up, reposition so I can see his face, and then sigh out loud again. "Whatever happens, I'm on your side."

He places his hands on my cheeks, still grinning. "And I'm on yours."

"I go where you go."

"If you lead, I'll follow."

We both smile now. And I lie back down on his chest. Content.

A little while later Pell gets up, adjusts his package in his pants, and grins down at me. "I have a pressing matter in the smithy."

I'm confused. "What kind of pressing matter?"

"Need-to-know basis. But…" He glances to the part of the forest path that leads to the outside. "Would you mind staying inside the tomb for the rest of the day?"

"Why?"

"I don't know what's going on with them, Pie." He kinda motions with a hand towards the outside. "But something is brewing. They're mad at me right now and I don't want them to take it out on you."

"You're not the only one they're mad at."

"All the more reason for you to stay inside."

"But I have to go check on Jacqueline."

He looks over at the doors. "That door pops you out onto the side of the mountain in town, remember? You can take a door, right?"

I nod. "Yeah. Sure. I hadn't thought of that, but it's a good idea."

"Good. Then I'm gonna go take care of business in the smithy and I'll be back later."

He bends down to kiss me, but instead of a little peck goodbye, it's a long, passionate affair. He even puts his hands on my head, like he can't bear to let go of me, and our tongues play together for almost a full minute.

When he pulls away and stands back up, he sighs. "I already miss you."

I kinda melt into the forest floor. And my eyes track his muscular back and furry legs as he jogs away, down the path.

I relax a little, kind of relieved that I don't have to go outside. I really like Pell's tomb. Mostly because I know it's safe in here. No one can hurt me inside this tomb. And I'm glad he suggested that I use the doors to travel because that's an excellent idea.

Also, a limitless one.

I get up and walk over to the line of doors. Most of them have a ring floating in front, but not all. The ones we've already used do not have a ring because Pell and I are still wearing them. Once you put them on, you can't take them off.

I think this is because once you use them, they are assigned to that door forever. Maybe there is some kind of reset spelling to make a clean slate of destinations, but if so, I don't know how to do it.

We've only used a few. The mountainside in Granite Springs, the bakery in Vinca, and Tarq's office in Vinca.

Plus one more. The one I used to leave the Bottoms. I'm just not sure which door this is because it wasn't planned and it didn't come with a designated ring. In my head, I thought it was the Granite Springs door when I came out. The one Pell controls with his lion ring. But if it was, then I don't know how that works. How would one get home from the Bottoms if the door leads to Granite Springs?

I dunno. None of this is the point of my deep thinking. The point is there's fifty of them in total so it won't matter at all if I use one to, say... go visit Tomas in the dungeon. Pell didn't say anything about seeing Tomas when he left. He just said he didn't want me to leave the tomb. And if I use a door, I won't need to leave the tomb.

Yeah, it's a little bit sneaky. But I'm not afraid of Tomas. I'm really not. Even if he turns back into his dragon self, I would still not be afraid of him. I would keep my distance, for sure. But that's just common sense, not fear.

I need a bath. And a change of clothes. I don't stay in the cottage anymore. Batty, Eyebrows, Cookie and a few others have taken it over, anyway. So I just moved my clothes and stuff here to the tomb. Pell has a makeshift bathroom here in the forest. It's got a shower. Well, it's actually a bag hanging from a tree that he fills with water. But there's no tub.

I was distressed about this at first, but then Pell suggested I just use the stream. It's not hot water, but the season in these woods feels like perpetual June. So it's cool water, but it's very refreshing.

I spent a whole day in the apothecary last week making different kinds of soaps, and balms, and tonics, following recipes in an old book written by an ancient alchemist called Pressia. There were several to choose from, but this one was very nicely illustrated. There were even illustrations of her. In color, even.

Now I gather my little basket of homemade products, take a bath in the stream, and dress in an outfit Eyebrows made for me for my job in Vinca—a pair of tan leggings that end just above my first knee joint and a super-soft, cotton-eyelet crop top.

Then I walk over to the next door in the long line of them and pluck the ring floating in front of it from the air, looking at it carefully. There is a design on it. Leaves. Typical. But as I stare at it, the design begins to change. The gold rearranges until I can make out the head of a dragon.

"Well." I smile and put the ring on. "That's settled, I guess." I will go see Tomas first. Because I have questions.

I open the door and stand there, staring into the shimmering, silver nothingness, trying to think up a spelling for a door to the dungeon. But a moment later the words are already spilling out of my mouth:

"A dragon's lair, a prison cell
Scales, and blood, and fiery hell
Take me there, reunite
Keep this from the monsters' sight."

And then there I am, standing at the bottom of the stairs, kind of impressed with myself, if I'm being honest. Because I wasn't thinking about keeping this little visit a secret, but now it will be.

Cool.

I smile, still pleasantly surprised that I'm actually good at this spelling shit.

"Tomas?" I say it quietly because it's very quiet down here. "Are you awake?"

I don't move forward. I might not be afraid of him, but it would be stupid to assume I'm safe down here. And if he's not his usual self, I can just back up and get out quick.

"I'm here." His voice is low and rumbly, like he was sleeping.

"Should I come back later?"

"No. I'm awake. Did you come through a door?"

"Yeah. Pell wants me to stay in the tomb. The monsters are… gettin' weird."

"Are they?" Tomas appears from the shadows looking like a dragon chimera who just woke up, which translates to… very sexy. Damn. His dark hair is all tousled, his cut muscles all tight so that your eyes just want to follow the ripple of his abs down to where his skin turns to red-orange scales. Even when he yawns, cavernously and without shame, stretching his arms high above his head, you can't help but stare at him.

Tomas is hot. And he doesn't even know it, which makes him even hotter.

I shake myself out of it. "Yeah. They are. They're… restless. Maybe?" I would like this to be the answer, but it's not. "I have a question."

"Hit me with it, sunshine." Tomas grins, unleashing dimples on me.

"OK. Well, when I was in Vinca with Tarq he came to my lab and showed me a book."

"Did he?"

"He did."

"What was in this book?"

"Pictures. Of the monsters." I nod my head towards the ceiling. "They were all in there. It was some kind of perp book."

"A what?"

"You know. Cops have books with pictures of known criminals. That's what this was. Tarq wanted me to identify the monsters."

"Did you?"

"No."

"Was I in there?"

"No."

"Why not?"

I smile. "Were you part of Vinca?"

"No. I've heard of it, but never been there."

"Well, I think all these monsters are actually from Vinca."

"Batty is, for sure. And Eyebrows."

"And Cookie," I add. "He was definitely from there."

"But all the others, too?" Tomas asks. I nod. "So what's the question?"

"Do you think…" I cringe. I don't want this to be true, but I already know it is. I just want confirmation. "Do you think they were actually meant to be prisoners here, Tomas? Like… the whole reason they were brought here was so I could lock them up in the Bottoms the way I did Callistina?"

And Nysta, I don't add. That wasn't really thought out, obviously. But I'm not sorry about it.

Tomas just smiles at me. "What do you think, sunshine?"

I sigh.

"You have a job here, correct?"

"Slave caretaker."

"Slave caretaker. You take care of slaves."

"Did we come to a consensus on that? Because I'm not convinced we did."

"Oh, we did. You take care of slaves."

"Which means they're—"

"Slaves."

"And I should—"

"Lock them up immediately."

"Tomas! Why didn't you tell me this?"

"Because maybe I wasn't in that book, but I'm one of them, darling. And I just found a loophole in my sentence. I didn't want to give it up."

"But now you're back down here."

"Yes. But it's by choice this time." He looks into the shadows. "Isn't that right, my love? We're here because we want to be here, aren't we?"

A growl rumbles from the corner, low and throaty.

"Is she—"

"Don't worry, sunshine. She's not ready yet."

"Not ready for… what?"

"To be her dragon self. It will take a little while yet."

"And then what happens?"

"She will be a dragon for a few centuries."

"Centuries?"

He frowns. "We have a slow maturation process." Then he brightens. "But that's OK. If I have to be stuck here forever, then I have all the time in the world to wait for her to be able to love me in this form."

"So you're…" I don't really know how to finish my question, so I wave my finger around in his direction. "Just a chimera now?"

"This is the final life stage for me."

"Final? You're not going to die, are you?"

"Darling, everyone dies eventually. Even Pell, one day."

A sudden sadness overtakes me and I wilt a little. "Well, I hope it's not soon, Tomas. I love you. I hope you know that. You and Pell, you're my people now. Oh." I hold up a finger and my eyes go wide. "I forgot to tell you. I bumped into my best childhood friend out on the country road."

Tomas guffaws. "You did what?"

"I know. Crazy, right? She's like the only person I have on the outside. Pell made me call her after my disastrous date with Russ Roth just to prove that I was real. And I told her I was in Granite Springs. So… well, it's a long, weird story, but she came here to find me."

"And she did." He grins.

"She did." I smile too.

"Well, bring her down. I would love to meet your friend."

"She's not here. We put her up in Granite Springs."

"I thought Pell said the devil was living in the bar?"

"He is. I guess. I don't know. But I put a spelling on Jacqueline to make her stay out of the bar."

Tomas is wincing.

"I know. It's not a perfect solution. But I can't bring her here. She doesn't know I'm a monster. And she's got kids with her. Right now, this is no place for kids."

"That's for sure. You said the monsters were restless. But they're giving you trouble, aren't they?"

"Trouble? Well…"

"They are."

"Yeah." I sigh. "They really are. Ever since the wood nymphs got here, they've been different."

"Ah, yes. The infamous Vincan wood nymphs. Someone, maybe Batty, told me about them. But that was a very stressful night, so I don't remember all of it."

"That's for sure." My eyes dart to the shadow behind Tomas where Madeline is hiding. She must see me looking in her direction because another low growl floats out from the darkness.

"Never mind her." Tomas waves a hand in the air, dismissing the growl.

I redirect to Tomas. "Do you remember setting Granite Springs on fire?"

"I do." His eyes narrow and his face changes. And this is maybe the first time I've ever seen the dragon hiding underneath when he's in his chimera form. His eyes flash yellow for a moment. Then there's like… like a mirage, or something. Blood-red scales form and disappear over his chest, arms, and neck. "They deserved it though."

And the moment after this declaration, the mirage fades and Tomas is Tomas again. Cheerful, optimistic, and sexy. He claps his hands together. "Now. What else can I do for you?"

I let out a breath. "Nothing, I guess. What can I do for you? Do you need help with anything, Tomas?"

"Is that a real question? Or a polite one?"

"Real. If you need anything, just let me know. You're not a prisoner here, OK? I don't care why they sent you here in the first place—whatever you did, thousands of years should be enough penance."

He presses his lips together.

"What? What do you need? Just spit it out."

"It's a big ask."

"Maybe. But ask anyway."

"OK, if you insist. I would like a door. One like that." He points behind me where my door, the one I came through from Pell's tomb, is waiting like a patient steed for me to exit.

"Huh. OK. Well, I've never given away a door before. I'm not sure how I would do it. But I'm sure—"

And then, like magic, the words are tumbling out of my mouth.

"A dragon's lair, bare to bone.
A door to where, and when, and home.
He can leave, and come, and go.
Be the dragon we love and know."

And poof. Like... magic, again... there is another door. With a ring floating in front of it.

"Holy hell, Pie! I had no idea you were such an adept!"

"Um." I just stare at the door and the ring. "Me either." Then I let out another long breath. "Tomas? Can I tell you something?"

"Anything, sunshine."

I point at the door. "I didn't do that. And earlier, when I put those ruby things on the walls?" My gaze darts over to the walls. They're glowing now. And just a moment ago, they weren't. I look back at Tomas. "I'm not in control of this. I'm not in control of any of it."

Tomas reaches out and places a hand on my cheek,

85

stroking it as he looks fondly into my eyes. "Of course you're not, Pie. None of us are. Do you think I want to burn things down? I don't. But what I want doesn't matter, does it?"

"Doesn't it scare you?"

He shrugs and pulls his hand off my cheek. "Maybe, back when I was new. But now? It is what it is. And for what it's worth, most of the last several thousand years has gone without incident. It's only recently that things became a problem again."

"Recently. Like… since *I* got here."

"Perhaps. But then again, perhaps not. It might just be my time, Pie. It might be something as simple as that." He grins and rubs his hands together. "At any rate, look at this beautiful door! And what is this? A ring? Is it for me? Shall I put it on?"

And, as always, Tomas's innocent, child-like wonder is contagious. And the troubled feeling inside me ebbs away like a wave leaving the beach. It'll come back. That's what waves do. But it's gone right now.

I pluck the ring out of the air and look at it for a moment. Do I recognize it from the bag? Not really. It's silver, like most of them. And fairly plain, with no stone. But there is an engraving along the outside.

"Does it say something?" Tomas asks, his voice low and reverent now.

I squint until the words come into focus. "It says… 'Be the dragon.'" I look over at him. "Please don't take that too literally."

He grins, then crosses his heart with a finger.

I offer him the ring and he takes it, eyes squinting, just like mine did. "Hmm."

"What?"

"'Be the dragon,' you say?"

"Yeah. Why?"

"That's not what I see."

"What do you mean?"

"It doesn't say that when I look at it."

"What do you see?"

"It says… 'Property of Pie Vita. Please return to owner when finished.'"

I huff out a laugh and shake my head at him. "That's not what it says."

"No. But it should. It's your ring, Pie. I'm simply borrowing it. Feel free to take it back if you feel it's necessary."

This is a warning. Well, no. Not really a warning. More like a *fore*warning.

He is going to do something with this door. Something big.

But not even Tomas knows what that big thing is yet.

"Where do you think it leads?"

I turn and face the door. It's closed, of course. "It will probably go wherever you want it to."

"How do I make it work?"

"Well, I do a spelling and the spelling tells it where to go. But I'm not really an expert. I'm sure there are many ways to make these doors work."

"I've never been a poet. But I will work on it."

"Where do you want to go, Tomas?" I'm a little bit sad when these words come out. Because I can feel him slipping away and it's not fair, really. We should have decades of friendship ahead of us. Days of tripping the hallways upstairs, and eating dinner together, and just… enjoying each other.

But I don't think that's how this ends and that's what this sadness is.

"I don't know," Tomas says. "I don't know what's out there." He looks at me, his eyes a little bit panicked. "What if I can't go anywhere because I've never been anywhere?"

And now I feel selfish for wanting him to stay here. He's a

prisoner. And like I said, no matter what he did thousands of years ago to land in this place, this punishment does not fit the crime. He deserves to leave and find his own life. "Maybe it's like the hallways? Maybe you just... trust it?"

He relaxes, smiling again. "Yeah. Maybe it is."

here is tension in the sanctuary as I weave my way through the tombs in the direction of the cathedral. I only get to marry Pie Vita once, so I'm going to do it right. She will wear this ring for the rest of her life and that means it should be special.

I am a talented blacksmith. I could bang out a ring in a matter of minutes. But I'm not going to do that. I want to take my time and, if there is any real magic inside me, I would like to put it in that ring and share it with her.

So I'm heading up to the apothecary library to get some ideas about this.

But the tension is distracting me.

There are monsters and nymphs everywhere. The party is over. It's not even happening down by the lake. And this was not my doing. Still, I can feel the blame.

I growl at a monster staring me down as I pass. "What? You have something to say to me?" I don't mean to use my new powerful voice, it just comes out. And things all around me begin to crumble.

The monster turns his head, unwilling to start a fight.

I take deep breaths because the anger inside me is so quick these days. I think the voice is tied to anger. Maybe I should look for a book on that too?

I come out onto the pea-pebble pathway that leads to the cathedral and immediately my eyes are drawn to the black tomb with the gold dome. Then they travel down to the black stone statue. A monster with gold horns.

I was in there. I heard Grant in there. But I heard Pie, too. Only it wasn't Pie.

What is going on with that thing? And the statue is creepy. It reminds me of many monsters, but mostly, it reminds me of Tarq.

Of course, I know it's not Tarq. Because Tarq's tomb is quite a ways away—not even on the same side of the pathway that cuts the sanctuary into halves.

But there is no way to deny that the tall, black statue with the gold horns and hooves shares a resemblance with my oldest friend.

Just thinking this thought sends a shiver of foreboding crawling up my spine.

But I don't have time for that tomb, or the monster who may or may not be inside it. So I shake it off and just walk past the tomb and into the cathedral.

There are no monsters in here. Not even a nymph. And, even though I don't want to admit it, I'm relieved. I don't want to have confrontations with them. I don't want to be their master, either. I just want them to leave me alone. I just want them to leave, actually.

I liked it when it was just me, and Pie, and Tomas. And fine, he wants a dragon-wife, the Madeline girl can stay too. I would be OK with that. But a hundred other people crowding us with their wants, and needs, and annoying parties?

Maybe I'm getting old? Am I acting like an old person? Why is 'sensible' synonymous with 'old?'

When I get to the top of the stairs there is no one in the new grand dining room. Just a bunch of empty tables. Well, they can't complain about that anymore, can they? I got them their stupid hay.

Vegetarians, my ass. Cookie just uses that hay to make his magical dishes.

Gross. Now I'm wondering how much of his magic I've eaten.

I'm never eating that food again. Pie and I will have to find a new grocery store. Even if the one in Granite Springs still has food in it, it can't be good food. Surely it's spoiled by now. There must be another town within the fifty-mile freedom limit that we can shop at for real food.

And now that I'm thinking about Granite Springs, I remember the woman. Jacqueline. And those kids.

I sigh, suddenly feeling a little overwhelmed with all the changes.

Even the apothecary is empty. And usually there is a whole team of fastidious monsters in here cataloguing things and filling up jars with the herbs and shit they harvest from the greenhouse.

But I'm glad they're somewhere else today. I'm not in the mood for anyone but Pie.

I grab a ladder, slide it over to the section of the library shelves where I found the book on bags, and then climb up. I have a feeling that the books up here are very old. And maybe old people are sensible and boring, but they are also wise.

Once up on the shaky scaffolding of the third level, I scan the spines. I'm just reaching for a book called *Breathing Life into Metal* when I see a name I recognize and pull that book out instead.

Pressia. She was the market nymph who wrote the book on bags.

I take it down to the ground floor, place it on the stone alchemy bench, and open it up. But then I get distracted by another open book that seems to have the same illustrations as the one I'm looking at.

I grab the other book, slide it over to me, and look at the

cover. *Soaps, Balms, and Tonics for the Magical Nymph.* Again by this Pressia woman.

Hmm. I think Pie was using this book. And is that weird?

I look up at the library all around me. There are thousands of books in this apothecary. What are the chances that Pie and I would both find a book by the same author?

I look back down to my ring book. It's called *Make Her Day Magical with a Magical Ring.*

"OK." I say this out loud. "What the fuck is going on here? I come looking for a book on how to make a magical wedding ring and one just... presents itself to me?"

I don't know who I expect to answer me. There is literally no one here. So no one does, of course. But I can feel some kind of presence.

Maybe it's the books?

"Pressia." I don't recall ever hearing about a market nymph called Pressia. Of course, who knows when she was alive, and I've been in here for thousands of years, so that's not unusual. I glance back up at the top shelf, and now that I know what to look for on the spines, I see many, *many* books by the market nymph Pressia.

She must've been someone important.

I open the book on rings. It's not a thick book. It's barely more than a pamphlet. But it's bound in engraved and illuminated leather. A very nice book for one specific task.

Still, it is what I need.

And the last time I came looking for a book—*The Magic and Mischief of Bags*—I found the one I needed too.

Hmm. It's the hallways, I think. Even though the apothecary isn't a hallway and nothing about this room has ever been variable. It must be the hallways directing me to the answer I'm searching for.

Then I get another idea. What if Pressia used to live here?

I pause, wondering if I just invented a conspiracy theory... or perhaps I might be onto something. If she was some kind of prisoner, or master, or slave caretaker of this place before I got here, then maybe she had a lot of time on her hands and she spent some of it writing books?

I've had dumber ideas in my lifetime.

But the way I remember things, the great alchemist Ostanes made this place to keep her secrets safe, and the gods panicked. The entire curse was created through a flurry of magical moves and countermoves by Saturn and Juno. But in a way that made everything more complicated, not less.

"Wait a minute." I pause. This was the story. I know that for sure. I've told this story to many a caretaker over the centuries. But it feels... rehearsed. Like I've literally said these same words, in that same order, dozens of times.

My mind goes blank for a moment. And then I just feel dumb. "Who cares?"

I take my book on how to make her magical day magical and leave the apothecary.

There is still time in this day to make progress on this ring and I don't want to waste it.

Again, when I pass through the maze of tombs, the monsters stare at me.

I don't acknowledge them. I don't even glance at them. I'm not sure I like the new voice and I one hundred percent don't understand the new voice. So I will do my best to control my anger—and my speech—until I understand it better.

Still, the tension as I make my way towards the smithy is palpable. Even more so when I step inside and close the door, because then all the tension melts away.

I sigh, put my apron on, start my fire, and sit down to read this book while I wait for the coals to get hot.

There's a whole bunch of blah, blah, blah about the history of weddings and rings—I stop here to growl. Because it mentions that the meaning of the wedding ring goes back to the god, Saturn. And I hate that guy. But I'm not going to let ancient history spoil my love for Pie and my quest to make her the perfect wedding ring. So I let it go.

There are several more pages—with quite nice illustrations—that describe how to write a vow, more blah, blah, blah. And then a small section on the power of a voice and a little marketing push for a book two in this series by the same author called *Kissing Magic on Your Wedding Day*.

Nice. I think Pie and I have the whole kissing thing down and don't need tips, but maybe I will check that one out later.

Finally, I get to the magic recipe. And of course, it's in verse.

To make your love a bit of magic
Forge a ring of pure metallic
Make it soft and malleable
And soon her heart will overflow.

Hmm. Pure gold is very soft and malleable. But it's too soft to use for jewelry. It would not retain a shape on her finger. I would have to add something to it.

I choose silver. Pure silver is also soft and will lose its shape, but the spell calls for malleability. And if I had to choose, silver is more in line with what I envision to be metallic.

I find a small rod of silver left over from when I forged the bag and a few minutes later, I have a ring.

The book has another poem to decipher, so I go back to the instructions.

Now you have her ring in hand
It's time to stamp it with your brand.
Give your power to her now
Breath, and words, and voice, and vow.

Well, that's not creepy. I mean, what are the chances that everyone reading this little book would have breath, and words, and voice power?

Something… is afoot.

Whoever this Pressia is, she wrote these books for me.

Maybe Pie, too, since Pie used Pressia's spells and recipes to make her soaps, and balms, and tonics the other day.

Yeah. I think I need to go up into the hallways and find this Pressia woman.

But first, I need to make a vow and finish the ring. I never did finish the bag—Tomas never gave his fire blessing. But I don't need anyone's help to complete this project.

I just need a good vow.

I grab a little notebook and a thin piece of charcoal, then go up to the roof and settle myself on the edge, gazing out in the direction of the lake.

It's so peaceful. Almost too peaceful. And that's when I notice that there's not a single monster or nymph in sight.

"Hmm. Maybe wishes do come true?" Then I catch a bit of light glinting off the polished gold surface of the black tomb's dome. "Later, tomb. I have a vow to write."

I think for a while, just relaxing in the sun. I lie back on the hot wooden planks of the roof and let my mind wander in thoughts and images of Pie.

I think of all the things I love about her. She's very pretty in a fresh-faced sort of way. But she's also funny, and good, and honest. And powerful. Pie thinks she came here power-less, but that's not true at all. That's not how power works. Not innate power, anyway.

It was always there, she just needed a little help turning it on.

Of course, she was always the Bird Whisperer. Then she was an eros lure. She was in Vinca for what, a week? And now look at her. The Magna Ducissa of Spelling. The Regina of Doors. And, let's not forget, the Tamer of Monsters. She's my little Package Pleasurer. My Junk Jerker. My Cock Coddler. My… OK, OK, OK. This is a fun distraction, but I need to write a vow.

And it needs to be perfect.

It might as well start with the word A, since Pie says that's how all the most powerful spellings begin. And it should embody the both of us. Attributes that describe us, maybe. And then, of course, I need to put some feelings in there and a promise about eternity.

I start jotting down words, getting a little lost in my process and feeling pretty good about it.

But then there is a commotion across the sanctuary, over by Pie's little cottage. I stand up and shade my eyes for a better look, then sigh.

Batty and that outspoken nymph, Isla.

I can't really hear what's being said, but I think there's an argument.

And now I'm angry again. Because this place is called a sanctuary and it's never been so full of strife.

It's not meant to be full of strife. It's meant to be a fucking place of refuge. And these damn monsters aren't appreciative.

This is what pisses me off. Their careless attitudes. Their contempt for my rules. Their frivolous parties and frat-boy insolence. And the irony is not lost on me. Wasn't I, just a couple months ago, defending my ways to Pie as something intrinsic? Wasn't I selling my monstrosity as something she was just supposed to accept?

Well... things have changed.

I've changed. This kind of behavior is no longer acceptable and I'm putting my foot down.

I shove the notebook and pencil into my pocket—pants really do come in handy—go back down the stairs, and leave the smithy.

Because I'm sick of these monsters and their interference in my sanctuary time is now over.

CHAPTER SEVEN - PIE

I *leave the dungeon* using my door and return to Pell's tomb. And when I get there, I decide I need to have some deep thoughts about rings and doors.

Because I just gave a door away. It even came with a ring and a spelling.

But the scariest part is, even though I was OK with doing that, I *didn't* do that.

The spelling just came out! The same way it did for the rubies in the walls.

"Pie..." I'm whispering to myself as I push through the woods and start counting doors. "You need to be careful. You have no idea what you're doing."

I agree with myself. Which is why I'm walking these doors. It takes me a while—there is a lot of brush to push through—but when I get to the end, there are only forty-nine doors.

I go back the way I came and just stand there in front of the doors that already have destinations, thinking about all the new, super-powerful magic I now seem to possess.

Not only can I walk through doors to other worlds, or this world, or... anywhere, maybe, I can also give doors away. They even come with rings and spellings. It's like a magical door kit. Everything you need to travel through worlds.

But wait, there's more!

I can manifest things—like glowing rubies in walls. I don't even know what that spell was about. Tomas and Madeline, obviously. But... yeah. I might've done something weird there.

And of course, I put a spell on Jacqueline and her kids to keep them away from the devil's bar in town. Not to mention the whole bloodhorn banishing spell I did to Russ Roth. But both of those were on purpose. There is a big difference between intentionally doing something and accidentally doing something.

It gets worse. What if... and I'm just spitballing here, but what if it's not an accident? What if someone is controlling me?

"This is bad."

And... oh, God. I wilt and my shoulders immediately drop into monkey-walk position. There's even more magic going on here. Because I can imprison people. No, even that's not right. I can *enslave* people. Because I can give them a Book of Debt.

What the hell? Also, what the hell is wrong with me? First Callistina and now Nysta? Why did I do that?

You didn't do that, Pie. The magic did it all on its own.

I don't want to think about the Bottoms. And even though I made a big deal about letting the monsters and nymphs see their debt books, I have no idea if they even have debt books. And even if they did, I've got no plans—like zero plans—that have anything to do with the Bottoms.

I don't want to go down there again. I don't want to go to Vinca again. And if Jacqueline wasn't in Granite Springs, I wouldn't want to go there either.

I just want to go home.

Which is funny, because I don't have a home. Pell's tomb is the closest thing I have to home these days. And I'm actually sitting at home right this moment. And yet... I still feel this pull. This longing. This indescribable desire for a place called 'home.'

My fingertips tingle and then, a moment later, my palms

begin to itch. I look at them, wondering what will come flying out next.

Moths?

Fireflies?

An image of Pell's statue flashes through my mind and then I'm picturing scarab beetles.

Wow. That's gross.

There's a part of me that wishes all this magic would just go away. But then, it's all kinda cool, right?

Except for the moths. And seriously, scarab beetles are a step too far.

I'm very powerful though. Is there a limit to my power? Or is it some kind of your-wish-is-my-command magic?

I don't know. I don't have enough information to know. As much as I hate to admit it, I will need to hit up that library in the Bottoms. Like it or not, there is a trip down there in my immediate future. And then I need to hit up the library in the apothecary too. Because I suddenly get the feeling that there is a lot more to Saint Mark's Sanctuary than I can even imagine and everything I need to know is probably up there on those shelves.

Then, as if I need another distraction, another question pops into my already muddled brain. What about all these doors with no destinations?

Most of the rings are just floating there in front of them. It's kind of handy. It means we don't have to keep track of them or force them into that bag—like that ever worked. But it's a little bit dangerous too. It's like leaving your car keys in the car. And these rings aren't even hidden under the mat. They're just floating in front of their doors like an invitation.

Perhaps these rings are specific? Perhaps one must be me, or Pell, to use them?

But it's far more likely that they can be used by anyone.

"Hold on." I actually say this out loud as I hold a finger up in front of me. Because they do have a lock.

The spelling. You have to have a spell too. It's like a kill switch.

This makes me feel better about leaving them here with no one to stand guard, but now my mind is all muddied up with ring theory. I need to figure this out before I can leave to talk to Jacqueline, so I run through what I know so far.

One. To use a door, you must have a ring and a spelling.

Two. Once you put a ring on, you don't seem to be able to take it off. It's yours. Maybe not forever—doesn't everything have a loophole?—but it seems to be the general rule that if you claim a ring, you claim a door.

Three. Some rings can combine and I don't know what that means yet. But my original slave ring combined with another ring to make the brassy moth ring I'm wearing now. And Pell's gold ring combined with that sparkly ring used for Tarq's office and became the lion ring he's wearing now.

Four. Doors can be given away. At the very least, I can do that. But Pell and I seem to be connected by these doors so he can probably give doors away too.

Five. Doors go to specific places.

But then I think about this for a moment. It's not really true, is it?

Right now, I'm wearing the ring with the pink stone. But that ring originally took me to the palace bakery. But during that trip I went to the Bottoms and—here's the really confusing part—when I left the Bottoms I came up out of the Granite Springs door.

I'm sure that happened.

So... what the fuck?

How did I leave here through the bakery door and return here from the Granite Springs door, which really should be called the Bottoms door?

It makes no sense. Which means it can't be a rule. Because what is the point of a rule that makes no sense?

Is there... perhaps a link between Saint Mark's, the Vinca palace bakery, and the Bottoms?

Maybe. Or maybe doors are like roads. They can twist, and turn, and take you many places. They can even take you to a new door without you realizing you've changed course, the way a country road might veer off at a fork. And that new directional door is not one of my doors because I have forty-nine of them here in Pell's forest, and I only gave one away.

"A map would be handy, ya know!" I say this to the forest sky, talking to no one in particular.

I glance at another door, the one that leads to Tarq's office. There is no ring for this door right now because Pell is wearing it. That means he controls it.

Then there was that first door I made that opened up to the candle shop in Granite Springs. I can see that door—I can see all the doors, actually. They are lined up in the woods, some of them mostly hidden by the boughs and leaves, but for sure they are all here. I just counted them. But that candle shop door is open, because I was going to use it, but it's not the candle shop. It's just a blank shimmer and the ring is floating there in front of it like all the other unused doors.

So this is another rule. Pell and I didn't step through that door. I took the ring off—which is good to know. I can change my mind and not use a door. As long as I don't walk through, I can take the ring off and keep the door passive.

New rule. At the very least, to connect a ring to a door, you must put the ring on. And to connect a door to a destination, you must recite a spelling, specific to that location, and step through wearing that ring.

I let out a long sigh. My brain is starting to hurt. And I'm not even done tallying up my current ring and door situation.

There is the door to Granite Springs that takes us to the hillside. This one makes no sense at all. It first appeared after we had sex right here in the tomb. But then it went away after that moth ring attacked me. But then we opened it back up again to go to Granite Springs. But then this is also the door I came out of from the Bottoms.

Except... Pell used this door to leave the smithy and come here. This is the first door that opened.

"Come on!" I whine up to the sky. "How does this make sense?"

No one answers me, of course, so I just continue with my inventory.

The moth ring and the slave caretaker ring are now the same and I'm wearing both. They seem to be connected to several doors, now that I think about it—the Vinca door at Tarq's tomb and the door that leads to Pell's tomb, which is also the door that got me here from the Bottoms and took us to Granite Springs.

I'm having a severe case of 'what the fuck' right now, but then I get another idea.

These two rings—Pell's gold lion ring and my brassy moth ring—are connected.

Not only that, they are connected to important places like the Vinca lobby, Pell's tomb, and Granite Spring.

"Oh!" I almost scream this. "Holy shit! The sanctuary gate!"

I think that's a door as well.

OK. I think I've accounted for all my doors. I am wearing three rings: The brassy moth ring, which is also the acorn slave-caretaker ring, which connects to Pell's tomb, Saint Mark's gate, Tarq's tomb that leads to Vinca, and Granite Springs. The pink-stone ring, which seems to control the Bottoms, and Queen Callistina, specifically, and also leads to the Vinca palace bakery. And now my new dragon ring, which takes me to Tomas and the dungeon.

And Pell is wearing two rings: His gold lion ring that leads to his tomb and Granite Springs. And his tiny sparkle ring that only goes as far as his first knuckle, which leads to Tarq's office.

I can't forget that I gave Tomas a door, and that comes with a ring, so... here is my conclusion.

Forget all those stupid rules. I only need one rule. The one rule that Pell came up with in the first place.

Magic. This shit is just magic.

Also, rings and doors are not like roads. They are like hallways. Specifically, upstairs hallways at Saint Mark's Sanctuary.

And I think, if someone was kind enough to give me a map, I would discover that all roads lead to Rome, i.e. *here*.

And then my eyes sweep over the long line of doors in Pell's tomb forest and I just have to laugh. Because of course they do. They are all right in front of me. And if they all lead here, they can lead to each other, as well.

I point up to the sky. "Ya could've just told me that! OK." I let out a long breath, bring my hands up, and make a sweeping motion to clear the air in front of me. "Focus, Pie. One thing at a time."

I need to get to Jacqueline. I need to make sure she's OK and figure out what to do with her next. I can't leave her in town, that's too precarious. And I can't bring her here, this place is downright dangerous.

So... a hotel? I remember seeing one across the road from that gas station Pell and I went to the night of my disastrous date. I don't really remember much about it. We haven't had to fill up the Jeep since then, and the truck holds a gajillion gallons of gas and it came with a full tank, I guess. Because it's not low. And we haven't really gone anywhere, so we haven't gone back to that gas station.

It might be a really crappy hotel, but this is my best bet at the moment.

I make a plan. Take the door to Granite Springs, pile Jacqueline and her kids into that bus, maybe steal a car from the used car lot so I can follow them to the motel, check them in using magic money, and then leave them there for the night—with many promises that I will come back tomorrow—and then come home and talk all this shit out with Pell.

Yep. This will have to do.

I walk over to the Granite Springs door, grab my leather jacket off a branch and put it on, then suck in a breath and walk through.

I pay attention to the journey this time. Because on the tomb side of this door I am a wood nymph chimera. And on the Granite Spring side of this door, I am plain old human Pie.

But I've never felt this change and I don't feel it now, either. Even though I'm trying to.

I come out on the hillside, just like Pell and I did that night we went on our date to the bar. It's not snowing, but there is a lot of snow on the trees. And even though I'm wearing a coat, I'm immediately cold because... yep.

I'm wearing the slutty schoolgirl outfit.

Why? Why must the universe torture me with my Halloween costume?

But my plaid mini-skirt and leather bustier are the least of my problems. No matter what story I tell Jacqueline, she's not gonna buy it. I could see it on her face when we left. She was going along with the whole abandoned coal-mine town thing just to make things easy.

But it doesn't make sense and Jacqueline is not stupid. Even if she wasn't over-educated, she would still see through this. She's street-smart and everything about our story was screaming bullshit.

I walk down the hill slowly and carefully because there's still a lot of snow up here. So I'm watching my boots, not looking at the town, when I finally make it to the bottom.

And then I look up and... "What the actual fuck?"

I say this out loud. Because what the actual fuck? I turn in a circle, then throw up my hands. "I give up. I seriously give up."

Why do I give up? Because there is no town here. No town! Not even the vestigial remnants of a town like the one Pell and I saw in the fog.

Just… forest.

And I'm in the right place. That's the side of the mountain where the candle shop was. And right there was the Honey Bean Diner with the apartment up top. And right there—

I stop and hold my breath.

Because right there is a man.

A *very* beautiful man.

"Hello, Pie. I knew you'd come back."

A very beautiful man, with a very musical voice, and the very greenest eyes I have ever seen.

Except that's not true, is it? I've seen eyes this green before, a couple times at least.

It's Russ Roth. Only he's… different. No uniform, for one. He's wearing a leather jacket with patches on it, like a biker jacket, and not like *my* biker jacket, which is a fashion statement. His looks old, and worn, and the patches have legit things going on. There are three thin rectangles over the right side of his chest, stacked on top of one another. The top one says 'Savage Springs.' The middle one says 'Him, Himself.' And the bottom one is a timestamp that reads '11:11.'

On the other side of the jacket is a winged heart. But it's not a sweet Valentine's Day heart. It's an anatomical heart, which kind of makes sense because it's placed over his heart. All around these red and gold patches is chaos. I don't know a lot about bikers, but I've seen movies. And I think these chaos patches are testimonials to events that one attends.

He's wearing a white thermal under the jacket and old, faded jeans ending in black work boots. His hair is a little longer, his face scruffier. But even if all these differences weren't so obviously on display, I would know that this is not really Russ Roth just by the way he stands. It's like… I dunno. Like he owns the world, or something. Nothing can touch him. Everyone wants to be him.

And even if I didn't already guess who he really was—the wings are a dead giveaway.

Well. Not a *dead* giveaway. When I picture a cupid, I see a fat baby with white wings and a cheap dollar-store bow and arrow. This guy here has black wings.

And just as I think that, he winks at me.

That's when I notice the crossbow.

He aims the crossbow right at me and I panic, stupidly stepping back with my hands up. "Let's just talk about th—"

That's as far as I get. The bolt slams into my heart and the next thing I know I'm on the ground, looking up at the sky.

A face appears above. "Why, I think you fell down. Do you need a hand up, sweetheart?"

I begin to smile stupidly. "Hi." This comes out like a whisper, with a little wave of my fingers, and shrug of my shoulders, and then I'm making kissing noises at him and—

Holy shit. Am I flirting with the fucking devil?

"Oh, no, no, no!" I snap out of it. "Fuck this!" I turn onto my hands and knees, get up, and run. But it feels like I'm running in mud. Like I'm stuck in one of those dreams. "*Noooooooo!*" I yell it as I look over my shoulder. But even the word is in slow motion. Because he's not the devil.

This is not a cupid, either.

This is an eros.

Perhaps even *the* Eros.

And he just smacked me in the chest with one of his love arrows!

I'm still running—still in slow motion—and a little bit tipsy. My head is all swirly. But there's a stuck moment here. A pause in reality, perhaps. Where I have time to think about that stupid love curse I put on myself when I went on that date with Russ.

And then I laugh. I'm talking a full-on giggle. And it's so... not the moment for this.

"Where ya goin', Pie?"

His words bring reality crashing back just as I break free of the slow-motion mud and book it back up the hill. His accent is that same hot and sexy Pennsylvania hick. Only this version of Russ Roth does not come off as some once-upon-a-time high school quarterback.

He comes off as... definitely a monster, but not the kind of monster I'm used to. Not the grumpy Pell, or naïve Tomas, or even the conniving Batty. He comes off as... *evil*.

Evil. With a whole lot of beautiful tucked inside for good measure.

I can see the door. I'm almost there. Maybe fifty yards. But when you're running up the side of a hill, fifty yards is monumental.

I know I shouldn't—I *know* I should not look back. But I can't help myself. I look over my shoulder one more time, just as I enter the trees.

But he's gone.

Then, when I look forward again, there he is.

I stop. Actually, I stumble and fall flat on my face, my palms automatically catching myself so I don't knock my teeth out. And when I look up, panting hard from my sprint and trembling from the predicament I've just put myself in, my eyes open in surprise.

Because from behind him, his wings are slowly unfolding.

Black wings. Massive wings. Not unlike Batty's wings, but also not anything like Batty's wings, either. They are feathered, and they are gorgeous, and I have an overwhelming urge to get up on my feet, walk over to him, and touch these wings.

But not just the wings.

Him.

Himself.

And then I am on my feet. And I am walking towards him. And I am reaching out like I *will* touch him—

But he puts up a hand. Actually, he wags a finger at me. "No, no, no, sweet Pie. You can look, but please do not touch."

"OK." My voice is weak, and breathy, and stupid.

"It's not that I don't like you. You're a sweet thing, aren't you? But I don't like winning by default, honey."

"Right." Still weak. Still breathy. Still stupid. And the weird thing is, my mind understands this. I totally get that I'm acting like an idiot and that this is all due to the eros part of him. But I can't stop it. It's like my brain and my body are two different people.

"I like a challenge."

"I can challenge you."

"I'm sure you could." He smiles at me, unleashing a dimple in the middle of that scratchy cheek of his, his eyes flashing the way Pell's bloodhorn shimmers like lava.

And I swear, my body almost goes limp. Like I'm swooning and about to faint.

"Now listen to me, Pie. Because I have your friend."

"My friend?" I'm confused.

"By the way, thank you so much for guiding her here."

"Guiding who?" This actually comes out of my mouth before I realize he's talking about Jacqueline. I want to bonk myself on the head. How did I forget about Jacqueline? She's the reason I'm here!

"She was going to find me, regardless. But you definitely simplified things."

I swivel my hips, raising a shoulder and tilting my head, like I'm shy. Internally I roll my eyes at my ridiculous flirting. But on the outside, I'm batting my lashes at him.

"Are you listening?"

"Oh, I'm listening."

"Good. I need you to run an errand for me, OK?"

"Anything. Just tell me what I need to do."

"Excellent. I need you to bring Tarq to me."

"Tarq?" My head is empty and airy, the word not making sense.

"The tall fellow with the giant black dick?" I just stare at him. He points to his head. "Horns? Dresses like a priss? Calls himself king?"

"Oh, yeah. Him. OK. Sure." I pause here to blink my eyelashes at him, smiling like a fool. "You want me to bring him here?"

"I do. I very much do. You see, we have business together."

"Business. Right." Why am I so breathless?

"And I'm gonna need you to do something else, as well. Just one more tiny thing. Can you manage that, my little lovely?"

"Manage? Of course!" Why am I so excited?

"Good. Now listen closely…"

His mouth moves, but I can't hear anything. It's like someone pushed the mute button. Still, I'm nodding my head enthusiastically. And this is not good. Because what if I'm agreeing to something?

The sounds come back and the devil's voice floats into my head like a dream. "So you skedaddle home now. Do what we agreed upon. Go fetch Tarq and bring him back to me. You see, he is not the king." The devil's massive black wings fly up over his head and his eyes glow like lava. "*I* am. I am the king of the royal beasts."

And then, right in front of my eyes, he grows a set of golden antlers.

I stand there for a moment, stunned.

Then I turn, and continue my way up the steep hillside.

When I get to the door I realize that his words are echoing in my mind.

Get Tarq, get Tarq, get Tarq...

"I need to get Tarq." This feels like the most important thing ever. "I need to bring him here."

So when I get to the door, and step through—that is the only thing I'm thinking about.

I come around the corner of a tomb and find Batty and Isla still arguing on the pathway. "What is going on here?"

The sanctuary trembles and another wall of a tomb crumbles to the ground.

That fuckin' voice. I didn't mean to use it. It just comes out whenever it wants. I'm not even that angry. It's more of an annoyance. And this destruction feels like overkill for an annoyance.

"Just the man we were looking for." Isla is still very in control as she approaches me and I catch a look of indignation on Batty's face as these words come out of her mouth.

She's trying to insert herself into some kind of leadership position and it's pissing him off, which delights me a little. But still, I put up a hand. "Just answer my question."

"I'll tell you what's going on," Batty sneers. "We don't want to be here anymore."

"Good! I don't want you here."

"We want to go back to Vinca," Isla says.

I narrow my eyes at her. "Back?" Then I narrow my eyes at Batty. "Is that where you're from?"

"Wow. You really are quite stupid. We're *all* from Vinca, Pell. Even you."

"I'm from Rome."

Batty almost snorts.

"What?"

"You don't remember anything, do you?"

Isla is looking at me like I'm an idiot. She glances at Batty. "Is he slow? I don't understand what's going on with him. At first it was kinda cute, but now—"

"Do not call me cute!" And again, the sanctuary rumbles. This time, many walls fall down and there are shrieks and gasps from a couple dozen nearby monsters and nymphs.

Isla puts up both hands with a scornful look on her face. "Sor-ree. God, you're so temperamental."

Batty side-eyes Isla. "Let me handle him. I'll catch up with you later."

Isla is about to object, like perhaps they are not done with the argument I strolled in on, but then she lets out a breath, shoots him some kind of knowing glance and backs down. "Fine. You know where to find me." Then she points at me. "We're going home to Vinca. *Today*, monster."

Not sure who Isla thinks she is, but she doesn't give me a chance to answer, or inform her that she is not the one giving orders around here. She just turns her back with a swish of her hair and saunters off.

I let out a long breath and look skyward, so tired of these people.

"You really don't know who you are, do you?"

"What?"

"You think you're"—Batty pans his hands down my body—"*this*. Don't you?"

I look down at myself. I'm shirtless—I hate shirts even more than I hate pants, but actually, the pants are growing on me. So I'm wearing them right now. They are leather because I like the leather. It's good for working in the smithy. "What's wrong with what I'm wearing?" Then I look back up at Batty and study what he's wearing, comparing us. "I look better than you do."

Batty has always been partial to clothes. Sometimes he wears capes, like he's Batman. Other times he wears a coat and nothing else. But today he's wearing a whole outfit: a t-shirt—it's tattered and ragged because it needed to be modified to accommodate his wings, and from the looks of the end result, he must've done it himself—and some kind of canvas pants.

"Not your *clothes*, you simpleton. You, as in… *you*." He waves a hand down the length of me. "You have no clue, do you?"

I sigh. "Clearly, I have no clue. So why don't you fill me in."

"How do you think you got here?"

"Ostanes made a book. A very powerful book—"

"The one Tarq had. The one you're hiding in your tomb."

"That book. Yes. There was a divorce between Juno and Saturn, they fought over their shit, blah, blah, blah. Moves and countermoves. Me, a caretaker, and the tombs." I wave my hand in the air. "Story time over."

"Well, I guess it went like that. But who do you think Saturn is?"

"A god. The god of… something. It's been a long time since I thought about this shit." I snap my fingers. "Oh. Time. Fuckin' time. He's the god of time. Which is why I'm still alive after two thousand years."

Batty cocks his head at me. "You *really* believe that."

It's not even a question. "Really believe what?"

"The god of *time*? Giving you… what?" He almost giggles. "Eternal youth?"

I shrug. "Fits."

Batty guffaws. "Boy, I'm not sure what really happened that day because, as you are aware, I had a hood over my head because they were about to chop off my wings, but what is your excuse?"

"Excuse for what?"

"For why you're so dumb."

"You know what?" I step forward and poke him in the

chest. He recoils in pain. Chest-poking is actually very uncomfortable, even if you're joking. But I'm not joking. I put in an effort.

"Ow, you asshole! I'm trying to help you, ya know."

"Help with what?"

His hands go out in a clueless shrug. "Help you get your life back? But you know what? I don't even care what you believe. We don't want to be here, Pell. We want to go back to Vinca. You had no right to make Tarq king."

"Well, it worked, didn't it? So I guess I did."

"You've fucked it all up! We had a deal with the devil! This needs to be rectified. I've been helpful and patient. Here's what's gonna happen." He actually puts a hand on my shoulder. I shrug it off and he retreats a step. "You're going to take us all back to Vinca. You're going to help us retake that city. You're going to—"

"No." I don't even say it loud, but again, the whole sanctuary rumbles. Many things crumble. And this is when I notice that all the things that have crumbled from my voice over the past day or two aren't being rebuilt. The rubble is just... piling up. I squint my eyes at Batty. "You're working with him, aren't you?"

Batty just laughs.

"You're working for the devil, aren't you?" I yell it and the tallest spire on the back side of the cathedral comes toppling off and crashes onto the decorative pavers lining the garden patio. Many wood nymphs and monsters go scattering out of the way, but one...

"Oh, shit."

People start screaming.

"Oh, my God!" a wood nymph shrieks. "He killed him."

"What?" I blink at the accusation and point to myself. "Me?"

She shrieks again. "He killed Freckles!"

Fuck. Freckles is one of Pie's favorites. He was the one

who made her all those tomb tokens. "I didn't—" But I can't even defend myself. Because now all the nearby monsters are yelling and no one can hear me.

Things begin to devolve almost immediately. Dozens of monsters crowd the little patio area, looking down at the feet of Freckles. That's the only thing you can see of his body. Just his hooves sticking out from under the enormous spire, cracked into three pieces.

It takes them like two heartbeats to process what they're seeing. And then every set of eyes finds me. I begin to back up towards the cathedral. "I didn't—"

"He killed him!" This is Isla. She screams it again. "He killed one of us!"

Us? So that's how it is.

I decide now would be a really great time to use the voice and crumble some more shit so I can get back to my tomb, but when I say, "I didn't kill him!" in my biggest, most powerful monster-Pell voice, there is no rumble. Nothing crumbles. In fact, I don't even think they hear me, because now they're rushing towards me like villagers with pitchforks storming a castle.

I turn, and I run.

I burst through the cathedral doors, take the center stairs seven at a time, and in twenty-six leaps, I'm in the grand hall. There are a handful of monsters and nymphs milling around the food on the dining tables. *Food I brought them*, I want to growl.

They look at me with wide, surprised eyes as my hooves skid to a stop on the polished marble floors. But then from behind me comes the yelling and the screaming.

"Murderer!"

"He killed Frecks!"

"Get him!"

And then those wide surprised eyes narrow down into slits and I know I need to get the fuck out of here. I could leave through the front door, which is a nice option, I'm not gonna lie. But Pie is still in my tomb and there's no way I'm leaving her here with these psychopaths.

One of the bigger monsters comes at me and I just barely skirt out of the way of his clawed hand as it reaches for my arm. And now I'm pointing in the direction of the real dining room and the variable hallways that lead to Tomas's dungeon.

I go that way, and then I have to make a choice—dungeon or dining room?

I choose dungeon.

Thankfully, the hallways don't shift in front of me, but I think they do shift behind me, because the yelling and screaming turns to confusion. And then all the voices get fainter and further away.

When I come to the winding dungeon staircase, I pause to check behind me, leaning on the stone wall with one hand, panting hard in the stuffy darkness.

But there is no sound. None at all.

I turn back to the stairs, grab a torch off the wall, and descend.

The first surprise is the lack of smell. Pie said there were eggs down there, so I was expecting the smell to be worse, not better.

But not only is it better, it's... kind of sweet. Like flowers.

"Tomas!" I yell it loud because I don't want to surprise him. I'm not sure what he is these days. Come to think of it, I don't think I've ever been sure of Tomas. "Tomas, can you hear me?"

"Pell? Is that you? Are you coming for a chat?" And then I see his handsome, smiling face peering from around the turn of the stairwell. "I wasn't expecting you. I would've tidied. Madeline is sleeping, of course, so she can't visit. But come. I'm wide awake, as you can see."

He beckons me with his hand to follow, then disappears around the corner.

I take a deep breath and let it out, look over my shoulder one more time, then follow him into the dungeon. "Tomas. The monsters upstairs, they think I—" But I stop because... "What the... is that a door?"

Tomas beams at me. "Can you believe it?"

"Where did it come from?"

"Pie gave it to me. She was just here."

"What?"

"Yeah. She came for a visit. And now you. I feel special." Then he glances at Madeline. "Don't we, love? Don't we feel special?"

My eyes narrow, trying to see into the shadows. And then, after a moment of adjustment, there she is. Madeline. Her body is covered in red scales, even her face, just like Pie said. She is stretched out across some large boulders. But then I realize those aren't boulders, those are dragon eggs. "Fucking hell, Tomas. What are you doing down here?"

"What do you mean?"

"And that door?" I turn to look at it. It's shimmery and blank so there's not much to see. "How did Pie give you a door?"

"Well, I don't know the specifics of the magic, but..." He shrugs. "I just asked for one and she obliged by spilling out a spell and popping out a door." He smiles brightly at me. "Isn't it wonderful?"

"Where does it go?"

"It doesn't go anywhere yet. I can use it any way I want."

"Well, make it go to my tomb. I need to get Pie out of here. I think we're going to Vinca." I look back at the stairwell and let out a breath. "Those monsters up there"—I turn back to Tomas—"they're out of control. They're all from Vinca. Did you know that Batty and the rest of them are from Vinca?"

117

"Of course." Tomas chuckles. "We're all from Vinca, Pell."

"You say this like it's common knowledge."

"Isn't it?"

"No, you—" But I refrain from calling him names, because I need him to give me that door. "You don't understand. Batty says *I'm* from Vinca."

Tomas tilts his head at me. Like he's a confused dog. "Are you saying you're not?"

"Of course I'm not!" This bellow of objection comes out as the voice. And once again, things begin to crumble.

Tomas looks alarmed, then rushes back into the shadows. "Madeline? Are you OK?"

A growl—a deep, throaty, angry, dragon growl—comes rumbling out from the darkness.

"Oh, good, love. There, there. Don't mind Pell. He's a little confused these days."

"I'm not confused!"

An entire wall on the far side of the dungeon just slips to the ground. Like it melted.

"Stop doing that! You're scaring Madeline."

I let out a long breath and pinch the skin between my eyebrows. "Can you please. Make that door. Take me to my tomb."

Tomas comes back out of the shadows. "I'm sorry, Pell. I can't do it."

"Why not?" The ground shakes beneath my feet.

"What are you doing?"

"I'm not doing anything. I'm not in control of this voice, OK? It just happens."

"Well, it's ruining my dungeon. I think you should leave now."

"Great. Just…" I wave my hand at the door. "Make it take me to my tomb."

"No." And this 'no' of his comes out very final.

"What do you mean, no? I'm the master of Saint Mark's.

This door belongs to Pie and me. We're in charge of the doors. And I want you to make it go to my tomb."

"Well"—Tomas folds his arms over his chest—"if you're in control of it, then *you* make it go to your tomb."

I narrow my eyes at him. We both know this won't work. I don't even have a reason why I know this won't work, I just… feel it.

"Tomas." I use a more reasonable tone. But still, things around me are degrading. I start again, almost whispering. "Tomas, listen to me. The monsters upstairs think I killed Frecks."

"What?" He's alarmed. "You killed Frecks?"

"No. I—"

"Frecks is dead?"

"Yeah, but—"

"Pell!"

"I didn't do it! My voice came out like it is now, and —" The stone floor under my feet is shaking. "And then the grand spire on top of the back side of the cathedral just… toppled over. And it took out Frecks on the ground. I didn't kill him, Tomas. I'm not in control of this voice!"

The entire dungeon shakes.

And then Madeline shrieks, and Tomas is even more alarmed.

And then a hissing sound comes from the shadowed corner. "Eggs. Eggs. Eggs."

"What's that, dear?" Tomas retreats back into the shadows and there is more hissing and some whispering. Then a gasp. "Oh!" Then he reappears. "You need to go. Now, Pell. You have cracked one of our eggs open! If you kill my baby dragon I will—"

He stops himself before the threat comes out.

But I'm angry now too. "I didn't crack your egg." The voice is different now. Still low and rumbly, but there is much more control. And nothing around me comes apart. "I don't understand this new power."

Tomas narrows his eyes at me. "Then maybe you should stop using it."

"Stop speaking?"

He just shrugs with his hands. "I think the eggs will be OK. But I'm mad, Pell. I have been living in this dungeon, as something less than a person, for thousands of years. And now I have a woman and eggs that are hatching, and I will not lose these things. Do you understand me?"

His voice changes as he talks and by the last part, it's very different from the voice of Tomas, my friend. It's low, and controlled, and powerful.

Suddenly, the room gets a little bit brighter.

I have always known he has power. At least when he's a real dragon and not some apparition. But Tomas is so... I dunno. Innocent. And kind. He really is kind. Also, optimistic. I know he burned the cathedral down, but that was his dragon form protecting his lair. And I know he burned Granite Springs, but that was his chimera form protecting Madeline.

But this voice he just used on me was something I've never experienced before.

It was a threat.

A very nicely worded, tightly controlled, polite-as-he-could-make-it threat.

"What is going on here, Tomas?"

"What does it look like, Pell?" His voice is normal now, and he pans a hand to the rubble that's starting to pile up around us. "Things appear to be coming apart."

"But what does it mean?"

"Might it be that the curse is coming apart as well?"

"But Pie said we can't break the curse or the sanctuary won't protect us anymore."

Tomas sighs, then looks at the shadow in the corner.

"Didn't you ever wonder what it might be like when your curse was lifted?"

I shrug. "I dunno. I guess. Long time ago, when I still had hope that it might be broken."

"Well, it appears that breaking the curse involves breaking the sanctuary. Don't you think?"

I swallow hard. Because I don't want to break the sanctuary. This is the only home I've ever known. I have some memories of my origins—unreliable ones, apparently. But I've been here for so long now, I'm not sure I *want* to leave.

"What did you think would happen, hmm?" Tomas is being kind, his voice soft and low. "Did you think you'd just walk out those gates and then come back when you got tired of your freedom?"

I let out a sigh, absently looking at shadows of flickering light on the dungeon walls. I squint, trying to understand what I'm seeing, then the room brightens again and I realize there are gemstones embedded into the walls. Huh. I shake myself out of it and get back on topic. "Well, maybe, I guess. I didn't think it would just... crumble away and disappear. I thought maybe—"

"You could stay here forever? Just come and go as you please?"

"Yeah."

"Do you really think that's how it works?"

Another sigh from me. I'm so tired of all this drama. "Probably not. But... my tomb, Tomas. And your dungeon?"

"We're going to lose them, Pell. We're going to lose it all. So I guess we had better decide where we go from here, don't you think?"

I don't answer him. I can't even picture a life outside this place.

"I cannot give you that door, Pell. I can't. I need it. Look around. We're almost out of time. I need to get Madeline and

121

the babies out of here. And that door is how I do that. You understand, right?"

We're staring into each other's eyes. His are a bit glassy. I'm not sure if he would really give up the door if I insisted. Perhaps he would because I am the master of Saint Mark's. But he would not want to. And if that's the case, there's no way I would be able to compel him without feeling like a complete shitbag later. So I nod. "I do. You keep the door. It was a gift."

And then I turn to leave.

"Well, I didn't say I wouldn't help you, Pell. I'm happy to help you get back to your tomb."

I turn back to him. "How?"

"Why don't you use a hallway?"

"You mean… the ones upstairs?"

"Well, they're not all upstairs, are they?"

"Oh. Right." I glance over to the winding stairwell that leads up to the main level. "But those hallways are different, aren't they?"

Tomas shrugs. "Why would they be different?"

"I dunno. I just assumed their only purpose was to rearrange the route to get to your dungeon."

"I think the hallways are based on expectations. Why don't you try expecting more of them?"

He's got a point. I really have no expectations of the hallways. I just thought they were… I dunno. Something to placate me. To keep me occupied. So he could be right. It could be that I have low expectations of them.

Or no, not them. Me. I have low expectations of me. "Still, I don't understand how this will get me to my tomb. I can find it in the hallways, I'm sure of that. But it's just a memory."

"Maybe you can command it to be more? Maybe that voice of yours just needs a little spelling to pop it into place. And you might try adding in some fire."

"What?"

"Fire, Pell. You're made of fire. Your horns are burning as we speak. You're practically lighting up the room."

I shift my eyes so I'm looking over my shoulder, trying to see my horns. They mostly go down my back, so I can't see much of them. But I can see enough. They're glowing. I'm the one making the room brighter. And this happened without my input when I perceived him as a possible threat. Like maybe it's a defense mechanism.

"Useless magic."

I look at Tomas. "What?"

"The hallways. It's all so… stupid, don't you think?"

I shrug. "I dunno. It's kinda cool."

"Cool? Do you really think that's what magic's about?"

My exhale comes out tired. "No. Of course not. It's about power."

"Exactly. And you've been given quite a bit of it. You have always claimed to be the master of Saint Mark's. You have bellowed about this for thousands of years. But you have never really explored what that means. It's time for you to grow up a little, Pell. It's time for you to take some responsibility. It's time for you to take back your life. Do you want to know what I've learned over the centuries?"

"Sure. It's not like I can't use the advice."

"No one is coming to save me. No one is coming to make me happy. If I want happiness, I have to find it myself. And if someone tries to take it away, I will have to fight for it."

A smile creeps up my face. Because Tomas has always been a happy guy. He's always looking at the bright side. He's always making the most of things.

And I've been doing the exact opposite, haven't I? I'm grumpy, and growly, and selfish.

And now I kinda just feel like shit.

"No one's coming to save you, Pell. Not the caretaker. Not

the gods. Not the monsters. So if you want to be happy, then it's up to you to *make* yourself happy."

We stare at each other for a moment. "Tomas—"

"No need."

I chuckle. "You don't even know what I was gonna say."

"I do, Pell. And you don't need to apologize for anything. We are who we are." He shrugs. "But sometimes it's good to take a second look at ourselves and make a decision to be someone else. Now go. You need to get to Pie. She has her own decisions to make, I'm sure."

"Will we see each other again?"

"Is that sadness? Will you miss me?" He walks up to me and pulls me into a giant hug. Squeezes me for several seconds, which is far too long for my comfort level. But when I try to pull away, he doesn't let go. "Just enjoy it, Pell."

So I do.

Because that was his answer.

This is it.

Like it or not, the curse has been broken. Or, at the very least, is in the process of breaking.

And he will go one way, and I will go another.

Where we end up is anybody's guess.

Finally, he lets go of me and steps back. "Don't give up on her."

"Who? Pie? Never."

"Never," Tomas agrees.

Then I turn and walk over to the stairwell. But then I turn back. "Hey. Congratulations, by the way. On the family." And then I smile, and I realize it's a real smile. "You deserve it, Tomas. You really do. I'm happy for you."

"And me you."

Then I turn back to the stairwell and begin to climb. Some of the steps are missing and there are gaping holes that I have to leap over. I try to see what's down underneath the dungeon stairs, but not even my eyes can penetrate that darkness.

Some of the steps have been reduced to sand. And it makes me wonder at the power of my voice.

Speech.

It's familiar to me. And it lines up with Pie's spelling powers too.

Weird.

But I don't have time to think about that just yet. I have to get these hallways to cooperate and that means I have to know what I want them to do.

When I get to the last step, there's a huge gap between me and the rest of the sanctuary. Like the dungeon is about to fall into some deep, dark abyss and forever be severed from the rest of the world.

And I guess this is it.

I take a deep breath and focus all my attention—and intention—on what I need.

Then I close my eyes and the words come tumbling out.

"The end of the line and now it's time
To take me where I want to be.
At peace with Pie, she is mine
And the hallways here are now the key."

s I walk through the door back to Pell's tomb, I find myself in a fog and I don't come out the other side. My mind is slow and muddled. But then, as the fog lifts, I hear a voice. Pell's voice.

"Pie?" It's echo-y and far away.

"What?" And that's my voice. But it's not coming from me. It's coming from somewhere distant and it's also echo-y and far away.

"I love you, Pie."

I smile, just as I hear my other self say, "What?"

And I sound surprised when I shouldn't be surprised. I know Pell loves me. It's probably the only certain thing about my life.

"Listen, I know you think you like that sheriff, but he's not your type."

Huh. This conversation feels familiar, but new at the same time. Is this the day I got my Jeep out of impound? The day I kissed Russ Roth? The day I learned about my debt? What is going on?

"How—" other me says.

Oh, I know what this is! It's a memory. Like in the hallways. That's so cool. My days are in the hallways!

Except this isn't how it went that day. I didn't even like Pell at that point. And he, for sure, was not proclaiming his love to me.

"He's not. OK? Just trust me. You and me?" He points to us. "We're the real thing."

He and I are the real thing.

Wait, what is happening here? Where am I? Didn't I just go to Granite Springs to find Jacqueline?

Ooooooooohh. Yeah. The devil.

I think he put a spell on me. Wait. If he's an eros, then he doesn't have to put a spell on me. I'm just going to be attracted to him the same way I was Russ Roth.

That's a really creepy power.

And then more of my little visit comes back to me. Not only did he entrance me, but he sent me on a mission. I am supposed to go find Tarq and bring him to Granite Springs. Which isn't even called Granite Springs anymore. It's called Savage Falls.

Kinda ominous, if you ask me.

Well. I have lots of opinions about what just happened.

One. No. No, no, no. I will not be fetching Tarq for the Devil of Savage Falls.

Two. Where the fuck are Jacqueline and her monster kids? My heart palpitates a little when the obvious answer manifests in my mind. Either the devil and I were in some kind of in-between, magical-dimension door world, and this was not the real...-ish world where Pell and I left Jacqueline, or the devil really does have her and now she's locked in a fog curse. Or something.

I sigh, so tired of other worlds. They were kinda cool at first. A little bit scary, but cool. Now, though? I don't see the point. It's too much magic for a girl like me. It's too much power.

Back to my list.

Three. Royal beasts. That's what he called... well, us. All of us monsters, I guess. Royal beasts. And I know that name. I know this name because it's written on the cover of the book down in the Bottoms.

Four. The fuckin' Bottoms.

I have not been back down to see Callistina since that day Tomas burned the town. There is a part of me that feels guilty about this because what if I'm supposed to feed them or something?

But then there's another part that really hopes she's starving to death.

She killed my Pia. And I get it. Pia wasn't... something *else*. She was me. But that's even worse. If Callistina really is my sister—and I have my doubts. I didn't see any proof. But even if she is, what kind of bitch kills off her sister's... like... *essence*, or whatever?

I hope she's starving. I hope she's miserable. I hope... all kinds of very bad things for her.

And now Nysta's down there too.

You're making a mess of things, Pie.

When those words manifest in my head, they come through in another voice.

My mother's voice.

You're making a mess of things, Pie. Of all the things I can remember about the woman who dropped me off at Child Protective Services when I was nine, this phrase is right up there at the top. One of the most familiar things about her memory.

You're making a mess of things, Pie. And that's why I'm doing this!

A door slams closed in my head and I'm startled for a moment. Because I had forgotten about that. I had forgot how she would lock me inside things. Hotel rooms. Cars. Apartments. Gas station bathrooms.

Everything was my fault. Everything. And her solution to my interference was to leave me behind. To just shove me through a door, close it behind me, and walk away.

A sudden sense of loss fills me up and makes me weak. Because isn't this exactly what I'm doing to Callistina? I shoved her through a door, closed it behind her, and walked away.

And now I'm doing it to Nysta. And I don't even know Nysta. She got on my nerves and my first instinct was to use my power to shut her up.

Nice, Pie. Way to be just like your mother.

"OK." I put up a hand as I say this out loud. "Enough of the Memory Lane bullshit, Pie. Focus. You're in the middle of the devil's mission."

Right. Five. Either the devil put me in some kind of trance when we met, or it was just his natural eros sex appeal working its magic on me. And that trance followed me through the door, but then wore off immediately once I was inside the door.

I'm still here in the not-trance standing in the not-door.

And now, conveniently, my earlier musing about the doors comes back to me. They are like hallways. I don't know why I just heard a conversation between Pell and me, but it really does feel like a hallway thing. So I think I'm right about this. The doors are like hallways.

Which means they might even be connected.

No. They *are* connected. And I'm in a hallway right now.

Somehow, some way, I walked through a door and ended up in a hallway.

"Welp." I throw up my hands. "There's only one way out of a hallway. You keep walking until you find a door."

So that's what I do.

I walk through the fog and hope for a door...

When I open my eyes, I'm in the Jeep.

And when I look to my right, Pie is sitting next to me.

"I'm not a witch. I can't break your stupid curse."

"You say that, but yet… here you are. How does that make sense?"

"I don't know. But I'm not a witch. I don't know any spells, I can't concoct any potions. And the breakfast doesn't count. Tomas told me how to do it. And it was just reciting words and waving my hand over raw food. I will not be helpful in any other capacity. So what we should do is—"

"Oh, you've been thinking about this, have you?"

"It was a quiet drive back, so yes, I had time to think. And I was thinking… we should just find another witch to help you."

I almost snort. "Should we? Should we do that?"

"Yes. One who does have some actual magic."

"What about your bird?"

"What about her?"

"She's not magic?"

"She's a psychosis. My personal hallucination. So no. She's not magic."

"Then why can I see her?"

"You don't see her. That's not my bird up in the ceiling."

"Just some random bird, huh?"

"Yep. Just another random bird."

I smile. Big. Because this, I think, might be the moment I fell in love with Pie. "OK. Fine. She's not magic, you're not magic, but you've stumbled into a magical person in town?"

"Exactly!" She sits up straight and claps her hands. "Oh, my God. You're not going to believe this."

"You're right, I'm not."

"But that sheriff? He's your guy! Not me!"

I almost frown. I think that's what I did the first time we had this conversation. But there's no way I can manage a frown. Not even if my life depended on it.

"Why are you smiling like that?"

"What?"

"You're... smirking. Why are you smirking?"

I pull the Jeep over on the side of the road.

"What are you doing? Why are you stopping?"

I don't know how this works. This is not how the hallways behaved in all the other times I've experienced them. So I don't know why I'm here, and why she's here, and why this is a memory, and why I can change it.

But then again, I never did visit myself up in the hallways, did I?

If this conversation is different than the original—and it is now, because I didn't continue the banter and she didn't confess to kissing Russ Roth—then what happens to the present?

I look over at her. "Pie?"

"What?"

"I love you."

She huffs. "What?"

"Listen, I know you think you like that sheriff, but he's not your type."

"How—"

"He's not. OK? Just trust me. You and me?" I point to us. "We're the real thing."

"What?" She practically gasps out the word. "What are you talking about?"

"You kissed the sheriff."

"Um..."

"You did. You told me."

"I literally didn't."

I sigh and lean back in my seat, smiling so big as I look out the windshield. We're in the forest and the sanctuary is nearby. This part of the road is all glamoured to keep it private from any wandering hikers.

I turn the Jeep off, open my door, and get out.

"What are you doing?"

I close the door, walk around the Jeep, and open her door.

"What's going on?"

I offer her my hand. "Come on."

She pulls away, shrinking back from me. "No. Get back in the Jeep. Let's go. The food—"

"Fuck the food."

"What? What about your *provisions*?"

"You're the only provision I need, Pie. Just you."

She smiles then, her defenses temporarily on hold. We were not friends in this part of our beginning. She still kinda hated me. Minutes from now, in the original version of this day, she will find out about her debt and everything about Pie Vita will change.

She will be vulnerable, and sad, and tired of losing.

But right now, she's vibrant, and happy, and maybe even a little bit satisfied.

I don't even mind that this satisfaction comes from her planned date with the sheriff of Granite Springs and subsequent curse-breaking—if only for herself, and not me.

I don't care what makes her happy.

I just want her to be happy.

"Do you trust me?"

She makes a face. "Why would I ever trust you? You tricked me into breaking your curse."

"I literally didn't."

She's caught off guard for a moment, confused, but not in a bad way. Not the way she was the first time this happened.

"'A story of a monster's curse. A Book of Debt and a spelling verse.'"

Her eyes narrow. "What?"

"'Blood, and horns, and doors, and trees. You and me, forever free.'"

"Why are you... what are you doing?"

"That's my vow. I just made it up."

"Ooookay. Should I know what that means?"

"No. We haven't had this conversation yet."

"Should I know what *that* means?"

I simply smile. And I can't see this smile, but I can feel this smile, and I know it's something different. Even for her, a woman who hasn't even known me a full day, she can tell that something has suddenly changed.

She twirls a single finger in the air. "Is this... something magical right now?"

"Yes."

"Well... are you gonna fill me in?"

I let out a long breath. "I'm stuck in the dungeon with Tomas. You're in my tomb. And the monsters are pissed at me for accidentally using my new voice power to kill Frecks. So I'm using the hallways to get back to my tomb. But they sent me here, to this day with you. And it's... well..."

She doesn't laugh at me. She doesn't call me a liar. She just stares up at me with those sky-blue eyes of hers and whispers, "It's what, Pell?"

"Nice. To be here with you before everything that happens next, happens next. And if I had known that we had such little time together—alone, I mean. Ya know?—I'd have done more with this day. I'd have come to dinner, not gone to bed. I would've taken you for a walk down by the lake. Maybe looked at the stars. I would've listened to you."

I can tell she's thinking wild things. Her eyes are darting back and forth, looking into mine. She presses her lips together and stays silent.

"In a couple days, we're going to be in love, Pie."

A smile slowly creeps up her face. "We're going to be in *love*?"

"It's soulmate kind of shit."

"Is it?" She giggles a little.

"It is. Because you're gonna do amazing things, and travel to another world, and cut off my horn, and save the sanctuary."

"Wow. I sound busy. What do you do?"

"I save you."

Her smile falters as the full meaning of these words sinks in.

"And then, in a couple weeks, we're gonna do it all again."

"Huh."

"And then we will get to this day—my day—and I will make a ring for you." The smile is back. "And get stuck in the dungeon. And ask the hallway gods to put us back together. And they will send me to this day. And you know what?"

"What?"

"I could live this day forever. This first day with you."

"Second, actually."

"Yesterday doesn't count. I was a dick."

"Oh, my God. You so were. But where am I again?"

"In my tomb. You made a spell to walk into it." Now it's my turn to smile. "You're an excellent speller."

"Ummm, OK. Well, thanks. I did win a spelling bee once when I was eight."

"And you know what the best part is, Pie?"

"What?"

"You say you're ordinary, but nothing about you is ordinary. You care so much, and you're so kind, and a good friend."

She blushes. "Wow. I feel like I should say nice things back. But I don't know you, Pell."

I offer her my hand again. "No. You don't. Not yet. But since we get this afternoon together, we could change that."

She looks at my hand, understanding that she has to make a decision. Then she looks up at me and allows me to help her out of the Jeep, pausing for a moment to glance around at the woods. "Where are we?"

"Just a short walk away from the sanctuary."

She lets out a long breath, like she's giving in to what I'm offering her, then looks up at me. "You know what I never knew before?"

"Tell me."

"How pretty Pennsylvania is. I've lived in this state all my life, but mostly in Philadelphia. Have you ever been there?"

"No. It's too far away. The curse won't allow it."

"Well, compared to here? To these woods and all the leaves and the colors and the hills?" She sighs. "I'd rather be here than there any day."

"You wanna hear a confession from me?"

"Sure."

"I don't want to break the curse."

"What? Why? But I thought you wanted to be free?"

"I am free. We both are. We just don't realize it."

"Hmm." She thinks for a moment, then says, "Then what's the point of me?"

"What do you mean?"

"Well, if I'm not here to break the curse, then why am I here?"

Something changes in the air. A shimmer, maybe, or the way the sun falls through the leaves of the trees. I don't know what happens, but something changes. The illusion is about to break and I'm not ready for this. I want a day, just a day.

To love her, and laugh with her, and forget all the stupid shit that's happening all around us in the real version of our lives.

And then I see it.

A door.

Pie notices me looking at something, and turns her head in that direction. "What is that?"

"It's... the end of this moment. I have to leave."

"Leave? But..." She looks at the Jeep. "How will I get home?"

"You're not really here."

She opens her mouth to object but no sound comes out and her body begins to fade away. A few seconds later, there is nothing left of Pie. It's just me, and this forest, and that door.

What else can I do?

What choice do I have?

I go over to the door and walk through it.

he fog around me morphs into the tomb maze behind the sanctuary but immediately, I know it's not real. I know this because I see myself standing with Pell in front of his tomb.

We are talking. And I remember this day. It was the first time I walked through Pell's tomb door.

"My statue is on the inside," Pell is telling me. "Just past the columns. You can't see it, but it's in the center of the inner chamber."

"How do you get inside?" I take a step back, surprised. Because these words came out of my mouth instead of memory Pie's. In fact, memory-Pie is gone and now I'm just… her.

"Well, if you weren't here, this black shadowy part"—Pell waves his hand at the black shadow just beyond the columns —"that would actually be the stoa."

"What's a stoa?"

"Oh. It's a walkway. The space between the columns and the inner chamber, which is called a naos."

"Wow." I look back up at the columns, remembering how in awe I was that day. "It's all very… interesting. But what is all that up there?" I point to the space above the columns.

I know what it is, of course. I have already lived this moment. But I don't want to pre-empt the conversation. I want to live it again. So I just let the memory play out.

"That's called the entablature. It's a scene carved in stone.

Which, now that I think about it, I actually haven't noticed in centuries."

The conversation goes on like that. Pell explaining things. Me trying not to feel ignorant. But I find that I don't actually have to participate in this conversation. It's like… like I'm programmed or something. Like this is something important that needs to play out, whether I'm actively engaging with it or not.

The next thing I know I'm climbing up onto Pell's shoulders. And a moment later, I'm precariously perched on the ledge just below the entablature, Sharpie in hand.

A wood, a buck, a nymph, and stone.
A way into a satyr's home.
A door appears, the nymph walks through,
And now their lives begin anew.

I'm really proud of that spelling. I think it might be one of my best. It definitely gave the best results.

I jump down, but when I look around, Pell is gone. The sanctuary is gone too. There is me, there is the tomb, and there is the fog.

I think this is my door.

And then there's nothing left to do but walk through.

So I do.

Pell's tomb is different than the others. It pretty much looks the same on the outside. Maybe a bit grander, compared to most. It looks like a proper Roman temple with columns and shit. And that courtyard space between the columns and the actual entrance to his woods, that's the stoa.

And inside the stoa is Pell's statue. Again, it's different than the others in the sanctuary. For one, you can't see it until you're actually inside the tomb. I've always wondered about this. Is it hidden because Pell can leave his tomb and none of the other prisoners can?

Or is it hidden for some other reason?

It's Egyptian, not Roman. So that's kind of a big red flag

that there's something going on here. And it's... creepy. Maybe that's just me. I have never liked ancient Egypt. I have never found it fascinating. Mummies, and curses, and tombs that want to kill you.

Take out the mummy part and this could be my life.

But I walk over to it now because I have never really given it a proper once-over. Pell doesn't like it either. He never wants to stop here. In fact, he doesn't even look at it when we pass by.

It only takes a casual glance to see all the differences though. He's sitting in a chair. Or maybe a throne? His head is in profile but his body is straight-on, a common trait of ancient Egyptian art and sculptures. And he's wearing clothes. A skirt, I think. A very short one too.

This makes me snicker, recalling his annoyance with my very first work outfit.

Unlike my office-appropriate skirt, his is brightly colored. Blue and gold, mostly, but with red accents. There are strappy sandals on his feet, the flat kind with laces that wrap around the ankles.

I smirk, coming up with all kinds of ways to tease him about this once we're back together.

But then I get serious. Because this statue has to mean something. Why Egyptian, when he's from ancient Rome?

Of course, there is an obvious answer. He's not from ancient Rome. He's from ancient Egypt.

I can get on board with this for a couple of reasons.

One. Pell has a very bad memory. He doesn't even remember who Saint Mark is. And that's just the start of it. There are gaps there. Lots of them.

And two. The hallway doors brought me here for a reason. Whatever gods, or magic, or curse is running these things wanted me to see this statue.

But these are the only conclusions I can draw. I think the rest is probably up to Pell.

I glance over my shoulder at the opening that leads to the woods, and decide it's time to go. My best, and only, friend on the outside has been kidnapped by the devil of Savage Falls. He did some kind of magic on me to make me want to bring him Tarq. Which... I'm maybe not entirely against. I just don't trust him. But I wouldn't ever hand Tarq over to the devil without telling Pell first.

And when I left the devil and stepped back through that door, I wasn't going to look for Pell and get his permission. I was going back to Vinca to get Tarq.

He spelled me. And he didn't even use a spelling to do it.

But the hallway-slash-doorway gods stopped this by putting me in a fog and showing me Pell.

Yep. We've got a mystery on our hands. And normally, I might complain about this. Maybe even do a little monkey-walking. But I'm not really upset about a new mystery. I'm actually looking forward to figuring things out. Because I'm sick of this shit. I'm sick of always being a victim of circumstance.

And if the gods of Saint Mark's Sanctuary want me to solve their little mystery, then it's the least I can do. Because before I came here, I was just floating. No purpose. No future.

And now look at me. I can spell the fuck out of things. And I can do magic. It's maybe not typical of how witches do it—or alchemists, for that matter—but I can do magic.

Pretty cool stuff, too.

I'm kind of a big deal. And I owe it all to Saint Mark's.

But I know my limits. There are a lot of gods, and monsters, and maybe even demons involved in this whole curse thing. There are magic books at stake. And prisoners. And debts.

Including mine.

Not to mention Pell and Tomas.

So I need to tread carefully.

And isn't it convenient that I have hooves now? Hooves that are very good at stepping carefully.

I snicker as I enter the woods, a little bit proud of myself for being so positive—even though Pia isn't here to prod me into that kind of thinking.

But the woods do not take me to the big tree that Pell and I sleep under. In fact, this doesn't look like our woods at all. It starts off thick and lush, but as I travel down the path the trees, and shrubs, and ferns become fewer and fewer until there's nothing but a gray wasteland.

"Now what the hell? Why does the freaking world have to shift around so much?"

The last part of my sentence echoes off in the distance.

And then the whole place goes dark.

I *come out of the door* and find myself in... nothingness. That's the only way to describe it. It's not even darkness, it's just gray, blah nothing. "Hello?" This one word echoes through the space, repeating itself over and over again until my 'hello' is just a hum.

"Hello?" Again, I listen for the echo.

I'm no expert in echoes, but I'm pretty sure that repeating echoes bouncing into one another mean that this is not an open space, but a confined one.

"OK, hallway gods." My words come out weary. "I don't know what this is, or what I'm doing here, or if this has a point. But I'm looking for Pie!"

I yell the last part.

It echoes. And echoes. And echoes.

And then... a faint voice in the distance. "Pell? Pell, is that you?"

"Pie? Pie, can you hear me?"

"I can hear you."

But she sounds so far away. "Pie! Where are you?"

"I don't know. It's dark! I can't see anything!"

"Follow my voice, Pie. And I'll follow yours."

"I'll try, but—"

She cuts off. I think she's scared. I hate it when Pie is scared. "You're OK, Pie. Don't worry. We can't be that far away."

"Oh, Pell. Don't say things like that. It's like tempting fate."

She really is scared. I can hear it in her voice. "Talk to me, Pie. Where did you come from?"

"What? I can barely hear you! Pell! Can you hear me?"

"You're going the wrong way. Turn around. Follow my voice."

"I can't see anything, Pell. Nothing. Nothing at all."

"OK. I'll come to you. Just keep talking. Tell me what happened. How did you get here? Did you get lost leaving Tomas's dungeon?"

"How did you know I was in the dungeon?"

"I went to see Tomas too."

"Hey, I can hear you better now."

"I'm coming to get you, that's why. Just stay where you are."

"Don't worry about that, I'm not going anywhere. There's nowhere to go."

"So did you get lost leaving his dungeon?"

"No. I went back to the tomb and then I went to check on Jacqueline."

Her voice is getting louder and louder as I walk. "And what happened?"

"The devil, Pell. The devil got me."

"What?"

"Oh, hey! It's getting lighter. I can see… well, nothing. But it's not black anymore."

"I'm getting close. I'm bringing light with me, I think." And then I see her off in the distance. Right where the gray meets the black. She's wearing her slutty schoolgirl outfit, but instead of being human—which she often is when she's in this outfit—she's still her wood nymph self.

"Pell!" She sees me. Then she's running, her hooves making a soft tapping on the ground. When she reaches me, she leaps, jumping into my arms and wrapping her long legs around me. "You found me."

"I never had any doubt."

She buries her head in my neck and lets out a long sigh as I put her down. "The devil got me, Pell."

"I think you should explain that."

She pulls away from my neck so she can look me in the eyes. "I went through the door to Granite Springs"—she points at me—"just like you told me to."

"I didn't tell you to go visit Tomas. Or give him a door. What was that about?"

"Would you like to hear my devil story? Or do you want to complain about my spontaneous and uncontrollable generosity?"

"Spontaneous and uncontrollable?"

"So you *don't* want to hear my devil story?"

"I do. Tell me the devil story."

The words spill out of her mouth and she describes the devil as an even more handsome version of Russ Roth.

"Handsome?"

"You do have to admit he's hot, Pell. There's no getting around that."

I wave my hand in the air, telling her to continue.

"Anyway, he did something to me."

"What kind of something?" I growl these words out in my new rumbling voice. And as I do that pinpricks of light appear above us.

Pie looks up. "What's that?"

"Finish the story of the devil."

She sighs. "Is it stars?"

"Pie! Focus!"

"Fine." She pouts a little. I really like it when she pouts. Her lips get all plump and sexy. "He put some kind of spell on me."

"What kind of spell?"

"Like a… one-track-mind spell. He wants me to go to Vinca and bring Tarq to him."

"Tarq? Why?"

"The devil says Tarq is not the king, he is. And blah, blah, blah… he controls the royal beasts. Also, he says I belong to him too."

"*What?*" Again, I roar this. And the voice is loud, and commanding, and reverberates around in the space. This makes the pinpricks of light glow.

Pie points up. "I think we should talk about that."

"How could you belong to *him* when you belong to *me?*" There's no stopping the voice. I'm getting hot about this fucking devil and this time the rumble produces a flash in the air. Then the grayness all around us takes on a yellow-orange glow.

Pie side-eyes me. "Are you doing that?"

"How. Can you belong to him? When you belong to me?"

And again, the world around us brightens.

"I think you're doing that, Pell. And I'm not trying to change the subject or whatever. The short answer to your question is that I don't know. I need to go down into the Bottoms and find the library. Tomas says there's a library down there. You can come with. Now"—she lets out a breath and twirls her finger in a circle above her head—"what's going on with this?"

I look up. There's nothing to see up there. The only thing that has changed is the light. The pinpricks must've expanded into the glow, because I can't see them anymore. "I don't know."

And now I'm confused too. Because the anger has left me, but the rumble in my voice continues and the glow around us grows.

"You're doing that."

I shrug. "Maybe." And at the same time that word comes out of my mouth, the world brightens again.

"No 'maybe' about it, Pell. You're making… light."

"Well. That's weird."

"Yeah." She chuckles a little, then lets out a long sigh, like she's relaxing. "What is this place? Where the hell are we? And how did we get here?"

"I was down in the dungeon with Tomas." Then I let out an exasperated breath because I momentarily forgot about the whole scene from the sanctuary and now it comes rushing back. "The monsters and nymphs are pissed off at me. So I had to make a run for it. I ran to the dungeon and the hallways rearranged so they couldn't follow me. Then I needed to check up on you, but I didn't want to go back out there. They're really pissed. So Tomas suggested I use the hallways to…" I don't know what happened, so I just throw up my hands. "Make a door or something. And then I ended up here."

"Huh."

"What's that 'huh' mean?"

She puts up a hand. "Hold on a second, mister. Why are the monsters and nymphs all mad at you?"

"Well, you're not gonna like this—and it was not on purpose—but Frecks is dead."

"What? How?"

"My stupid voice." And when I say this, the rumble comes back and the world flickers. "See? I don't know what's going on but this voice is… destroying things out there."

"That doesn't explain what happened to Frecks."

"So the voice came out, and the whole place trembled, and then the spire fell down off the cathedral and… Frecks ended up underneath it."

"Oh, no." She pouts her sexy lips again. "He was the one who made me all the portal door dragon-scale jewelry."

"Good thing we don't need those anymore."

"Pell!"

"Sorry. But… but they're getting on my nerves, OK? I'm

tired of them." This comes out too loud and with too much anger, so the world around us flashes and then...

Pie's eyes go wide when she looks up at the sky. Which is... now a sky. She points to it. "What the hell is that?"

"A sun?"

She looks at me. "What's it doing here?"

I just shrug. "Dunno."

Her eyebrows crinkle and she stares at me. She glances up, and around, and her eyes land back on me. "You... lit up the world."

"Hmm."

"Hmm? That's all you have to say about that?"

"I doubt it was me, Pie. It's the hallways. They're fucking with us."

"I don't think so, mister. Do it again."

"Do what again? I'm not doing anything. I'm just talking." And the moment the word 'talking' comes out, the sky turns blue. A very pale, gorgeous shade of robin's egg blue.

Pie's eyes go wide and a smile creeps up her face. "You're *doing* that."

She might be right. I test it out. "I'm doing that!" I say it loud, and add some growl as we both stare up at the sky. But nothing happens. I look at Pie and shrug. "I guess that's that."

But she points to the ground and whispers, "Look."

Well. I stand corrected. "Is that grass?"

She steps lightly, her hooves sinking into the lush green as she walks a few paces away, then turns, beaming a smile at me. "You're... creating something, Pell! Do more."

"No. I don't want to. I want to get rid of the monsters." The grass grows longer. Right in front of our eyes. "I want them out of my tomb!" A little tree pops up from the earth.

"Say more. What else do you want?"

"Umm... I want that devil to go away. I want you—" I let out a long breath and whatever is happening around us pauses. "I want you, Pie. You and me. I even made you a ring."

"What?" Her eyes go blinky and wide. It's a cute look. "Do you have it on you?" She's eyeballing my pockets. "Let me see it."

"No. It's a surprise. You can't see it. And besides, I have to make a spelling for it. To give us good luck and long love."

Now her face goes all melty and soft. Like I'm making her swoon. I like to make Pie swoon, not only because she's more likely to say yes to sex when she's all swoony, but also because she's just… cute.

She steps towards me, reaching for my shoulders. She leans up on her tiptoes, bringing us nearly eye to eye. And then she kisses me right on the lips. Words pass between us in a whisper. Her words.

"A love, a life, a world, a sun
You and I are meant to run.
Make the forest our place to roam
And we will have a forever home."

We pull apart and all the tiny trees around us are now saplings.

"Did you mean to do that?"

She lets out a sigh. "No. It just came out. It's been doing that all day. That's how Tomas got his door. I didn't really agree to that, the words just tumbled out and there it was."

"New powers."

She agrees with a nod. "For both of us, Pell. Your voice makes worlds."

"Not really. Only in here. And this place isn't real. Outside, Pie, the sanctuary crumbles when I use the voice. And at first, I didn't think this was a big deal. Wouldn't be the first time it fell down, right? But then I noticed it wasn't repairing itself."

We stare at each other for a long moment.

Finally, Pie says, "What does that mean?"

But she's not slow or dumb. She knows what it means.

She just wants me to say it out loud. "I think... I think the curse is breaking."

"Really? Well, that's great!"

I'm not displaying the same excitement.

"What?" she says. "Why do you look that way?"

"You said we can't break the curse because this is where we're safe. Remember?"

"I do. But"—she smiles—"everything ends eventually, right? No one is very happy with the sanctuary right now. And it's not even impenetrable. Batty flies over the walls."

"Batty. He's on my shit list." The voice rumbles again and now the saplings are grown.

Pie pats my chest. "Yeah. But that's OK. Because I don't think they're supposed to be here."

Now she's frowning so I frown too. "Where are they supposed to be?"

"Well." She makes one of those clenched-teeth smiles. "I think they might belong in the Bottoms."

"In the prison?"

"Yep. I think they go down there. That's another reason I need to get to that library. I haven't been down there since... you know, that whole 'enslaving Callistina' thing. But I've made a mess of things." These words make her pause and look sad for a moment. I'm just about to ask what that's all about when she continues. "I need to face what I've done. I can't run from it forever."

"Wait. So you're telling me that you're going into debt for a bunch of prisoners?" This pisses me off. And all the trees grow huge, their boughs creating a canopy that now shades us.

"Maybe?"

"So we have to put them all in prison."

I might smirk a little too much here because Pie says, "As fun as that would be for you, it's not fun for me. I'm not in charge of… justice, or whatever. I have no idea what these people did to be in that perp book of Tarq's."

"Perp book?"

"Yeah. He had a book of defectors. And all our monsters were in there."

"Well, there you go. They are criminals. They belong in the Bottoms prison. We should send them there right now."

"No."

"Why not?"

"Because one, we've got some alone time here, and two, we need to think this through. What about the devil?"

"What about him?"

"He's holding Jacqueline and her kids prisoner."

"Oh. You didn't mention that part."

"I should've. But I'm stressed. He wants me to bring him Tarq."

"Well, that's not gonna happen."

"What if he kills them? I can't just leave Jacqueline in the hands of the devil."

"He spelled you, Pie. That's… not nice. He's not nice. I don't think we should worry about him."

"Well, that's because you didn't see him. He was…" She sighs.

I recognize this sigh. "He was *what*?" And boy, these really are some growly words. Flowers pop out of the grass. Like… a whole carpet of them.

"Hot, Pell. He was hot. Like—"

"So fuckin' hot?"

She giggles. "Yeah. But don't worry. His spell didn't work on me. I stepped through the door, pretty intent on getting Tarq and hauling his ass back here, but then I stumbled into a memory of us and whatever hold the devil had on me just kinda… faded away."

"Ohhh." My mood lightens. "When I was in the hallways, I had a memory of us too. That day in the Jeep, when you

JA HUSS

came from town the first time and learned about your Book of Debt. You were so cute that day."

She frowns. "Was I cute? Or was I just kinda dumb?"

"Pie."

"What?"

"Always cute."

Her frown disappears. "Well, I don't quite remember it that way. But my memory was of me writing that spell over your tomb door. Now that"—she winks at me—"that was a day to remember."

"Do you think we had these memories at the same time?"

"I think we did. I think that's what broke the devil's spell. I heard your voice and it snapped me out of it. And look." She points to the sky and the trees all around us. "We're doing something here, don't you think?"

It's hard to deny. This place was gray nothingness and... well, now it's not. Now it's a lot like the woods in my tomb. Not exactly like the woods—it's too young—but it's still growing. "You know what?"

"What?"

I'm still looking up and around, but then I lower my gaze to find Pie's eyes. "I think this is my tomb." Then I squint my eyes at a tree. "I know that tree."

"You know that *tree*?"

This makes me chuckle. "Pie, I'm a creature of the forest. I've been living in the same home for two thousand years. Why is my personal relationship with the trees such a point of contention with you? Wasn't I right about the trees on the other side of the Granite Springs door?"

"You were."

"I'm right now too."

"Fine. You can be right. Tell me how you know that tree."

"Look." I take her hand and walk over to the tree. "Do you see this broken branch right here?"

"Yep. I do."

"See where it's connected to the trunk? It's star-shaped."

"OK."

"Well, that's how it started. Just a broken branch that left behind a star-shaped scar. But over a couple thousand years it turned into a huge hole. Still star-shaped. If we ever get back to my tomb, I'll take you to see it. I lived in it for a while. Maybe seventy or eighty years."

"So why did you move out?"

I think about this for a moment. It was a pretty long time ago. "Hmm. I don't really remember. I think I just wanted more space. But the point is"—I touch the scar on the tree—"this is how it started. I remember that very clearly."

"So…" Pie slowly turns in a circle. "We're in your tomb."

"I think so. I think all we have to do is wait."

Pie's turn completes and she's looking me in the eyes. "What are we waiting for?"

"Time, Pie. To catch up, I guess."

"So we're in the past right now."

"A memory."

"But we've never done this before. And aren't the hall-ways just there to show you something has happened in the past?"

I can't really agree or disagree. "I guess."

"So that means…" She starts to spin in her circle again, looking up at the sky. "That means something else is happening here." She looks down at me. "And we should go look for it."

I hold up a finger. "Alternatively"—she giggles as I take her hand—"we could just sit down here"—I kneel, taking her with me—"and enjoy a little break."

Now we're both kneeling. And I have to suck in a breath when I look at her. Because the golden glow from the sky is casting a light over her that makes her appear… luminescent.

"In fact," I continue, "I think we should… maybe… make some new memories."

"Let me guess. You think we should have sex, don't you?"

"Woman, it's like you're inside my head at all times."

"You kind of have a one-track mind. It's not that hard to read it."

"Is that a no?"

"It's not a no. But"—she smirks and shrugs her shoulders—"I'm not really in the mood."

When Pie says she's not in the mood it's my cue to put her in the mood. I turn towards her, leaning in as I take a step to erase the small distance between us. As I do this, one hand slips around the velvety skin where her lower back meets her ass while the other hand slips over her hipbone on the opposite side, caging her in my arms.

Her eyes are dancing with delight just like her little hooves do when she's excited. "We should stay focused."

"Oh, I'm focused."

"On business, I mean."

I reach up and stroke her cheek. This sends a little shiver through her body and she does a little shake. "We're stuck in a hallway, Pell."

"We're not stuck. We're just... visiting."

"The devil is after me. My best friend is missing."

I lean into her neck and press my lips against the soft, soft skin just below her ear. "We could make a door anytime we want. And we can make that door take us anywhere we want. Saving Jacqueline is a matter of good timing and nothing else."

"Good timing?"

"Twenty minutes, Pie." I whisper this in her ear. She has good points. It's hard to justify sex when her friend could be missing. But that doesn't mean I'm not gonna try. "Don't we deserve twenty minutes?"

She sighs and goes soft. And then her hands are on my shoulders, pressing down. Encouraging me to kneel.

I look up at her, grinning as I lower myself to my knees and find my mouth right at her bare belly button.

"We should be quick." But then she bites her lip. Her tell.

I flip her little skirt up—my eyes still locked on hers—and stick my tongue out as I lean in between her legs and pull her cute red-tartan panties to the side.

The moment my tongue sweeps against her sweet, sweet folds Pie grabs my horns with both hands and throws her head back.

My hands grip her hips as I lean in, flicking my tongue just enough to tease.

"OK." She breathes this syllable out. "Fine. You win —oooooohhh!"

I chuckle as I slide the finger I've pushed up inside her in and out. Then I lean my face into her stomach, letting my shaggy cheek skim along that velvet boundary just below her belly button. She squeezes her legs together and twists her body a little—a signal that she is about to explode if I don't pull back.

I don't pull back.

I like to get Pie off immediately. Get the first orgasm over with so we can slow down for the next few. And I'm just picking up the pace with my finger, ready to do that, when she scoots to the side, breaking the moment.

"What are you doing?"

"I know what you're thinking." Her face is flushed pink and her breath is coming out eager and heavy. "You're thinking that you can get this first one over with—"

"Pie."

"And then we can slow down and just linger in the sex—"

"Pie."

"Like we've got all the time in the world."

"Don't we? We are in the hallways."

She grabs my horns, pulls me up so I'm standing, then reaches for my cock through my pants. "This is a quickie, mister." Her fingertips slip into the waistband of my pants and she tugs me forward. A moment later, the button is popped and the zipper is down.

When her hand wraps around my cock and pulls it out, I nearly moan. "Well. I'm not sure what your point is, but I'm on board."

Pie smirks. "Here's my point." She lifts her long, long, sexy leg—unfurling it at the knee until her hoof is pointing towards the sky—and then she sets her ankle down on my shoulder. Grinning. "Quickie. Go."

Dare I look down at the scene she has painted for me?

Oh, hell yeah, I do. One hand wraps around her ankle on my shoulder, while the other slides down her inner thigh, my eyes following the progression of my fingertips.

The soft, pink folds between her legs are glistening and full. And when I look up into her eyes, I lick my lips.

"Later." She giggles this word out. "We can do all that slow stuff later."

"Fine." My voice is husky and low. And then I place my hand over hers, the one still wrapped around my cock, and push inside her.

She immediately moans. And then her other leg draws up, her knee pressed against my hip as I move forward and back. Not fast though. She wants a quickie, fine. But I'm gonna take my time.

Her hands play with the loose curls of hair that just barely touch my shoulders while her mouth presses against mine in a kiss that is both urgent and careful at the same time.

And this is how I love her.

We come at the same time, we moan each other's names, we make whispered promises that we absolutely mean.

I'm going to keep this woman forever.

We're going to live a life that is full, and long, and blessed.

I can see it all in my head. A paradise far, far beyond the curse that has trapped me for the last two thousand years.

Pie's legs drop back to the ground and then we just lie down on the grass. She angles her body into mine, one leg draped over my hip, one hand on my chest, one cheek on my shoulder.

"I thought you said we were in a hurry."

She sighs. "We are."

And then... we close our eyes and whatever hurry we were in disappears.

And in its place comes something else...

CHAPTER THIRTEEN - PIE

PIE

The sharp voice of my mother jolts me out of my slumber.

Except I'm not sleeping. I'm not in a forest with Pell. I'm standing in a dirty hotel room. Two beds, both unmade, and only the crackling blue light of the TV flashing across the dingy walls for illumination. There is a crack in the blackout curtains across the one window and through this crack, past the snow- and salt-stained glass of winter, is the flashing chaos of Christmas lights strung up outside.

On the other side of the room is a closed bathroom door. A sliver of bright light leaks out at the bottom where the old, frayed edge of carpet meets the cracked tiles of the bathroom beyond.

The bathroom is where the yelling is happening. "Now look what you've done! You're making a mess of things, Pie!"

I remember this place. We lived in this hotel for a little while. In my child's mind, it was forever. But looking back now, it probably wasn't more than a few months. We did spend Christmas here though. So I can place the year. Six, I think. I was six.

My mother is shaking me in that bathroom. I haven't thought about this night in... well, maybe since the night it actually happened. But now that I'm here, seeing it again as a living memory, it's all very fresh. Like it really is happening here in the moment for the very first time.

My mother is also screaming at me because of Pia. "That bird does not exist! She's not there, you idiot! You moron! You're making it up! And if you think you don't have to listen to me... well..."

I was sitting on the edge of the bathtub, Pia clutched in my hands, just looking at my toes slipping in and out of an oversized pair of leather boots as my mother grabbed my shirt at the shoulders and shook me.

"And you can play crazy all you want, but we know better. Where is the ring?"

Ring? I lean in, trying to hear more. Because I don't remember anything about a missing ring when I was a kid.

"It was on your finger! Right here! Right here!" She's screaming these words. I look around the room, concentrating on the walls for a moment. Wondering how thin they are. Wondering if the people on either side of this room can hear the yelling.

But there is a lot of noise coming from outside and on the other side of the walls. I can make out babies crying, and men yelling, and doors slamming. Wherever this hotel is, it's not a place for tourists. It's a place where you pay by the week. It's a place where families go when they have no other choice.

It's a place where a small girl from another realm ends up with a woman who is not her mother.

I am not this woman's child. I think I've always felt this, but never quite believed it until now.

I do not belong here.

"I can't do this anymore!" she yells. "Do you hear me? I can't do this anymore! I should leave you here. Just walk out. Just leave and never look back! Merry Christmas to me!"

"What a bitch." I barely mutter these words out. But the woman who is not my mother must have superpowered hearing or something, because she pauses her rant. Then the door comes swinging open.

"Well." She plants her hands on her hips. "It's about fucking time you showed up! This brat is ruining everything!"

For a moment, I'm sure she's talking to me. But then a man is stepping through me, like I'm just a ghost or an apparition. "You don't need to yell at her, Lisa." His voice is calm, and deep, and soothing. He pushes past her, into the bathroom, and then kneels down in front of little me.

I am sitting on the edge of the bathtub, just like I remember it. But everything aside from that is new and unfamiliar.

For one, I'm wearing a red and yellow tartan uniform. Something a child might wear to a private school and not the short, sexy kind one puts on for Halloween.

But it's not any kind of school uniform I've ever seen. The skirt is very long and pleated. Like if little-girl me were to stand up, the skirt would fall all the way down to my ankles. On my feet are a pair of brown leather boots, like the ones in my memory, but also very different. They are too big, that's true, and my feet are slipping in and out of them. But they are square. And for a moment I wonder if the legs underneath that skirt are covered in fur and the feet inside the boots are actually hooves.

But no. My toes appear. And even though I am not the little-girl me, I can feel her wonder every time the toes poke up from the dark boot and wiggle. She is… amazed by them. Even in the midst of all this yelling and stress, she is fascinated by her own toes.

The skirt and boots aren't the only things wrong with this uniform. There is a sash across my chest made of deep scarlet leather. And there are little medals on the sash, like something from a Girl Scout uniform, except they're not crudely sewn patches. They are made of gold, and silver, and maybe bronze. And they are cast, or carved, or something, with tiny illustrated details and words printed in another language around the edges. There are ribbons, too. Gold and red satin. And tassels on my shoulders. My blonde hair is nearly white and it has been painstakingly plaited in a very elaborate way with glittering gold and red threads woven into the hair so that even in this dingy room with gross fluorescent light, my hair sparkles with the slightest movement of my head.

The braids fall down on either side of my body, almost to my waist, and the ends are decorated with a red satin hair tie accentuated with a gold lion medallion.

There is a cape made of a deep-red velvet covering one half of my upper body and a gold clasp that cinches it to my uniform at the shoulders.

I blink, stunned at the little girl who is me. Because I don't remember this. I don't remember any of it. In my memory it was my mother—the yeller—and me. And we did stay here in this hotel, but I don't remember this man.

And I don't remember my outfit being so... regal.

No. *Royal.* Royal is the right word.

Suddenly, I switch places. I am no longer a grown woman watching like some unaffiliated third party. I am the small, stolen princess sitting on the edge of the bathtub holding a soft, warm, squirming Pia in my palms.

I look up at the man in front of me and gasp.

"There, there, Pie." The name comes out *Pahhhh.* Because his accent isn't Philly. It's Western PA hick. And he has the greenest eyes I will ever see. He is Russ Roth, but not *the* Russ Roth from Granite Springs. He is the doppelganger from Savage Falls.

He is the devil.

With the same handsome face, and the same deep, soothing voice, and the same power of attraction. With a gentle sweep, he slides the back of his hand down my cheek, dragging my tears along for the ride. My stomach feels like it's flipping upside down and doing somersaults. But at the same time, his touch turns my fear and sadness into something else.

It becomes... acceptance, maybe. Or... surrender. That might be a better word.

"It's OK, darling. It's all gonna be OK. All we need are answers, little sweetheart. Then you can go home. Wouldn't you like to go home? Hmm? Spend Christmas with your family? Doesn't that sound nice?"

I look back down at Pia and she says, "Where are we, Pie?"

"I don't know."

"You don't know what? You little brat!" My mother—who is obviously not my mother—thinks I'm talking to her, not Pia.

"What does he want to know?" Pia squeaks.

"I don't know."

"See!" The woman is pointing at me, but she is talking to the devil. "She's a moron. A retard, or something."

"Don't call her that!" The devil stands up when he barks these words out, his green eyes flashing with anger. "How many fuckin' times have I told you not to call her that!"

He makes to strike my not-mother across the face. But at the last second, when she's cowering back against the sink, he changes his mind and takes a deep breath instead.

The woman holds her breath, eyes wide, scared now.

"Go wait out there." The devil points to the messy bedroom and the woman scoots her way past him and out of sight.

The devil closes the door. Then he turns back to me and kneels back down on the gross bathroom tile. He puts both his hands on his thighs and lets out a long exhale. "Pianna. Look at me, sweetie."

I don't want to look at him. When I look at him, he makes

me feel funny. And then he makes me feel sick. Every time I look at him, I want to throw up.

He places his finger under my chin and tips my head up. Finally, feeling like I don't have a choice, I meet his gaze. I gag and shake my head until he lets go of my chin and allows me to look away.

"It's not your fault."

I don't know what he's talking about, but I'm listening now. Because all day the woman has been telling me that everything is my fault.

"You can't help who you are. And you're just a little girl, so it's not even like you can change it."

I let out a long breath. It's my turn to sigh deeply.

"But if you tell me the secret words, Pie, and you tell me where you put the ring... then I can change things. I can change everything for you."

"You can send me home?" My voice is small, and shaky, and scared.

"Yes." The devil is delighted. Finally, I have spoken and taken an interest in what's happening. "Of course I can. If you just tell me the words and give me the ring, things will go back to the way they were. And don't we all just want things to go back to the way they were? Hmm?"

I don't know about this. I don't know where I come from. Even though I am inside my little-girl self in this moment, I don't understand what's happening. Not the important parts.

I do understand, now that I am in this body and not passively watching from the outside, that I am not a human. And that I did have hooves, or something other than human feet, when I woke up and put these boots on. They are not boots made for human feet.

And I understand that I have been kidnapped. That I am someone important. Or, at the very least, the daughter of someone important. Even if I had not been told that

Callistina was my sister, I would be able to piece this together just by looking at the outfit I am wearing.

I am a royal beast and I have been taken.

The devil tries to take my hand, but I resist. I'm still clutching Pia in my palms. When he insists, Pia flutters up my arm, crawls her way up my cape, and settles into the collar of my uniform near my neck.

He pries my hands open and out comes a fluttering of moths.

He stands up and steps back, his hands in the air, like he's warding them off. "Fuck! Fuck!" He says this over and over again. Then he's got a lighter in his hand, flicking on a flame. Then, one by one, the moths are burned away to dust.

When they are dead and the room is still, he lets out a long breath, shoves the lighter back in his pocket, and says, "Now that was not what we want from you, Pie."

"I don't know how that happened."

It's true too. When these words come out of my little-girl mouth, I mean them. I am as confused as I've ever been about the stupid moths.

"Where are the fireflies?"

"Fireflies?"

He places a hand on my shoulder and shakes me, not too hard, but hard enough to make me jump and gasp. "You know what I'm talking about."

The bathroom door opens and my not-mother pokes her head in. "I don't think she knows," she says. "The moths came out the moment I pulled her through the door. I think this place changed her."

"We don't have time for this place to *change* her, Lisa. This was your idea. You said it would work. And now…" He sucks air past his teeth. "Now she's *human* and all her magic is missing."

"She had the ring, though. I know she did."

"Get out."

Lisa is not my mother, but she's not a monster either. I don't even think she's magic. I think Lisa is a human. Probably a human who got caught up in the eros love spell. And the two of them came up with this whole kidnapping plan, but something happened and it didn't go the way they thought.

That's what I get out of this short conversation between the two of them.

My not-mother backs up and once again, the door closes.

The devil bends down, takes my hand, holds it, and points to my finger. "The ring. See? That's where the ring was, little Pie. Right there on your finger. You can see the outline."

I look down at my hand, and sure enough, he's right. There is a pale band of skin around my ring finger where something recently was, and has been for a long time, but is missing now.

"What happened to the ring, Pie?"

"I don't know."

"Did you take it off? Hmm? And maybe leave it somewhere?"

I shake my head no.

"Then what happened to it?"

"I don't know."

I really don't. I can't even imagine what ring he's talking about.

Well, maybe that's not true. I have a lot of rings these days. Any one of them could be the ring he's talking about.

He's frustrated with me. I can tell. But he's not mean, like the woman I will end up calling Mother. He doesn't yell, or stomp, or threaten me. He just... talks. In a nice, soothing, low, rumbly voice that makes me like him.

"You were in the ritual this morning, remember?"

I actually don't. I have no memories of this other world where they took me from. And by the way—'ritual'? What the hell?

"You were in the room with the gods, remember? And you got a gift. A bag of rings. Does that sound familiar?"

Well, it's certainly interesting. Because my history seems to be a muddled mishmash of lies and half-truths. And this little revelation right here falls into the category of half-truth.

Ostanes claimed to be my real mother. But I'm not feeling it. Still, she is connected to me in some way, that I do feel. But the bag of rings more than kinda fits. It fits pretty damn good. Because I do have a bag of rings.

But I certainly didn't back when I was a child.

"Remember?"

I shake my head no.

"You know the words, Pie. You know them. What did Ostanes say to you? And which god gave you the rings? Was it Saturn?"

I don't answer him because I'm so confused right now.

Why the hell would Saturn give me a bag of rings?

"And then," the devil-man continues. "You were in the room with all the people—remember the people? And the royals? Hmm? This sounds familiar, right?"

It really doesn't.

"And the gods. They were all there. You had the bag of rings—plus the one on your finger." He stops here to place his finger under my chin again and tilt my head up, trying to force me to look him in the eyes.

I won't do it.

He doesn't push, just continues with his recap of what, apparently, happened earlier in the day. "And then, Lisa and I opened the door and brought you here. And we did that, Pie, because we need. Those. Rings."

So. That's how it happened. I guess it's nice to finally know the truth. They kidnapped me from some ritual—which could've been a life-saver, now that I think about it. Whatever kind of ritual it was, it couldn't have been good.

Then somehow, they opened a door, grabbed me, and took me back through it.

They took me out of my world and brought me to this one so they would have time to coax the spelling words out of me and find that stupid bag of rings. But I never did tell them the words because they must not have known that in this world, the magic is impotent.

Humans, and this world we live in, are not magical. Not the way they are in Vinca and other places.

So something went wrong with their little kidnapping scheme.

Something happened on the journey from there to here. Something happened to me, and my magic, and my memory. And I never did give up those words. There was no way I could. Because when I walked through the door I came out the other side a human girl, and no longer a royal beast.

I'm suddenly outside the bathroom. I don't really recall what happens next in there. A little more coaxing from the devil, I guess. But nothing more than that.

I think he knew too. I think he figured it out. But instead of telling Lisa that the whole thing was a bust—they would not be getting my magic and whatever plans they had made were now moot—he just... left.

He left her, and he left me, and then... I simply became someone else.

And if Pia hadn't been in my hand when they took me, I might never have woken up.

I might've just slipped into being that other little girl who had no magic and saw no talking birds, and didn't get dropped off at CPS three years later after the devil ran out on my new mother and she finally came to terms with the fact that he had left her behind and now she was gonna do the same to me.

I look at my mother now, eyes darting to the closed bathroom door as she puffs on a cigarette. She is pretty in a used-up kind of way. Like her life was rough. And that's why she is rough now too.

And I guess I should give her some credit. Because she hung in there for three years. She took care of me for three more years before she'd had enough and finally walked away. And actually, I still have her number. She never really disappeared. Not completely.

I was a little piece of string that attached her to the devil.

Every now and then she came to see me at the foster homes. Not many times. Maybe... three or four. But the last time, it was my eighteenth birthday and I was walking home that night with Jacqueline. We'd been partying a little. A few beers, that's all. We were buzzed, sloppily walking down the sidewalk towards the three-story row house we called home, singing some pop song off-key, happy as a couple of discarded teenagers could be.

And there was my mother. Standing in front of our stoop, smoking her cigarette. Nervous smile on her face as she watched me for a reaction.

There were a few awkward moments between her and Jacqueline. A few snide comments, too. Jacqueline was buzzed and her tongue was always sharper when she was drinking. But she went inside and left us alone. And my mother talked to me outside my foster home for five whole minutes.

She asked how I was. She asked me if I ever saw my father. And back then, I didn't even have the foggiest idea of who she was talking about. But now, of course, after this hallway memory, she was talking about him.

The devil.

Who was not my father any more than she was my mother.

She was looking for him, I guess. And I was her only point of contact.

But up until I met Russ Roth outside Saint Mark's that

second day of my curse, I didn't have a single memory of that face the two of them share.

I wonder if Tomas was right about the payment for my enslavement. He told me that my parents would've been compensated once my curse began. But which parents? The ones of this world? Or the other one where I originally came from?

If it was this one, then imagine the surprise on my mother's face when she won the lottery or whatever. A windfall. I think that was the word Tomas used. She would've gotten a windfall.

And maybe she felt it was just luck. Just dumb luck.

But if the devil was acting as my father in this world, and he got his windfall, might he not have figured it out? Might he not have put two and two together and that's how he got to be the devil of Savage Falls?

I let out another long breath as the bathroom door opens and little me walks out, clutching Pia to her chest. And in this moment, I have the most uncontrollable urge to go back. It almost makes me sick.

To go back, and be little, and be with Pia. And do it all again.

Because yeah. These two jerks walked out on me.

But I was never alone.

I was *never* alone because I always had Pia.

And I get it. Pia is just me. Just the magical part of me. Somehow, when they pulled me through that door and I came out the other side as a human instead of a beast, my magic was packed up inside the body of a little bird.

Callistina didn't kill Pia. Because Pia can't die. Pia is me.

But I feel her loss so hard.

And this loss makes me want to do horrible things to my gryphon-chimera sister.

That's why I haven't gone back down to the Bottoms.

Because when Callistina 'killed' Pia, all she really did was give me my magic back.

And with this magic, and these rings, and these doors—I can do things.

Spectacular things.

Or maybe horrible things.

Maybe I will do horrible, horrible things.

CHAPTER FOURTEEN - PELL

glow passes across my eyelids and I slowly come out of a deep, sound sleep. When I open my eyes the first thing I see are fireflies. They are crawling out of Pie's palm, which is resting on my chest, and their tiny feet are tickling my bare skin as they crawl away and then lift off into the air.

When I look up, there are hundreds of them. Maybe thousands. And the whole forest, all around us, is aglow from their little bodies.

One of them breaks off from the group, heading into the darkness of the trees. Then another follows. And another. Then dozens. Until there is a little stream of fireflies up in the dark sky. A little pathway, maybe. Something we can follow, perhaps.

"Pie." I whisper it. "Pie, wake up. Look."

She moans a little, then goes stiff and sits straight up. "Horrible!"

"What? No, sweet Pie. It's not horrible. Not at all."

"What?" She looks around, confused. "What are you talking about?"

The fireflies are still pouring out of her palm. And she looks down, maybe feeling them, and just stares at them for a few moments. Like none of this makes sense.

Which it doesn't.

She looks at me with wide, surprised eyes. "The moths, Pell. The moths are *bad*."

Now I'm confused. "What moths?"

"You know. The ones I used to—" She pauses, watching the fireflies still pouring out of her palms. Then she looks at me again. "The ones I used to banish Saturn, or whoever. They're not… me. Not the real me. The real me is…" Her eyes drift upward and she points to the stream of light. "That. Them. The fireflies are my real magic. My good magic, Pell. The magic they wanted to steal."

"Who? What did I miss?"

"A dream. Or… no. A memory. I fell asleep and then I woke up in a hotel room. It was the day they took me, Pell. My mother and the devil."

"The devil? As in the guy waiting for me in the Granite Springs bar?"

"Him. He was there. He was part of the kidnapping. And I wasn't always a human."

"Well, we knew that, right?"

"Yeah. But I'm not a wood nymph chimera, either. I'm a…" She squints her eyes, then sighs. "I'm like Callistina. I'm one of those lion things. I'm one of those royal beasts."

She starts describing the scene to me. The yelling and the little uniform she was wearing.

Royal beasts.

This keeps popping up so there has to be something to it.

This whole time that Pie is talking, fireflies continue to pour out of her palm. She absently itches them with her fingernails as she retells her story. But it must get overwhelming because she throws up her hands and yells, "Stop it!"

The fireflies do not stop. In fact, they grow in number, the river above us getting thicker and brighter.

"Why won't they stop? There must be millions of them up there."

"I think they're trying to tell us something."

"What? What are they trying to tell us?"

I point to the river. "I think we're supposed to follow them."

Pie sighs. "Oh. Well, OK. Should we do that?"

"Feels like the next necessary step. But... we don't have to go right away. I don't think the fireflies are in charge of anything. They're just a map. And maps will wait until you're calmed down."

"I'm calm."

I side-eye her.

"I am. It was just... unsettling. My mother and the devil. And you know what the really gross thing is? He wasn't mean the way she was. But then he left. He just walked out on us. And my mother—Lisa—she took care of me for three years even though I wasn't hers. I was just... a leftover kidnapped kid who never panned out. He never came back. But she did. Several times after she dropped me off at CPS. That's why I still have her phone number. Though I have never called it, so who knows if it still works."

"Hold up. The devil was nice to you?"

"Yeah."

"But you told me that he put a spell on you. He told you to bring him Tarq."

"Well, I thought that was him. It looked like the same man. But the devil looks like Russ Roth too. And they're definitely not the same guy. So maybe there are several of them? Maybe lots of them? And maybe all those eros men look alike?"

"Maybe." I say this out loud but I don't really mean it. I think they are all the same. Even Russ Roth. I think something is going on with Granite Springs. Or Savage Falls. Whatever it's called. I think there's something to that place the same way there's something to Saint Mark's. Maybe there are no hallways in the town, but it's definitely got a split personality.

And we did find a bonafide blood dragon living in its midst.

That's gotta mean something.

Pie gets to her feet and then offers me a hand. I take it, smiling. Then I pull her close, slip my hands around her little waist, and lean into her neck. "We'll figure it out. So please don't worry about it."

She rests her head on my shoulder and sighs, and we sway a little bit. Like we're slow-dancing to our own private tune.

Finally, after several quiet minutes of this, Pie says, "Where do you think the fireflies will take us?" They are still pouring out of her palms, their little feet tickling my upper arms now, little pitter-patters before they take flight and join the river in the sky.

"There's only one way to find out." I pull back from Pie and smile, then offer her my hand.

She gives it to me. And when our palms touch, the fireflies in that hand stop.

"Hmm," Pie says.

Hmm indeed.

We walk under the stream of flickering light, following it into the forest. And then, after we come around a bend and pass a large tree, we find our door.

It's made of fireflies.

"Wow." Pie smiles, her face lit up with the power of her inner glow. "That's actually kinda cool."

It is. I can't deny it. There must be millions and millions of fireflies all bustling together to make that door.

"How do we open it?" Pie asks. But before I can answer, she's already reaching forward with the hand I'm not holding. The fireflies continue to pour out, but they don't mesh into the door. They make a handle.

Something tells me this door is for her, and her alone. Pie doesn't hesitate. She leans forward and then we're walking through. I just barely have enough time to wonder if the door will let me pass when we're already on the other side.

Music blaring. Bodies moving to the beat. Little dots of flashing lights are spinning around the ballroom and when I look up, I get lost in the constellations being thrown off a disco ball.

"Wow." Pie laughs this word out. Then she looks down at herself. "Oh, my God. What the hell am I wearing?"

I chuckle. Maybe I don't recognize the exact year, but I know the decade. But then I see the banner on the other side of the room and all the details slip into place. "Look." I point at it. "You are the height of nineteen eighty-two fashion."

She laughs now. A full-on laugh. "This is the ugliest dress I've ever seen!"

She is wearing a greenish-blue—let's go with iridescent turquoise—mini ruffle dress with a ruched bodice and puff arms. Her long human legs are covered in black, diamond-patterned tights and her shoes are the same color as the dress, but have giant black bows on them. I hide my smile with my hand, not wanting to laugh, but she is fuckin' adorable in retro glam.

"Hey!" She slaps my arm playfully. But then she points at me with narrowed eyes. "Why do the gods dress me up like a joke every single time and you always look so hot?"

I look down at myself, not feeling very hot, but then shrug. "The tux is eternal. But look." I lift up my iridescent turquoise silk tie. "We match."

"Oh, my God, we do. We're too cute, Pell." Pie's shoulders relax and she smiles as she takes in the room. The whole place is decorated in midnight blue and silver. Streamers, balloons, and more teenage bodies than I've ever been in one room with before.

"Oh!" Pie exclaims. "I get it! It's prom!" She looks at me, very excited. "I never went to prom."

I know what prom is. I've been around. But I've never been to one, so I just shrug. "Me either."

Pie hooks her arm in mine. "This is fucking awesome!" She tilts her head up and looks at the ceiling. "Thank you, hallway gods!" Then she squeals. "Look!" The perimeter of the room is rectangular, like most ballrooms. And the outer edge is lined with dozens and dozens of sparkling chandeliers. But all down the middle there is a domed ceiling and it has been painted to look like the midnight sky splattered with silver stars. But that's not what she's pointing at. "There they are! The fireflies are here. And you know what that means?"

There are indeed fireflies up there. Thousands of them. All happily twinkling like they're not caught in a fake sky. "We should find the next door?"

"What?" Pie looks crushed. "You don't want to stay?"

"I do." This is a lie. "But… there are some pressing matters to take care of, Pie. Should we—"

"We should. Look!" She points to other side of the room where the banner is. "The theme is 'Firefly Nights.' And the fireflies are up in the ceiling. This is a sign. Pell! A sign!"

"A sign of what?"

"It means we have work to do here."

I narrow my eyes at her. "You just want to go to prom."

She deflates a little and pouts her lips. I really hate deflated Pie, so I immediately give in. "OK. Fine. We'll go to prom."

"No." Now she's moping. She's doing that posture she calls the monkey walk. "Forget it. We don't have to stay. It's dumb."

I spin her towards me. All the kids around us are bopping their heads around and playing their air guitars like… well, like it's the Eighties. I place both my hands on Pie's cheeks and smile at her. Immediately, her posture changes.

"Pie. Would you like to go to prom with me?"

Her whole face brightens, but then falls a little. "Not if you're gonna hate it."

"I'm not gonna hate it. I'm gonna love it. You know why?"

"Why?"

"Because I've never been to prom. It wasn't a thing in my day. We did a little blood sacrifice to celebrate our coming of age—"

Pie slaps my chest playfully. "Shut up. That's so gross!"

"I've been missing prom, Pie. I need this in my life."

"Now you're just making fun of me."

"You're not listening."

She huffs out a breath and plants her hands on her ruffled, glam-skirt hips. "Pell—"

"Pie." I make serious eyes at her. "I'm being very serious now. I need prom. My life will not be complete." She giggles. "Would you *please* go to prom with me?"

She tilts her head, two seconds away from giving in.

"We're all dressed up. You look like... you're ready for... a mermaid Bon Jovi concert."

She nearly spits on me.

"And I look like... well"—I smile smugly and shrug—"your date." I offer her my arm.

Her eyes narrow. "You're going to dance with me?"

I sigh.

"Pell! If we go to prom, we have to dance. And it's not even like we can leave, anyway."

"What do you mean we can't leave?"

"Look. No doors."

I look around and, sure enough—even though this is a ballroom, and every ballroom I've ever been in always had several ways to get in and out—there are no doors. "Huh."

"Yep. See? We're meant to be here. It's a gift, Pell. Like our bar date in Granite Springs."

Kind of a bad example. That date flipped our world upside down. But... she's looking around with excitement in her eyes. And, well, she does deserve a nice night in the hallways. Plus, we're already here and if we were really needed in some other part of the sanctuary right this moment, wouldn't the hallways just kick us out?

For sure, they would not hide the doors if they didn't want us to stay.

Pie turns to me and mouths the words, *Dance with me*.

I'm cringing. But, obviously, I'm going to give in. But just as I open my mouth to say OK, the music abruptly changes to a drumbeat and a deep bass rhythm. 'I Love Rock 'N' Roll' begins to play and every girl in the room squeals with delight and starts rocking their hips and snapping their fingers, singing along.

Pie looks at me, her sky-blue eyes lit up. "I know this one!" She rocks her head a little, imitating the girls all around us, then tugs on my hand as she sings along. "One dance!" She makes praying hands, clapping the tips of her fingers. "Please! Just one. Then we'll go do important grown-up stuff."

Here's the problem with 'I Love Rock 'N' Roll.' It's a fist-pumping, scream-the-words-off-key, anthem song. Not a dancing song. But I let her drag me into the crowd and watch her transform back into the teenager she probably never was.

She recites the lyrics to me—and I swear, I have never seen her this happy. This carefree. This... young. I mean, I know she's twenty-five human years old, and that's very young, especially compared to me. But this is a different kind of young.

This is... youthful. And innocent.

It's not even like I noticed that she was world-weary, either. Until now, that is. Until I see her how she should've looked at seventeen. And now there is no way I will deny her this night. Even if she wants to make me dance to Joan Jett.

"'Come on'"—Pie is swaying her shoulders and beckoning

me with a crooked finger as she and all the teenage girls around her belt out the words—"'dance with me.'"

I'm just reaching for her hand, ready to just… whatever. Whatever she wants, I mean. Because she's mine, and we're here, and this is a once-in-a-lifetime thing and… yeah.

Whatever she wants.

But then she squeals again. "Oh, my God! Look!"

She's pointing across the room. I see a crowd in the corner and I squint, trying to see what's gotten her so excited.

Pie takes my hand and pulls on it as she jumps up and down. "It's a photobooth! Only not the cheesy kind of photos with gross animated backgrounds. But the cool kind that only come out in black and white!"

A photobooth.

"Please, please, please, Pell!" She's making praying hands again, clapping her fingertips. "Can we take a picture? We need mementos."

"A keepsake," I murmur, more to myself than Pie.

"Yes!" She practically squeals this.

"It's not something I've ever thought about before. I'm not sure that a photograph of me actually exists in this world. Or… any world. I can't recall a single time I've ever posed for one."

"So this is"—she sighs—"your first photograph?"

"Yeah. I never saw the point."

She twines her fingers with mine and gazes up at me adoringly. "That's because you've never had someone you wanted to share a past with."

Which makes me smile. Maybe even melt a little. Because she's right. Being with someone you love isn't just about the present and the promise of a future. It's about sharing a past.

I gaze down at Pie just as adoringly. "We absolutely need a photobooth picture."

"Yeah." She tightens her grip on my hand and pulls me off

the dance floor just as Joan Jett, and every teenage girl in the ballroom, belts out the last verse of the song.

We reach the photobooth area just as another song comes on. Pie tilts her head, listening. Like she's trying to place it.

"What are you doing?"

"What?"

"Why do you have that look on your face?"

"This song. I think I've heard it before."

"You think? This is the Go-Go's."

"The who?"

I laugh. "'We Got the Beat?'"

"Yeah, that's this, right?"

"Oh, my God. How do you not know the Go-Go's?"

"Pell. We're in nineteen eighty-two. I was born in nine-teen ninety-eight. And how do you know all these songs, anyway? I thought you were infamously antisocial."

"The radio. Top 40 countdown. Every fuckin' Sunday."

"The *radio?*"

"It was a thing back then. Grant used to work on El Camino in the back parking lot and he always had the radio on. I heard it from all over the sanctuary."

"And the Go-Go's caught your ear?"

"They had a good beat and were fun to dance to." I'm smiling all the way through those words.

"You're such a dork. And I think it's cute that you call his car El Camino."

"What do you mean? That was its name."

She just pats my chest and mutters, "Cute." Then she points to a table of props where a group of teenagers are sorting through glitter glasses and feather boas. "Props or no props?"

"Whatever you want, sweet Pie."

"I say no props." She places her hands on my shoulders and leans up on her tiptoes to kiss my mouth. In the middle of the kiss she whispers, "Just us. That's all we need, ya know? Just us."

When she pulls back, I grab her around the waist and tug her towards me again. "Pie." I say this seriously because I'm being very serious. "It's going to be us forever, and ever, and ever."

"I know."

We spend a moment lost in each other's eyes. And then someone pokes me.

I turn and find a massive teenage boy—obviously an athlete—with cropped blond hair, clean-cut face, and piercing green eyes. He nods his head at me, then points to the booth. "It's your turn, dude."

I smile and turn Pie around, then glance over my shoulder at him as she leads me into the booth.

He looks familiar. Like maybe we've met before at some point in the past.

Or hell, maybe I've seen him in the present. He's got a Roth look to him. Like maybe he's Russ's uncle, or father, or cousin-in-law. And isn't it interesting that he could see us? I mean, sometimes the hallway people do see us, but usually it's only after we've been interacting with them too much. Like they want to ignore us, but can't.

Pie and I haven't been interacting with anyone here. And we were just quietly standing in line, talking between ourselves and waiting our turn.

Pie steps into the booth and tugs me in behind her. But just before she swishes the red-velvet curtain closed, I spy the Roth kid still staring at me.

Then he's gone and Pie is pushing me to sit down on the tiny bench. I barely fit in here, and the only way she fits with me is by sitting on my lap.

She wraps her arms around my neck and presses her cheek up to mine. "OK. We get five pics. They're gonna come like flash, flash, flash, flash." She blinks her fingers each time she says the word 'flash,' very animated about this photo-shoot. "So we need to decide. Do we want to pose or be natural? Look hot and sexy or make goofy faces?"

I reach over, press the green button, and then start kissing Pie.

She giggles at first, and *flash*!

But then I cup her face and take her mouth, and *flash*!

I take my kisses to her neck and she tips her head back, exposing her throat so I can nibble my way down her neck, and *flash*!

Then I grip her shoulders as she opens her eyes and stares down at me with a hunger that makes me hard, and *flash*!

The next moment, she's got her fingers in my hair, tousling it, and she kisses my cheek as we both stare straight ahead, and *flash*!

Done.

We come out of the booth, kinda breathless. And it feels like everyone in the ballroom is watching us. It feels that way, because they are.

"Ut-oh," Pie whispers. "I think they've realized we don't belong here."

"Yep." Then I look across the ballroom and sure enough, there's a huge double door. "It's time to leave."

Pie sighs. "Well, it was fun while it lasted." Then she looks up at me. "Do you think this is our goodbye tour, Pell?"

"Goodbye tour?"

"Yeah. The band is breaking up. The sanctuary is crumbling. The curse might be over. This might be the last chance we have in the hallways."

"Huh." I am unexpectedly sad about this.

"Oooo!" Pie squeals as the booth spits out our photo strip. She grabs it from the little silver cage and blows on it, just in case it's still wet. Then she sighs again. Only this time, it's a swoony sigh. "Look, Pell. It's really us."

She holds the photo out for me to see and I sigh too.

Because even though the hallway gods have dressed us up in these ridiculous clothes and turned us human, we are not human in the pictures and we are wearing our usual stuff. Me, shirtless and muscular. Pie in her nemesis outfit, the scarlet-leather bustier pushing her breasts up nearly to her neck. Her horns are dotted with illuminated fireflies and mine are glowing lava orange.

And the pics?

I take the strip from her hand and study them, one at a time.

Fuckin' adorable. All five of them.

She takes it back, then rips the paper in half.

"What did you do that for?"

She hands the bottom one to me. "I dunno. I just don't think we should keep our only pictures all in the same place. You keep this half and I'll keep the other. Just in case."

I raise an eyebrow at her, ready to ask her what 'just in case' means. But she just smiles at me and slips her half of the photo strip into her bosom.

"You do realize you've ripped the third picture in half? And that was the sexiest one."

"If we ever want to look at it, all we have to do is put it back together."

I smile, kinda loving the whole romantic aspect of what she just did. And then I slip my half of the photo strip into my jacket pocket, feeling pretty good about things. Until I glance up and realize all the teenagers are still looking at us.

I find the Roth kid and sneer at him. "Is there a problem?"

"Yeah." He steps away from his friends. "Who the fuck are you?" He's not just talking to me because his eyes dart from me, to Pie, and then back to me. "And what are you doing at our prom?"

Pie steps in front of me and puts up a hand. "We're just passing through. We were just leaving. Come on, Pell."

"Pell?" the Roth kid says. And as my name comes out of his mouth, his eyes go very narrow.

"Come on, Pell." Pie is tugging me now. "Let's just go."

She pulls me towards the huge double doors on the far side of the ballroom. We're weaving our way through the crowd—everyone has stopped dancing and they just stand there on the dancefloor, watching us—when the brightly-colored strobe lights go out and the whole place goes dark.

Some of the girls scream. Some people laugh.

But everyone goes still. Including Pie and me. She and I stop in the middle of the dance floor, only halfway to our exit.

And then the lights come on again, but just one. And it's centered over us.

And in that same moment, a new song starts playing.

'Ball and Chain.'

"Ut-oh," Pie murmurs. "This isn't good."

This is not good for many reasons. One of which is that this song won't be released for another eight years. But the other, more pressing matter is, of course, the person it's connected to.

Another light comes on, this time up on the DJ stage. And sure enough, there he is.

The devil.

"Welcome to Firefly Nights. Leaving so soon?"

The whole crowd of teenagers begins to murmur. But then, a voice. The Roth kid. "Uncle Eros!" He's pushing his way through the crowd, but after a few steps, bodies simply part for him like he's Moses in front of the Red Sea. "They crashed our prom!"

Suddenly, everyone is taking exception to the fact that Pie and I have stumbled into the hallway memory of their dance. They blurt out insults and threats, pressing forward towards us.

I take Pie's hand and squeeze it. "Don't panic. We're outta here."

"Oh, not before I have a little chat with your woman, *Pell*," the devil says. When he says my name, it feels like the room narrows, and shrinks, and there is suddenly just a tunnel of light between him and I and no one and nothing else exists anymore. "Or should I say, *my* woman?"

There is a tingling in my body that registers as attraction. The eros in him. It works even on a monster like me.

But I've been dealing with eros for thousands of years now. I understand the feeling and I have developed ways to fight it. Ironically, the most effective way to deal with an eros is to think about the one that came before. Make the memory of an attraction compete with the emergence of a new one.

So I think of my other caretakers. I cycle through them, concentrating on how they made me feel the first time we met. Stewart, Jonas, Michael, Ignacious, Antonius, Luther, Milo, Odo.

Then Grant.

The devil grunts, sensing his lack of power over me. Frustrated, maybe. But then he turns his attention to Pie. And this is when I realize that she's leaning forward, like she wants to be closer to the devil and she's trying to wriggle her hand out from mine.

"Pie." I jerk her back. "Pie, look at me."

"Huh?" She doesn't look at me. Her eyes are only for him. She starts pulling towards him again, not even aware that she's doing this.

"Pie!"

"Like I said, Pell." The devil's glowing red eyes are trained on me now. "She's my woman. She has always been mine. Even before I plucked her out of her world as a small child and pulled her into this one."

I'm lost here. I don't know what he's talking about. But it doesn't matter. I'm sure whatever worldview-altering revelation he's got planned for me is coming, no matter what happens next. But that doesn't mean that Pie and I have to stick around for it.

I growl at him. "Get back, devil. We're leaving." And the whole ballroom shakes and quakes from the power of my voice.

The devil laughs. The 'Ball and Chain' song makes a skipping sound, like the needle just jumped across the record. A lamentation about ten years and a thousand tears blares from the gigantic speakers protruding from the ceiling, the hard-luck song starting over from the beginning.

The teenage girls scream and move back. The teenage boys, though? Nah. They start pounding their fists and walking towards us. Closing in, like it's me and Pie against them.

"Keep going!" the devil yells. "More! Please!"

"More what?" I ask this out loud, even though I'm not really asking.

But the devil answers. "The voice, monster! The voice is crushing your curse." Then he winks at me. "And your walls. Pretty soon there'll be nothing left and I'll just be able to walk right in." His joy morphs into disappointment. "But I can't wait for 'pretty soon.' I have business to attend to. So step away from my little dessert and let her do her job."

"Which is what?" This time I don't try to use the voice, but it comes out even stronger than before. One of the many, many sparkling chandeliers falls and crashes onto the black and white checkered floor, shattering shards of glass in all directions.

Now the girls aren't just screaming—they're running. An instant later they realize there is only one door and it doesn't belong to them, it belongs to us. So try as they might, they cannot get the door open.

The devil laughs. And in this moment, all I feel is regret. Regret that Pie and I ran out of that bar back in Granite

Springs. Regret that I didn't kill Russ Roth when I had the chance.

I know—like my brain understands—that this is not Russ Roth. This devil is some... distant relative, maybe. But it doesn't matter. It's the bloodline. Hopefully, it ends with the curse. I am by no means happy that the sanctuary is crumbling from my own voice. But if I can take out that eros bloodline in Granite Springs, maybe it'll be worth everything I lose.

"You really don't know who she is, do you?" The devil laughs again. "You think she's... this?" He makes a motion with his hand, indicating Pie, who is still trying to tug her hand out of my grip. Still leaning towards the devil at the top of the room. I hold tight. There is no way I will let go. If she gets across the room to him, I will be going with her.

"I know who she is." I don't. But I'm putting together some clues. "She's a royal beast."

The devil's eyebrows knit together just for an instant. If I wasn't studying him so closely, I might've missed it. But I didn't miss it. He's troubled by my words. "You think you're clever, do you? But I know better. You don't know who she is any more than you know who you are."

He's probably right about that. "Well, here's something I know that you don't. 'A ball, a night, a swirling light. Fireflies in their flight. Make a path, lead us there, through the door escape the snare.'"

Every word rocks the ballroom. Chandeliers sway wildly and a few even crash to the ground. Pandemonium ensues, people running and screaming. Not just the girls this time.

And then the fireflies up near the ceiling gather together in a great swarm, their light bright like the sun. Bright enough to make everyone cover their eyes and turn their heads. Even the devil.

But not me. I blink through the blinding whiteness, tug

hard on Pie's hand, and then follow the fireflies as they create a path to the door at the back of the room.

The devil roars, his voice powerful like mine. I look over my shoulder, stunned. Because I wasn't expecting that. And if I'm being completely honest, his voice is more terrifying than mine.

More chandeliers crash to the floor, shards of glass skittering across the tiles. A few slam into Pie and me, making her gasp. But the pain must wake her up out of the devil's stupor, because she stops fighting me and turns, now running with me.

"What's happening? I think I lost time!"

"Just run, Pie. We need to get through the door!"

The devil roars again, and this time the entire dome ceiling comes tumbling down on top of everyone. Chunks of plaster hit me on the head and back, but I push Pie under me, protecting her from the worst of it.

The fireflies open the door for us and when we're but ten feet away, we leap—the same way we did through the door on the mountainside of Granite Springs. We pass through and the door closes behind us as we crash to the ground.

But then, in the calm after the storm, I can hear the song. Faintly, but definitely there.

'Ball and Chain.'

He's following us.

ell and I both crash to the hard, slate floors on our knees and skid a good seven or eight feet across the new room.

Pell is frantic, his yellow eyes wide as he looks at me. "We can't stay here."

"What just happened?" My head is so foggy and every time I blink, I see a negative image of the devil on the back of my eyelids.

"The devil got you, Pie. He got into your head. Fuckin' eros. Someone should've ended them long ago. But we don't have time for that now. We need to keep going." He points to the next door just a few few away across the small chamber, which appears to be a library.

I am momentarily distracted by the books. Well, more than momentarily. I have a compelling urge to go look at them. I even start crawling that way, not even bothering to get to my feet. But Pell pulls me back by an ankle. "Pie! Pay attention! Snap out of it!"

"What?" I turn to look at him, breathless and confused. "The books, Pell. I need to get to those books."

"No! We have to keep going. Can't you hear it?"

"Hear what?" I strain my ears.

"The song, Pie. Can't you hear the song? It's him. He's gonna follow us. We need to go."

"But the books! I think I might need some of these. Look! That one says *Royal Beasts!*"

"No time. We can't. He's coming."

"How will he get through the door? It's gone."

Pell turns his head to look back the way we came. "Huh."

"Yeah. We should stop here and—"

"*No*." He cuts me off with a deep rumble of his voice. And this is a very firm 'no.' In fact, it's so firm, it kinda clears my foggy head and wipes away most of my compulsion to get to those books. "No," Pell says again, this time without the rumble. "He's coming. I don't know how his powers work, but he can change entire towns, Pie. And you're under his spell. If these books are important the hallways will show them to us again. Now *let's go!*"

He doesn't give me a choice. Even if I wanted to resist, and I don't—not really—I would not be able to because Pell stands up, pulls me to my feet, and uses all his strength to drag me across the room and pull me through the next door.

We crash into a hallway. Like... a legitimate hallway of what appears to be a mansion that lives in a world of gloomy light and cloudy shadows. It reminds me of romantic English literature.

"Fuck," Pell murmurs.

And I get it. Because this hallway that lives in some historical Jane Eyre mansion is filled with doorways. All of them closed.

Pell looks at me, still holding my hand. We're still wearing our ridiculous Eighties prom outfits. My puffy shoulders are a little bit deflated and his tie is very crooked, but my pumps are still on my feet and he still looks like a movie star about to save the world. "Which one do you think?" He pans his hand towards the line of doorways.

"Um." I look them up and down and just shrug. "Does it matter?"

Pell gets distracted, tilting his head up like he's listening to something. "Shit. The song is following us."

"What song?"

"'Ball and Chain.' Remember?"

I shake my head. "I can't hear it."

"Well, I can. And it's his calling card. I don't know why, but it's a signal that he's not far behind. I think the hallways are protecting us, but they're not really trustworthy, ya know?"

"Where are we? Like, I was coming through the door to your tomb when this all started. And you were..." I trail off because I can't remember.

"Coming out of Tomas's dungeon."

"Right. So. Are we even in the hallways? How does it connect to your tomb?" But then I sigh, remembering my earlier thought exercise about doors and hallways. Then I look down the line of doors in this hallway and try to put the pieces together. "The doors and hallways are connected." I look at Pell. "Don't you think?"

He nods. "It has to be that way."

I look back at our options. "Maybe it doesn't matter?" I walk over to the nearest door—Pell kinda tugging me back by my hand, but not enough to deter me—and then I just pull it open.

There is nothing on the other side.

"Well, that's not ominous."

I shoot Pell a 'no duh' look. Then I open another one. Also darkness. Then another. Just black. Pell and I do this for all the doors nearby and find that they are all just... nothing.

Then he puts up a hand. "Don't panic. I think this is good."

"How the hell is this good?"

"I think these doors need a spelling. And this is good because if we use the door and assign a spelling and a destination to it, then no one else can use it."

"I don't think it works that way."

"Which part?"

"The part about how no one else can use it."

"If the doors close behind us, then how can they follow?"

I think about this. It's all very confusing. And the rules surrounding the doors and rings are a lot like the rules of Saint Mark's Sanctuary. In other words, none of it really makes sense. There isn't much logic happening. It's just a mishmash of… whatever. Like the rules just get made up as we go.

Pell is looking at me like he can read my mind, his yellow eyes a little bit narrowed, his fangs showing, but not in a growl. "Moves and countermoves," he says.

"Maybe," I reply back. "But then again, maybe not."

He looks up at the ceiling and then looks at me. "The song is getting louder. We need to make a decision."

"Well." I turn to the door nearest me. "It's all the same, one or another, I suppose. So it doesn't matter which door we choose. Where do we want to go?"

"Back to my tomb. That's the only safe place."

"All right. Let me—" Well, I was gonna say 'think' so I could come up with a spelling. But I don't even get the full sentence out before the spelling is just spilling past my lips.

"A monster man and pretty girl.
The path they take a twisty swirl.
Into a world where they have been
A who, a what, a where, a when."

Pell looks confused. "Where does that—"

But that's as far as he gets. Because the door opens of its own accord and we are pulled through like we're being sucked up into a twister.

he song is still playing in my head, but when I open my eyes and find myself looking up at a canopy of trees, it fades. And when I take in the fact that I'm lying on the forest floor, even the echo of it disappears completely.

My smile is immediate and my words come out in a laugh. "Pie! You did it!"

She moans next to me. We're still holding hands so I bring hers up to my lips and kiss her fingers. Then I roll over and touch her cheek. "Wake up, Pie. We made it. We're back in the tomb."

She moans again, her eyelids fluttering for a moment.

"Come on, Pie. Wake up." We've never come through a door this way. It felt like we were caught up in a tornado or something. And I have no recollection of actually coming through the door. Just a vague sense of wind and then darkness.

But we are here. And here is most definitely a forest.

I look around, taking a moment to orient myself as Pie takes her time waking up. I don't recognize any of the trees, but... there are a lot of trees in my tomb. Tons. And it's not like I make regular rounds or anything. I usually stick to the same places.

"Pell?" Pie moans out my name.

"I'm here, Pie. You're OK. It was just a weird trip through the door."

She opens her eyes, kinda breathing heavy. Then she sits up. I sit up too and place my hand on her back.

This is when I realize she's naked. And a wood nymph chimera again. Her long blonde hair is even longer in her monster form. It goes all the way down to her waist.

"Where the hell are we?"

"In my tomb."

"No." She tries to get to her feet, but can't quite make it.

"Just rest for a moment. You're disoriented."

She doesn't listen. Not uncommon. So I just get up off the forest floor with her and hold her steady by the elbow.

After a deep breath she scans the forest. "This isn't your tomb, Pell."

"How would you know?"

She throws me some side-eye, as well as a smirk. "I don't recognize these trees. And where are the doors? And the keys? Nope. The spelling was off. Well"—she tilts her head a little as she looks at me—"no. Maybe not off. And it's not like I actually had anything to do with it. That spelling was... automatic. It said..." She pauses to think back. "'A monster man and pretty girl. The path they take a twisty swirl. Into a world where they have been. A who, a what, a where, a when.' That's not your tomb. That's... who the fuck knows where. Whoever is controlling my spelling just basically threw us into the magical ether."

"'A who, a what, a where, a when.'" I repeat the last line, suddenly getting a sinking feeling.

"Yep." Pie throws up her arms. "We could be anywhere." She looks around and huffs. "And no doors in sight. Now what?"

"Well." I hook her around the waist with my arms and pull her close. "I can't hear the song, so the devil's not following us. And... are we in a hurry?"

"Are we in a hurry? I dunno, Pell. Saint Mark's is crumbling, Tomas is hatching dragons, the monsters want to kill you for killing Frecks—"

I point at her. "I didn't kill Frecks. It was just an accident."

"Does it matter? They are pissed at you. Meanwhile, the cupid devil is making me swoon like an idiot, I've locked up my sister and Tarq's woman in a debtors' prison, and my BFF—my only F on the outside, in fact—has stolen a bunch of throwaway kids and is now missing or being held prisoner by the swoony eros asshole. Who, by the way, was the one who kidnapped me when I was six and then walked out and left me with *Lisa*"—she sneers this name—"my not-mother. Because I..." She throws up her hands. "I dunno. I didn't have what they needed, or couldn't be used the way they wanted me to." A long, tired exhale follows after these words. She blows out a breath, making her bangs fly up. "And you know what pisses me off the most?"

"Tell me."

"My name."

"What?" I grin and hug her close. "What's wrong with your name? I love your name."

"I know. I love it too. But it's not my name. All this time I have been Pie. Cute. Whimsical. Eccentric. And now I find out that my real name is Pianna. Pianna, Pell? That's—"

"Not bad," I say. She shoots me an incredulous look. "What? It's really not."

"It's gross. And not at all whimsical. I'm not even me anymore. I have no idea who I am."

"What are you talking about?"

"Me, Pell. All these years I have been Pie. Weird Pie with the talking bird. And now look at me!" She throws up her arms. "*Pianna*. With no bird. I'm just... normal. Worse than normal. I'm boring."

"Boring?" Now it's my turn to be incredulous. "Pie. Please."

"And here's the funny part. Ironic, actually. It's always

ironic. But this is what I wanted, remember? I wanted to be normal. I wanted a boring life. And now look, here I am. And—"

I put my hand over her mouth. She struggles, pushing it off, and then sputters out, "What the hell was that for?"

"You need to stop talking and take a look at yourself."

"What?"

I take her hand, then take a step backwards, like I'm appraising her. "Pie. Please. You're the most gorgeous wood nymph chimera I've ever laid eyes on. Your fur is so soft and your horns are sleek and slim. Don't even get me started on your ass and your legs. You're like something out of a fuckin' book. Some fairytale creature."

"This is not even me!"

"What do you mean?"

Now she just deflates. At first, I think she's being dramatic but then she covers her face with her hands and falls to her knees in a bed of soft ferns.

I kneel down next to her. "What's wrong? I don't understand what's happening here."

She removes one hand from her face and looks at me with a single teary eye. "I'm not a wood nymph chimera, Pell."

"Of course you are. Look at you."

"No. You don't understand. I don't know what this is, but this is not what I looked like back where... wherever I'm from."

"So you're human."

"No, Pell. I'm not a human, either. I'm fucking gryphon!"

"But what's so bad about that? I'm sure I'll love you just as much in your royal gryphon form as I do your sexy wood nymph form."

"No. You don't get it."

"Then tell me."

She sighs, then shakes her head a little. I'm patient. I give her time. But the moment stretches on and I get a sick feeling in my stomach. I'm just about to prod her along when she finally spits it out. "I was promised to Tarq, Pell."

I know this. He kind of told me this before I made him king. But... "It's not like that, Pie."

"Isn't it?"

"He's not going to make you marry him and have his child."

"Isn't he?"

"He's not. And if he tried, I'd kill him. That would be the end of it. I'd just kill him."

"Kill the king, Pell?"

"He's not my king."

"You made him king. You spelled him into that position. And by the way, that spelling? It's... wrong."

"What do you mean?"

"All the syllables were off."

I'm confused. I didn't actually make that spelling up, it just floated out. Kind of like the way Pie's spells have been materializing on a whim.

"'I take the power of this ring. My best friend Tarq is now the king.'" She narrows her eyes at me. "It's wrong. And what ring? Did you give him a ring?"

"No." I hold up my finger with the ring. "This one. The too-small one. But obviously, it's still on my finger, so I didn't give it away. But there was a crown. I'm not sure where it came from, but there it was. Poof. On top of his head."

"I'm not a hundred percent sure what's happening here. And I'm not pretending to be any kind of expert on magic, or spellings, or rings. But—*but*—I'm pretty sure there is some kind of royal beast agreement between Tarq and me. And I'm starting to get the feeling that this is some kind of done deal."

"I get what you're saying. And…" I don't want to admit this, but Pie is way beyond soothing with half-truths or even lies. "And I do agree that there is most likely some kind of royal decree about you and Tarq. But that doesn't mean it has to happen."

"I think you're wrong."

"Why?"

"Because the devil, Pell—the devil sent me on a mission to bring Tarq back to him. Something about Tarq not being king."

"See?" I smile at her. "His power is just… pretend."

"No. I mean, probably, yeah. But that's not the point. The point is that the devil wants Tarq and me together with him. I think this decree—whatever it is—comes from the devil. Callistina is no one. She's definitely not as powerful as me or how could I just put her in prison? It's the devil, Pell. I think he took me from my family and my world back when I was six because…"

She pauses and just looks at me, the end of her sentence hanging in the air between us.

When she doesn't finish, I say it for her. Because I already know what she's thinking.

"Because you belong to him."

She nods. "I think he's being truthful about that. He controls me, Pell."

"Yeah, but he's an eros. He's got that power over everyone."

"Does he have that power over you?"

"No, but—"

"He has some claim on me, Pell. And I think he has some claim on Tarq too. And I also think that he's the one who wants the godling prince."

"Godling." I whisper the word. Because I remember this now. Tarq and I were having this same conversation in his office that night everything went to shit for the second time.

And he was so... I don't know. Pissed is a strong word. I don't think he was pissed off at me, but he was frustrated with me. Because I didn't understand what was happening. He said, *You were there.*

But I don't remember it.

And isn't this the problem?

I don't remember things. Everyone seems to know more about me than I do.

I don't remember things.

"The devil made a bargain with someone. Maybe my parents, maybe Tarq's parents—who knows? But he made a deal and Tarq and I are part of this deal, Pell. This is where it's all heading."

"Well, then the solution is simple. We can't go back. We'll just... go to the doors in my tomb, pick one, and use the ring to take us somewhere safe."

"Yeah. I'd agree with you. If my best friend wasn't being held prisoner by the devil."

"You don't know that."

"Well, she's missing. We left her in Granite Springs. Two blocks down from the fuckin' devil's bar. And now the town is gone and he's in charge of my future."

I sigh and walk over to a fallen tree and take a seat, putting my head in my hands because I have a thumping headache.

Pie comes and sits down next to me. She puts a hand on my furry leg and leans her head on my shoulder.

"OK," I say, dropping my hands and looking over at her. "I see the logic. But you're missing a big piece of this puzzle."

"Which is?"

"Me." We stare at each other for a moment, our eyes dancing back and forth as we search the windows to our souls. "You haven't taken me into account yet."

"So where do you fit in?"

"I don't know."

She scoffs. But it's kind of a laugh. And then she wraps her hands around my upper arm and sighs into my chest. "You were the best prom date ever."

"Shit." I pat myself down. "Did we lose our photobooth pics?"

"Well, we're naked. So... yeah. That fuckin' sucks. I liked those pics. I planned on staring at them for centuries, at least. They were gonna get me through all the hard times."

"There aren't gonna be any hard times."

"Please, Pell. This is the story of my life. It's just... crap. Bad things happen to me."

"Well, not all things were bad. I get that being a slave caretaker to a satyr chimera isn't exactly your dream life, but we've made it work."

"Speaking of slave caretaker"—she sits up straighter and looks me in the eyes—"when I was talking to Tomas earlier he said I was the caretaker of slaves."

"What do you mean?"

"You know. Like... I'm not a slave caretaker of you or Saint Mark's. I'm really a caretaker of the prisoner slaves down in the Bottoms."

This makes me tired. Life is wearing me down. I can feel it. It's slow and gradual—so much so that it's hard to pinpoint the moment when things passed a point of no return. But we're there. The line has been crossed. There is no going back now. The fuckin' sanctuary is crumbling, the curse is breaking, and nothing is going to turn out the way I want it to.

Not that I've spent any amount of time dreaming of what freedom from the curse looks like. I haven't. I gave up hope on breaking my curse hundreds of years back, at least. But in the beginning, I spent a lot of time daydreaming about what comes next.

What comes next?

Losing. That's what comes next.

It's funny, too. This whole voice thing with me, and Pie's spelling, and even Tomas being able to leave the sanctuary as a human—it felt so much like winning a few weeks ago.

But it isn't. Wasn't then, either.

It's just… we didn't understand what was happening.

My voice is destroying the sanctuary.

Pie's spelling is just drawing her closer to her real destiny.

And Tomas… Tomas isn't ever going to stop being a dragon. No matter how many different bodies he inhabits. He is… an evil thing. And I'm not saying that to be disparaging. I like Tomas. Maybe I even love Tomas. But he's a fuckin' dragon. I think he's held it together pretty well over the centuries. He's found ways to cope with his innate nature.

But it won't last.

We are who we are.

And maybe we'd have a chance to fix shit if we actually understood ourselves.

But we don't.

I have no idea who I am. I have no idea who Pie is. I have no idea how Tarq fits into things, or why the devil is chasing us, or what the fuck all those prisoners are doing down in the Bottoms. Hell, I can't even get down there. I've tried. The door Pie says she came through from the Bottoms is actually the door she opened using the pink-stone ring to get us into the palace bakery.

So I don't even know. I have no clue what the Bottoms is about.

"Why are you so quiet?"

I look over at Pie and just sigh. "The Bottoms. And the door that leads there. And how nothing is what it seems."

Pie squints her eyes a little. "Do you need to see it?"

"The Bottoms?"

She nods. "Do you need to see it to believe it?"

"No. I believe you. If you say there's a hidden prison filled with tomb monsters, then there is."

"OK. But you didn't answer the question. Do you need to see it, Pell? Because I'm pretty sure I can get us back there."

"You don't want to go back, remember?"

She nods, but her shoulders slump. "I don't. I don't want to go to the Bottoms, I don't want to go back to Vinca, and if I'm being honest, I don't even want to go back to Granite Springs. But..." Her blue eyes meet mine.

"But what?"

"But I think I've been running this whole time."

"Running from what?"

"The truth? The devil? My mother?" She shrugs. "My past, Pell. Because it's catching up with me and there's nothing I can do to stop that."

"Yeah." I let out a long, tired exhale. "I'm starting to get that feeling too."

"There's a part of me," she continues, "that wants to just forget everything. To find a door, and a ring, and say a spelling, and take your hand, and pull you through with me, and start a brand-new life."

This plan makes me smile.

"And we could do that, I guess. But... what about everyone we leave behind? And I'm not just talking about Tomas, either. Or Jacqueline. I mean the prisoners, and Madeline, and all those monsters in Vinca. I don't like Callistina. Even if she is my sister, I don't want a future with her in it. But even if Tarq is the bad guy I imagine him to be, not even I could walk away from him now. Even if all the people we're involved with are horrible and did terrible things to be put into the Bottoms, or used as pawns in another realm, or end up being held by the devil's magic—they're still part of our story, aren't they? And doesn't that mean we have some responsibility to them?"

My smile falters halfway through her monologue. And by the time she's done, I'm in a full-on frown. She's right though. I can feel it. Whatever is happening to us is part of the plan. I don't know whose plan it is. Saturn? Juno? Ostanes? Tarq? The devil?

But does it matter?

One might think to themselves, *I will not do the devil's bidding. I will not be a part of it.*

But what if you have no choice? What if the only reason you exist is to play your part in the story?

"And if we're in a story," Pie continues, "don't we owe it to the story to see it through to the end?"

I look Pie in the eyes and shrug. Because it's the best I can manage. "We're going to lose, you know that, right?"

She looks away and lets out a breath. "Feels that way, yeah."

"They're gods, Pie."

"They are." She looks back at me. "But we're monsters. And there's some synergistic, or maybe even symbiotic, bond between gods and monsters, right?"

I smile as she talks.

"Right, Pell? It's all through history. Gods and monsters. I mean, think about it. If there was no Medusa there would be no Perseus."

"That's Greek."

Pie laughs because I kinda sneer that out. "OK. Well, whatever. If Saturn didn't have a monster nemesis, then… well, he's stupid."

Now I laugh. "Nemesis is actually a goddess. Not Roman, though. She was like… karma. When people got too full of themselves she would knock them down."

"Well"—Pie is frustrated—"if Saturn doesn't have a monster, if he didn't fight his way out of some great… shit show, or whatever, then who cares about him anyway? Why is he so fuckin' famous?"

"He ate his sons."

"What?"

"Yeah. There was a prophecy, I think. Saying one of his sons would usurp him."

"So he *ate* them?"

"I did mention he was a dick, right?"

"Ewww."

"But I would say, that if he did have... like a nemesis, or whatever, it would've been another god."

"Which one?"

"I don't know. But he's a jealous fool with no self-esteem. That's why he eats his sons. He's just full of fear and doubt. He is threatened by the power of others."

Pie makes a face. "Anyway. Forget him. My point is... monsters are powerful too. And we're monsters. So we've got skin in this game, right?" She sighs. Like maybe she wants to believe this, but she's not quite there.

"What you're really saying is... you want to fight back." She nods. "You want to save everyone." She nods again. "Even though we both have this feeling that we're totally gonna lose."

"Listen, I get it. We're... out-powered. We're not gods. My little analogy with Saturn doesn't work, so there's no fate in any of this. At least as far as us coming out winners, anyway. But still, Pell, we can run. And we can probably get away. Maybe have a really great, normal, boring life together. And don't get me wrong, that would be perfect. But wouldn't we just spend the rest of our days wondering what happened to everyone? Wouldn't it drive us nuts?"

"Wouldn't we feel like cowards, you mean?"

She bunches up her shoulders. Like... *If the shoe fits.*

"So what should we do? Go back to the tomb?"

"I think we should go to the Bottoms, and even though I don't want to, I should talk to Callistina. Then look over the Books of Debt. Maybe even... set everyone free."

I cringe, but want to hear more. "OK. Then what?"

"Obviously, we have to go check on Tarq, and Talina, and all the girls."

"What about the other monsters? And the wood nymphs? They want to go to Vinca too. Are you saying we should just give everyone what they want?"

"Why not, Pell? I mean, who the hell are we that we get a say in the lives of others? Why should we have power over anyone?"

"Because maybe they're a bunch of assholes and by keeping them locked up the worlds are a better place?"

"But is that our job? Shouldn't there be a god or something who sorts all that shit out? Shouldn't everyone just be free to live their own life?"

"But what if these monsters hurt people?"

"Then hopefully they cross the wrong person and get what's due to them."

"Sounds a bit like anarchy."

"Or"—she points at me—"natural order."

"I think there's a fine line between shirking one's responsibility and going with the natural flow of things."

"I think you're right. And we're walking that line, whether we want to or not. But if I have to choose, then I choose to set them all free. Because if I keep them prisoner, then I'm... well." She throws up her arms. "I'm their keeper. And I don't want to be a keeper. I don't want to be a caretaker of slaves. I don't want to be anything but Pie."

"Yeah. I totally get it. I don't want to be anyone but Pell."

Pie gets up from the fallen log we're sitting on and takes both my hands. "So we're in agreement?"

I love how she is no longer self-conscious about her monster body, even though she's naked. Her hair is so long, it's almost always covering up her breasts. And I understand better than most how the velvety fur that begins at her hips and spreads down over her ass and legs can make a person feel clothed, even when they're not.

But it's more than that now. She has embraced her monster side. Which is, probably, her true self.

And that makes me blissfully happy. Because it has always been my dream to fall in love with a woman who is like me. And I really never thought that would actually happen until Pie walked through my prison-cell door.

Being in love with her, and her in love with me—well, if that's all we get out of this, then we win.

I stand up and slide my hands over her hips, gripping her ass and tugging her close so that her breasts are pressing into my chest. I lean down and kiss her. We spent an eternity doing this, our tongues dancing, our imaginations going wild with possibilities, our bodies heating up like maybe—

Pie pushes me back, giggling. "Sex, sex, sex. That's all you ever think about. Are we in agreement, or not?"

She's impatient. She wants an answer. But I just want to look at her.

"Pell!"

"Fine. Fine. I'm on board. Let's go to the Bottoms and—"

But just as these words are leaving my mouth something comes whizzing through the trees and slams right into Pie's heart.

She gasps. Clutching at the arrow. Her eyes wide and shocked.

I'm in shock too. Just… staring at the blood seeping out of her chest.

And then the song is playing in the trees. Floating along boughs and whispering through leaves. *Take away this ball and chain…*

Pie falls backwards and I'm reaching for her. Ready to pick her up and carry to safety.

But my hands don't get there in time and in the end, all I grasp onto is a bit of empty air.

Because Pie has disappeared.

PART TWO

A little girl in a foreign land
Is worth more than her bird in hand
She has no self, it's all a lie
The proof is always in the pie.

CHAPTER SEVENTEEN - PIE

hen I hold Pia in my hands, she takes me to other worlds. She takes me to a place where it is endless summer. Where the sun shines and there is no such thing as piles of black snow on the side of the road. Where the peaks of mountains rise up from the horizon and the sky is the color of silver unicorns.

It's not a real place. It's just a fantasy. I know this because she takes me to a good place—I think. I have good feelings about it. And that's just not how the world works. You're not allowed to be happy. You're not allowed to be good. You're not allowed to earn things, or save things, or get more.

Ever.

You're not allowed.

You must be poor, and sad, and lacking. Because if you're not, someone will come along and take it all away from you. If they're just regular mean—like Mother—they take one little thing at a time. They take this, and then that, and more, and more. But only little bits. So it takes you a while to realize you have nothing left.

But if they're really mean, they just take it all at once. They rip you away from everything you know, and turn you into someone else, and then they hate you. And they make everyone else want to hate you too. And they feel good when you're hated, and poor, and sad.

That's what I've learned about life since I came here.

But Pia isn't trying to hurt me the way everyone else is. She's trying to make me feel better.

"I'm trying to make you remember." Sometimes she says that. But it's kind of dumb. There's no point to living in a fantasy.

"That's not true. You used to love the pretty pretends." She says that too.

But I don't understand what she's talking about and anyway, she's the only thing I love. Only her. But she doesn't belong here. I can feel her slipping. Every time Mother asks me about Pia and I deny she exists, Pia gets... fuzzy. Smudgy. Like glass, but not that clear.

But I'm sure, if I keep doing this, one day she will be like glass and she will just disappear. I don't know where Pia comes from. I don't know where I come from. Every day that I get further away from that night sitting on the edge of the bathtub I become fuzzy too. I am a smudge. And one day I will be glass.

The only time I feel better is when Pia is strong. And Pia is only strong when I make Mother mad. When I talk about Pia, Mother gets furious and this makes Pia strong and strong Pia makes me feel—not good, but better.

"Today is your birthday."

I look down at Pia in my cupped hands and try to force a smile. I don't feel better and Pia knows this. When I'm unhappy, she's unhappy too. And the last thing I ever want to do is make my Pia sad. So I play along. "It is?"

Pia chirps at me. A 'yes' in her little-bird language. "You're seven now."

"Seven." I am barely even whispering, but of course, my mother, who is driving the car, hears me.

"Are you talking to yourself again? What have I told you about talking to yourself, Pie? You can't do that here."

I'm not talking to myself, of course. I'm talking to my Pia. But I've explained this to her a thousand times and it just makes her angry. *There is no bird! There is no magic! You are nobody!*

She will yell this, or growl this, or sometimes even shake me by the shoulders.

So. Fine. There is no magic and I am nobody.

I can agree with that.

But I will not deny the existence of Pia. I will not be the reason that Pia fades to glass.

I know I do not belong here. I know I am not this girl in the car. I know that I was someone else once. I know that I am lost.

I know all these things but I can do nothing about them. The only thing I'm in control of is refusing to deny the existence of Pia.

If I lose her, I lose everything. Forever.

Sometimes I think I've already lost it. Sometimes I feel crazy. Mother calls me crazy all the time. But sometimes I just feel like a liar. Did I really come from another world?

For a while I had my clothes. The red and yellow checkered skirt. And the medals, and the ribbons, and the shoes that didn't really fit. But Mother threw them away months ago and now they are just another smudge in my memory.

And even when I hold Pia tight, and we slip into that other place where the sun shines warm across my cheeks and makes yellow streaks across the inside of my eyelids—it's fading.

There used to be a castle, and Pia and I would wander empty hallways. There used to be a city too. I would stop on a bridge between two towers and look out across the streets and buildings. It was an empty city. No people. No activity at all. But still, I had it. I had that castle, and those hallways, and those streets.

And now all that's gone. I can't see them anymore.

Maybe I made it all up?

Maybe Mother is right and I'm making Pia up too?

Everything is fading and soon it will be nothing but glass.

My mother stops the car and opens her heavy door with a loud creak. A moment later the seat flings forward and she is beckoning me to get out. "Hurry up, Pie. School started an hour ago. You're late."

I'm not the one who's late. She's late. But Mother doesn't like to be corrected.

When I don't move fast enough, she reaches into the back seat, grabs my arm, and tugs me out of the car.

It's freezing outside. I'm not sure how to count time here in this place—I don't understand minutes or hours, let alone months and years. And this makes everyone think I'm stupid. This is not my first school. And everyone at the last one called me stupid. Even the teacher called me stupid once. This was the school I went to when we were living in the hotel after my father disappeared.

I know that man is not my father. But what else do I call him? The stranger who kidnapped me from a place with skies the color of silver unicorns?

Anyway. I don't know what an hour is. I tried to wrap my head around time when the teacher talked about it in last school but every time I asked a question, the kids laughed and the teacher looked at me funny. I would say things like, "Which hour is Earth Hour?"

And that was it. Because the teacher said, "Earth Hour, Pie?" They made fun of my name too, always snickering and calling me different kinds of pie. "Earth Hour? What are you, a baby witch?"

The other kids went wild with fits of laughter. They called me Baby Witch for weeks.

And then… I just gave up on time. So I don't understand how late we are.

I gave up on everything, really.

I slip as I get out of the car. My boots got left behind in the hotel room. Not the boots I came with—those were shaped funny and didn't fit—but the ones Mother got me from the store that smells like soup. So I'm wearing sneakers that have a hole in the toe and I fall onto the slick, snow-covered parking lot in front of a building that looks every bit as dingy and sad as the last one I went to.

The cold turns to wet and when Mother yanks me up by my arm, I look around to my backside and realize there is a now a big wet spot on the bum of my soup-smelling pants.

Earth Hour, Wind Hour, Breath Hour. I say these things over and over in my head because they are starting to get smudgy.

But sometimes my head gets too full of things that don't make sense anymore and then I have to stop remembering. Because I only have so much room in my brain. And there must always be a place for Pia.

"Hurry!" Mother grabs my arm and begins to pull me across the sludgy parking lot towards the building. Pia crawled up my coat sleeve while I was being forced out of the car and now she is snuggled up against my neck, burrowing into me to keep warm.

What would I do without her?

We approach a door and I get that fluttery feeling in my stomach.

Doors get me excited. Because doors go places. And every time I walk through one my heart beats fast for a moment. I can't seem to stop the hope that on the side of that door will be the place where I belong.

It just… never happens that way.

But it happened that way once. I'm sure of it. In my head there is still enough room for the Door of Vinca City. I don't remember what it looked like. And that name—Vinca—is very smudgy these days, so I don't know what that is, either.

But there was a special door. A door that… did things.

And I went through it. Father-man took me through it. I know he did. That's how he got me here.

I'm pretty sure, at least.

But on the other side of this door is just a boring office. We've been in lots of these since the father-man left. One time we were getting food stamps and something called welfare. Another time we were going to the doctor and I saw a man who asked me questions about my imaginary bird.

I tried to explain Pia to him. I thought he was listening. For a moment I even thought he could see Pia because he was nodding his head. But then I heard him tell my mother that he was going to give me pills and I would need to be monitored.

I had to stay overnight for this monitoring. They took me to a room, and they gave me little white bitter pills that made me sleepy. And a little while later Pia went away.

I started looking for her. Crying and crawling around on my hands and knees. Checking under beds and behind curtains. Pleading with them—with anyone who would listen —to please help me find my bird.

They wrapped me up in a tight coat and set me on the bed facing up. I couldn't move, but it didn't matter. Because I was too sleepy to care.

When I woke up, Pia was back, chirping and being happy, and telling me that everything was going to be OK. All I had to do was tell everyone who would listen that she does not exist.

I said no and they kept me in that place for a whole eternity.

One day Mother came back and said I had to come with her. But every morning after that, when I would wake up in our small, ugly, smelly hotel room, she would remind me that there is no such thing as Pia.

She would want me to say it too. "Say it, Pie. Say it right now or you won't get any breakfast. Say it! 'There is no such thing as Pia.'"

If I didn't say it, she would throw things. And then she

would leave. And sometimes she would not come back until I was very, very hungry.

Then I started to wonder if perhaps one day she might never come back.

And so I would say it. And Pia would become smudgy. So the next day I would have to take it back. Then Mother would disappear until I went hungry.

So I would say it again.

And Pia would become smudgy.

Then Mother would disappear until I went hungry.

THREE YEARS **later I understood time.**

Three years later I understood a lot.

Doors never went anywhere good, winter was gloomy and cold, schools didn't teach me anything I really needed to know, and parents were worthless.

Three years later Mother dropped me off at CPS and never came back.

Well, for all intents and purposes, she never came back. But she lurked.

For a while I even understood why she was lurking.

The father-man and the skirt I was wearing that night in the bathroom were lingering in my memory. The way my toes didn't quite fit in those boots. The idea that I was from somewhere else.

But even that got smudgy after a while and I started to forget things.

And then one day, my past was nothing but glass.

I OPEN *my eyes* and find myself in a forest. I blink, then squint. Because the sun is bright and rays of it have found their way past the upper canopy of leaves and are shining right into my eyeballs like frickin' lasers.

I sit up, confused. "Pell?"

Then I remember what happened and look down at my chest. There is an arrow sticking out of me.

Kind of.

It didn't penetrate. Which is also confusing, because I remember the pain when it slammed into my heart. It was like everything around me went bright white and then there was a shock. Like... like someone just hit me with one of those defibrillator things they use in hospitals.

I bump the arrow with my hand and it falls into my lap unceremoniously. The whole thing is pretty anticlimactic.

I pick the arrow up and look at it. It has a long shaft made out of some kind of lightweight metal. Graphite comes to mind, even though I don't really know what that is. The word feels right. Anyway, it's not made of wood. I think that's the important part.

And the arrow isn't some crude piece of chipped rock. It's fuckin' serious. Like... steel. And it's not just a flat point, either. It's more like an elongated star with barbs all over it. Like, if this thing found its way inside you, you would be better off leaving it where it was because pulling it out would take a chunk out of your body.

So why didn't it kill me?

And who shot it?

I stand up and look around for the hunter. Pretty sure I know who it is since an eros devil has been stalking Pell and me all day and doesn't that fuckin' cupid come with arrows?

I'm pretty sure he does.

But when I look around, there is no one here.

A sudden tingling in my palms momentarily distracts me. And when I look down at my hands I am simultaneously revolted and frightened because my skin is pulsating and undulating like something is on the inside, trying to get out.

I take steps, and steps, and steps backwards trying to get away from the things stuck inside me.

But of course, they're *inside* me, so there is no getting away.

Suddenly, the skin breaks and slowly—like slow-motion fucking slowly—the tiny legs of insects appear from the brand-new openings on each of my palms.

The gasp escapes my mouth, even though I already understand what's happening. Understanding isn't the problem here. I get it. There are moths and fireflies inside of me and this is part of my magic.

But understanding and acceptance are two very different things.

They come out feet first, tentacle-like legs probing and feeling for the flat skin on the other side of the hole. Then, an instant later, a head, and a body, and then the wings are unfolding and before I know it, the first two moths are out and flying away.

Almost instantaneously, there are more. And more. Just nothing but more. Hundreds, thousands, maybe even hundreds of thousands of moths begins unfurling themselves from the openings in my palms. They fly forward into the forest, making a trail through the trees.

I just stand there for a moment, palms up and arms outstretched to keep the creepy fuckers as far away from my body as I possibly can, watching them swirl like a sideways tornado, carving a path through the woods.

It goes on and on like that. Never-ending. Like there is an infinite number of magic moths living inside me. I don't know what to do. I try closing my hands, but then they push against my palms, trying to squeeze out. And oh, my God, it is the grossest feeling, so I open my palms again, giving them the freedom to spill.

I just stand there watching them, feeling revolted and fascinated at the same time.

"House of Moths." These words come out of my mouth unbidden and they bring the magic with them. Because for a moment I am standing in the truth-or-dare room and I'm looking down at a drawing on the floor. A circle divided up into pieces like a pie. And there are spaces for three people to sit.

House of Bucks—Pell.

House of Dragons—Tomas.

House of Moths—me.

But just as quick as it came, the vision—or hallucination, if we're being totally honest here—disappears and I'm just a wood nymph chimera standing in the woods, looking out at a sideways tornado of moths spilling out of my hands and disappearing into the trees like they are boring a hole into the side of a mountain.

I take a step forward and suddenly, the stream of moths stops.

My lips make a little 'o' shape and I pause, unwilling to even breathe, as I wait to see what happens next.

Is it over?

But nope. They're back. Just spilling out of my hands.

I take another step. There is a downed tree right in front of me, so I climb over it.

The moths stop.

"Huh." I plant my hands on my hips, just staring at the tail end of the tornado as it winds its way through boughs and leaves. But then the moths start up again and quickly fill in the gap.

Obviously, these little fuckers have intentions.

"All right," I mutter out loud. "I guess I should follow them."

When I take another step forward I am rewarded with understanding. When I follow them the twister of moths stops. When I stop following them, they assume I am slow or stupid and need a push, so they start spilling out of me again.

"Fine." I sigh, pushing my bouncy blonde hair out of my eyes. "I'll play along."

Because I don't seem to have a choice.

But also, what else am I gonna do?

I don't know where I'm at. I don't know what I'm doing here. So why not just follow the magic moths coming out of my hands?

I've made dumber decisions in my life.

I continue walking and this is when I notice that my slutty schoolgirl outfit has changed. It's no longer black and red and it's no longer covered in pilled-up fuzzballs and made of scratchy, synthetic whatever. It's red and yellow now, like the outfit I was wearing when the devil and my mother took me from whatever world I came from and plopped me down in this one. And the fabric is soft, and thick, and made of some kind of exquisite wool.

The bustier has changed too. Not scarlet, but a butter-colored yellow leather that is even softer than the skirt. I have a sash now too, perhaps the same one I was wearing that night I was taken, but I don't think so. There are just as many medals and ribbons on this one, but it is much bigger, fit for a woman and not a child.

I hold the sash up, trying to see the medals better. They all have a different design. And once again I am reminded of Girl Scout badges. I was never a Girl Scout. That's laughable. But there were girls in my various schools—before my mother sentenced me to foster care—who were part of this after-school cult. I mean, club.

Wow. Where did that word come from?

But then I'm reminded of a conversation with Pell several weeks back. *I was the object of a minor cult in my Roman days.*

I don't think he meant it the way we use the word 'cult' today. I think he just meant he had followers. Worshippers? Which actually does mean it was a cult, I guess.

I find that distressing though. Not sure why, I just do.

People used to worship Pell?

It's… creepy.

But who am I to talk? I have insects crawling out of my hands.

But the point is, there were many gods back then and people could pick and choose who they wanted to give their loyalties to. And if the gods are real—which seems to be the case from what I've seen, so I'm gonna go with that—then if people asked them for favors, the god might grant the favor.

Not that Pell was a god. But he's definitely more than human. So I guess I understand it.

Anyway. Back to the medals. One of them might actually be made of gold because it is shiny and heavy. This one has an engraving of a lion on its hind legs with fighting forepaws. I think this particular lion has an actual name. But I don't know what it's called.

I pause here to look a little more closely at the medals and realize almost all of them have a lion in the motif. And while they are mostly made out of gold, there are some that appear to be silver or maybe even bronze. These do not have lions. The silver ones have crude starfish-looking stars and the bronze ones—there are only two of these—depict fire.

My palms begin to tingle again and the moths start pouring out.

I shudder, then start walking to make them stop.

It's so gross. So, so, so fuckin' gross.

My stomach twists and turns as I picture the moths emerging from my hands and I have to force myself to think of something else as I walk because I don't want to stop and throw up.

Something else is new about my outfit. It's not super-long the way it was in my new-to-me memory of that kidnapping night. That skirt went well past my feet. I think that's because it was made for a girl who had monster legs and not human legs. This one is not that long but it is definitely below the... hock. Which kinda translates to ankle, I think. Except there's more space between the hoof and the hock, obviously.

If I were describing this skirt on a human it would fall well below the knee.

And while I'm looking down, I notice that I have boots on. And knee socks. Or hock socks, as it turns out. They are gold and come with long red tassels peeking out from under my skirt that flip and flop as I walk. The boots are different too.

And of course they are. I'm once again reminded of that kidnapping night, when I was sitting on the edge of the tub lifting my foot up and out of my too-big boot, wiggling my toes like they were a brand-new novelty.

My original body probably had hooves and the boots I was wearing that night must've been made for hooves, not feet. That's why they were too big.

These boots are made for hooves too. Except they are not too big, they are slightly tight on me and I would actually like to take them off, but if I stop walking the moths will revolt and I will barf. So I just keep going.

So. I take stock of my situation as I follow the mothnado. I am a monster. That's comforting now that my memories are coming back. Because I was never supposed to be a human and I'm getting used to this wood nymph chimera body. I like it, actually. I like the velvety fur that starts at my waist and covers my hips and ass. I even like the longer fur on my lower legs. I have little feathery bits just above my hooves. And I love, love, love my hooves. I like the way they are split and how this lets me grips things when I'm climbing over rocks and shit. And I really like my hair when I'm a monster. It's so bouncy and long. Plus, I'm only an average-height human but I'm a tall monster. I'm in lust with the shape of my legs too. They're so long and slender. I feel like a ballerina.

My monster body just... fits. Especially when I'm next to Pell. He and I just go together. We're like the total power couple.

All this acceptance of myself feels really good. Because I've spent most of my life hating who I was—or maybe who I wasn't—and now I feel like I can just be me.

It's all very refreshing.

Except for the moths. I might be able to get on board with insects living inside me if they would just stay fireflies, but more often than not, it's moths that come crawling out. And moths come with dark intentions. I'm not making this up, either. I've read a bunch of alchemy books in the apothecary and all the ones with moths engraved on the covers are creepy and talk about things like curses, and hexes, and generally doing bad things.

I pause my introspection when I realize that the forest has become dotted with large gray boulders. I have to jump and climb over these boulders, which is not as easy in boots as it would be if I wasn't wearing them.

Just a little while later the boulders are dominant and the trees are becoming sparse. Like I've changed altitude and the tree line is coming up. I'm not any kind of environmental expert but I took biology in two of my high schools. I didn't care for the whole internal organs thing, but I did enjoy the botany. And I remember the tree line was like a demarcation into the tundra life zone on a mountain.

So I'm on a mountain. Yeah. This place feels like a mountain even though I hadn't noticed that I was walking uphill or anything. The air is becoming crisp and cool and the underbrush—which was ferns and stuff when I first woke up—is not much more than low-growing moss. Soon, the trees become spindly and sparse and as I walk I realize there really is a tree line because I come to the edge of the forest and find myself looking out over a cliff.

I am high, high up. This is definitely not PA. Or Pell's tomb. His place didn't exactly feel tropical—Saint Mark's didn't really feel tropical either—but it was thick, and lush, and warm, and humid.

There is like... no air up here. Which is a contradiction, because there is a lot of wind blowing my hair in all directions.

I sigh as I look past the cliff to another mountain top. "Well." I'm huffing. Mostly from the walking but also, I'm just ticked off. I throw up my hands. "What the fuck? How am I supposed to get over there?"

And that's when I notice all the moths have disappeared. And even though I have stopped walking, they are no longer crawling out of my hands.

"Maybe we can just fly?"

I don't move. I stand completely still as turn my head so I can see my left shoulder. "Pia?"

"I mean, we do have wings."

"Pia! You're here!"

She tsks her tongue at me. Which is distracting. Do birds even have tongues? "Why are you acting weird?"

"What?"

Pia actually sighs. "I'm tired of this journey, Pie. I want to go home."

Home. This word echoes in my head. Home. "We can go home?"

I don't even know where home is. Or what it is. Or what's waiting for us when we get there.

"I told you not to drink that lionberry juice this morning. But do you ever listen to me? Noooo."

I smile, then giggle a little. She's still the same Pia.

"Now your head is all foggy and I told you we should've turned left back there at the smithy."

"The smithy?" This reminds me of Pell. And suddenly, I remember that we were in the forest together and someone shot me with a fuckin' arrow. I'm just about to blurt out all kinds of dumb plans to get back to him when Pia says, "So. Flying, right? We've agreed?"

And now a set of wings unfurls from my back. And they are not just any set of wings, either. I can barely see them, but it's pretty fuckin' obvious that these wings are something spectacular. For one, they are gold. And I'm not talking gold-*colored*. I'm talking gold leaf or something. Because they are shiny, and metallic, and when they flutter in the wind, they make tinfoil sounds.

One thing does worry me though, just a passing thought in my hallucination—that's what this is, right? It has to be. But the worry thought is—do these things actually work? Because they look... ceremonial. And if I'm gonna jump off a cliff—

Whoa, whoa, whoa. Who says you're jumping off a cliff?

I close my eyes, confused about pretty much everything and a little bit scared. Because some things are coming back to me now. Not just the memories of my childhood, either. But Pell, and the tombs, and the monsters, and the devil.

Who is my father, but thankfully not my father.

Oh, God, what if he is my real father?

No. I shake my head. I don't think he is. He stole me, that's what he did.

But I am an eros, aren't I? Isn't that how I got into Saint Mark's in the first place?

I feel like I'm coming full circle here. Like two ends are about to meet up and make something solid. But I'm not quite there yet, so really, it's just a feeling of absolute confusion. And a dash of feeling intrigued. Because I have no clue what's happening right now.

Pia, apparently tired of waiting for me to make a decision, jumps off my shoulder and soars out over the valley between mountaintops. "Race you!" she calls.

Before I even second-guess myself, I'm running. And then I jump—no. Really, it's more of a dive. I dive headfirst into the air. Soaring, but not really.

There is this moment when I know for sure that this was a mistake. That these stupid gold-tinfoil-covered wings absolutely do not work and were only meant to be part of a costume. And now I am going to fall millions of feet and splat on the rocks below and... well, that's the end of me.

But thankfully, in the next moment, the wings lift, taking my whole body with them, and we catch a wind. And then I'm soaring after Pia.

She is a little dot in front of me and I do not take my eyes off her. I just stare at her tiny body and press my arms against my body like I'm diving through the wind after her.

What happens next is a mystery. It feels like a skip. Like a skip in time, or place, or whatever. Because one second, I'm marveling at how the wind feels under my wings and the next, the ground is coming up to meet me.

I'm a hundred percent sure I'm about to splat myself on the smooth, gray cobblestones, but I don't. My legs are moving—running, actually. And when my feet hit the ground, I'm upright and on the move.

Pia flies back to my shoulder and lands with little patters of her feet.

I turn my head to look at her and I sigh as I come to a stop. "I'm so glad you're here. I've missed you so much, Pia. You have no idea how sad my heart has been since you died."

She actually shoots me a birdy look of confusion. "You need sleep. That party was too much."

"What party?"

"This is not going to go well. I can already tell. Maybe we should skip it? Do you think they would hunt us down if we skip it?"

"Hunt us down? What the fuck does that mean? And what are we skipping?"

Pia is staring off to my right, so I turn to see what she's looking at. And then she just takes off and flies away in that direction.

I'm about to call her back, but that's when I realize that we've landed in some kind of courtyard that is walled in on three sides and filled with horses and carriages. Not like the dusty horses and carriages you see in Western movies with cowboys and shit. I'm talking royal wedding kind of horses and carriages.

And this is when I realize that my head is kinda foggy. And I only realize this fact because it suddenly clears up and I am one hundred percent in the moment.

"Holy fucking shit. Where am I?"

But there's no one to hear me because Pia is far away now, already passing through the one open end of the courtyard.

I follow her. Not flying though. Just jogging a little.

My legs feel different. I can't decide if they are more or less springy.

They feel... stronger in a weird way. I'm not sure. I just know they feel different.

Pia disappears once she's through the open courtyard gate. A huge, huge wooden gate made of a very light blond wood. And when I pass through the gate, and see what's on the other side, I actually stop in my tracks and gasp.

And once again, the words, "Where the fuck am I?" spill out of my mouth.

Because this is a castle. A freaking castle. I'm talking made of gold blocks of stone, and those parapet things or whatever they're called. And huge banners, and flags, and tall-ass flagpoles, and more fancy carriages, and horses, and a fountain that is spurting something very bubbly that looks like champagne. And on the other side of that fountain is the most massive set of stairs I've ever seen. Pia is already flying up them.

For a moment I'm afraid that she will go inside and leave me here. But the door to the castle is closed and she stops, hovering in the air, then turning to look my way. "Hurry!" she calls. "We're late!"

"Late for what?" She can't hear me though. Because these are distracted, mumbled words and I'm really just thinking out loud.

I run. Right past the carriage and horses, around the fountain, and up the stairs. And when I get to the top Pia floats over to my shoulder and once again settles there. "I'm so tired. I'm going to sleep for weeks. What are you waiting for? Open the door!"

The door.

I like doors, don't I?

Or no. Do I hate doors?

Why do doors give me a weird feeling?

I push the door open and see nothing but fog and I am instantly annoyed. Maybe even pissed. I move forward, muttering, "What the fuck? If this stupid place is a trap—"

My rant comes to an abrupt stop. Because the moment I cross the door's threshold it brightens around me like it's some kind of technological device. The light flashes, causing me to close my eyes and put up a hand as I am momentarily blinded.

And when I open my eyes again, I find that the fog has disappeared and in its place is a whole other world.

I'M NOT EXACTLY **surprised** about the new world in front of me. I've gone through my share of magic doors at this point in my life, but everything about the next moment feels... different.

And this is not a feeling I recognize.

My perspective changes. That's the only way I know how to describe my viewpoint. Or maybe the room grows? It's a massive room and the ceiling height of the great hall in Saint Mark's cathedral doesn't even come close to how tall this room is. It's like giants live here.

And there are people! Well... chimeras! And not any old chimera, either. No frat-boy satyrs or half-naked wood nymphs in this place. Nope. They are the lion chimeras. Like Callistina.

For a moment I'm sure that this door has deposited me directly inside the Vinca palace because that is my only point of reference for castles. But I wasn't in Vinca when I walked up to the door. And sure, the door probably scooted me through realms, or whatever. So it's still possible that this is Vinca. I guess.

It's just... so not Vinca.

It's nothing like Vinca. And aside from Callistina and her guards, I've never seen so many lion people.

And the clothes. My God, the clothes.

There is a row of young lion-girls along one wall. They are maybe... I dunno, sixteen? Not fully adult women, but not children, either. And they are all wearing lavish skirts. I'm talking skirts made of layers of silky tulle and chiffon, making them flare out from their bodies. They are a rich mustard color and go all the way to the floor, but I can just catch a glimpse of the golden sandals on their feet that are paws. There is a lot of elaborate embroidery at the hem and gold thread weaved into the top layer of fabric. They shimmer like jewels as they stand there along the wall, cupping their hands to their mouths the way girls do when they gossip.

On top they are wearing silky blue camisoles and short jackets made of thick fabric embroidered with a blue and tan floral pattern. And more gold threads are woven through the design.

They are all blonde and their long hair flows over their shoulders in gentle waves. Like it is water falling over a cliff. And they each have a very small set of golden antlers peeking up from their heads.

Like Callistina, they have fur everywhere. But not shaggy fur, like Pell. The velvety kind. In fact, they look like they are covered in a pale-yellow velvet. And this whole look is so luxurious and tempting, I almost walk up to them and start touching everything.

In fact, I'm taking a step in their direction when I hear a familiar voice say, "Pianna! I've been looking everywhere for you!"

I turn in that direction and there she is. Callistina. Looking the same in many ways, but with smaller antlers and much, much younger than the woman I left in the Bottoms prison.

"What are you doing here?" She grabs my hands and bends down, looking me right in the eyes. Then she lets out a long breath, like she was worried about something and now she's relieved. "You scared me."

"Why?" Oh, my God, my voice is different. It's high-pitched and sounds like Pia. And then it hits me. I under-stand why my perspective was so off when I came through the door. I'm a frickin' *kid*.

I look down at myself, recognize the red and gold tartan

uniform or whatever it is from that night in the hotel bathroom, and then look back up at Callistina.

She's dressed like all the other teenage lion-girls along the wall. And her blue eyes are so sparkly and pretty that for a moment I forget that I hate her and maybe even want to get revenge for her killing my Pia.

"I was afraid you ran away," she says. "And then I was afraid you didn't."

"What?" my little-kid voice asks.

She squeezes both of my hands. "I would take your place if I could. You know that, right?" I kinda want to pull my hands away, but she's gripping them pretty good. "You know that, right?"

I don't. But... I feel like playing along is the only real option here. Because, as usual, I have no idea what the fuck is going on.

"I wish—I pray, Pianna—that I could be the one to go."

"Go where?" It slips out and I'm instantly sorry and want to take it back. If this were a movie and I was not in it, just watching a little girl who is out of time and place, I would be like, *Come on! Get with the program! You're out of time and place, you need to act like everything's normal!* This is a major complaint of mine when I watch time-travel movies.

But anyway...

"*Pianna.*" Callistina is using one of those exasperated voices on me. "We've been over this." Then someone claps from across the room and Callistina's head practically swivels off her neck as she looks towards the sound.

"Line up, girls!" More clapping. "It's almost time."

The woman is also a lion person. But she's older, has a full rack of massive golden antlers, and has a spinster-y look to her. She's not wearing the elaborate pretty dresses like the other girls, but a very proper, tailored, neat suit-dress thing. Long skirt—red and gold tartan, like mine, but not frilly or full. Very tight against her body. And a matching jacket. Like she's the power CEO of... teenage lion-girls, apparently.

Suddenly, the spinster's eyes find mine. And a moment later she is a train coming right at us with a sour look on her face as she shakes her head. "No. No, no, no! What are you doing here?"

Callistina bows low and lifts her skirts with one hand, averting her eyes. "I was just taking her to the throne room, Mistress Ryella."

"She should've been there already! She's missing her god's last words!"

"We're going right now. I'll be right back." She bows again and then she's dragging me across the smooth, pink, polished floor.

I have to run to keep up and once again I am stuck on how my feet feel. There's something wrong with them. And this realization starts up a sick feeling in my stomach, like there's something bad going on here and I just haven't caught on yet. In fact, even though this place is very grand, and beautiful, and filled with fancy rich lion-people, it's got a bad vibe to it.

"Oh!" I say this, but not loudly. So no one really hears me. But it just occurred to me where I've seen these clothes before.

In Vinca. The dress that Eyebrows made me for that last day. And the outfit that Tarq was wearing on that first day. He was pretty pissed off when I showed up in those clothes on Fireday, calling it royal garb. Like I wasn't allowed to wear it and people were going to have fits over it.

But turns out I *was* allowed to wear it. Or at least it's possible I was allowed to wear it. According to the fact that I am in some kind of palace and related to a girl who is allowed to dress this way.

Callistina is running and dragging me like we are fleeing a fucking war zone down a hallway made entirely of windows when I just happen to look to the side and catch a glimpse of myself in the windows.

I stop. I'm talking full fucking stop. I stop so hard, Callistina loses her grip on my hand and half-stumbles, half-trips a few paces forward before she can halt her momentum.

But I don't pay any attention to Callistina. Because I only have eyes for *me*.

I am not Pie.

Not in any form whatsoever.

I am something… foreign.

I am a lion, and I have wings, but they are not made of gold foil. They are made of honest-to-God feathers. And the moment I notice them, they unfurl from my back and stretch out to an enormous length. And my hands—I swear, these were not my hands a minute ago, and this was not my body a minute ago, either—but my hands are covered in golden velvet.

And this is when I realize why my feet feel wrong.

They are not feet.

They are not hooves, either.

They are *paws*.

My hair is still blonde, my eyes still blue. But there are no horns. Just tiny nubs that might one day develop into a spectacular set of golden antlers.

I can't even speak. I just… point to the reflection in the window with my mouth open.

"Pianna! Put them away!" Callistina starts shoving my wings back into place, trying to fold them up. "You know Father hates the wings. It just reminds him of all his mistakes. If you show them in the throne room—" She sighs, irritated, as she continues to shove them back into position, and I feel like I'm fighting her for a moment, but I'm not doing it on purpose. "Please, please, please, Pianna, do not show him your wings! Now let's go. Mistress Ryella is going to beat me silly tonight if we mess up the Caretaker Ceremony!"

These words echo in my head. Then I look up at my sister. She *is* my sister. Maybe I didn't feel it at first, but seeing her here, it's so obvious. And in the present day—well, she's a prisoner in the Bottoms thanks to me. But she's a queen. A freaking queen. And she's mean. And it kinda sucks that I didn't know her back when she was young because in this time, she seems to really care about me. And in the future—or the present, depending on how you look at it— she hated me. She did not want me there. It's like my sudden appearance was going to ruin her good thing.

But anyway, back to that word. "Did you say... *caretaker?*"

"Pianna, I'm so, so sorry this is happening. I really would take your place. But I am firstborn and you are secondborn. And this is just how it is. I know you're scared." She stops and grabs my shoulders, then looks nervously down the hallway in the direction we came from, then looks me in the eyes. "Listen to me. OK?"

I nod.

"You're going to be fine. And do you know how I know that?"

"How?" Maybe I'm morphing into this past version of me, because I can hear the fear in my voice, even though I'm not fully internalizing that I'm in some kind of immediate danger.

I mean, this isn't really real. It's some kind of hallway trick. I'm not really here. I'm... still in the forest with Pell. We're exhausted from having sex, and running from the devil, and generally sick of being in charge of shit, I think. So I'm not really afraid. But I can hear it in my voice.

Maybe I'm not afraid now. I'm grown up. I have already lived through whatever comes next. But the little girl I'm inside of has no idea what's coming.

Callistina shakes me. "Because you are *Pianna*, Second

Daughter in the House of Fire. And that means you are special. More special than any of the others. And tonight, you will be the toast of the Realms. They are coming here for *you*, little Pie."

When she says my name—my real name—she places the palm of her hand flat against my cheek.

"You will go home with a king tonight. You will live in a palace grander than even this. You will have teachers from all the Realms. And you will marry the most handsome prince and live a charmed life of beauty and riches."

Hmm. Since I am a kid in this... dream, memory, whatever this is... and I am an adult in my real life, I can say with one hundred percent certainty that this is *not* what happens to me.

Callistina must read the doubt all over my face. "Trust me, Pianna. Father has only invited the most respected of all the kings. No gods will be bidding tonight. You are to go to a king. That is the rule this time."

Well, that's a relief.

Not.

Since obviously I didn't go home with a king! And what the actual fuck? *Bidding*? Is this like a child-bride thing?

Of course, I know it isn't. Or maybe it was, but it didn't turn out that way. The *devil* got me. And this is where it all happened. And then he took me to Pennsylvania, and turned me into a dumb human, and my life became a CPS-foster-care nightmare.

And speaking of the devil—the *eros* devil—isn't he some kind of love god? So what the actual fuck? Just lies, lies, lies coming out of Callistina right now.

"Your palace will be your sanctuary." Callistina is still talking. I have kinda tuned her out, but when she says the word 'sanctuary' I pay attention again. "No one will be able to hurt you there. The magic you will have, tiny sister..." She takes a moment that she really doesn't have to spare to gaze fondly into my eyes. "Your magic will be unstoppable. Father is going to make sure of it. And one day, we will meet again and we will be…" Her eyes go up and look around, like she's being sneaky. Or about to tell a secret. "And we will be," she whispers, "the most powerful sisters in all the realms. OK?" She's still got her hand on my cheek, and she strokes it for a moment, sighing. "You'll see. It's all been planned. Now let's go. I'm taking way too long and Father is going to be so angry."

I sigh as she begins tugging me down the hallway once again. Then we turn a corner and my mouth actually drops open in awe.

Because now we're in a huge room filled with massive doors. I'm talking twenty-five feet high, at least. Like they were made for giants.

"OK." Callistina stops in front of the first door, out of breath. Then she licks a finger and wipes a smudge off my cheek. "You go in—"

"Not by myself!" And again, I can hear the fear in my little-girl voice.

"Fine. I'll take you in. But I can't stay. I'm needed. I have to give you away during the Caretaker Ceremony."

Oooooooohhhh. Hmm. So that's the part all the beautifully-dressed teenage lion-girls are playing tonight. They are giving away their little sisters.

Which is… gross.

"Are you ready now?"

I look down the line of doors and for some reason, I am compelled to count them. There are twelve. This number means something, but I can't immediately put my finger on it. And then I'm out of time. Callistina knocks on the door, making it open of its own accord.

And then we walk through into yet another world.

The throne room **is just as grand** as the rest of the palace, but it is surrounded by fog. And even though Callistina was giving off the impression that our father would be in here waiting for us, there is not one man acting like a god and sitting on a throne.

There are four of them.

I let out a long exhale of frustration. Because of course there are four of them. One is just too easy.

They are each sitting upon a grand throne and pretty much all look alike. Older, bearded—though not long beards, kinda short—and wearing various forms of godlike garb. Variations of togas and...I squint my eyes at the man sitting in the first throne on my far left. Because he's different. His clothes are Egyptian. And immediately, my mind goes to the statue of Pell inside his tomb.

"Oh, fuck." This comes out in my little-girl voice before I can stop it. But thankfully, the four gods on the four thrones are roaring different things at Callistina, and they don't hear me.

Four. And they each have a banner over their throne declaring who they are.

The one from Egypt is called Ptah. He is wearing mummy wrappings. But they're not old and gross, the way I normally picture mummy wrappings, but bright, bright white. And they cover every bit of his body, with the exception of his face, which is covered in green skin, and his head, which is covered in a bright blue cap.

Fucking Egyptian gods were so weird. They're the ones who looked chimera too. I'm not all up on the whole pantheon or anything, but I do remember alligator men, and bird men, and dog men being among the strange depictions of these gods.

And this makes me pause. Because... yeah. Chimera. I feel like a revelation is coming about this whole thing.

The next one is called Cronus. Who, if I remember correctly from studying ancient gods in fourth grade, was a titan. A primordial Greek god who came before all the ones we know so well.

Then Zeus in chair three. Everyone knows him. He's the god of gods.

And then, of course, the one we love to hate—Saturn on the far right from ancient Rome.

There are three more little girls in the room too. All dressed just like me. They are kneeling on fancy red-velvet pillows in front of the thrones with their foreheads pressed to the marble floor.

Of course, the pillow in front of Saturn is empty because that's where I'm supposed to be. And just as I work this out, Callistina drags me over there and whispers, "Kneel down and place your head on the floor until they tell you to stop."

I do this. Reluctantly. I'm getting sick of this memory. How do I get out of it? Just... find another door and walk on? Will that work?

Doesn't seem likely. I feel like this memory is playing out for a reason.

Once I'm kneeling on my pillow, I side-eye Callistina as she bows low, lifting her skirts the way she did with Mistress Spinster. She bows her head and says, in a loud, clear voice, "I beg your pardon, gods. My little sister got lost. But she's here and now I must go."

"Off with you," the Egyptian guy says.

"Be gone," Zeus roars.

And then Saturn says, "Thank you, child," in a voice I do not equate with the Saturn of the future. His tone conveys genuine affection for Callistina.

Callistina retreats, the door closes, and then the gods are arguing in loud, rumbling voices. They each get up from their thrones, pacing back and forth across the room.

I don't even know what they're arguing about. Their words don't make any sense to me.

I chance a look to the girl to my left and she rolls her eyes, which makes me smile and roll mine back.

Gods, we are saying. *They are so tiring.*

Then she says, "They're mad about your rings," just loud enough for me to hear, but not loud enough for the sound to carry beyond the argument going on all around us.

"What rings?" I ask back.

She makes a face at me, like I'm being stupid, then focuses her eyes on the floor. Conversation over.

"This is my gift to her and you have no say!" That's the Egyptian guy.

Why would he be giving me rings? And are we talking about the same rings? As in bag of magic rings that opens doors?

"It's dangerous," Cronus bellows.

"It's far beyond any gift we are giving to the other daughters," Saturn adds.

"And she is just a nobody," Zeus says.

The Egyptian guy—Ptah, who I have never even heard of —seems unconcerned. "It is my gift. And that is the end."

"You act like you're still in favor," Zeus challenges. "You're no one now, friend."

"As if you are?" Saturn's jab is sharp and loud. "The world is mine. And there will be no successor to me."

Hmm. Interesting. Because didn't Pell mention something about Saturn feeling threatened by other gods? And is this... I chance a look up to study them. Is this some kind of line of succession?

Egyptian, titan, Greek, Roman.

It *is.*

They are equals. But... oh, shit! I think I get it! Their cults have died out. No one worships them anymore.

None of them. Not even Saturn. So joke's on him, I guess. They have been discarded.

Well, in my future, anyway. In my future none of these gods matter. There are plenty of religious cults, that's for sure. But as far as I know, none of them bother with the ancients.

Then the twelve doors also make sense. The Twelve Olympians? There must be equivalent gods in each of the throne rooms. And each of them is—selling, maybe?—a daughter?

For what reason, I have no idea.

Maybe to... dilute the magic? And keep them all equal? To save face, maybe?

It's as good an explanation as any, I guess.

Or maybe, since we are being given to kings, it's to keep their cult going in different realms?

Just as likely, I suppose.

So how the hell do I go from this moment to sitting on the edge of a bathtub in a hotel room with the devil?

Dunno. But I'm like a hundred percent sure that I'm about to find out.

Suddenly, the arguing stops. And then, the next thing I know, there is a pair of white mummy feet standing in front of me.

He's going to give me the rings.

And just as I think that, a woman's voice—a voice I have definitely heard before—interrupts things.

"What are you doing?"

And the whole argument starts all over again. This time in the presence of Ostanes.

OSTANES.

Yep. Shit is happening and I'm about to get answers.

The gods are all making their case to her about why I should not have the power of these rings. And when I chance a look up to gauge how things are going, I find her staring at me. Like she knows I'm not a little girl called Pianna. Like she knows I'm really Pie.

"It cannot be done. It's too much," she proclaims.

But the white mummy feet are still standing directly in front of me. This god, Ptah, he hasn't said a word since she entered. And the next thing I know he's tapping my shoulder.

I look up and stare at the green-skinned mummy man, who commands me to stand up with a flick of his finger.

I stand, looking around at all the gods, then finally up to his green face.

"I have a gift for you."

More protests. But this god doesn't seem to care. He simply smiles at me, withdraws a bag from his mummy wrappings—the very bag that Pell and I found in place of my Book of Debt after we brought the forest monsters into the sanctuary—and he bends down.

He takes a ring out of the bag and asks me for my hand. I extend it and he pushes a little ring onto my finger. "This one you keep." Then he ties the bag to a loop at the waist of my skirt and stands back up. "It is done."

The room, which had gone eerily quiet, erupts into a new cacophony of objections.

But, as Ptah said, it is done.

I'm still standing there—the only girl standing—and I feel the heat of Ostanes's stare. So I look at her. She is frowning. But then she smiles.

And it is this smile that explains everything. Call it intuition. Call it suspicion. I don't care what it's called, when I look at her I see through her. As in her intentions.

She wants my rings.

And when I look at the rest of them—except for Ptah, who is sitting back on this throne, casually picking at his pristine, white wrappings—they are staring at me with... hunger?

Not for me, of course.

None of this has anything to do with me.

They want my rings too.

This is the magic. These rings were given to me by some god I've never even heard of. Some old, long-forgotten, washed-up and nearly useless god.

I'm sure, as a child, I had no idea what was happening. I didn't have the context of the future to put all the pieces together. I'm equally sure that I had no idea these gods— including the one calling himself my 'father,' not to mention Ostanes, who has told me she is my mother—were using me in some kind of... conspiracy.

Perhaps Cronus, Zeus, Saturn, and Ostanes are all in it together.

But I doubt it.

You don't have to be some magical empath to feel the vibe in this room.

These people are enemies through and through. And once again, Pell's words come to mind. If Saturn did have a neme- sis, it would've been another god.

This is it.

I'm looking at... the *why*. Why is my life so fucked up? Well, it all starts here.

These damaged gods are so full of themselves. So pumped-up with self-importance. So sure they are necessary —even after humanity has left them behind—they are scheming. And worse, they are using little girls to fulfill these schemes.

Suddenly Ptah stands up and roars, "That's enough!" His voice is so deep and powerful, it shakes the room and I am immediately reminded of Pell.

And then my mind is swirling with questions. Where is Pell? Is he on some memory trip too? Or is he still back in the forest, wondering what the hell happened to me?

"It is time," Ptah says. "Get on with it."

"He's right." Ostanes walks over to me and takes my hand. The smile she shoots me is a bad impersonation of something warm. She's not even looking at me, I realize. She's not even thinking about me. Her eyes are on my bag of rings.

She must notice me watching her because she snaps out of it. "Hurry up and bestow the remaining gifts. We're late."

Each of the other three girls is told to stand. The one in front of Ptah—I'm assuming she comes from his House—is given a single red apple from Saturn. It reminds me of the poison apple from Sleeping Beauty, but I'm sure there's some kind of magic in there.

The one in front of Cronus is given a crown of roses by Zeus. They are black and the whole thing is heavy with thorns. One of them pricks her head when Zeus places it and a little bit of blood drips down the side of her face.

The one in front of Zeus is given a wand made out of silver and topped with a yellow stone from Cronus. She is the only one of us who smiles. Like she thinks her gift is so special. And... well, maybe it is. But I don't think she knows that. Not for sure.

Unless the three of them are also reliving their slavery-day memory, I'm the only one who understands the gift. One day, a long time from now, I will use these rings to control doors that lead to other places.

"One last thing." Ostanes lifts her hands in the air in a dramatic way that accentuates the bell-shaped sleeves of her intricately embroidered robe. And then she says, "'Four girls, a room, some gifts and thrones. Four gods each know their place at home. A mother gives a book of words, locked up tight in the beaks of birds.'"

And suddenly, there are four little red-capped sparrows flying around Ostanes' head in a circle.

"We did not agree to this!" Ptah is outraged. He stands up, practically shooting daggers at Ostanes with his eyeballs from across the room.

Ostanes waves a hand in the air. "We didn't agree to your little key stunt, either." She snaps her fingers and the four birds fly to us girls and land on our shoulders.

"What does this mean?" Zeus asks.

"It means," Saturn says, "that the birds contain the magic of the gifts."

"What?" Cronus—who is a mean-looking guy anyway—stomps over to Ostanes with his hand open. Like he might wrap it around her throat. "Take it back."

"No." And I have to give Ostanes credit here. Her 'no' is firm. "There has been trickery in this room." Her eyes slide over to Ptah, who glares back. "The purpose of the gifts is to equalize you. And your gift"—she's talking to Ptah—"unbalanced everything. So I will lock it up. None of these girls will use their gifts unless they can figure out how to release it from the birds."

I let out a long breath and for some reason, it comes out loud. Loud enough to make everyone look in my direction. Even the other girls.

"Sorry," I mutter.

A moment later the protests resume, the room filling up with angry accusations.

But things are starting to make sense for me. This is where Pia came from. This is how I got the power over the rings. Saturn could be my father and Ostanes could be my mother, but it's far more likely that it happened the way Pell told it.

Whatever us lion-girls are, we are a product of science,

not love. And if Ostanes is my mother, she is the mother of these girls too. Because I am certain that we are just a consequence of her alchemy.

I'm guessing that each of the twelve doors I saw had four gods in succession inside. I'm not any kind of god expert, but if Ptah, Cronus, Zeus, and Saturn are in this throne room, then there is another throne room with other sets of successive gods. Apollo, or whoever. Venus, maybe. I really don't know any Egyptian gods. Ra, or something. And the only other Titan I remember from school is Rhea.

But it doesn't matter if I can name them. I'm certain this Caretaker Ceremony has something to do with... equality.

So it's possible that Ostanes is the only mother alchemist. Possible, but not likely. I'm guessing she's in charge of us four. And each room filled with damaged gods has their own alchemist who is doing the same. Producing chimera offspring to use in a war of power.

In fact, maybe Pell's divorce story—which always sounded kinda stupid, if I'm being honest—is true? Surely Juno is in one of these other rooms. And maybe she and Saturn really did have a thing and now they are in some kind of chimera-monster war?

It would not surprise me. I mean, the Egypt guy just fucked everything up by giving me a bag of magic doorway rings. Is it so outlandish that the gods in other rooms would be warring and plotting in a similar way?

Power corrupts. And absolute power corrupts absolutely.

This whole production is a way to spread the power out and create a game. To give them something to do, maybe?

They are old gods. Unnecessary gods. But they are still gods. And for whatever reason, their influence needs to be equal.

Like this is some kind of... treaty.

Yep. I like this reasoning. It feels very close to true.

But, of course, we're talking about gods here. So I'm not really surprised that no one seems to be playing by the rules.

Suddenly, the room is quiet again. All the yelling has stopped. Like the gods and the alchemist have reached some kind of agreement.

And I wasn't paying attention. *Good job, Pie.*

Little Pia snuggles up against my neck and I am filled with warmth. Then Ostanes claps her hands. "Let's go, girls. Your big sisters are waiting to give you away."

At this point, I'm ready to go. I understand the rings, I understand Pia, and I think I even understand the gods. So why keep going? I already lived the life that comes next. I'd much rather be back in the forest with Pell's arms around me so we can talk all this shit out and make a plan to go forward.

What's the point of visiting the past, anyway? It's dumb. And do I really need all the details of how the devil stole me?

THE THREE OTHER **girls** and I leave the gods behind and fall into a single line behind Ostanes. There are other short parades, just like ours, coming out of other doors. And I feel pretty proud of myself for getting this right. Because each is led by an older woman who is probably an alchemist.

We all file into the glass-lined hallway that Callistina dragged me down and we are a very long line. Some quick multiplication tells me we are forty-eight girls, to be exact. Plus the twelve alchemists.

Pia is warm and comforting against my neck. I look over my shoulder at the lion-girl behind me, and she's shooing her bird away. It flies in circles above her head, like they are magnetically attached.

She does not look pleased about her new BFF. I want to tell her it's gonna be great. Just wait.

But actually, it wasn't great. It kinda sucked.

I mean, Pia was the one who got me in all the trouble. It wasn't on purpose, but still, my life would've been a whole lot easier if there was no Pia.

This line of thinking makes me feel ungrateful and ashamed. Because without Pia, I would've really gone legit crazy a long time ago.

We leave the glass hallway and file back into the great room where I started this journey. The teenagers are still lined up along the wall and we are told to go join our sisters and be quiet and good while we wait.

I walk straight over to Callistina and she bends down to hug me. "What did you get?"

"A bird."

"What?"

"Ostanes gave us all birds to bind our magic."

"What?" Callistina looks appalled. "Why the hell would she do that? Didn't Father stop her?"

"No. I guess…" I lift up the bag of rings at my waist. "That Ptah guy gave me a bag of rings and—"

"What!" This time, Callistina exclaims it. And it's so loud, the whole room stops talking to stare at us. She places a hand on my shoulder and turns me around so that we're both facing the wall and no one can see us talk. "Start over, Pianna. What. Happened?"

So I tell her. I tell the whole story. And all she says is, "Tell me Ostanes's spell. Exactly."

"Well." I sigh. I really don't remember it all, but then, just like this morning in my real-life world, the words come spilling out. "'Four girls, a room, some gifts and thrones. Four gods each know their place at home. A mother gives a book of words, locked up tight in the beaks of birds.'"

"What birds?" Callistina seems really upset over this new development. She looks around, presumably looking for the other little lion-girls who were in the throne room with me. "I don't see any birds."

Another clue.

Callistina can't see Pia.

Well, at least it's consistent. So far, the only people who have been able to see Pia are Pell, Tomas, the monsters of Saint Mark's, and the entire realm of Vinca.

"Where are the birds, Pie? I don't see any birds."

I point to my neck. "She's right here. Snuggled up against me."

Callistina shoots me a look. It's a look I am very familiar with. It's a look that says, *You're crazy.*

And so it starts.

"And what book?"

Well, my first guess is that it's *the* book. The source code, or whatever. But it could also be my Book of Debt.

I don't answer Callistina. I'm over it. I think I got what I need. I'm ready to leave now.

I start looking for doors. There are a lot of them, actually. But then I look at the main door. The one I came through.

Even though, in all my hallway experiences, we have never left a place the same way we came in, I'm starting to think this isn't a hallway, but an actual magic door.

So it makes perfect sense that I need to go back through that door to get back to Pell in the forest.

And Pia too.

Other Pia. Pia who has been constantly with me for nineteen years. Not the one who just got spelled into existence.

I look around, calculate the distance between where I'm at and the door. I approximate it to be about fifty feet. I'm no track star or anything, but I think I can sprint this, open the

JA HUSS

door, and get through it before anyone figures out I'm escaping.

The element of surprise is on my side.

And I'm just about to take a first-step mad dash back to my real-world life when the lights go out, music starts playing, and Callistina grips my hand tightly.

Escape thwarted.

Happy future dubious.

Stuck in a slave auction.

Story of my life.

"HERE WE GO." Callistina is still gripping my hand tight. "Don't be scared. It's all going to be OK."

Maybe if I really was a kid her words might placate me. She seems sincere. Which is kind of surprising since she was all bow-down-before-your-queen back in Vinca. I have to remember though—she's just a kid right now too. There are almost two decades between this moment and that one.

But anyway. I'm not a kid. I'm a grown-up who's been through a lot and I know what comes next and it's got nothing to do with being OK.

We are lined up in the hallway two by two and when the pair in front of us begins walking, so do we. Even though I know where I end up—sitting on that bathtub looking down at Pia. Who is brand-new today. That's kind of a cool detail—I still don't understand how the devil and my mother actually get me out of here. I mean, there are no humans here. And I get that the devil isn't human—he's an eros or maybe *the* Eros. But my mother is a human. So my mind is spinning with possibilities of how the two of them manage to get me out of this world and into that one without a single person in this place stopping it.

This is when I realize everything has gone eerily quiet in front of us. It's like everyone is holding their breath. And just as I think that, Callistina inhales loudly. Like she knows what's coming and it's a big, big deal.

Is she excited? Is she terrified? I can't tell.

But I don't have to wait long because the pair in front of us passes through the door. And then we're there, right on the threshold. And that silence—I'm stuck in it for a moment. It's a little bit comforting. But also foreboding.

Because it's the silence I feel just before I step through a magic door. And the space on the other side of that door has nothing to do with the space on this side of the door.

We cross over the threshold and my foot hasn't even touched the ground yet when the screaming and yelling fills the world.

Callistina squeezes my hand and even though I can't hear it, I know she lets that breath out. Excited.

Because people aren't just yelling and screaming. They are cheering and we are in some kind of ancient arena, the kind you might find in Rome or Greece. The kind left over from long-ago times.

Someone with a big, booming voice yells, "Princess Callistina, Princess Pianna, House of Fire!" Like we're at a debutante ball and must be announced.

The crowd cheers. For us.

I look around, my eyes wide and wild, trying to understand what is happening here.

Are we in the Coliseum? Are we being thrown to the lions? Are we going to be killed by gladiators?

No. Nothing like that. Nothing like that at all. The room is actually not that big. There are lots of people, for sure. All chimera. I'm not a hundred percent sure, but from here all the men look like satyrs and all the women look like nymphs. And they are crowded together—shoulder to shoulder—on the center floor. And in the middle of that crowd is a small circular platform and over their heads is a bridge made of wood that leads towards where all the lion-girls are standing lined up along the outside edge.

But there are other people in the room too. These people sit on chairs on elevated platforms that are terraced up the sides of the circular space. They are chimera. But... different. And this difference isn't just in their clothes, or their jewels, or their crowns.

It's... everything. No satyrs, that's for sure. But there are minotaurs. I thought Tarq was sleek and sexy? Well, he is. But he's just one of many here. And they're not just mino-taurs, either. There are lots of different kinds of chimera. The most attractive and regal combinations of humans and famous monsters from ancient times that I have ever seen.

No one in this group of people is shouting. They are stoic, and regal, and dressed like royal beasts.

This thought makes me pause. And then I get a little sick to my stomach.

"Ooo!" Callistina pokes me. "There he is. The Prince of Vinca. House of Bucks."

"Prince of Vinca?" I actually say this out loud, my little-girl voice surprising me for a moment. "Who's that?"

Callistina winks at me. "Your future husband, if things go to plan."

"Which one is he?" I already know I'm not going to marry the stupid prince. But it doesn't hurt to check him out.

"There."

My eyes follow the length of Callistina's finger and I find... "Holy fucking shit."

"What did you just say?"

"Umm." I look up at my sister. "I said... he's... a hairy... bucking..." I sigh. "Never mind. But I know him." And I do.

Because the Prince of Vinca is a teenage Tarq. I've even seen this version of him. It was when we were running through the forest during that first trip into the hallways. Oh, my God. Is Pell here too? I scan the crowd, but can't find him.

Callistina pokes me. "Know him from *where?*"

"Vinca." I give up on the pretense. It's not like any of this matters. This is a memory. It's a wrap, as they say.

"You've never been to Vinca, Pianna."

"Well, Callistina, actually, I have. I've not only been there, I worked there. I'm some kind of spelling prodigy and Tarq— I mean, that prince guy? He was my boss. And guess what? You were the queen."

She smiles, giggles, plays with her hair. "That's quite a dream you had."

She's really not listening. "It's not a dream. It's just… the future." I look around, bored. Ready to go. The only door I can find in this place is the one we came through.

"What do you mean, the future?"

"The *future*, Callistina." I look up at her and meet her gaze. "I'm not a kid. I'm twenty-five. Somehow, some way, the fucking devil stole me from here, took me to a realm called Pennsylvania, left me with a strange woman called Mother, and…" I throw up my hands. "Then I got stuck in a monster's curse, learned to do magic, banished Saturn—"

"Father?"

I roll my eyes. Can she be any dumber? "Then I went to Vinca to work for the prince over there and became a spelling prodigy. And then we stole all the wood nymphs and took them back to Saint Mark's so Tarq could be the king and I could put you in debtor's prison for killing my Pia."

Callistina's eyebrows are so furrowed in confusion, she's got a unibrow. "What in the name of the House of Fire are you talking about?"

I point to the bag of rings tied to my waist. "And these? They open doors to other places. That's kind of how I got here. In a roundabout way. And actually…" I sigh again. "Can I just… go now? If I can just get to a door—"

Callistina sputters and gasps. "Pianna. This is your Caretaking Day. It's the first day of the rest of your life! You're going to be—"

"I'm going to be a homeless foster-care kid in Philadelphia. I'm going to ditch a lot of school, go hungry a lot of nights, pass time getting drunk with college kids I don't actually go to school with, and then be hunted by the devil."

She places a hand against my forehead. "You've gone ill." Then she looks up and around. Not finding what she's searching for, she taps the teenager in front of us. "Where's Mistress Ryella? My sister has gone sick."

And then again the lights go out. But this time a spotlight immediately lights up the small circular stage in the center of the room. There is cheering, and clapping, and then Mistress Ryella walks across the little wooden bridge and stands in the center of the tiny stage with her hands clasped together.

Immediately, people go silent. So silent you can hear everyone breathing.

In this silence Callistina says, "Don't worry, Pie. I'm going to put a stop to this. You can't go through with it. Not while you're ill!"

Yeah. I just sigh a third time. "You do that, Callistina. You do that."

Meanwhile, this whole shit show has already started. Mistress Ryella's platform is slowly spinning in place so she can address the entire room at the same time. "Thank you for joining us today for another Caretaker Ceremony for the finest younger sisters in the second generation of gryphon chimera." There is a smattering of polite applause, but Mistress Ryella doesn't wait it out, so it dies quickly. "As you all know, the alchemists of the House of Fire have spent thousands of years perfecting the *lioness*." She really emphasizes that word. "And as you are also aware, gifts tend to accumulate in the secondborn of each new protocol. And these lovely lionesses here today represent the finest the House of Fire has ever produced. We breed these magical children with *you* in mind, so that they may enhance your line and bring forward your power." She pans her hands towards the kings and queens in the tiered section of the stadium. "But before we get started, a shout and a clap for the gods and goddesses who made it all happen."

Mistress Ryella raises her hands up in the air and claps. Just as the lights come on high at the top of the stadium.

"Huh. Like... skyboxes," I mutter. Private rooms so they can have business meetings while their little genetically-engineered daughters can be sold off to placate royal families. Nice touch.

Even though I'm now disgusted, and bored, and so ready to go, I can't help but scan the faces up there.

Gods.

It's... kind of impressive. I mean, how many people in this world—or any world, for that matter—get to see the ancient gods in person?

This is the moment when some of what's happening to me finally starts to sink in.

I am not human.

OK. I've had a few weeks to get used to this idea. But it's more than that. Not only am I not human, I am... *special.*

It feels weird to even think this about myself for lots of reasons. Mostly because I've never been anything but weird. And maybe some people are evolved, or whatever, and to them weird and special are the same thing, but that's not how I felt about it.

I was weird in the kind of way that puts people off. And this off-putting became a part of me. When you're that girl you have two choices: You can change the deepest levels of who you are and pretend to be someone else. Or you can just give in to it.

Maybe some can embrace the weird. Celebrate it and turn it into something unique.

But I wasn't that kind of weird girl. I was the sick kind of weird girl.

No one embraced me. No one accepted me. I mean, Jacqueline did, obviously. But by the time we met, Pia was not something I talked about. I was hiding who I was. Jacqueline liked the public face of Pie Vita. She had no idea what was going on inside my head.

And all the people who came before her tried to talk to me about depression, and offer up diagnosis after diagnosis to help me come to terms with—not who I was, but what I was *not*.

They wanted to medicate me.

Even after I started lying about Pia and pretending she didn't exist, they could still tell that I was... *wrong*. That I didn't belong.

And I guess they were right. Because I am a genetically engineered lion chimera who was made by the alchemist to the gods, and was born into a... what? Royal family is not the right word.

Royal... menagerie?

Closer.

The intentions of this Caretaker Ceremony might be to pair us up with some member of the families of royal beasts sitting in the tiered sections of this room. But we are not like them. Our bloodlines were manufactured. We are products. Possibly even made to order.

Special. So special that now I don't feel like I belong anywhere.

House of Fire.

It reminds me of the truth-or-dare room in the hallways. House of Bucks. House of Moths. House of Dragons.

And this bothers me too. Because Pell is so much more than some random male animal. And I am not the sum of those moths. And while Tomas is a dragon, he is faceted. Like a cut diamond. I mean, for all intents and purposes, he's a shapeshifter. He's so many things.

And now I'm mad at that hallway room. Because what gives those hallways gods the right to define us?

What gives anyone the right to define us?

It's bullshit.

I guess everyone's allowed their opinion. Whatever. But I'm so used to being misunderstood, and mislabeled, and called all the different kinds of crazy that I'm practically immune to it.

And anyway, I'm not crazy. I'm completely sane. It's the world around me that's gone mad.

But at least now I have finally gotten the truth. And it's not very romantic, and not very humanizing, and not very comforting. But it is the truth.

I snap back to the presentation and realize my eyes are still tipped up to the gods. They all stand and there's a lot of shouting from the people in the center of the room. They are asking for things. "Give me a good life. Save someone from sickness. Give us a good crop." And they are clapping, and laughing, and cheering.

Fucking gods.

Who made them boss, anyway? It's not like they're in charge of anything. So they have powers, or whatever. And riches, obviously. And followers. Cults, as Pell would say.

And the stories. Can't forget the stories.

And then there's the little fact that they're immortal.

Or are they?

Tomas said something interesting when I was in the dungeon. He said everyone dies. Even Pell, one day.

And if that's true, then these gods will die too.

Or maybe not die, but fade away.

Egyptian. Titan. Greek and Roman.

There are a lot more myths and legends of gods around

the world where I come from. Thousands and thousands. I mean, India has a shitload. And China. And Japan. The Vikings. The Native Americans. Well, pretty much every culture has their own gods, right?

So why are these four pantheons so special?

Maybe they're not?

Maybe they just spent time in the wrong world the same way I did?

Maybe the people who saw them there got the wrong impression.

And maybe… maybe someone figured out that they didn't belong in that world. And when that happened, they stopped being gods and just became… weird.

The kind of weird that warrants… *banishment*.

This revelation is like a sun exploding in my head. The idea that the ancient gods were kicked out of my human world resonates so perfectly with me, I get a little dizzy.

Damaged gods. That's what they were.

So they left that world and came to this one.

Maybe through a door.

Maybe through a hallway.

This place where they can still position themselves above all others, and command the royal beasts, and do their alchemy, and have Fireday, and Earth Hour, and ten-day work weeks. Where dragons have been forgotten, and the common chimera are the peasant class, and they can offer little magical gryphon girls up to the ruling class to make them feel special too.

The people at the bottom—the ones on the floor in the center of the room, the ones clapping and cheering—they throw them scraps. Because you can't have all-powerful gods if you don't have obedient kings to do your bidding. And you can't have obedient kings without serfs to do the work.

It's disappointing, really.

It's like that moment when I was talking to Grant in

Granite Springs, that night of my disastrous date with Russ Roth, when he offered me the secret of money and success.

But it was really a bribe. Nothing but a payoff. *Join our ranks, Pie. Be one of us and you will get rich.*

And it's so gross to me.

But it doesn't explain what they're *doing*.

I don't get it.

Pell's voice is suddenly in my head and the words 'moves and countermoves' bounce around in my brain.

Is that all this is? A never-ending climb to the top?

The gods control the royals. The royals control the chimera. The chimera control... well. Society, actually.

Without the chimera, there would be no workers. Without workers, there would be no royal beasts. And without royal beasts, there would be no gods.

Surely they must know this.

The cheering stops and the gods take their seats. I study the faces of the common people on the floor. How excited they are to be here. To see this. To be a part of a world that must only exist in their wild imaginations.

And they are satisfied.

It's Vinca. Not literally. But it's the same way there. They let the mixed chimera work their menial jobs. And I'm not disparaging the work they do. The Vincans I met were all pretty important people. And yet every Fireday they would subjugate themselves to the queen. Every Fireday they would bow down in order to lift her up.

The queen.

The teenage girl who is holding my hand, in this very moment, squeezing it tight to let me know she cares.

But that is almost twenty years in the future using the time I'm accustomed to. Right now, the chimera on the floor seem pretty satisfied. And they are not subjugating themselves. They are clothed, and smiling, and cheering. There is no hint of revolution.

Maybe something happened between this day I'm in right now and the future when I was learning to spell in Vinca?

Maybe the chimera learned something about the gods or the royals that changed their minds about their role in society?

And maybe the gods decided that would not do.

Moves and countermoves.

"WELCOME *to the Caretaker Ceremony* for the House of Fire!" Mistress Ryella is back in control after all the relentless cheering and applause for the stupid gods. "So that the ceremony can move along as efficiently as possible, we ask that you please hold your applause until each girl's caretaker has been finalized. Then, and only then, can we properly celebrate her bright future."

There's muttering in the floor crowd. But it's not the discontented kind. It's tacit agreement. *Yes, yes, yes. We must all hold our applause until each little lion-girl's sale is final.*

Don't they understand that this is wrong?

It's a rhetorical question, obviously. They don't. This is just... normal.

"First up," the mistress continues, "is House of Fire number one."

Number one? She doesn't even get a name?

"Engineered by the alchemist Brinn"—there is gasping, ooohing and ahhhing—"from the bloodlines of the oldest kings—"

I stop listening and just pay attention to the little lion-girl who is being led to the wooden bridge by her big sister.

When she gets to the bridge her sister leans down to hug and kiss her. Then she is given a little shove and begins to cross the bridge where the small circular platform awaits her in the center of the room, about a foot above the heads of the chimera on the floor.

When she reaches the platform, she pauses, then carefully steps on to it and immediately she is slowly spinning so everyone in the room can get a proper look at her.

Including me. I study Number One, who is breathing heavy and looking around with wide eyes. We are all wearing the same get-up. And we all basically look alike, as well. She looks like me—I mean, not twins or anything, but same hair, same eyes, same skin, same uniform.

But I do notice something a little bit different. She's got the sash on, which covers her golden-yellow leather bustier, which is really more of a corset since she's *six*. But her sash has different medals and ribbons.

Just as I'm thinking about this the mistress starts calling out her talents and I realize that the medals correspond to these talents. "Proficient in spelling and well on her way to excelling in potions, she has been gifted the power of sight by the goddess Venus."

There's clapping here. A few people forgot the rules. And Mistress Ryella shoots the crowd on the floor a warning look, so it dies down quickly.

Then she says, "First bid, please."

This is when I notice that the royal beasts in the tiered seating between the gods and the people each have an older lioness standing beside them with an auction paddle.

Several paddles go up at once and there is basically a bidding war. I don't understand the money, so I don't really keep track of that. But the whole thing only lasts about thirty seconds.

Then she is proclaimed, "Taken," by the mistress and carefully retraces her steps back down the bridge where her very excited sister whisks the little lion-girl towards a hallway and they disappear.

Number Two has already been called and is stepping on to the platform when my attention returns to the ceremony. It's the same routine. She has also been engineered by the alchemist Brinn and her gift was bestowed on her by the goddess Aphrodite.

Each alchemist has created four girls for each of the gods, or goddesses, in the line of succession.

Ostanes presides over group three and I am Number Eleven. When Number Nine is announced people forget the rules and begin cheering wildly. She's the one Saturn gifted a red apple and I learn that it contains the power of truth-telling.

This almost makes me snort. Saturn handing out truth is next-level irony.

Number Nine's little sparrow peeks her face out from her neck, her little beak moving, and I know the girl can hear the bird because her eyes kinda flit down towards her shoulder.

But no one seems to notice this. And Mistress Ryella doesn't mention the caveat about the power of the apple being locked up in the beak of this bird.

Hmm. Interesting.

So the royal beasts have no idea that the magic little lioness they are buying can't even use her gift.

Wow.

It's like ten pieces of my life puzzle just slid into place.

I got the bag of rings. I can open doors. I can spell.

But I couldn't. Not really. Not until Pia and I were separated. And once she was dead—

Holy fucking shit.

I look up at Callistina. She's not paying any attention to me, she's so absorbed in the ceremony. But I told her the truth. I told her about the birds. Hell, I told her the actual *spell*!

And, obviously, it means nothing to her today. She thought I was crazy.

But in a few years' time, when the other royal beasts have figured out that Ostanes put a spell on us girls to bind our gifts—yeah. She would know that what I told her in those moments before the ceremony was all true.

And somehow, she becomes queen. Perhaps taking my place after I was kidnapped by the eros devil? And then what? She commanded Tarq to look for me? Is that why she had Tarq hunting wood nymphs?

But how did she know I was a wood nymph chimera?

Maybe she didn't.

Maybe that part was a guess.

Meanwhile, back at the child-slave auction... Number Ten has just been sold and the next thing I know, my number is called.

"Ready." This is a statement, not a question. Callistina isn't even looking at me. She's holding my hand, but all of her attention is on the stage. She takes a step, but I do not take a step with her. And when she realizes this, she turns, her face fierce and stern, her words coming out through clenched teeth. "Do not mess this up, Pie. If you've got a fever or have gone ill, you need to be strong and brave. Everything is riding on this moment." Then she squeezes my hand very hard, so hard I wince and almost cry out.

But then her grip loosens and before I can even respond to what she just said, she looks back at the center of the room and takes a step.

This time, I walk with her.

No one claps or anything, but the moment I leave the shadows lining the edges of the circular room and enter the light, they are murmuring. My eyes sweep over the people on the floor. Their wood-nymph faces. Their satyr horns. They cup their hands over their mouths to make whispered comments and maybe it's just that I wasn't paying close enough attention to the lion-girls who came before me, but this feels... weird.

Like they know me.

Like I am somebody.

When we get to the wooden bridge Callistina lets go of my hand, bends down, and places a new medal on my sash. None of the other sisters did this, I'm sure of it.

I don't know. Nothing is making sense anymore. I'm lightheaded, and my stomach feels queasy, and Pia is chirping at me, her warm feathers pushing against my neck. But I can't understand her.

When Callistina straightens back up there are even more murmurs and the people directly in front of me even gasp.

Someone loudly whispers, "It's the mark of the Saints!"

What? Saints? I don't know what this is about, but I'm very sure anything to do with saints right now is a bad thing. I look down, trying to find the new medal. And then a whole bunch of whispers erupt in the room. But then Callistina squeezes my hand tight again. "Go. Now."

And then she turns and leaves me there at the edge of the bridge.

Mistress Ryella is off to the side now, no longer center stage on the little revolving platform because we are the stars of this show. But she's close enough to me that I can hear her say, "Walk. Now."

So I walk. A moment later I'm on the bridge. Two more after that and I'm carefully stepping onto the rotating platform. It's not moving quickly. I would barely call it a spin. It's very slow, the way a car might revolve in a car show. But stepping onto it instantly makes me dizzy and I have to hold my breath and focus very hard to keep from falling over.

"House of Fire Number Eleven," the mistress calls out. "Engineered by the alchemist Ostanes and from the bloodline of every single god and goddess present in this room—"

That's all I hear because the whole place erupts in shouts.

It's so loud, and the room is spinning, and my head is pounding, and my stomach is sick, and my knees are—

And then I lose all my thoughts. Not because I pass out, even though I want to. But because there he is. Right there, on the floor in front of me, bare-chested, and tattooed, and blonde, and green-eyed, and… winged. And Mistress Ryella is talking about my bag of rings when these same wings suddenly unfurl, creating a great wind. And then the devil rises up in the air and floats there right in front of me.

People begin to scream and push towards the edges of the room, trying to get away from him. I hear someone say, "Watch for the arrow! Get out of the way! The *arrow*!"

And then there it is.

The fucking arrow. Coming right at me and slam! It hits me in the chest.

I wait. For death? To pass out? Something.

But nothing happens.

Well, nothing happens to me.

But the room is chaos.

I stand there looking down at the arrow that has—once again—penetrated my heart. And I feel nothing. No pain. There's no blood. It's like I was never hit. Except for the fact that a fucking arrow is sticking out of my chest.

"What is this?"

I don't know who says that. But it doesn't matter. It's just the first of dozens of objections. All of which are coming from the gods and goddesses from the top tier. All of which are basically saying the same thing.

"What are you doing?"

"The nerve of you!"

"You don't belong here, Eros!"

"Get out!"

Even the royal beasts are fleeing, climbing over seats and each other, trying to get to the edge of the circular room.

Welp. I was wondering how it happened and here it is.

The devil smiles at me. And I smile back, giggling. Maybe even blushing, because I feel my face go hot.

"Hello there, Pie. It is my pleasure to finally meet you."

It is so weird to hear his PA accent here in this realm, that's all I can think about. Well, that and how pretty he is. And how I want to be with him forever. And never stop looking at his—

"Oh, for fuck's sake." I actually say this out loud.

And the best thing is, the devil laughs.

But then Saturn is descending from the top tier like— well, a god, I guess. Being all demanding and godlike. "You have been banished. Get out."

"That's funny," the devil says. Then he looks at me and squints his eyes. "I'm not the devil, sweetheart. Wrong pantheon, I'm afraid. I'm Eros. Your new caretaker."

"The hell you are!" I don't know who this woman is, but she comes from the top tier as well, so... a goddess, I presume. "Number Eleven is a joint project. She has already been promised to the royal beasts of Vinca in exchange for *access*."

Everyone is still in the room. There are no doors except for the one us lion-girls came through, which is a fire hazard. But the people are all still here. They are just pinned back against the wall. In fear for their very lives, I think. But this last comment gets them animated again.

"Promised?"

"How is that possible?"

"Access to *what*?"

"Isn't this an auction?"

"It's rigged! I told you it was rigged! But do you simpletons ever listen?"

"Silence!" Saturn roars. Immediately, there is silence. I think he used the voice on them, because the whole room rumbles the same way it does when Pell uses that voice. And when I look to the back, through the shadows, I can see that they no longer have *mouths*. There is just bare skin there. Like they all just stepped out of a Japanese horror movie.

Well, that escalated quickly.

The rest of the gods and goddesses have now all arrived and have formed a ring around me, Saturn, and Eros. These gods and goddesses all join hands.

And that's not a good sign, either.

"Get out, Eros. You have been stripped."

This comes from Zeus. But it's not very effective. I'm going to assume that he's insinuating that Eros no longer has power. But he's here, inside this exclusive slave auction, looking pretty damn powerful with those wings.

Plus, he's just so beautiful. I get weak knees at the sight of him.

Fuck's sake, Pie. That's the magic! Snap out of it! This is the moment you've been waiting for. The final piece of your puzzle. Do not miss it because of some magical swooning!

I blink and shake my head, trying to overcome the spell of his arrow, or his face, or whatever.

It works. A little. My head clears just enough to hear his threat.

No. Not a threat.

A spell.

"A little girl, made of gods.

A debt comes due,

The perfect time.

All agreed this girl is mine!"

But just as these words come out of his mouth, all the alchemists—including Ostanes—come together with lips moving as they conjure up balls of light in their hands. And together, as they manipulate the fire in their palms, they say—

"A banished nobody in the hall.

A man with wings dares to call.

A god he was, no longer true.

If he wins, he loses too!"

And then everyone is yelling. The gods and goddesses, the royal beasts, the other lionesses waiting to be sold, and even the people on the floor pressed up flat against the outer rim of the wall.

They yell the spell in a chorus.

And then they start making up new spells. There are so many words, so many commands, it's almost too much to comprehend. But I hear things that catch my attention. Just fleeting sounds. Not even passages. I have no idea which words belong to which spell, belong to which god or goddess, or royal beast, or lioness, or alchemist.

All I know is that all of these spellings are directed at me and Eros. They are closing in on us. Making a circle around us like they are a bunch of fucking witches. Hands out as they cast their doom and despair up on me.

The whole room is now filled with words. They float there, in the air in front of me, like real things. In color, even. Blue, and orange, and red, and green. I see the word 'moth' spelled out. 'Monsters.' 'Slave,' 'insanity,' 'woods,' 'hooves,' 'horns,' 'nymph,' 'saints.' I see 'despair,' and 'poverty,' and 'orphan.'

Suddenly my whole body begins to vibrate. It's intense, and scary, and then, in this chorus of curses and spellings, I am screaming. Because when I look down at myself, I am changing.

Flickering between all the different ways I can be Pie. The lioness, the wood nymph chimera, the human. And more. Many, many more that I don't even have words to describe.

This is when a bit of truth hits me.

It's all moves and countermoves, just like Pell said.

Only it didn't happen the way he said and it's not about some stupid book.

It's about me, and these vengeful and forgotten gods, and the alchemist who made me, and this banished Eros who wants revenge for being discarded. And all these floating and colorful words are my life foretold. I was to be bought by the Vincans and promised to Tarq. And even though no one here mentioned a godling, I already know about the godling. Because Tarq told me himself. These gods and goddesses had a plan for me and it was big magic.

A new line of gods, maybe.

A new line of rulers.

One with more power, perhaps.

One with no chance of being superseded at the whims of the humans who bow to them.

No chance of being discarded like an eros on Judgement Day.

Because I was something... terrible.

I *am* something terrible.

I· am some purposeful genetic engineering with the bloodline of all the gods, across all time, running through my veins.

They were up to something when they made me. Up to something no good, something so big that the only way to set it right was to ruin me before this magic ended up in the wrong hands.

They chose to ruin *me* to save *themselves*.

What a bunch of assholes.

And then, just when I think it can't possibly get any more fucked up, out of literally nowhere a door appears in front of me. Mere inches away. From the door comes a hand. A hand that grabs onto my leg, pulling me through, screaming, as I gaze upon the smiling, excited face of my *mother*.

I look behind me, reaching out for someone to save me from the terrible fate I've just been sentenced to, but it is Eros who takes my hand and I pull him through the door with me.

And there you have it.

The beginning is now known.

PART THREE

The little girl's reality.
Holds the door—both lock and key.
Traitors always become your friend.
But they will kill you in the end.

CHAPTER EIGHTEEN - PELL

he song fades, but it's not comforting in the least. Because the world around me begins to fade too, going gray, then dark, then black.

"Pie!" I yell it. And my voice is powerful and rumbly. But nothing shakes. Because there is nothing here.

He shot her. The eros. The devil. He shot her. And then he took her.

I am growling. A new kind of growl, one that matches the new kind of voice. "I'm going to kill you, Eros. I'm going to hunt you down, through time itself if that's what it takes. And I'm going to kill you."

I stand there in the black, waiting.

Waiting.

Waiting.

Minutes pass. Hours. Days, weeks, years, centuries.

"No gods now?" I ask the dark. "Nothing to say? You think it ends this way? You think this is how it ends?"

It does not end this way.

I have been in the dark before. Pie and I both have. And this is a comforting thought. Because I don't know where she is and I don't know what's happening to her. The only thing I do know is that eros got her.

And this is probably a big problem. Because he might not be just any old eros. He just might be *the* Eros.

And *the* Eros is a god.

A lesser god, for sure. But still, a god nonetheless.

But I'm still in the hallways and that means I still have hallway powers. And my hallway power is creating things with my voice.

No. That's not actually right.

The voice is just the mechanism. But the actual power came from my emotion. I was getting mad about that fucking eros.

"Fucking Eros." I grumble it out loud, looking upward for light. Nothing shakes, but a tiny light blinks on above me.

I'm just about to get excited about this, but then it blinks off.

"What the fuck?" Now I'm annoyed.

Then the light comes back on.

Then it disappears.

Then it comes back on.

I squint up into the darkness and then... yeah. I smile. Then I'm laughing. "It's a firefly."

Which makes me feel... I dunno. Right, for some reason.

Well, I know the reason. Fireflies are part of Pie. And even though she's missing right now, she's also still here. That's what this firefly means.

Why the hallways decided to split us up, I have no clue. But if they're in charge, and this firefly is a sign that she's still close by, then I can push the fear to the back of my mind and concentrate on the now.

I need to make this place into something. But not just any something, it should be intentional. Because I don't know what the hallways are up to and leaving them in charge of shit feels like a bad idea.

So I need a spell.

I think about what I want—to go home, and be with Pie, and be safe together. It's not asking much. But, then again, it kind of is. So I need to word it just right and not make the same mistakes I did with making Tarq the king. I mean, it worked, but Pie pointed out some very important shortcomings in my Tarq spelling. Shortcomings that could matter greatly if someone were to challenge it.

I don't want to be challenged with Pie. Especially when there's an eros out there claiming her.

This thought momentarily sidetracks my spelling progress because it makes me angry. Not that he's claiming her specifically. That's stupid. She's mine. But that he's a fucking god and he's messing with me.

Why can't they just leave me the hell alone? I'm so over it. I want them all to just fuck off forever.

All right. That's all-important stuff, but for later. Right now, I need to hook back up with Pie, find answers in the Bottoms, probably go visit Tarq, save Pie's kidnapping friend, and... put people back where they belong.

If this curse is over—and by the state of the sanctuary, I'm pretty sure it is—then I fucking quit.

Deep breath. Close eyes. Exhale. Be calm. Think. Compose.

OK. I open my eyes and begin:

"A Pie, a Pell, a forest tomb.

Our family home where magic blooms.

Under the trees with lights above.

Take us back and give us love."

Damn. That's a good one. I'm a hundred percent sure this will work and I'm not wrong. The sky begins to form just like it did earlier. Light, then grass, then trees start growing.

I sit down on the lush ground and I'm just about to lie back and relax as my new world takes shape around me when—

"Shit." I get back up. "Shiiiiiit!" Then I look up at the sky, like there's a god up there waiting to hear my complaints. "There are no palm trees in my tomb! It's northern hardwood, you fuckheads!"

Which means... this is not my tomb. "You bastards!" I shake my fist at the sky like a crotchety old man. "Why are you fucking with me? Why can't you just *TAKE ME HOME*!" I roar this and every bit of magic inside me roars with me. My hands begins to heat up and when I look down at them, they are glowing and fire is coming from my palms.

Whatever is happening, it is powerful. Because the whole new world actually blinks out of existence and I'm just about to start celebrating when it blinks back.

Only now, I'm in the fucking desert and to my left, just over the top of a sand dune, is… a pyramid.

The next thing I realize is that I am on the move. I'm talkin' bookin' it kind of moving. My legs are running hard. And it's not that easy to run up a sand dune. Still, I feel powerful. And my hooves seem to find their grip in the sand with ease.

It's normal. Kinda. But it also feels different.

Then I realize that I'm in this body, and I think I'm in control, but no. I'm not. I'm like a passenger in the body.

And the next thing I realize is… someone is chasing me.

I look over my shoulder—still very much running my hardest—and see a whole gang of… not sure. Not quite sure who these people are. The word 'Bedouin' comes to mind for some reason. Long dusty robes, faces swathed in dirty fabric, sticks or maybe swords held high in the air. And they are screaming as they chase me.

Don't speak Bedouin. Not even sure that's a language. But despite this, one thing is very clear—they are not just chasing me, they are after me.

Something changes. I can't quite describe it, but it's like one moment I'm the passenger and the next I am consciously driving the car. Sucking in air in short, ragged gasps. Desperate to breathe because my muscles are screaming like I've been running for hours and I'm about to drop.

I get to the top of the dune and then I stop short, unsure what to do, and kinda trip forward. Then I'm rolling down the sand dune.

This roll feels like it goes on forever and I'm relieved. It's a little reprieve for my legs. Plus, rolling down a huge sand dune is a lot quicker than running, because when I come to a stop and look up, I've gained some ground on the Bedouins.

But. There's always a but. Now that I'm this monster—I am still a monster, right? My hand goes up to my head and yep, sure enough, those are my horns. OK, but the problem is that when I was a passenger, I didn't need to know what the fuck was going on. Other me was driving the car.

But now that *I'm* driving the car, I have no idea what to do next. And even though the Bedouins are a little further behind, they have not given up on their quest to kill me, or maim me, or whatever the hell it is they want to do with me.

And—this is a very important point, in my opinion—I have never been to Egypt and I'm pretty damn sure that's where I'm at. So I don't know why I'm running from these people or what my plan was for escape.

The only possible option I can come up with is to just keep running.

So I get up and that's what I do. I run up the next huge sand dune heading in the direction of the pyramid.

I try not to look back because I know that slows you down, but I'm no longer running with ease. In fact, the sand on this dune feels more like mud. It's almost like dream-running. I pause here—mentally, not physically—to send up a little 'please, please, please' to the gods. *Please. Let this be a dream.*

But if it is, it's not over yet.

The Bedouins are only about ten paces behind me when I hit the summit. I'm more in control this time, and my intentions are to dive down the dune and do another roll to gain a little ground, but the moment I start to go over I realize that it's a trap. And I am fucked. Because on the other side of that dune is a whole line of warriors who look a lot more serious than the ones chasing me.

I skid to a stop on the far side of the dune, sand cascading down like a waterfall from my feet. And then the warriors jump up screaming with staffs raised and I duck my head, covering it with my arms, and sink into the sand.

Seconds. That's all I have left.

But then the strangest thing happens. The warriors go right past me and they reach the top of the dune at the same moment that the Bedouins reach the top. And there is a mighty clash!

And then... fighting.

I just sit there in the sand—breathing so hard my chest and throat are burning with the effort—and watch the battle as the muscles in my legs tremble.

What the hell is happening?

"Come on!" I yell. "You fucking gods! You're a bunch of assholes!" Again, I'm shaking my fist like an old man. "One break! One stupid break!"

"I'll give you a break!"

I turn at the voice over my shoulder, look up, and just barely manage to fall backwards as the curved and gleaming blade on the end misses my face by less than a finger's width.

I cover my face with my forearm and duck my head, getting ready for the next blow.

But... it never comes. Instead, I get laughter and a strong hand gripping my shoulder to pull me to my feet.

When I look up and meet the gaze of the warrior, I smile and laugh—because it's Tarq! He looks a little different. Younger, for sure. Like... way younger. And his horns are very dusty. Almost discolored. But pretty much everything else is the same. He's cut, and muscular, and big. And wearing pants and boots, which is not a look I remember about him, but... who cares. It's Tarq!

I'm still smiling like a fool when I exclaim, "My friend! What the hell are you doing here?"

"Saving your ass in war games. *Again*."

I look behind me. "War games?" Then I notice that no one

is really being hurt. There are guys on the ground, but they're playing dead, not really dead.

"Come on." Tarq is still gripping my shoulder and he spins me around in the direction of the pyramids. "We won this one. Thanks to you."

"Yeah?" I'm still breathing hard, still trying to make sense of things. But it's the fuckin' hallways. So why bother? Though it does kinda bug me that I'm here as a participant in the memory instead of an observer.

That's not usually how the hallways work.

"That was a great idea—lost in the desert by yourself. They'll never fall for it again, but who cares. Worked like a charm this time. The coming-of-age boy gets his win. Your father's gonna be thrilled when he gets back from the House of Fire."

My *father*?

Well, this is new. I'm a product of genetic engineering. And while I'm sure that there is some sort of genetic 'father'—everyone needs a genetic father—I'm also pretty damn sure that there was never a man in my life who I *called* Father.

Also, this is not a memory. I've never been to Egypt. Never. The only other places I've been in real life outside Saint Mark's are Rome and Western Pennsylvania.

Of course, this is not unusual for the hallways. They take you anywhere they want. But not as a *participant*. Because that's the point, right? You're not really there. You're just passing through the past. You get to enjoy it, and drink, and eat, and dance. But you're not *there*.

And right now, I most definitely feel like I am *here*.

The memory of how I got here comes rushing back to me and I stop in my tracks. "Pie!"

"What?"

"Fuck." I look over my shoulder, trying to see the first dune that I came over, like maybe she will be there. But of course she's not. She was shot by the eros with an arrow and she disappeared. Then I was in that forest, and did that spell.

"The spell!" I turn to Tarq, who is looking at me with worry. "The fucking spell. 'A Pie, a Pell, a forest tomb. Our family home where magic blooms. Under the trees with lights above. Take us back and give us love.' What part of that says ancient fucking Egypt and war games?"

Tarq just kinda blinks at me. "Are... you OK?"

"No! No, I'm not OK. I'm fucking sick of this shit!"

"Sick of what shit?"

I exhale. Loudly. Then throw up my hands. "This is just great. Just. Great. What am I doing here?" I yell this at the sky. "You fucking bastards! I said 'take me home!'" Then I just kinda blink. Because... "No. No, no, no. This is *not* home."

"Pell?" Tarq is really starting to look worried. "Who are you talking to and what the hell is going on?"

What do I say? I mean, there is no way to explain this story.

"Ohhhhhhh," Tarq says. "I get it."

"Mmmmm... Nnnnooooo. I really don't think you do."

"You had another episode, right?"

"Episode?"

"Time skip? Isn't that what you call them? It's been a while. Unless you've been keeping them secret from me. And seriously, that's not cool. Don't keep secrets from me, Pell. If you're hallucinating a life with a wood nymph in a fantasy realm called Pennsylvania, that's... well, not *fine*, per se. But we can deal with it. As long as you don't keep it secret."

"You know about Pie?"

"That's her name, right? She sounds great and all, but my friend, you're getting married tomorrow. You don't want Pressia to find out about this fantasy girl. You're gonna be hitched to her for the rest of your life. Don't start day one like this. So hush it up, man."

"*Pressia?* Did you just say Pressia?"

Tarq laughs. "I think you've been in the heat too long. Come on." He claps me on the back. "Let's go home. There's a feast in your honor tonight, brother. It's your coming-of-age day and your last night of freedom. Let's make it count. We can worry about hallucinations and delusions after the wedding."

Tarq talked enough for both of us the entire walk back to the palace.

Yep. *Palace.*

I just stayed quiet and spent the entire time trying to fit all the pieces together. Pressia is the market nymph who wrote all those books in the apothecary. And even though I didn't study them hard or anything, the illuminated images on those pages were beautiful enough to leave a mark in my memory. I can picture her face, and her clothes, and her words were both poetic and powerful.

But how the hell does this makes sense? And if I know Pressia, and she has books in the apothecary—so many books it would've taken decades, if not centuries to write— this means… this means she was *there*.

With me?

Before me?

After me? That's not really logical. But not much about my life has ever been logical.

Tarq walked me through the palace. In fact, he walked me all the way to my apartments. I think he's worried about me. And he has every right to be. Not only have I been having premonitions, or hallucinations, or delusions about Pie in this timeline, but there was no way to hide the fact that I was very confused.

I think that's why he talked so much on the walk back. He could tell there was something wrong with me and he didn't want to put me on the spot.

He's such a good friend. I know Pie doesn't like him, but she just had a bad first impression. Tarq is loyal. Just spending one hour with him in this hallway memory was enough to put me firmly back on his side.

I mean, I'm not gonna choose him over Pie or anything like that, but I'm not going to turn my back on the only true friend I've ever had.

Aside from Tomas, of course. Maybe we weren't close until Pie came, but we were constants in each other's world for two thousand years. That counts.

But this Pressia thing. It's bothering me. And the part that's really kinda flippin' my world upside down is the idea that she was there.

With me.

That maybe it's not just where the name Saint Mark's comes from that I have forgotten. Or the fact that Tarq and Pie were some kind of marriage promise. Or all that black-smithing I used to do.

Those are pretty big things. And I still don't know what Saint Mark's is all about.

So… is it possible that there was someone with me in the sanctuary all this time? And perhaps that someone was Pressia? Not just the slave caretakers?

My brain can't deal with that. Because what would it mean?

Am I obligated to go find her? And if I am, what then? Are we married?

Do I need a divorce before I can marry Pie?

I get up from the chaise I've been lying on and walk over to the large, covered terrace to gaze out at the village around the palace. It's a nice palace. Open rooms with lots of atriums. Intricate mosaic tiles on the floors. Columns lining breezeways made of stone. And pools. Lots and lots of little plunge pools. There's even one in my apartments.

The pyramids are off to the left from my vantage point. There is a lot of farming going on here, and a lot more water than one might expect in the desert. But it's not really the desert. Those dunes I came out in were just a very small part of this landscape. An anomaly. An attraction, maybe. Somewhere you go to play war games with your buddies. Who are not Bedouins, but regular monsters, just like Tarq and me.

In fact, almost everything as far as my eyes can see is lush, and green, and growing.

A commotion off to my right diverts my attention from the landscape to a group of humans. There are a lot of humans here. In fact, as far as I can tell, they outnumber the monsters by a factor of many. They are pretty much all I saw inside the palace as Tarq walked me to my apartment.

Down below, in a courtyard that is open to the sky, they are bowing with praying hands towards an approaching procession of single-axle carriages pulled by teams of oxen. And further back there is a line of walking monsters—hands bound together, feet in shackles, and being pulled along by ropes attached to the last carriage. They stumble, like they are about to pass out. But they keep going because they have no choice.

Something about these prisoners feels very familiar even from this distance. And that's when I see him. Batty, or whatever his real name is. His huge black wings are drooping so low, they drag on the dusty ground behind him like the tail of a too-long cloak. And once I recognize him, I recognize more. Eyebrows, and Cookie, and Frecks.

Poor Frecks. I really do feel bad about that.

Why they are here, and how they became prisoners of this god-man who is my father, I have no clue. But, of course, it's an important detail. A detail that I probably once understood, but now don't.

The carriages in front pass through the massive columns and come to a stop in the middle of a mosaic five-pointed star on the ground.

The door to the first carriage is opened by a servant, who bows low when a man gracefully exits. He is everything I imagine when someone says the words 'ancient Egyptian god.' Hard, muscled body that reminds me of stone. Eyes focused with intent. Power flowing off him like it's a scent.

I don't really possess the vocabulary to properly describe what he is wearing because as far as I'm concerned, I've never been to ancient Egypt. But he's not wearing a shirt. There are plenty of decorations on his top half though. Arm and wrist bands and colorful, jeweled chokers around his neck. He's wearing a skirt, heavily embellished and made of something gold. And in his hand is some kind of scepter. His face is painted like the statue of me in the stoa of my tomb.

"Shit." I mutter this out loud. Because I had actually forgotten about that fucking statue. I never liked that thing. It never made sense to me. And I had a compulsion to just walk past it as fast as I could every time I entered the tomb.

But that statue is a connection between me and this place that I hadn't thought much about over the centuries.

Then again, I haven't thought about much at all over the centuries, have I?

It's almost like forgetting was part of my curse.

Even so, I'm pretty sure this guy here is 'Father'.

Just then there is a loud knocking on my apartment door. I leave the terrace and when I open the door there is a group of human men on the other side.

The one in front bows low. "Your Highness. Your father has returned and is requesting your presence in the throne room. We will get you ready."

I sigh, ready for this hallway experience to be over. I want to find Pie. I want to set things right with the other monsters. And I want to fix the sanctuary, not let it crumble into pieces.

But I know better. If the hallways want to trap you in the past, you're just gonna be trapped in the past. So I swing the door open wide and beckon them all in with a wave of my hand.

THE HUMANS WASH me very thoroughly. Dozens of them come in with large pots of steaming-hot water and they pour it into a massive copper tub, filling it so full that when I get in water splashes over the sides and trickles down slabs of perfectly angled marble to a drain in the floor.

Then they are all over me with soft, soapy cloths. Scrubbing me, and shampooing me, and massaging me.

Which, if I'm being honest, is quite nice. It's a pampering I've never gotten from any of the slave caretakers. Not even Pie—who does like to soap me up in the shower—has ever paid such close attention to my cleanliness.

Once that's done, and I step out, there is a white cotton robe waiting for me. They hold it open and when I slip my arms inside, they close it around me. It's short enough that it doesn't really cover my lower half, but once I am led over to a chair that sits in the sun, I understand why. They comb my furry legs as they dry in the sun, while others massage my horns and hooves with pastes that smell like cinnamon. Another massages oil into my shoulders and chest and all of this feels so good, I close my eyes and almost fall asleep.

It takes these humans hours to get me ready and it

reminds me of something else I had forgotten. How *slow* life used to be. How deliberate, and purposeful, and careful everyone was about ceremony.

Modern life is nothing like that. And even I, a monster who has been locked up in a curse for two thousand years and pays almost no attention to what's happening beyond my walls, could feel this change as it was happening.

Because that change was both recent and quick. Like a switch was flicked and the whole world was suddenly different. Well, recent if you're immortal, as I seem to be. A hundred years is nothing on my timeline. But for a human, I guess it was kind of gradual. So gradual, perhaps they didn't even notice.

But I certainly did. I don't care for the frantic pace of society these days. So this deliberate and careful preparation of me by the team of humans is almost a relief. And it allows me time to think and… maybe not make plans—is there any point to that? But it gives me a sense of peace that whatever is happening here, maybe it's not so bad.

When all the pampering is over, they direct me to stand up and then I am dressed. I watch as they bring things out. Arm bands, and jeweled chokers, and the gold skirt. And when it's all done, and they put a piece of metal in front of me that has been polished into a mirror, I realize… I am him.

I am the statue of me in the stoa of my tomb.

And I am *young*.

No more than thirteen. Maybe even twelve.

No beard, of course. But no hair, either. Just a skullcap of fuzz. Like it was just shaved this morning.

This realization should not surprise me. And I would not call my reaction surprise, exactly. It's more like… a slap in the face.

A sharp, painful realization that I have been tricked. And it has taken me two thousand years to figure this out.

In other words, I am embarrassed.

Batty was right. I have no idea who I am.

And of course he was.

He was here.

He *is* here.

I stare at myself in the mirror for so long, the humans become uncomfortable. Then they place a headdress over my head—and the name of this piece of decoration even comes to me. Nemes. It is striped blue and gold. There is a medallion affixed to it that rides the center of my forehead. The medallion has a winged lion in the center of it and the words 'Peace unto you' written in Latin around the top.

It's the lion of Saint Mark. Also the lion of Saint *Mark's*. Not to mention the lion on my ring. Which is not on my hand at the moment because I won't stumble into that magic for another two millennia.

There is big meaning in this lion symbol, but I don't have time to figure it out because the humans take the mirror away and proclaim me ready.

Only four humans leave my apartments with me. Two in front, two in back. Like an escort. And they are not the same humans who cleaned and dressed me. They are armed, and they are older, and they are big.

They are guards.

And I am... what?

A prince? Maybe. But not likely.

A god? Also maybe. More likely.

A god*ling*?

Yep. That's the word I'm looking for. The word Pie used when she was talking about some pact she has been put in with Tarq. Their child was to be a godling.

Something more or less than a god?

I don't know.

But tonight is my coming-of-age ceremony and tomorrow is my wedding to a market nymph called Pressia.

And right now I am going to meet a father I never knew I had.

So I force myself to stay calm, and breathe deep, and walk.

I just walk.

Soon enough, we stop at the threshold of a massive set of doors. And I hope, just for a moment before they are opened, that there will be something else on the other side. Some other world, or memory, or maybe, if I'm very lucky, the sanctuary.

But when have I ever been lucky?

On the other side is a colossal room that completely embodies the whole... *vibe* of the ancient worlds. Something made for giants. I've been living next to a place we call 'the cathedral,' so I'm no stranger to grand things. But this room —it stuns me silent for a moment.

"Come, my son." The voice is something I recognize. Not the voice itself, but the rumble it evokes. It doesn't shake the room, but it wants to. It's just that this place is made of monolithic stones.

My attention returns to where it belongs. The god-man himself, sitting on a throne about fifty yards in front of me. I walk forward, squinting my eyes as I try to make out details.

I know this place. Well, kind of. It looks like something I've seen in photographs across time. A temple, I guess. With the massive columns painted with stories in hieroglyphics and the mosaic floor in the pattern of concentric circles.

It reminds me of the Temple of Memphis. And then, just as I think the name of this ancient city, another memory bursts forth. Not the Temple of Memphis. The Temple of *Ptah*.

This is Ptah. The god of the beginning. The creator of everything. The one who comes before. The blacksmith.

I am the son of Ptah.

My feet are moving as I think all this and by the time I get the first line of guards, something comes over me. It's another switch, like the one I had when I was running. Only this time, it's different and I find myself kneeling on the tiled floor, then pressing my forehead to the ground with my arms spread forward in front of me and my palms flat on the ground.

I am in the presence of a god.

Maybe even *the* god. Though I suspect all the others might object to that characterization.

The next thing I know the god is walking towards me. He taps my shoulder. "Rise, son. We don't have a lot of time and things have gone... *awry*."

I look up, then stand up. I am young but I am not small. Much, much taller than the guards around me. But this man, he towers over me. Like the scope of these ancient halls, and doors, and temples wasn't to prop up his image, but was necessary so he could pass through.

I mean, he's not an actual giant. But he's like a good eight feet tall and chiseled like a fuckin' statue.

I don't know what to say. *Hello? How was your trip?* I understand that I'm here to learn about who I really am, but beyond that... I have no clue what's going on.

Luckily, he puts his hand on my shoulder and guides me to a open doorway leading to an interior courtyard garden and begins to speak before anything becomes awkward. "I'm sorry to say that plans have changed, Pell. The Caretaker Ceremony—"

Caretaker? I get stuck on that word for a moment. And then I've missed something because he's saying, "So there will not be a wedding."

"What?"

"I know. She's perfect for you. And godlings, son. Oh." He sighs, almost moans. "The godlings the two of you would've produced. It would've been... divine."

He pauses here as we stand in front of a reflection pool

covered in blue lotus so he can look down into my eyes. His are yellow, like mine. And I see myself in this man. A little bit, at least. Obviously, he is not a satyr and I am. He has no hooves, or hocks, or fur. But I see my face in his. And even though I am basically still a child and my manly form is probably a decade away, at least, I see my mature build in the chiseled muscles of his shoulders.

"But you have a more important role now." He places a sincere hand on my shoulder and gives it a little squeeze as he says this.

"What role?"

"You'll see. Enjoy yourself tonight. Have fun with Apis. Do all the things you had planned and don't worry about it. We'll discuss it again tomorrow."

I want to say, *Who the fuck is Apis?* But instead, I ask, "What about Pressia?"

He shrugs and looks away, almost bored. "Bed her tonight, if that's what you want. There will be no godling now." Then he claps me on the back and walks away.

I don't follow. I don't think I'm supposed to because the guards who were flanking us turn and walk away with him. A deliberate separation.

So I just stand there for a moment, not sure what to do next.

Something is happening here. Something big. Something that will explain who and what I am and what all this has to do with my curse.

Because this is why the hallways brought me here.

To see the truth.

ONCE I ACCEPT **that this trip** through the hallways has a purpose, I feel a little better about things. Do I need the truth at this point? No. Not really. I don't care anymore. And I can actually see the logic in forgetting. Even if it wasn't part of the curse, what's the point of rehashing old things?

But I don't think the hallways will let me go until I get through whatever is coming. So I decide to be proactive about this. Possibly make it all happen a little quicker.

I go looking for Pressia first because even though I now know we don't get married, she bothers me. All those books in the apothecary bother me.

And as I wander the many spaces inside the palace wall in search of her, memories of this place come back to me and I get a very strong feeling of déjà vu. Plus, all the humans are very attentive. I don't think I have my own servants or anything, but the humans are everywhere and they are constantly bowing to me and asking if I need anything. So when I ask for Pressia, one takes me to her apartment. He bows low, then backs away and retreats down the walkway the way we came.

I face the door, take a deep breath and knock.

I am greeted by an older human woman with dark hair, black eyes, and a scowling mouth with red lips. "You are not supposed to be here. The wedding—"

"The wedding is off."

"What?" She gasps, clutching her heart. "This is not true."

"It is. There will be no wedding. Something has come up."

"That's not possible! It's been arranged since birth."

"You should go talk to my father. I will explain everything to Pressia myself." I step aside, giving her a not-so-subtle hint that she is going to leave and I am going to enter.

She sputters a few more times, but there is nothing left for her to do but comply. She scurries away, cursing under her breath.

I enter the apartments and close the door.

There is a huge main room. Very elegant and proper. Not my style at all. But for a girl, it's nice. Very… pink. And across this expansive room is an open door through which I can see a bed with lots of mosquito netting draped around the frame.

From there, I can make out soft voices, so I head that direction. I pause at the door, not looking in—it seems a little forward to just appear at a girl's door in this time and place. So I knock. "Hello? Pressia?"

"Who's there?" The voice is… not quite right. And when I peek into the room, it's immediately apparent why it's not quite right.

This is not a woman. This is not even a girl. She is a child. Maybe seven. And she's on the floor, kneeling on a lionskin rug, playing with dolls.

"Pressia?" I say it again.

She stands up, surprised. And nervous, too. Because she fusses with her dress—also pink—and then gasps. "Oh!" And she drops to her knees, pressing her head against the floor the same way I did in front of Ptah.

"No, no, no. Get up. Please don't do that."

She looks up at me, meets my gaze, but does not get up off the floor. "You're not supposed to be here. We're getting—"

"We're not." I cut her off because I just want to get this over with now. Clearly, she is not the answer I was looking for.

"We're not?" Her whole face crumples. But she does not yell, or throw things at me, or even mutter a single word of complaint. She just bows her head back down to the floor and tries to breathe normally, but fails.

I sigh. She's crying. "It's not you," I start, but then almost laugh. Because love, man. It hasn't changed a bit. "It's really not you, Pressia. And get up. Please. I just want to ask you some questions."

She doesn't move, but I can tell she's trying to stop her crying before she shows her face again, so I try to be patient.

I'm not very patient. But after two minutes she finally looks up at me with a smile. Her eyes are glassy and tears are covering her cheeks, but she's smiling. She gets to her feet, does some kind of curtsey and then lets out a breath. "Yes, my godling. What can I do for you?"

And this is when I see the woman she will become. Proud. Smart, obviously. And *composed*.

She might've been playing with dolls three minutes ago, but she is not a little girl. Was maybe never a little girl. She is a princess of some kind and there is absolutely no chance at all that she is a market nymph.

I knew it. I knew it the moment I saw her in those books.

But she disguised herself. Somehow.

Well, that should not surprise me. The woman who wrote those books was a very accomplished alchemist. Changing one's looks is basic stuff.

"Pressia, where do you come from? And how did you get here?"

Her eyes widen with surprise. "You… want to know things about me?"

"Of course."

"But… you told me not to talk in your presence."

"Well, that was… not very nice of me. I'm sorry. I want to know these things. Please tell me because I'm short on time."

She curtseys again. "Yes, my godling."

"Pell. Just call me Pell."

"Yes—*Pell*." It wasn't easy for her to say that. The manners have been ingrained. "Well." One more curtsey for good measure. "I'm from Vinca, of course. But that's not what you're asking, because you know that."

Vinca. Fucking *Vinca*. Why does this place keep popping up? What is the deal?

"I come from all the goddesses. Every line of succession. And the alchemist, Lyrica. But you know all that as well."

So very smart and composed. Because these are the exact questions I am asking about and she is wise enough to disguise her answers as silly to hide my ignorance and spare me embarrassment due to my rank of *godling*.

I'm actually sorry I will never know the grown-up woman called Pressia. Because she would be a formidable ally.

"So what else can I tell you, my—I mean, Pell?"

"Have we met before?"

"Just the one time through a curtain." This time she does not add the disclaimer to spare me the shame of ignorance.

"What are they doing? With us, I mean. Do you know?"

She glances to the outer room, perhaps looking for her chaperone, who I am now certain is the alchemist Lyrica.

"She's gone. I sent her to talk to my father about the wedding. Or lack of one, as it turns out."

Pressia—all four feet of her—relaxes and smiles at me. "They are breeding us to produce the next godling, of course. A little prince for Vinca."

"Why though? When they have Tarq and Pie?"

Her eyes narrow and her face changes. "You *know* them?"

"*You* know them?"

"Of course. I made them up."

"What? Well… I don't know about that, but I do know them. I'm… from the future." God, that sounded lame.

But this seems to be an acceptable answer to her, because she smiles big now and then laughs and claps her hands. "I did it! I really did it! All my friends said, 'No way, Pressia! No way will you ever change your future!' But did I listen? Gods no, I didn't! I just did my magic and poof! My life has changed!"

I actually laugh. Because all her feigned maturity disappears and she morphs into a seven-year-old before my very eyes. And finally, the word 'cute' has found its proper home in this tiny girl.

"I knew I could." She plants her hands on her hips. "I'm powerful, Pell."

"Oh, don't I know it. You will write books in the future, Pressia. Hundreds of them."

She gasps again. "Really!"

"Truly. You are a great alchemist. I have all of your books in my apothecary. I used the one on bags to tame some magic rings."

"Stop it!" And she slaps me on the chest. Which she can't even reach without going up on her tiptoes.

"But what *are* you?"

"What do you mean?"

"In the future, in those books, you drew pictures of yourself."

"Ooooooh. What did I look like? Tell me, please."

"Well, like this. But... you were a market nymph."

"Was I?"

"I guess. Are you a market nymph?"

"No! I'm a godling, silly. Like you. Except a girl. Of course."

"But what is that?"

"Wow. Well, we're made from all the gods. Actually, not all. You were made from all the gods and I was made from all the goddesses. Did they curse you? Is that why you're slow?"

The chuckle cannot be stopped. "Yes, for sure. But my memory, it's all messed up. So I don't understand anything. My hallways brought me here and—"

"Hallways! They're real!" She snickers. "And I thought I made them up!"

"What?"

She points to her dolls. And the dollhouse, which now that I look at it has a suspicious likeness to the... "Holy fucking shit. That's my sanctuary!"

She claps her hands. "I did it! I made it all real." Then she grabs my hand and tugs on it as she jumps up and down. "How did I do it?"

I shrug. "You're asking the wrong guy. But... wait. If you made up Saint Mark's—"

"Oh, my goddess! It's even got the same name?"

"You came up with that stupid name?"

"I had a dream about the future. Some man who wrote a book that went famous."

"*The* Saint Mark? Who wrote a gospel in the Bible?"

"He's real too!"

"And the lions?"

"Oh, those silly lions. They're everywhere, aren't they? They pop into all my fantasies. So, anyway. What's the question again?"

What *is* the question? "Oh. Right. What are they doing? If they've got Pie and Tarq to make their godling then why do they need us?"

"Oh." Her face falls and goes serious. "Yeah. That's a problem. It wasn't, when I thought it was a fantasy. But now that it's real..." Her blue eyes meet my yellow ones. "I dunno. What could it mean?"

"Well, just off the top of my head here, that... maybe... perhaps... we're not *necessary*?"

"Right." She spins, walks across the room, then spins again. "And the wedding is off, you say?"

"Definitely off. Something happened at some Caretaker Ceremony and all the plans have changed."

"Hmm. That wasn't in my fantasy."

I sigh. I like her. She would be a nice friend. But I'm so sick of this mystery.

"Perhaps"—she raises a finger—"perhaps this is not my fantasy."

"I'm not following."

"Perhaps... I just... tapped into the... truth? Maybe?"

298

"You mean like you have some kind of psychic power or something?"

"Psyche. Do we like her? I never did. She came to visit me once, asking all these questions about her man, and I found her kind of mean. Don't you think she's mean?"

"Not Psyche the goddess. The word. Which means… um. *Oracle*." I snap my fingers. "Yes. That's the word I'm looking for. Maybe you're an oracle."

"Oooooooh." She likes this idea. "Perhaps I am an oracle." Then she frowns. "Is that more or less powerful than being someone who can turn fantasies real?"

"Less, I think. But still very helpful."

She sighs. "Well, yes. I agree. And I write books, you say?"

"Very helpful books, Pressia. It's like…" I chuckle. "It's like you knew the future and wrote books that I would need. Too bad I just noticed most of them today. I could've put an end to all this bullshit two thousand years ago." But then I reconsider. "Well, then I would've never met Pie. And we wouldn't be in love."

Pressia gets a swoony look on her face. "Tell me more. I want to hear all the romantic details."

"Um… yeah. That's not gonna happen. You're like… seven."

"Like you're so mature. And I'm old enough to be your wife!"

"Sorry, kid, you're really not. But anyway. This was a very helpful conversation."

"Well, I'm glad I could help. But what happens to us now?"

"That's what I'm trying to figure out." And just as those words leave my mouth, a voice calls Pressia's name from the outer room.

"Lyrica is back." Pressia makes a motion of zipping her lips.

JA HUSS

"Right. My cue to leave. But I promise, I will be back when I get answers. I won't forget about you."

But as I walk away, I know this is a promise I do not keep.

It's a lie.

I know it's a lie because I *did* forget about her.

I actually forgot about her for thousands of years.

And then I get a little stabby pain in my heart.

Because whatever happened to her after this, she did not forget about me.

She wrote me books.

Books, and books, and books to guide me through the end of this curse.

*After I leave **Pressia*** I go looking for… Apis. I know this name. Not the guy, though he is a stunning double for Tarq. But I know this name. Or should I say, I know this god. Because Apis was an ancient bull deity who actually made it past the succession into the Greek pantheon. A sort of middleman between the top rulers of the times and… whoever.

I only know this much because a past slave caretaker— Odo, I think—was trying to trace my lineage and was concentrating on the line of succession of apis bulls. Because after the transition from Egyptian gods to Greek, there were many of these bulls. They built a whole—almost labyrinth— of tombs in… Memphis, I think.

It was kind of a weird thing too. Especially the transition into the Greek pantheon. Because the Greeks didn't have chimera gods. Or full-blooded animal gods. And the apis was both of these things. A real chimera—maybe even Tarq's double—in the beginning. And then bulls. Black bulls with special white markings. They—the people—they see these bulls the same way the Tibetans do the Dalai Lama. It is born, it is confirmed to be Apis. And when it dies, it reincarnates into a new calf body and they look out for the special markings to declare it the next Apis bull.

That's about the extent of my knowledge. But none of that matters. The only thing that does matter is that I am now pretty sure this Apis guy is the stone statue in front of the black tomb back at the sanctuary.

A Tarq knock-off.

The only thing he's missing is the golden horns and hooves. But when we were in the desert together this morning, he was dusty. Very dusty. So it's not much of a stretch to assume that those horns and hooves of his are indeed gold.

So obviously I need to get his story. Because so far, the hallways aren't opening up any doors to take me home.

Like it or not, I'm stuck here until the mystery of my beginning is unraveled.

*I ASK MANY, **many*** servants for the whereabouts of Apis, and they all give me an answer.

"He's in the black courtyard."

"He's out by the reflecting pond."

"He's with a woman in the east tower."

And about a dozen more places. I check all of these places and there is no Apis.

It's not until I go back to my apartment that I discover where he really is.

In my fucking rooms.

When I come in, there he is. Sitting—no, lounging—on a chaise in front of the terrace being fed grapes by a naked wood nymph chimera sitting in his lap.

They might actually be fucking.

"What the hell?" I slam the door behind me. "I've been looking everywhere for you."

The woman jumps up, shimmies a skirt up her legs, and leaves my apartments without a word.

Apis jumps up too, his dick still hard and rocking between his legs. Pie is right. It's gross. But luckily, he finds his pants, pulls them up, and leaves them unbuttoned as he walks across the room to help himself to my fruit bowl. "I've been here for hours waiting for you. Where the hell have you been?" He dangles a bunch of grapes over his upturned face and plucks one off with his teeth.

I don't like him. I thought he was Tarq and he's not. And for some reason I feel justified in holding that against him. "Visiting Pressia. Telling her that the wedding is off."

He's not surprised. So he already knew. "Yes. I got that message. Now what?"

"What do you mean?"

He walks over to me. "We're still partying tonight. Coming-of-age hasn't changed." Then he punches me in the arm. "Gotta get you laid."

I don't have the patience for this. I'm not interested in the party, or bedding a woman, or this place, to be honest.

Maybe I do come from here, but who cares? That was thousands of years ago. I'm pretty much just an American dude from the woods of PA at this point. Even if we are breaking the curse, I'm not going back to Rome. There is no place for me there. And Egypt is even more foreign than Rome.

This whole thing is stupid.

But instead of getting angry, I just sigh. Because there's no place for me anywhere. Not even Pennsylvania. I'm a satyr chimera. There will be no slipping into a normal life.

"You're thinking very hard, brother."

"What?"

Apis points at me. "What's on your mind?"

"Nothing."

"Pell. I know better. You're worried about something. What is it?"

"Well, for starters, what happens now? And don't say 'the party' because I don't care about the party."

"Tomorrow, you mean?"

"Yeah. And Pressia? What's gonna happen to her?"

Apis tilts his head at me. "Do we care? She was your broodmare, Pell. Not your soulmate."

"But... do you know?"

"What happens to you?" He shrugs. "Well, I did some spying and found out what happened at the Caretaker Ceremony."

"Really? What?"

"A little lioness was kidnapped by an eros!" He can barely contain his laughter.

"What?" Fuckin' eros. Why is he messing with my life like this? I mean, it's been two thousand years and he's still interfering. *Why?*

"Yeah. That guy. He can't take no for an answer, can he? Showed up, tried to steal her, and then a door popped open and off they went! Can you believe it?"

"What do you mean 'off they went?'"

"She was pulled through the door, Pell. By a disembodied hand. And she took the eros with her. Princess Pianna. That was her name."

"Pianna? You mean *Pie*?"

"Yeah. Little thing, about six, maybe. My brother was

JA HUSS

gonna wed her tomorrow." Then he points at me. "Same day as you. And... wow. Now both weddings have been called off. That's some coincidence, isn't it?" He frowns, his brows furrowing. "Hold on. Wasn't your dream girl called Pie?"

"Yes."

"She's the one you're after? My brother's promise?"

"Your brother? Tarq?"

Apis side-eyes me. "I only have one."

I turn away from him and run my hair over my shaved scalp. It's not smooth, it's got stubble. Which kind of reminds me of Pie's ass.

This thought lifts my mood, just a little bit.

And I've gotten some answers. My mind begins to wander back to our first trip up in the hallways. We were in the woods, running. And then we were kids. This is what Pie said, though I wasn't there.

Well, I was, I guess. But not as myself. I wasn't even an observer. This was her dream inside the memory. Or... something.

But the important part is that Pie was right. We *did* live at the same time. "How long has it been since I've seen Tarq?"

Apis shrugs. "I dunno. Maybe... last summer at the temple?"

The temple. I recall this from Pie's description of that memory as well. She saw a temple through the forest with her moth eyes. "Was Tomas at the temple?"

"The nasty blood dragon? Of course. Without the stupid dragon Ostanes would be powerless. She needs his blood the same way she needs yours." Then he grins at me and points to my horns. "You're not dumb enough to do what he did, so at least you know they'll never lock you up like that."

Wait. Did he just insinuate that Ostanes is bleeding Tomas out for magic blood? And also imply that they've been doing that to me too, except I've been cooperative? "Lock me up like *what?*"

"Like the fuckin' dragon. Like those stupid monsters they walked into the palace today. They're on their way to the Bottoms too."

"The monsters. The prisoners?" I turn away, shocked. Though I don't know why I should be. I know there are prisoners in the Bottoms. And Pie just told me that she thinks our monsters belong there too.

And maybe I don't know a lot about those guys, but I've been around them for over a month now and I do know one thing. They have magic. Big magic. Not just Batty, either, who brought Madeline back to life as a dragon. But Cookie makes some pretty magnificent magic food and Eyebrows can tailor the fuck out of royal fabrics.

She's stealing our magic. That's what Ostanes is doing. But how? How did we get here? Or, better question, how did *I* get *there?* To Saint Mark's?

How did this day turn into that place?

Because this is where it all started, obviously.

Maybe I should go back to Pressia and get her little oracle ass to spit out more answers?

But I don't do that. I already know I don't do that. Because I never see her again and she writes me books to guide me through the curse.

I turn back to Apis, who has been staring at me as I work this all out. He's starting to get suspicious. I can see it on his face. "Are you OK, Pell?"

I'm not. I'm confused, I'm conflicted, and I'm tired of this. I want these answers and don't want these answers. I want to go home, and hug Pie, and maybe even chat with Tomas, and forget about all this stuff.

I want my sanctuary back.

I want my curse back.

I want all the monsters to leave, I want Pie to do some spelling to hide Saint Mark's from any and all prying eyes, and I want us to live in our curse forever.

And it's not gonna happen.

It's over. The curse has been broken. Why else would the hallways have me up here stumbling into answers to questions I never really had?

"Pell?"

Apis is looking more than suspicious now. It might be panic. And I have to remind myself that he's not on my side. Whatever is happening to me here in this palace, it's not good. And he's OK with this. If this were happening to Tarq, I would not be OK with it. Friends protect each other. And whatever Ptah is using me for—breeding the next godling, bleeding me out for bloodhorn magic, whatever it is—Apis has no objections. He is not going to protect me.

"Sorry." I sigh the word out as I massage the middle of my forehead with my fingers. "Life is just changing pretty quick, ya know?"

"I get it."

"And I don't know what comes next."

"Well, I do."

"What?" I turn to look him in the eyes. He's not my friend, and I want my friend. I know Pie doesn't trust Tarq, but I do. And I want him to be here so bad right now so we can figure this out together. But this jerk is all I've got.

"We get drunk, of course." Apis is either simple or conniving. He has a one-track mind tonight. But it is my coming-of-age so it's hard to tell if he's just looking for a party or pacifying me with booze. He's got a decanter in his hand. He holds it up and shoots me a charismatic look. "Let's get this party started. We can think about the rest of that shit tomorrow."

I don't want to be here tomorrow. I want to leave right now.

I walk over to the closest door, open it up, and hope.

But there's not a new world on the other side. Just a bedroom.

I walk to the next door, do the same thing—and find the same thing.

"Pell."

I walk to the next door, open it up, silently praying to the hallway gods to just give me a break and take me home.

They're not listening.

"*Pell.*"

I just exhale and turn to Apis. "What?"

"What are you doing?"

"Looking for the door home."

"What?" He's chuckling. "Did you start drinking without me? Don't pass out before dark, friend. I've got a special surprise for you later."

Pass out before dark? Finally, an option I can deal with.

So I walk back over to Apis, take the decanter, put it to my lips, and down a good measure of the drink inside.

It's wine and it smells like the forest and tastes like the past.

Apis claps me on the back, roaring with approval.

Fuck it.

I do need to get drunk.

I will get drunk, and pass out, and maybe, if I'm lucky, I will wake up at home.

I tip the decanter to my lips again, and this time, I finish the whole thing.

I DO NOT WAKE **up at home.**

I'm not even sure I wake up. My eyes are open, but I don't even know where I am.

The room is… a tent. Which makes me chuckle. Because it's like a billowy tent made of very feminine fabrics. And it's purple.

I laugh again as I spit the word out. "Purple."

And I'm on pillows. Giant, velvety pillows. The air is thick with incense. And when I inhale, it makes me cough. Then my head spins.

It's not incense.

And for some reason, I find this so funny that I guffaw up at the tent poles.

"And then…" I look to my left and find Apis with a gryphon chimera writhing in his lap. They are fucking, and he's just looking at me like it's no big deal as he tells his story. "Do you want to know what happened then?"

"Tell me," I manage through my laughter. "Tell me. I'm dying!"

"Then they started spelling her! Oh, my gods, Pell. Tarq was fuming in his letter. He said they cursed her, and cursed her, and cursed her. And then they turned her royal gryphon ass into a trashy little wood nymph chimera and then—*then*…"

"Wait." I stop laughing. "What are we talking about?"

"W-w-what?" Apis chokes this out between fits. "The little girl. That fantasy of yours. What did I call her earlier? Oh! Tarq's broodmare!" Meanwhile, he's still fucking the gryphon chimera in his lap, his fingertips gripping her hips so hard, her velvety, golden skin is turning white.

That's when I notice that there are several more gryphon chimera around us. One is rubbing her hand up and down my leg. I push her off and she goes flying backward into another mound of plush pillows, squealing with protest.

"What'd you do that for?" Apis asks.

I stand up, shake my head to try to clear the intoxication. It doesn't help much because the tent is thick with the smoke of opium.

I cough, stumbling to the edge of the tent, searching for the flap of a door. It takes me several seconds to find it. And by this time, Apis is up and next to me. "Pell, what are you doing?"

I push through the flap, sucking in fresh air.

"Pell!" Apis follows me, grabbing my arm.

I turn on him, baring my teeth. I'm a teenager, not a fully mature satyr with anger issues. So this threat is nothing like it will be in the future. But it's enough, because even though Apis is older, more muscular, and more formidable than me, he backs off.

I growl at him. "Finish the story."

"What story?"

"The little gryphon girl. What happened to her?"

"Is this what's got you all upset?"

"Answer the question."

"They cursed her with spells. The eros was taking her. He's been banished from the pantheon, Pell. He's not entitled to the riches the rest of us are."

"Rest of *us?*" But that's not what he means. And this is when it becomes clear. He's not talking about me. I am not one of the 'us.' I am something they are *entitled* to. Because I am not a god. I am a god*ling*. Something less. Something more, though, too.

Because I am magic.

I am… a tool.

"What kind of curses?"

He shrugs. "Tarq wasn't specific, if you're asking for the spellings. He just said they took away her gryphon magic. But it wasn't hers to keep, anyway. All the magic of animals belongs to the temple. But I don't have to tell you that. You know this better than anyone."

And there it is. The proof. Not only that they see me as something less, but it's worse than that. They see me as an

JA HUSS

animal, not a person. "They turned her into a wood nymph chimera?"

"So sad, right? But that's not the worst part."

"What else?"

"By the time she was pulled through the door, she was a *human!*"

I turn away, trying to get my bearings about where the fuck I am. Trying to fit all these pieces together. Trying to understand what it all means.

I get it. To these people, I am a magic animal to be used for my bloodhorn. It makes sense. But Pie? This is how she ended up with that shitbag of a mother, it has to be.

This Caretaker Ceremony cursed her to a life as a human in a world where there is no magic.

But is that really true? Because PA, from my perspective—and especially my little area of it—is overflowing with magic.

Apis puts a hand on my shoulder. Squeezing. Mimicking comfort, or understanding, or sympathy.

But he feels none of those things. I can tell.

The Apis bull, from one of the lesser-known legends, was *feared*. No. Wrong word. In that legend, people were terrified of him. And when he died, they did numerous ceremonies to make sure he would never return. Things like pull out all his organs—even his heart—and put them inside jars. Which was something they often did with mummification. But in the case of Apis, they used twelve jars, not just four. And they didn't mummify his body, they burned it inside the sarcophagus before sealing the lid and filling the cover with inscriptions. Spellings. To curse his remains and keep him contained.

They didn't even store the jars in the same tomb. They took them hundreds of miles away and buried them in different places, just like the legend of the god Osiris. In fact, there is some speculation that Apis and Osiris were the same god.

These jars were never found, so modern people don't even know how much he was hated. It's just something I had known, but had forgotten, and now remember.

Later, the personality of Apis was conveyed into a black bull with specific white markings. And that's how the myths stayed. The original Apis—and the fear he evoked—faded into obscurity and the blessing of the stupid bull became something more palatable.

But I am not in the company of the bull.

I am in the company of the god. One of the most powerful ever known and whose cult outlasted *all* the others.

I turn and look at him. "What are you doing?"

He screws up his face, then puts his hands up in some kind of innocent shrug. And this, I realize—this... charm, or charisma, or enchantment he's doing—is all an act. "I'm getting you drunk, brother."

"We're not brothers. You only have one, remember?"

"Hmm." He smiles. Smugly. "Maybe the better question is... what are *you* doing, Pell?" Then he narrows his eyes at me. "That is you, right? Because I don't see much of you in those yellow eyes of yours lately."

This is a dangerous moment. Because he knows I am not some young, wide-eyed, willing participant who can be pacified with drink and sex. Maybe it's just a gut feeling he's getting due to my odd behavior and admissions about a dream girl named Pie. But maybe it's something else.

"You asked about Pressia earlier."

Fear. That's my first reaction. But I get a hold of it. "What about her?"

"She's been taken care of."

"How?" My voice comes out with the rumble of power.

This makes Apis smile. "There it is."

"There what is?" I decide to play dumb.

"The power. The next level. The destruction."

I can't breathe at the moment. Because he's right. That *is* the purpose of this voice.

Destruction.

"Let's get to the point, shall we?"

"That would be great." My voice is still booming. "What happened to Pressia?"

"Funny thing, actually. She"—he shrugs—"seems to have disappeared."

"Disappeared how?"

"Through a door. And that's another funny thing. No one has had door magic in millennia. And suddenly, there are two of them in two days. First your little lioness *Pie* gets pulled through one"—he sneers her name—"and now your little broodmare conjures one up out of nowhere. Isn't this a coincidence?"

"Maybe."

"Or maybe not."

"I thought you wanted to get to the point?"

"I do. But… not quite yet. Because this is the pre-show, Pell. The main attraction is still upcoming."

And then a hand comes over my mouth from behind, and before I can stop myself, I suck in air. Only to get a healthy dose of poppy oil.

I'm falling backwards. And Apis is looming over me as my head begins to spin. "Don't worry, brother. It's all gonna turn out just the way it should." He smiles down at me. "And don't worry about the little lioness. We have ruined her forever. She will not be a problem. And by the way, just so it's clear, she was never yours, Pell. And now she never will be."

The poppy oil kicks in hard, dulling his words and making him fuzzy.

The next thing I see is blackness.

I WAKE **up slowly to the sound of drums**. Loud, thumping beats in a slow, almost suspenseful rhythm that bounce off the insides of my brain, making me cringe. My eyes are closed, not quite ready to cooperate, and I don't try to move. Can't, actually. I'm upright, standing, but I'm tied to something. A pole, maybe. But even without opening my eyes I understand that there are flames all around me. I can see the flickering yellow and orange through my eyelids and the heat coming at me from all directions is intense.

It doesn't hurt, though.

And I'm not surprised at that. I am a man of fire, after all.

The drums abruptly stop and a voice booms out, taking the place of the beat. It is Apis and he is spelling something into existence.

"A HORN, *a hoof, an eye, a bone.*
Forgotten gods will now be known
Two thousand years we bred them well
Beasts of magic, blood, and spells.

THE BLOODHORN *of the monster Pell*
Full of might and the fires of Hell
He gives it to us, he makes us blessed
And we take it from his beastly flesh

SO HEAR US NOW, *you overlords*
We did your bidding, we endured
The gods of future and of fate
Will grant us power to create."

. . .

EVEN THOUGH MY eyes are still closed and the poppy oil, not to mention the words of Apis, have subdued me and made me slow and foggy, I can sense that there is big magic going on all around me. I don't need the sudden rise of flames and heat to signal that. Whatever is happening in this room, I am… connected to it.

"No." This voice in my head is so clear. And it belongs to Tomas. "No, Pell. You're not connected to it. You *are* it."

I struggle, just trying out my bindings. But the chains are tight, their strength perhaps even magnified with magic. I am unable to move.

"Not true." Again, it's Tomas. "You're the biggest power in this room, Pell. Chains? Please. When have chains ever contained you?"

Never, actually. I can't remember a single time I've been in chains.

"Exactly. Just… take a breath. Clear your head. You still have about two minutes before they cut it off and take your horns—"

What?

"Yes. Your magic is in your horns. They're just going to take the whole head, though."

"I thought I was getting married?"

I didn't mean to speak out loud, but it happens. It's not loud, barely a moan, but it captures the attention of Apis, because he answers me.

"That was before your little lion girl escaped through a door, my friend. That threw us off the track. So, apologies, brother. But this is how it has to be."

I take a deep breath, like Tomas suggested, and then force my eyes open. It takes several moments for me to even focus, let alone find the face of Apis.

"There he is." Apis is grinning at me. "Welcome back, friend."

"Friend?"

Apis chuckles, then looks around, which makes me look around too. All the gods and goddesses are there, a ring of power standing around the edge of the small, circular room. The flames are coming from their palms, dancing along their fingers and rising up into the air.

In the middle of this circle are me and Apis. But we are not alone.

Saturn, Zeus, Cronus, and Ptah mark the four corners within the magic circle.

The top of the pyramid, so to speak. The capstone of sorcery. The succession.

The whole purpose of this—of me, actually—clearly manifests in a sudden and shocking revelation.

They are dying. All of them. A new religion is rising up, taking their place. And they are dying.

Dead already, really.

I play Apis's words back in my head. *Two thousand years we bred them well. Beasts of magic, blood, and spells.* And now I fully understand. They have been preparing for this day.

Perhaps they foretold it. Perhaps they heard it from an oracle thousands of years ago. But they have been preparing for this day.

And someone just fucked it all up.

The breeding wasn't done yet. Pie was supposed to breed with Tarq and I was supposed to breed with Pressia. And perhaps those children of that next generation were the real sacrifice—because that's what's going on here, let's not kid ourselves.

I am about to be sacrificed.

But there will be no final generation of royal beasts to give to the overlords in exchange for a fresh beginning. A new rise of old gods, if you will. Because Eros took Pie. He slipped her right out of this world and put her in the human one.

And Pressia has disappeared. Definitely an oracle. How she got a hold of a door, I will probably never know.

But I don't need to know the details to understand the grand scheme.

This is their last chance.

Me. I am their last chance.

My bloodhorn sacrifice could be enough to satisfy the overlords and give them back their power.

But if all the old and damaged gods are in this room with me—the major ones from the succession, at least—then who is controlling all this?

Who are *they* begging for relief?

"Come on, Pell. Come on!" Tomas's voice is back in my head. He sounds a bit exasperated. "Think hard, my slow friend. Think! Who controls things where we come from?"

At first, I don't understand. But my mind clears a bit and it suddenly hits me.

"The hallway gods."

"What?" Apis is staring at me.

"It's the hallway gods."

He looks confused. And of course he does. He doesn't know that I have lived with gods for two thousand years. He has no idea who I am.

I mean, *I* hardly know who I am, but I certainly know where I come from. I certainly know where I've been. And I understand that time is tricky and the hallway gods have been holding my memories.

Not *from* me.

But *for* me.

Because whatever has been happening to me in that sanctuary, it took time. A lot of time. And maybe, just maybe, I've been waiting for the right girl to come along and give me a little push.

And now here I am, ready.

"Let's get on with it," Saturn bellows. "Do it."

Apis nods at him like an equal, not a servant. He turns to face the damaged gods and raises up his arms. Everyone in the room raises their arms too, the flames from the outer circle throwing shadows on the wall. Climbing, evil shadows that lick the ceiling and haunt the air.

"You're almost out of time now," Tomas says. "Better get cracking."

Cracking how?

"Magic, Pell. You know how to do it."

Well... this is true. I do understand magic. A lot more than I used to before Pie came. I have a new voice.

"That's not enough," Tomas informs me. "To use a door, you need a ring."

I look down at my hand, and yep. Still got the ring.

"It's not enough," Tomas repeats. "To use a ring and a door, you need a *spell*."

A spelling, of course.

All the gods begin a chant. It's loud, and rumbling. Like they all have the same voice I do.

Their words are spilling out. "'A horn, a hoof, an eye, a bone...'"

And this panics me. "Tomas! Where do I go? What do I do?"

I yell this loud enough for Apis to hear me. He falters in his chant, looking at me strangely, probably working out that there's more magic in this room than he knows about.

Because Tomas is here. Maybe not corporeally, but Tomas exists in many forms. And he *is* here.

But there's nothing Apis can do now. They are now reciting the second line of their spelling. It's in progress.

"You go *home*, Pell! You go home! And you better do it quick!"

Home.

The sanctuary.

My life.

My world.

My everything.

But not just my everything. My every*one*.

So just as the the gods finish the third line of their spelling, I begin my first. And it rumbles out of my mouth with the power of a desperate man, shaking the room and making all their magic shrink back in fear. The chains holding me break with a crack that lights up the room. And I am on fire.

Literally on fire. Casting new shadows on the walls.

My hands come up and a ball of light appears between them just as the words I have read a million times over two thousand years come spilling out of my mouth:

"'A horn, a hoof, an eye, a bone. A man, a girl, a place of stone. A tick of time, a last mistake, keep them safe behind the gate.'"

And as soon as I'm done, I stand there among the once-great gods and goddesses, a line of succession that goes back nearly eight thousand years, all silent and shrinking now, and I laugh.

Because it was *me*.

I am the maker of my own curse.

Just when I'm about to breathe a sigh of relief—honestly, it's more like total satisfaction—a new fire appears between my hands, but I'm not controlling it.

And then, before I know what's happening, I'm spelling again. Only this time, like Pie earlier in the day, these words come out of me without my bidding.

They are powerful.

They shake the whole fucking world.

They rumble the room and make the old gods fall to their knees, cowering with hands shielding their faces.

"Love is *mad and love is heat,*
    Can win you wars or hand you defeat.

318

It claims the heart, the mind, and soul,
Can make you weak or make you whole.

DAMAGED GODS, savage saints,
And royal beasts locked in restraints.
Hold them hostage, in between,
A hallway's never-ending stream.

CURSE you good and curse you all.
My blood and fire will make you fall.
Revenge is cold, and dark, and deep.
But in the end, it is still sweet."

AND THEN, when I look up, the shadows on the walls take on a new shape.

Wings.

A bow.

And an arrow coming right at me.

It strikes me in the chest hard and fast, knocking me forward, and the next thing I know, I am stumbling through a door.

PART FOUR

Love is not enough to change.
The ending of a man of fame.
Give it up, you won't succeed.
Because your love is based in greed.

CHAPTER NINETEEN - TOMAS

*A*fter I watch Pell go back up the stairs and into his hallway adventure, I turn with a sigh, a good feeling surging through my heart, like everything is going to work itself out.

The next thing I know I'm being attacked. Madeline headbutts me straight in the chest and I go reeling backward, arms flailing, eyes wide with surprise, and a laugh bursting from my lungs.

I land hard on the stone floor and then slide a good while until finally I crash headfirst into the wall on the other side of the dungeon.

"You did this to me!" Madeline is wailing, coming at me with claws drawn, one hand held high like she's about to swipe it down my face.

I scramble to sit up, and then I clap my hands for her. Because I was afraid that this was it. That she was going to be lost in the transition for centuries and all I'd be left with would be her base instincts. "My love! You're back!"

Honestly, I don't mind base instincts. So this resurgence of her old personality is just a bonus.

"*Back*!" She screams this as she takes that swipe, aiming for my eyes. But I'm a good ducker and scamper out of the way. "Look at me! Just…" She glances down at herself, gets a little lost in the blood-red scales all up and down her arms, then looks back at me and bursts into tears.

"Oh, Madeline." I walk forward, ready to give her a hug.

She puts up a hand, palm out, in a full-stop motion. "Get the hell away from me, you freak!"

"Now, now. Let's not start name-calling yet. We've got thousands of years of honeymoon to get through first."

"Are you insane?"

"Not at all. Why do you ask?"

"What the hell is happening!" This is not a yell or even a scream. This is a shriek. She's losing it.

"Madeline, just calm down."

"Calm down!" Her eyes are wild and roiling with fire and brimstone, alternating between red and yellow. Which is normal. All blood dragons have lava eyes. "One moment I'm... I'm... well, not exactly a normal girl, but pretty close, and I'm dating a hot guy—" She begins to sob.

I reach out, but she snaps her teeth at me. Which are considerably sharper now, so I take a step back.

"—and then..." She begins to hyperventilate. "Then... then the next thing I know, I'm being shot—"

"That was not me, darling. That was Russ Roth."

"—and then... then..." Again, she pauses to give a breathy display of confusion. "Then I'm... this!" She points to herself.

"I know," I say. Softly. It feels like it fits the moment. "You were dead."

"What?" She blinks at me.

"Dead. The bullet killed you, darling."

"No. Because clearly"—she's shrieking again—"I'm still here! And I'm a fucking *dragon*!"

I hold up a finger to point out an inconsistency in her observation. "Not quite yet, my love. It's a long transition and you—"

"Shut! Up!"

OK. Clearly, my sweet Madeline needs a moment to process. So I zip it.

We stare at each other for a moment, her wild eyes and my loving ones. Honestly, I just want to wrap my arms around her and give her a good, long squeeze. But as I'm thinking these thoughts, she snarls at me.

This makes me smile.

"What are you smiling about? There's nothing to smile about!"

"Oh, there is so much to smile about. You have no idea how long I've been waiting for someone like you."

She holds out her arm. She's covered in scales. But for some reason, she's fixated on this arm. Probably because that's where the scales first started to appear long before I showed up. "What is this?"

"You're a dragon, darling."

"No."

"Yes."

"You did this to me."

"I didn't. I wouldn't, Madeline. I like you. I would like to spend the rest of my life with you. But you can't just turn someone into a dragon. You know that, right? You know that. It was inside you before I got here. The scales."

Again, she glances down at her arm, then looks back up at me, waiting for… something.

"But hear me, dear. Even if I could do this kind of magic, I never would." I shake my head at her. "I *never* would."

She starts to cry again. But this time, when I approach, she doesn't have the will to push me away. So I put my arm around her, lead her over to the nest, and help her sit down on the edge. Then I fold her into my chest and stroke her hair, which was always a beautiful strawberry color, but is now an even more brilliant shade of fire.

We sit there like that for a good while. She's got her face buried against me and she continues to sob, but quietly now. And I watch the eggs as their outer shells ripple with colors as they transition between wicked shades of thunderstorm blue, seafoam green, and bruised purple.

Eventually, she rests her head on my thigh with her face turned away from me and asks, "What happens now?"

I let out a long breath. "Well. Everything."

"That's not an answer. What happens to *me?*"

"You will... change completely."

"Explain this."

"You will turn into a dragon."

She sits up a little and faces me, blinking. "You mean, like you?"

This is what she wants to hear. That she will jump right to chimera stage. But... that's not how it works. I don't even know what I am. Maybe one gets to be a man again after a few thousand years of burning things down, being imprisoned, turning into a part-time ghost, and then being a full-time chimera.

But then again, perhaps that's not how it works at all. Perhaps what happened to me is just a right-time-right-place kind of thing.

"No. I don't think that's what comes next, darling."

She's growling now. "Then tell me what does!"

"You will turn into a dragon."

She's shaking her head. And while I would prefer that we not have this conversation for a few decades, she's asking. So it's my duty to tell her.

"You will grow big. And long. And wide. And one day, you will have wings and a burning sensation inside you. And then, when you're not even expecting it, you will open your mouth and out will come fire."

She just stares at me. Unblinking. Like she's trying to wrap her head around all this. Then she's shaking it. "No. No. This is not going to be my life. I would rather kill myself."

I gasp. "*Madeline!*"

"What?" And again, she's snarling. "I don't want to be a monster like—"

She doesn't say it. But she doesn't have to. "Like me, you mean."

She breathes. That's all. Doesn't answer.

"Well, I'm not trying to be mean here. I'm really not. But when one is dwelling in the realm of *fantasy*"—it comes out a bit mocking, because I've got feelings too, but then I rein it in —"one needs the truth more than ever. And here is the truth, my dear Madeline. You were already a monster. You were born a monster, just like the rest of us."

"Rest of... us?" Her poor face. She's so vulnerable and confused. "Rest of who?"

"Well, Pell and me, of course. And Pie. And, well, all the monsters here at Saint Mark's. It's our sanctuary."

"A sanctuary for monsters?"

I pan my hands wide with a smile. "Welcome, Madeline. Welcome to the monsters of Saint Mark's. You will be perfectly safe here—" But no sooner are these words out of my mouth than I realize it's a lie.

"What?" she asks. "Why did you stop?"

"Well, truth be told, it's not safe here. The curse is ending, the whole place is crumbling, and honestly, shit's really fucked up."

Again, she blinks at me. But then, a moment later, a chuckle rumbles out of her. Like it came from deep within her belly.

I manage a smile as well.

"I don't think I've ever heard you swear."

"Well, I already have a reputation as a boorish and vulgar fire-breathing lout. So I try not to swear in front of ladies if I can help it. But it's the times and all. They are a-changing."

"So I'm basically fucked."

"Fucked." Now it's my turn to chuckle. "Yep. But"—I hold up a finger—"think about it, Madeline. Aren't we all? I mean, we are, of course. But isn't everyone fucked? It's all pretty fucked."

She blows out a breath, rests her head back on my thigh, and relaxes. "I guess. Life before this was…"

She trails off and doesn't pick up.

I could fill in the blanks. A little, at least. I could point out that Uncle Jim was an asshole who had a very low opinion of her. I could point out that she comes from a line of eros. This is certainly true. And I could point out that no one at Saint Mark's has anything to do with her dragon genetics.

But she knows all this, even the part about Big Jim. So there's no point in bringing it all up.

"And the eggs?"

"Mine. From a long time ago."

"You had someone else? I mean, before me?"

"No. All dragons lay eggs. It's the only reproductive strategy that works. Often, there is only one or two of us alive on the earth at any one time. We'd just die out if there had to be two of us to lay eggs. But to hatch them, you need two. They do last for thousands of years, obviously. And once two dragons are in close proximity of the eggs, they mature quite quickly. It's actually a horrible way to reproduce, but it's the best we can do."

"We're going to hatch them, aren't we?"

"Well, of course."

She sits up now. All the way up so she's actually sitting next to me. "But… the world."

"What about it?"

"You said it wasn't safe here. And it was crumbling."

"It is." It comes out tired.

"So what's the point? If they're just going to die?"

"Oh, they're not going to die."

"How do you figure?"

"Well, actually, I haven't gotten that far yet."

"And we're going to die too."

"Absolutely not."

"How do you figure?"

"Well…"

"Let me guess. You haven't gotten that far yet."

I'm just about to wilt, because she's right, but then I remember something important. I jump up to my feet and point across the dungeon. "Oh! We have a door!"

Madeline gets up as well and we both walk over to the door. I closed it after Pie left. I didn't like the shimmering nothingness on the other side. It looked like a wall of mercury.

"Pie gave it to me. Actually…" I pause to think about this. "I'm not really sure it was Pie."

"Who is Pie?"

"Oh, I forgot. You haven't met anyone yet. She's a magnificent alchemist. One of the best ever. She commands rings, and doors, and spellings—"

I'm about to go on and on about Pie's merits when Madeline growls again. Only this time, it's not some newborn dragon growl. It's serious.

And when I look over, I have just enough time to skip back out of the way before her considerable teeth try to snap me in half.

She follows, waving those claws in the air, trying to take my face off. Her eyes are pure lava now. And I realize that I fell into a too-comfortable comradery with my dear baby dragon here. And I forgot what she really is.

A monster.

It was nice to have another real conversation with her. But that's not her. Not anymore.

And this is my reminder.

Maybe tomorrow she will snap out of it again and remember what she used to be. And we can talk for a little while, discussing what comes next.

But then again, it might be a thousand years before we have another chat.

I retreat up the stairs, only going far enough that she doesn't follow, and then I sit on a step, once again alone.

AFTER A LONG WHILE I go back down the stairs and peek around the final turn, much like Pie did earlier today. Madeline is sleeping on top of the eggs, arms and legs spread wide, her dragon instincts to protect the next generation kicking in.

When I step back into the room, I notice that the gemstones embedded into the walls are glowing a little. They haven't done that since Pell left. But it gives off a nice glow, making the dungeon, and the blood dragon in it, look soft and romantic.

It was nice to have that talk with Madeline. Maybe she will never remember it, so it's more for my benefit than hers. But I feel better for having explained a little, at least.

But then my eyes drift down to the eggs and their muted colors.

Madeline had a point. The world is no place for tender babies. And even though newborns from eggs are fully formed, just very small, they will be able to breathe fire by the end of their first day.

That's another reason why we are so few. It's not like they'll come out looking like me. Or Madeline, for that matter. She's a genetic anomaly and I've already lived through all the life stages these little beasts will be presented with.

We're hard to hide once we're born.

And the sanctuary is crumbling. Even Pell had to admit it. It's not going to last much longer.

Which means we can't stay here. Not if we want to live. And despite Madeline's desperate threat to harm herself, if she can just hang in there long enough to get past this beast stage, she will see that…

But even I can't muster up that level of delusion.

Will she become like me?

I don't know.

It's just as likely that she will be a beast forever, with no concept whatsoever that there is any other way to exist.

And if this is what happens to her, won't this happen to the children too?

Maybe she's right? Maybe this is not a place to raise a family.

Which means… I must take us somewhere safe.

And, of course, that was always my reasoning for asking for a door. But I hadn't actually thought it through when I made that request to Pie. I just knew I had to leave.

I walk back over to the door and this is when I notice something weird.

The doorknob has fallen off and is sitting on the dungeon floor. It's glowing a soft shade of pink. My eyes track up to the walls, where the gemstones are also glowing a soft shade of pink.

Then I look back down at the doorknob. "No. It can't be."

I walk over to the wall, grab the nearest gemstone, and pluck it right out.

And do you know what it is?

A doorknob!

I go back over to the door, push it inside the hole where the doorknob goes, and then turn it.

THE DOOR OPENS AND—ON the other side is a little girl.

She's got long, blonde hair, a sweet, sweet face, and a fancy light-green dress that looks like Eyebrows made it from royal fabrics and that falls all the way to the floor. There's a golden-yellow sash around her waist.

Atop her head is a crown of flowers, on her wrists are bracelets that clink, and around her neck is a gemstone that looks suspiciously like a dragon-dungeon doorknob.

She's playing with a dollhouse. And she's got little dolls that look like monsters. There's one like Pell, and one like Pie, and there's even a dragon. And that's when I notice that it's not a dollhouse at all.

It's Saint Mark's Sanctuary. In miniature.

Her head tilts in my direction and she squints. I haven't walked through the door, so I don't think she can see me. But she certainly can sense me. "Are you going to hurt me?"

I step through and smile. "Never."

She giggles. "I already knew that." Then she holds up the dragon doll. "It's you, right?"

I shrug. "Where am I?"

"You're at the palace."

"What am I doing here?" I don't know why I'm asking her, she's a child from another realm. And, of course, I know why I'm here. I came through the door.

"I think you're looking for something."

"I am, actually. A safe place to take my family."

She frowns. "Well, that wouldn't be here."

"No. I suppose not."

She points to my hand, which is still holding the doorknob. "Do you have more of those?" Then her fingers go to her neck. "Or did you come to ask for mine?"

"Oh." I let go of the doorknob. "No. I have plenty. Hundreds, actually."

"Really?"

"Truly."

"Where did you get them?"

"Pie."

"Pie?"

"My friend. She gave me the door too. Well, she gave me the knobs first, then the door. But I didn't ask for the knobs. She just sputtered out a spelling and, well"—I throw up my arms—"there they were."

"Lucky. I don't have a door for this one." She points to the gemstone around her neck. "But I know it can take me somewhere."

I look back at my door. My one and only door. Then I look back at the little girl. "Do you need to leave?"

"Not yet. But probably soon."

"Where would you go?"

She bits her lip, then looks at her dollhouse. "There." She points at it too.

"That's where I come from."

"Really?"

"You can come back with me, if you want. But I have to warn you, it's not safe there anymore. We have to leave too."

"Well, thank you for the offer, but I can't. Not yet. Someone is coming to see me and I have to be here when he arrives."

"Is he good?"

"I think he is. But I can't know for sure."

"Well…" I don't know what else to do. This is the wrong doorknob, obviously. "I guess I should be going."

"Can you leave me the door?"

I wince, looking at my door. My one and only door. "I don't know how to do that."

"Can you just… tell it stay when you leave?"

"But I'll need to use it again. I'm searching for a safe place for my family."

"Oh. Well, doors can go more than one place, you know."

I brighten at this news. "Can they?"

"Oh, yeah. They're like hallways." She giggles. "I don't even know what that means. I just... see words in my head and then, if I think it's important, I tell people about it."

"Like hallways," I repeat. Maybe she doesn't understand her words, but I certainly do. "Where I come from"—I point at the dollhouse—"hallways can take you places. But only memories. Not real places. That's why I need a door. This is the first doorknob I've ever tried. So I should probably be getting back so I can try out more."

"And you'll leave the door?" Her expression is cheerful and her tone is light. But she's worried underneath. "All you have to do is remove the doorknob before you leave. Then you'll keep this place and"—her fingertips play with the gemstone at her neck—"I can use it too. With my doorknob."

I think about this for a moment. "It's like a bookmark?"

The little girl giggles. "It's exactly like a bookmark. Then you can come back. All you have to do is use the same door-knob. It's been assigned now, and you remove the doorknob when you leave."

"How interesting. It's like a ring, then."

She smiles at me, her whole face lit up. "Oh, yes! It's almost the same thing. But rings need spells and they are not preassigned. Doorknobs don't need spellings. They already know where to go."

"Of course. That makes sense. But if I leave the door here, might someone find it? Someone we don't want to find it?"

"Oh, don't worry about that. They're invisible unless you have a doorknob or a ring. It's a key, you see."

Invisible. I can't help myself, I look around, wondering how many there are in this room. I wonder if I'm standing at the threshold of one right now and I just don't have the right tools to see it.

"There are possibilities everywhere, Tomas."

I squint at her. Because I don't think we introduced ourselves.

"Possibilities," she says, slowly twirling in the center of the room with her arms out, "and opportunities. I bet there are thousands right here in the palace. But we don't have the rings or doorknobs to see them."

She walks over to the window and throws the curtains open. This is when I realize we're in the desert somewhere. There are pyramids in the distance, and a hot wind comes through, blowing bits of ribbon and paper across the floor.

The little girl turns to face me again, her cheeks pink with excitement. "They're everywhere, don't you see?"

I just stare at her for a moment, trying to figure her out. But then I answer, "I do see." And I smile at her. "And look at you. How clever you are. You're like a little encyclopedia, aren't you?"

She's laughing when she replies. "I don't know what that is."

"A little fountain of knowledge. A little computer." I point at her. "You're like a phone. Filled with information and small enough to carry in a pocket."

We both laugh now. And all the worry and tension drains out of me for a moment.

"I like you," she says. "Maybe we'll see each other again one day."

"I'm sure we will."

It's something one says to be polite, but as I turn away from her, pull my doorknob out, and walk back through the door, I find that I really mean it.

*I EXIT **the door back in my dungeon*** and suddenly, and for the first time ever, it feels so hot and stifling in here, I find myself backing up the moment my feet hit the stone floor.

But the door behind me is just a curtain of shimmering silver because I'm holding the doorknob in my hand. So there's no escape.

And it's not like I even want to escape. It's just... there's something about my dungeon that feels... different now. And it's not just the sticky, humid air or the lack of ventilation.

It doesn't feel entirely mine anymore.

Which is fine. I'm not selfish. I'm willing to share. Especially with Madeline and the eggs.

But it's more than that.

For thousands of years I've been the only one down here and now I've got company. But it's not that people have been added, it's more like... I've been erased.

Not entirely, of course. But a little bit. Yes. A little bit of me has been erased to make room for a little bit of them.

Interesting.

Anyway. I shake myself out of this introspection and walk over to the wall. Then I put the gemstone back where I got it and scratch a note in the stone just above it to keep track of where it goes. I didn't get the girl's name, so I call her "Smart Friend."

Madeline growls behind me from her corner of shadows. I turn, squinting my eyes to see her better in the darkness. She's... gone again.

I like that she's a dragon. Rather, I *will* like that she's a dragon. One day.

It's just... it's going to take so long for her to mature and be something more than a fiery beast. Thousands of years, probably. I'm willing to wait, that's not my problem. It was so nice to have a real friend. A girlfriend. A partner. Someone to talk to. And I know I have Pie, and Pell, and the monsters, but I want Madeline.

The *other* Madeline. Or even *future* Madeline.

Present-day Madeline is nothing but anger and fire. And that's fine. I've been there. All dragons go through this. It's just that she and I aren't even the same species at the moment.

Which is also fine. Neither are Pell and me. Or Pie.

But… we were, weren't we? Madeline and me. We were the same. Just a few weeks ago we were going on dates, and talking, and laughing, and falling in love.

And now we're… strangers, really.

And the babies won't be any better. They will take just as long to come out of their instinctual destructive stage and be something I can relate to.

It's wrong to want to skip the journey and get right to the happily ever after, I know this. But I can't help myself. I feel like I've *been* on the journey. I've done it. And now that I'm on the other end, I'm going to have to do it again.

It just doesn't feel fair.

And, really, how important is it that dragons destroy things with fire for a thousand years before they mature and come to their senses? Isn't it a waste?

Madeline said so herself. She said she'd rather be dead. Which is awful. And now it feels like my duty to snap her out of this, or perhaps push her forward. The babies, as well.

I scan the wall of gemstone doorknobs and feel like the answer is right here in front of me. One of these destinations includes the future.

But which one? If I try them all I'll be here for a thousand years. Maybe that's overly dramatic, but it will take a long time.

Just as I think these words, the sanctuary above me rumbles and shakes, making little rocks crumble off the celling and rain down on me like hail.

I don't think we have much time. I think I need to hurry this process along.

Which makes me think of my ring. I raise my hand up to study the ring. It's silver and mostly plain. Except for the inscription, which is telling me to *Be the dragon*.

Being the dragon is a bad thing.

Isn't it?

Is that all we are? Nothing but destruction?

Why bother, really? Why bother with such a creature? Surely we have some other purpose in this world. We must.

I sigh. These are all thoughts for another time. Right now, I need to find a safe place for us.

Once again, I stare at the wall of gemstone doorknobs. If I just pluck them out, one by one, it's nothing but luck and chance.

But if I perhaps put some direction behind this plucking then maybe we can skip the journey and—

Another rumbling from the sanctuary above pauses my thoughts. I look up, then immediately regret it because crumbling pieces of ceiling fall into my eye and I have to rub them out. But as I'm doing this I have an idea.

A spelling.

Yes. That's brilliant. If I use a ring, and a door, and a doorknob, *and* a spelling—well, what could go wrong? It seems like an unbeatable combination, if you ask me.

The problem is, I'm not much of a poet. So this might take a while. I wouldn't want to get this wrong, now would I? I could send us somewhere terrible.

So I need a very good spelling. Something spectacular.

I walk over to the nest and settle on the edge, letting my attention wander while I stare at my beautiful, bruise-colored eggs as everything above me starts to fall apart.

*ONCE I SIT **down*** and direct my attention to rhyming words with meaning, I find that I am a very creative person. I told Pell I was complicated, and look, it's true. One never knows what one is capable of until one tries. Isn't that how the saying goes?

At any rate, here is what I come up with:

A man of honor, I have been
I deserve a place, a den.
A home where family can reside
A lovely place for my new bride.

It's good. I like it. Gets to the point. I have earned my place. Paid my dues, so to speak. And now the gods of doorways should give me a reward.

But when I go over to the doorknobs and try to pluck one out of the wall, it doesn't budge. "What the—"

Exasperated, I try to pull harder, to no avail.

Perhaps I should use the spelling to loosen it a bit?

It's worth a try.

I stand in front of the wall of gemstone doorknobs and clear my throat. Then I say my spell.

The doorknob right in front of me begins to glow, like they were earlier, and I clap my hands, so proud of myself for figuring out the magic of doorknobs.

But then... it disappears.

"What the—" I just stare at the empty space where the doorknob was, blinking. Then I look up at the ceiling as I talk to the dungeon gods. "What is this? Are you punishing me for terrible writing? That's not fair! I never went to school for this! I'm an amateur! I should be judged as an amateur!"

I shake my fist at the ceiling as well.

The ceiling, however, does not respond.

Well. I go back to the nest, settle down on the edge, and think up a new one.

Bastard gods. Who do they think they are, expecting me to be perfect on my very first try? Jerks. All of them.

Still, I am rather good at this. So in no time at all, I have a new spelling. I walk over to the wall, take a deep breath, focusing on one particular doorknob—I figure this cannot hurt my chances—and then spit out the new words:

I am good and I am great
I respect the gods of gates.
(Not really, but does it matter?)
I have a woman and some eggs
Crack them open and give her legs!

I really emphasize the legs part because I think Madeline should skip her menacing, evil dragon stage and skip straight to the chimera stage, if that even exists. What can they do but say no? What do I have to lose by asking?

And again, the doorknob glows and I get excited.

But then, again, it disappears. Poof! Just gone!

"Oh, come on!" I wail at the ceiling. "It wasn't that bad! And she was born a human." Technically not true. "She was born a chimera!" I shake my fist at the ceiling. "She has earned a break just like me!"

The dungeon gods do not respond.

"Very well." I take a deep breath and inject some resolve into my rapidly deflating state of confidence. "I shall try again."

I go back to the nest, sit down, and think up another one.

This one is much better. And as I walk over to the wall of doorknobs, I decide to pay a little homage to the dungeon gods for their wisdom in denying me the first two times.

Third time's a charm, though. Everyone knows that.

"You dungeon gods really know what you're doing, don't you? So wise, and… perfect… and…" Fuck it. "Here we go." I focus on the doorknob gem with intent this time, narrowing my eyes and clenching my jaw.

Oh, gods of greatness and of gifts
Give me a new life and make it swift
Thousands of years I have served
Loyal, humble, and reserved.

This time the whole wall glows brilliant red and pink, kinda blinking in and out, throwing off magnificent shadows.

And I'm jumping up and down, clapping my hands with excitement, practically patting myself on the back, when they *all* disappear.

My mouth drops open. "What the—"

I refuse to believe it.

This cannot be happening.

How could I have the world at my fingertips in one moment, and then be woefully stripped of all opportunity the next?

"It's not fair!" I yell this at the dungeon ceiling. "And you know what, you shitbag gods? I'm tired of this! I'm done. I will save my family and you will help me, or I will—"

In my experience threats are almost never the way to go. So I pause here and take a breath. I turn away, pace a little, mumble curses—but only to myself—and calm down.

Clearly, I am going about this the wrong way.

Perhaps my overly... how should I put it? Overly... *boastful* blustering is a bit much?

I am not really a man of honor. I mean, I want to be. This is my goal, of course. It's just the life I've lived hasn't given me a lot of chances to be a man of honor. I'm not really good or great, either. That's a goal of mine as well. But I'm not evil. Not anymore. I've been passively neutral for a very long time now.

Shouldn't that count?

Apparently not.

"But I am loyal!" I shake my fist at the ceiling. "I'm very, very loyal! I will do anything to help save my friends!"

But... would I? I mean, Pell did ask for my door and I did tell him no. But it's the only one I've got. And there was another route to his tomb. It's not like it was the only answer. Just the obvious one.

I feel justified in denying him.

And it's not like I haven't done anything around here. I've saved the sanctuary. Twice! Even Pie said so.

"If I could do more," I tell the gods of dungeons, "I would!"

And just as I say that, a single, sparkling gem doorknob appears back in the wall.

It's a game. These words come out of my mouth, unbidden, as I stare at the single, glowing doorknob on the wall. For a moment, I'm slightly elated. Slightly. Still guarded. Because, of course, this is all a game and I'm being set up for something.

Not to mention that particular doorknob is the very one I've already used. It's the one with the designation "Smart Friend" scratched above it on the stone.

I throw up my hands, exasperated. "Well, what am I supposed to do with that? Play dolls and have tea with the little girl? How is that going to save Pell, and Pie, and the sanctuary, and the monsters, and *my Madeline*!"

I roar the last part. Angry now.

They're playing with me.

Like always.

This is the story of my life.

I walk over to the nest, sit down, and rest my elbows on my knees, propping up my chin with my fists. "Is this the point, then? Make me feel defeated and helpless? Worthless?"

"What?"

I jump up, surprised at Madeline's voice. Then relief floods through me. Because I really thought that last conversation was, well, our last. For a very long time, at least. "Madeline! You're awake again."

"Was I sleeping?" She peers out at me from the shadows, her face covered in those blood-red scales.

I exhale, tired. "No, darling. You're... changing."

"I can feel it. It's bad, isn't it?"

My first instinct is to lie. I want to comfort her. But comfort built on lies isn't comfort at all. It's... betrayal. "It is, love. You're going to be a dragon. And being a dragon is pretty much the most horrible thing that could ever happen to someone."

She chuckles. But it's clear she's in pain. "It can't be that bad. You're not horrible."

"Oh"—I sigh—"but I am. It's just... I've had a few thousand years to ripen and consider my actions before I give in to the monster that lives inside me. But you, darling. You've got thousands of years ahead of you before you will get to this point."

And in that time, she will learn to hate herself. Everything about who and what she is will fill her with self-loathing.

I wish we had let her die.

It would've been the right thing to do.

But I was selfish. And in the middle of destroying things. And Batty didn't save Madeline for me, actually. Did he? No. He saved Madeline to *stop* me. To pacify me. To make me stop destroying things.

He saved her in order to save everyone else.

And just as I think this, Madeline growls at me and slinks back into the shadows, reverting back to her dragon state.

I walk back over to the still-glowing gemstone in the wall. And this time, the words that come out of my mouth are pure of heart and have nothing to do with me.

A girl she is, through and through,
Not a dragon, nor a shrew.
A life of joy she deserves,
Give her that and I will serve.

The doorknob gemstone glows a bright gold color and then it begins to blink.

Could this be it?

Is the secret to ask for things, not for yourself, but for others?

I reach for the knob, holding my breath, and when my fingertips wrap around it, it loosens in my palm and I pull it out of the wall.

I let my breath out as well. And then I walk over to the door, plug the doorknob in, and—with zero expectations about what might come next—I open it.

I CAN'T SEE **what's on the other side** of the door. It's just a muddled blur. But this door is all I have. It's my last chance to save the family I so desperately want. So what else can I do but walk through?

I pass over the threshold of the door and end up in...

I blink a few times, trying to put it all together.

I've been here.

I step away from the door and look around, then smile as

I take in the hookah in the middle of the small room. This is the truth-or-dare room. The very one where I had my first kiss on a dare from Pell.

There is still a wheel of sorts painted on the floor. A circle divided into twelve parts, with three of the parts labeled, just as they were before.

House of Moths.

House of Bucks.

House of Dragons.

We played a game in here. And at the time, I figured that's all it was. A game. Something children do. Not a *Game* with a capital letter G, something gods use to move monsters and people around on their playing board.

The room has not changed since Russ Roth appeared downstairs and we had to rush out. There are fancy velvet pillows strewn about and I picture the three of us in here, just before that stupid sheriff made his way into the sanctuary and everything changed.

I walk around and pick them all up, putting them back on the equally fancy chairs. Then I stare down at the stupid wheel on the floor and ponder what it might mean.

"Well." I sigh. "Wheels are for spinning. That's one option."

Except it's not a real wheel. It's a painted one.

But just as I think that, the whole thing shimmers below my feet. Like it's got a secret. Like, perhaps, it *can* be spun. I tilt my head a little. All the while the twinkling continues, and then, almost as if it's an illusion, it changes, just a little, with a tilt of my head.

When I turn my head back, it goes back to normal.

"So. Stupid wheel. You *are* hiding a secret."

Obviously. Since I didn't ask to come here, it was the will of the doorknob gods.

They put me here for a reason. I vowed to serve, didn't I?

345

A little spark of hope lights up my heart. Because if they brought me here to serve, then that means... could it be?

Could they be considering my request to help Madeline along on her transformation?

I press my hands together in gratitude. "Oh, thank you, thank you, thank you. I will not let you down. I will not. I will figure this out and I will do my part. I promise."

They, of course, do not answer me.

Not for the first time I wonder if these gods are even real. I mean, couldn't this all just be coincidence?

No.

I feel this to be true. I have never seen the actual gods, only the damaged ones. And then, unless my memory is failing me, only the ones Pell is tangled up with.

But still, I feel them. Not all the time, but certainly there *are* times when their attention is very much focused on me.

And this is one of those times.

Suddenly, and without warning, the air all around me begins to shimmer as well. And then the next thing I know, two doors are appearing. Doors that were always there, just unseen.

And who comes tumbling out?

Well, naturally, the only two people who could.

PART FIVE

So here we are, the end is near
On the line, things you hold dear.
Love, and lies, and magic spells.
Choose your path and choose it well.

CHAPTER TWENTY - PIE

*M**y mother's grip on my ankle is so tight**, I can actually feel a bruise forming.

This is how it all started. She and that stupid eros kidnapped me and sentenced me to a life I was never supposed to live.

And now she thinks she's gonna do it again?

I don't fuckin' think so.

Just as I slip through the door, I pull my leg back and I kick her in the chest with the flat bottom of my boot as hard as I can. She gasps, losing her breath, lets go of my leg, and goes reeling backwards into dark, empty space.

For a moment, I smile, filled with satisfaction.

But it's only for a moment. Because in the next moment I am spinning and reeling through the darkness after her.

"Noooo!" I'm screaming it just as light appears in the distance.

A door. And I am spinning my way towards it.

I wriggle and twist in the blackness, trying to change my trajectory. But it's no good. And the next thing I know, I'm over the threshold. I come tumbling out into a room, slide across a polished floor, and then crash into a... velvet pillow?

I blink a few times, then look up. "Tomas?"

He laughs out loud and comes towards me. "Pie! Oh, Pie! You're here!"

He picks me up off the floor, but just as I get to my feet, there's a flash in the room.

349

"Oh, dear," Tomas says.

"What's that?" My heart is racing and my mind is spinning just like my body was a few moments ago. I can't quite place where I am. I mean, that was the craziest hallway trip ever!

And then I'm thinking, *How did I get into the hallways again?*

Another flash, and then a crash, and a bright white light. I cover my eyes, but when the flash is over, I open them and see—

"Pell!" Tomas is elated again. "Look! We're all here."

Pell is just as confused as I am. He looks around, trying to understand what's happening. "Where am I? How did I get here?" He squints. But then his yellow eyes find mine. "Pie!"

I rush over to him and help him up off the floor and that's when I recognize where we are.

I look at Tomas. He shrugs with his hands. "I guess we'll be playing a game again."

"What are you talking about?" Pell is still catching up. I have no idea where he's been, but I have a sneaky suspicion that his trip through the doors and hallways was a lot like mine.

Weird.

And... true.

"Look." Tomas is pointing at the floor. "It's the truth-or-dare room. There we are in the wheel."

And sure enough, he's right. This is the truth-or-dare room. And on the floor is the same wheel. House of Moths. House of Bucks. House of Dragons. And this is very much looking like a game.

I groan. But my dismay doesn't last long because I have so many questions. "But Tomas, how did you get here?"

"How did any of us get here?" Pell asks.

"Oh!" Tomas is in good spirits, unlike Pell, who seems to

be getting grumpier by the second. "It's a long, sad story. I had a fight with the gods. They won and here I am."

"What are you talking about?" Yep. Pell is way beyond grumpy. He growls these words out like he's about to take a bite out of someone.

"Well…" Tomas scratches his head, like he's got something to tell us, but doesn't want to. "I was messing around with the doors, and spells, and the doorknobs, making demands I really didn't have a right to make. And then…" He sighs. "Then I made a promise."

"What kind of promise?"

"Pell." I put a hand on his chest. "Calm down." Pell's eyes flash yellow, but underneath my hand his galloping heartbeat begins to slow.

"Sorry," he grumbles. "But my trip in the hallways was pretty fucked up."

"Oh, tell me about it. I mean, my trip was fucked up. I learned exactly who I am and how I got here. This isn't even me, you guys!" I point to myself. "I'm a fuckin' lion!"

"You don't really look like a lion to me." I glance at Tomas and find him squinting at me, confused and caught up in the literal meaning of my outburst. And just for a moment I have an urge to yell at him the way Pell does.

But Pell beats me to it. "Not right *now*, you simpleton!" He growls these words out. And they come with that new voice of his. "She means in her hallway life!"

"Actually"—I put up a hand—"no. It was my real life. Uggghhhh." I shake my head, exasperated and tired of not understanding who and what I am. "It was real, Pell. And it was a shit show, OK? An absolute shit show! They were selling me to… Prince Tarq, or whatever!"

Pell softens with my building frustration. He even offers me a sweet smile that comes with a melty look in his eyes. "Well, if it makes you feel any better my trip into the hallways ended up with me *cursing myself into this whole mess*!"

"What?" Tomas says.

"That's right! I'm the one who put us here! I spelled the whole thing into existence because they were going to kill me and use me to make big magic and I just started sputtering out… bullshit!"

I lean in to him, placing my head on his shoulder, ready to give him the sympathy he needs. "Oh, Pell, that's—" And I was going to say 'cute,' because of the pun. Bull and shit. Because he's a bull. Never mind. It doesn't matter, because I don't get that far.

The room blinks into darkness and Tomas says, "Oh, what fresh hell is this?" And then the center of the room bursts into flames and a deep, menacing voice fills the void around us.

"Your spells are good, but so are mine.
I lead you through the hall of time.
This place is but a dream I dreamt,
Caught in the world I did invent."

And Pell says, "Dammit. I forgot about him."

And I say, "No! Fuck this shit!"

And then… there he is.

The fuckin' eros.

But not a real person. He's a shadow on the wall. Flickering up the sides like the flames in the center of the room.

"Finally," the shadow says. "We're all in the same place at the same time. And thank you very much for completing all your tasks so well."

"*What?*" This time Pell's growl makes the whole room rumble.

I'm just about to ask the same thing. I even open my mouth, but instead of a question, a spelling spills out instead…

"A HORN, *a hoof, an eye, a bone.*

A book, a jar, a moth, a stone.
A crown, a fire, a golden ring.
The cheated man who would be king."

AND THEN, before anyone can say anything about that weird outburst, Pell is spelling too.

"WORDS ARE power and breath is time.
He sits and waits, commits no crime.
Make him stay and make him wait.
Cold is justice served too late."

AND THE MOMENT Pell is done, Tomas picks it back up:

"SPIN the wheel and seal your fate.
Make a choice, walk through the gate.
But once inside there is no out,
Journey on without a doubt."

THE FLAMES in the center of the room grow huge, licking the high ceiling. And then, poof! They disappear and in their place...

Well. I plant my hands on my hips. Because there he is.

Only this time for real.

I'm talking black wings, and the crossbow, and the arrow, and the whole black leather get-up that has actually never appeared in any of my mental images of how a cupid looks, but whatever.

The Eros is here in the flesh.

JA HUSS

He claps. Not a Tomas clap, which is always delightful. One of those slow claps. The mocking ones.

And in between these slow claps he says, "Thank you. Thank you. Thank you. Well done *you*."

The three of us are actually speechless. And we look at each other, throwing meaningful glances that are saying, *Do you know what he's talking about?* and *No, do you?*

We don't. We don't have a clue.

Eros slowly turns in a circle, meeting each of our stunned gazes as he does this. Then he chuckles. "Well, I can see an explanation is in order. Shall we begin so we can wrap this up?"

"Wrap what up?" Pell's growl is back and so is that voice.

"Oh, just calm down there, godling. I'm getting there. But let's not jump to the end just yet, OK? I've been waiting two thousand years for my moment and you will let me have it."

"So get on with it," I deadpan. "You're *boring* us." I'm not sure where that came from. It's more along the lines of something Callistina might say. But it seems to delight Eros.

"Oh," he exclaims. "I love that haughtiness, little royal lioness. Soon, my dear. Very soon you will forget all about your human life. There will be no scars. And I didn't bother you a bit, did I? No. I didn't. I left you to live your life."

"You *left* me," I growl—and can I just say my growl is on par with one of Pell's?—"to be raised by a lunatic who locked me up in mental institutions and then abandoned me to Child Protective Services!"

"All because of that stupid bird. Who wasn't even real, little Pie. She was just a curse."

This makes me angry. Because Pia wasn't just a curse. She was my friend. And Callistina killed her to release the curse and free up my magic rings.

Wow. My life is really fucked up.

"And you." Eros points to Pell. "You were the perfect vessel. No." And now he glares at Pell. "You did not curse

354

yourself. Don't be ridiculous. You couldn't come up with a three-stanza spelling if your life depended on it. You don't know a single rule about spelling, luckily for me. Because it means that Tarq is *not* the king. Was *never* the king."

We just stand there, trying to work it all out.

Then Tomas says, "Well, what about me? Don't you have something to say to me?"

Eros shrugs. "Not really. I don't know why you're always hanging about. You're not a part of this."

I make a face. Because how is that true? Tomas is in the room. He got here using magic. So...

"Anyway." Eros swipes his hand through the air, like he's clearing it. "On with the business. I need you to bring me Tarq." He's pointing at Pell. "And I need that done immediately." Then he points to me. "And I need you to pair with Tarq and spit me out the godling I was promised two thousand years ago. And if you both do that—"

"Whoa, whoa, whoa." Pell puts up a hand. "Godling?"

"Yes. A godling. I was promised one by the gods for leaving the pantheon. From a pairing of my choosing. And I chose Tarq and Pianna." He smiles.

"Then why did you fuck everything up?" I ask. "Why didn't you just leave me alone? Why pull me out of that world and put me in the human one?"

The eros's face goes dark and menacing. Then he points at me. "Because I knew."

"You knew *what*?"

"I wasn't there in the gifting room, but I know what Ptah did. He gave you a bag of rings."

I'm not sure why I pat my waist where the bag was attached to my belt when this gifting took place, but it's an automatic gesture. Of course, there is no bag of rings there. All the rings are in Pell's tomb.

"And that bag of rings was a bad-faith effort to wriggle out of our deal. If I had left you alone, as you put it, then you would've grown up with those rings, and you would've been surrounded by royal alchemists, and they would've taught you how to properly use them."

Properly use them. So is he implying that we're using them incorrectly?

"That didn't happen, did it? No. And while it did take me a very long time to catch up with my own magic, we are here now. And we can resume where we left off. Which was you marrying the royal beast, Tarq, and producing me a child to use to start my own House." He pauses to smile. "House of Love. How do you like that? It's good, right?"

Pell and I just stare at Eros, trying to envision this future.

But Tomas has a question. "Don't you need an alchemist to have your own House?"

Eros looks over at Tomas, points at him. "Correct. I do." Then he looks back at us. No. He looks back at *Pell*. "Don't you worry about that. I know where one lives. A very, *very* prolific and talented alchemist is caught up in the curse." For a split second, his eyes dart to Tomas. But it's so quick, I almost think I made it up. "And once this is all over, I will collect her too. And then…" Eros pauses to envision his own future, I think. "Then life can begin again." His face goes dark for a moment. But then he smiles. It's almost warm, too, which is kind of gross. "Then I will release your curses. And you can do whatever you want."

"But again," Tomas says, "what about me?"

"Go away, you stupid dragon. You have no purpose here. I'm not dealing with you. I'm dealing with *them*." He's pointing at Pell and me.

Tomas continues to question this, but only muttering under his breath.

"Your plan has faults," Pell says.

Eros directs his gaze to Pell. "Does it?"

"What are you going to do about the other gods? They're not gone, they're just…" Pell throws up his hands.

"Lost, I think. Saturn has certainly found a way around whatever rules they're living under. Shouldn't you dispose of them?"

"Dispose of them? Why in the ever-loving fuck would I do that?"

"Don't you want to be the one and only?"

Eros throws his head back and laughs. "One and only? Pell. Come on. What is the point of playing the game *alone*? No! I will not be disposing of them. We are going to reclaim what was ours to begin with."

"Vinca," I say.

"To start with. But not just Vinca. All the worlds will be ours this time. We will control all the doors. Because, dear Pie, with you comes the rings. I will be the new Ptah. I will be the new Cronus. I will be the new Zeus, and the new Saturn. They will proclaim Eros the God of Gods. And I will rule the worlds forever and all the other, newly demoted, gods will bow to me and do my bidding."

"Well, that's not creepy at all, is it?" Tomas mutters this.

But Eros ignores him and barks at Pell, "You will go bring me Tarq." Then he points at me. "And you will stay here—"

"*No!*" Pell's objection is so loud, and so furious, and so final, that the whole *world* shakes. The floor beneath our feet, the ceiling above our heads. Plaster is crumbling and tiles are breaking and then he says it again. "No!" And his voice—the power behind it—it shakes Eros. Not literally, like the room. But internally. It's just a moment. Just a fraction of a second, but I see it.

He's afraid of Pell.

"*Yes*," Eros demands back. His great black wings fly up, threatening us. "She *will* stay. And you *will* do my bidding."

"How about I stay?" Tomas raises his hand. "I volunteer to stay."

Everyone ignores him. "This is not happening," Pell says, his voice still booming, but not shaking reality the way it

357

was. "She is mine. You have already promised that we will be free after we do our tasks."

"But I need insurance, Pell, that you will do as you're told. And she is the only thing you seem to care about."

"Well," Tomas says, "he cares about me too. We *are* best friends."

Eros doesn't even look at Tomas. His eyes are locked in a battle of wills with Pell's.

Pell looks away first and I wilt a little. Because I don't want to stay with Eros. But then Pell says, "So bind her to you. Isn't that what you do? Hmm? Throw arrows at hearts and change the future? You weaponized love. That's the real reason they banished you. You had too much power. You could, with a single arrow to the heart, change the course of everything. Because when you're in love, you will do just about anything to keep that love safe."

Eros smiles. "You're more perceptive than I thought, monster."

"They were afraid of you, weren't they?"

Eros's smile turns diabolical. "So. Very. Afraid."

"So bind her to you," Pell repeats.

Which is a gross idea. Ugggh. So gross. I don't want to be in love with the eros.

I'm just about to speak up and declare my objection when Eros says, "You know very well that I am immune to love."

"Well," Tomas says, "that's very, very sad. You never get to fall in love? Wow. I would never want to be you."

Eros shoots Tomas a dirty look before redirecting his attention back to Pell. "You know I can't do that."

"So... bind her to me."

"What's the point of that? You're already in love with her."

"It means I will do anything to save her. And the only way to save her is to bring you Tarq."

"And here I was, thinking you were smart. All of that can

be accomplished if I simply keep her with *me*, monster. Now—"

"You're missing the point."

"Am I?" Eros laughs. "Then enlighten me."

"You're a liar. You're a cheat. You kidnap little girls and abandon them in foreign worlds. You're selfish, and self-centered, and evil. Because love is the most powerful emotion and you use it like a weapon."

Eros is still chuckling. "You say that like this is a bad thing."

"Which means I don't trust you."

"Nor I you. So what was the point, exactly?"

"I have a power as well."

"Do you now?"

"And if you force Pie to stay here with you, I might have to use it to just… wipe the world clean and leave it at that."

Oh. Shit. He's talking about his voice.

"I might just be a monster. And I might only be a godling. But you know what I can do."

"But the question is, will you?"

"That certainly is the question."

"You won't."

"I will. You see, Eros, if you're going to double-cross me, what's the point?" Pell throws up his hands. "Why work so hard to get my happily ever after if you can't be trusted? Why not just… end it all right now? I could do it. *You know I can.*"

And these last few words come out with so much power, his voice so loud and commanding, that the floor splits open underneath the eros and he goes tumbling to his knees, his great, black wings flying up to catch him before he actually falls through the hole in the floor.

Eros hovers there, mid-air, so angry at Pell, it's coming off him like heat.

"*Mine.*" Pell says this with the same power. And suddenly, there is a chasm between us and the eros. An endless pit of darkness ringing the center of the room, with Eros right in the middle of it.

A threat.

For a moment, no one dares to say anything, or move, or even make a face.

Then the eros disappears, making the room dark again. A flame of fire rises up from the newly opened chasm, making a shadow on the wall.

Not a man, not a god, but just a voice dancing in the flames...

"REVENGE IS sick but oh so sweet.
Burning hate makes me complete.
I have no love for men or gods
I use it to enslave their bonds.

SPIN THE WHEEL, truth or dare
And all your lives will be spared.
If you follow all the rules
And deliver me the beastly fool.

UPEND THE WORLD, make me the king.
Tarq and Pie, a new godling.
And I will leave you all behind,
And be myself with my own kind."

THEN HE UNLEASHES an arrow and next thing I know, it hits me in the chest! I stumble backward. Then there's another bright flash, more darkness, and... he's gone.

And we are standing in the truth-or-dare room again, looking at each other with confusion.

"*He cursed us,*" Tomas says. "That was a curse, right?"

"Did he just bind me to Tarq?" Pie asks, looking down at her chest where the arrow should be, but isn't.

"Spin the wheel?" I'm looking at her when I say this. "Did you catch that part of the spelling? We're supposed to play truth or dare?"

Pie lets out a groan. "What the fuck is wrong with these people? Why do they have to talk in riddles? And I swear to God, if I'm in love with Tarq, I'm gonna be fuckin' pissed!"

"Well, at least the two of you are playing the game," Tomas groans. "I'm irrelevant. How am I supposed to serve the doorknob gods and save my Madeline if I'm irrelevant?"

Pie and I both look at him. "What?"

"The doorknob gods."

"Tomas." I'm growling at him again. He really gets on my nerves sometimes. "We don't have time for your petty problems. Our whole world is precarious right now. We have to figure this out."

"Figure what out? Go get Tarq and take him to Eros. Pie has one baby—she can manage that, right, Pie? Simple. Done. Your curses are over. Meanwhile, my Madeline is changing into a dragon and will be sentenced to thousands of years of distressing turmoil and self-loathing. I think my problem takes precedence here. Don't you, Pie?"

We both look at Pie, who has a strange look on her face.

I recognize this look. "Pie—"

She immediately puts up a hand. "Just hear me out! We can't just give him Tarq."

"Why not?" Tomas asks.

And I'm in agreement. "I thought you hated Tarq?"

"I do. Well"—Pie bobs her head a little—"I don't hate him. That's a strong word. I just never trusted him."

"Wait." I point at her. "*Are* you in love with Tarq? I mean, I was hoping he would try that, but do you have real feelings for him?"

Pie snaps at me. "What?"

"You were hoping for this?" Tomas asks.

"Well, he needed a reason to let her come with us, Tomas. I wish it had been me, but he wasn't going to just hand her to me. He needed insurance. So I planted a seed about a love arrow."

"You planted a seed to make me fall in love with *Tarq*? Who, by the way, we're not handing over to Eros."

"Oooh!" Tomas exclaims with wide eyes. "A twist. You *are* in love with Tarq."

"No! It's just…" Pie looks confused for a moment, then a little bit scared. Because he did bind her to Tarq. We all heard the curse. We all saw the arrow. Pie rallies, though. She, like Tomas, has always been a dreamer. "I'm not in love with Tarq. It's just… what happens to Vinca if we keep meddling in their magical business?"

"Do we care?" Tomas asks.

"Not really," I admit.

"What about Talina? And the girls? And everyone else? They won't have a king, they won't have a queen—"

Tomas points at Pie, chuckling. "Oh, I forgot you have her locked up in the Bottoms."

"Tomas!" I sneer.

"That's what I mean," Pie continues. "We can save

ourselves, I guess. But what about everyone else? Aren't we caretaking them anymore?"

"Were we ever?" Tomas asks. He and I both shrug.

"We were, you guys. We can't just forget about them. That's not how stories end."

"Don't they end in happily ever after?" Tomas asks.

I agree with him again. I might have to rethink my frustration with Tomas. He's on point today. "They do. And if we win, we get our happily ever after."

Tomas laughs. "It's like we're living in a fucking fairy tale, isn't it?"

This makes Pie pause and look confused for a moment. "Do you guys even *read* fairy tales?"

We make faces at her.

"You can't just save yourself. That's not happily ever after! You have to save everyone."

"Well, that's just stupid, isn't it?" Tomas. He's kinda funny today. "Saving everyone is impossible. And I do read fairy tales. They often have horrible plotlines. Children being pushed into ovens. Beautiful girls being locked in towers. Spinning gold for trolls."

But Pie is not giving up. "It's not stupid. It's heroic. And *helloooo*! Accomplishing the impossible and being heroic is the whole point of happily ever after! Fairy tales end with a hero doing heroic things. Like cutting open the wolf's stomach to release the grandma, and slaying the—"

She stops.

Tomas tilts his head at her. "Were you going to say 'dragon?'" He looks at me. "Was she going to say 'slay the dragon?'"

I roll my eyes at him, then look at Pie. "Well, it's a nice speech, Pie. But—"

"Hold on." Tomas puts up a hand. "Heroic, you say?"

"Yeah!" Pie brightens, not sure if she's happy he's let the

dragon-slaying go or that he's latched on to the idea of heroism. "Heroic. Isn't that the point of all this struggle?"

"Is it?" I ask. "Isn't the point to break the curse and live our best lives?"

"No!" Pie stomps her hoof. "It's not going to end this way. We have monsters to think about. And Jacqueline, Pell!" She pulls on my arm, pleading with me. "I can't leave Jacqueline!"

"I will need to change my vote."

I growl at Tomas. "There is no vote."

"Of course there is." He grins at me. "There's always a vote. Isn't there, Pie?"

Pie is making one of those clenched-teeth smiles, which means she knows I'm getting angry, but she's gonna do whatever comes next anyway. Then she shyly raises her hand. "I vote we be heroes."

Tomas raises both his hands. "I second and third and declare the motion passed."

All I can do is sigh. Because if this is what Pie wants… well, then that's all I need to know, I guess. The whole point of my life is to make her happy. Still, my agreement comes out with objections. "Have the two of you forgotten about spinning the wheel?"

Pie shrugs with her hands. "What wheel?"

"This one." Tomas points at the floor where there is, indeed, a wheel. Just not a real wheel. "Too bad the hookah's gone. I bet it had all the answers."

Now he's giving me a headache.

"Ooo!" Pie raises a finger. "I bet that's how we get home."

"Why wouldn't we just walk out the door?" I point to the door. Which… was there the last time we were here, but isn't now. When I look back at Pie, she's smirking. "Hey, all I wanted to know was how it fit into the spell."

"'Spin the wheel, truth or dare, and all your lives will be spared. If you follow all the rules and deliver me the beastly fool.' I'm pretty sure spinning the wheel takes us home.

Because obviously"—Pie points to the missing door—"there is no door."

"What about the rest of it?" Tomas scratches his chin. "I can't remember the first part."

But Pie can. "'Revenge is sick but oh so sweet. Burning hate makes me complete. I have no love for men or gods, I use it to enslave their bonds.'"

"They fucked him over," I say. "I don't want to get into the whole stupid story of where I came from and why I'm here, but that eros was there."

"He was there for me too." Pie is frowning. Like she's recalling her trip down Memory Lane. "And he's not just an eros. He's *the* Eros."

Tomas nods. "Yes, I figured."

"Well, long story short, the old gods got… old. And people forgot about them. So they formed some kind of pact, I think. To keep some power. But only twelve from each pantheon."

"And let me guess," Tomas says. "They didn't include Eros."

"They did not."

"So he's what?" Pie shrugs. "Just a… jealous dick?"

Tomas smiles. "Sounds about right. And what about the last part, Pie?"

Again, she's got the words ready. "'Upend the world, make me the king. Tarq and Pie, a new godling. And I will leave you all behind, and be myself with my own kind.'"

"Well, that's a promise of… trust?" Tomas offers.

"He'll keep his promise and let us all go if I have Tarq's baby."

Pie says this with… "Are you being wistful?"

She screws up her face as she looks at me. "What?"

"You just said 'Tarq's baby' like you were looking forward to it."

"I did not!"

"You did, Pie." Tomas is nodding in agreement.

Pie's mouth drops open. "I'm not in love with Tarq." Then she points at me. "But if I am, it's your fault! You planted the seed!"

"OK." I rub my temple. I really do have a headache. "Forget about Tarq. I'm sure there's a way to fix that in the future." I eyeball Pie as I say this just to make sure she agrees. She nods. Not enthusiastically, but I'll take it. "Eros wants revenge on the gods who fucked him over. It's a pretty simple task, actually."

"Is it?" Tomas isn't so sure.

"Well, he told us how to do it. All we have to do is bring him Tarq."

"And you're OK with that?"

I narrow my eyes at Pie a little. "I thought you hated him."

"Hate is a strong word. And it's not about me, it's about you. You're supposed to be loyal."

She's deflecting because she doesn't want to admit she's now in love with Tarq. But again, I need to focus. So I stay on point. "I *have* been loyal."

"Forever, Pell! Loyal *forever*."

Tomas and I look at each other. He's on my side. "Forever is a rather long time, Pie. And Tarq is the only way out."

She blows out a breath and throws up her hands. "Fine. You sell out your friend. But I'm not selling out mine." She points at me. "And I'm saving the monsters too. Even if they are assholes now that we can understand them."

"Agreed," Tomas says. "Now about this wheel." He points to the floor. "I'm guessing we need a spelling to get it working."

I'm so annoyed, so I'm growling again. "Why can't there just be a fucking door?"

"Just go with it, Pell, and—" But that's as far as she gets. Because a spell comes spilling out of her mouth. "'A buck, a moth, a dragon's wheel. A time to win and a time to heal.

Stand in the middle, turn around. And you'll be headed homeward-bound.'"

Tomas and I make faces of approval. He walks to the center of the painted wheel. "You're a very talented speller, Pie."

"Thanks. But…" She joins Tomas in the center of the wheel. "He kind of insulted us. He practically called us spelling amateurs."

"He did," I agree, walking forward towards them. "But he was talking to me, not you." We stand back to back, facing out. "Now what?" Tomas asks.

"'Stand in the middle, turn around.'"

We start shuffling our feet in a tight circle, keeping our backs together. And I'm just about to call this whole thing stupid when we really start spinning. Like feet-off-the-floor spinning. Faster, and faster, and faster, like a tornado.

And then…

We fall right on our asses.

But there's a bit of a soft landing. Not much, it's only my forest grass. But it's enough.

And… we're home.

"Hey! Where's Tomas?" Pie is already getting up.

She offers me a hand and I take it, then point at her and say, "Cute," which makes her blush. "He's probably in the dungeon. That's his home."

"Hmm. Well, I'm glad I didn't go to my cottage."

"Why would you go there? This is your home."

She snuggles into me. "Awww."

"OK. So. Let's get this show on the road. We'll go to Vinca, grab Tarq—"

"No!"

"Now what's wrong?"

She points at me. "You go to Vinca. I go to Jacqueline."

"Pie?"

"Hmm?"

367

"Fuck that."

She chuckles. "Why?"

"Because the fuckin' eros is with Jacqueline. When we go see him, we go together. In fact, we should do everything together. All the time."

"Agreed. Except this time." I'm just about to object when she puts up a hand. "Fine. Jacqueline can wait until we have Tarq. But I also need to go set all the monsters in the Bottoms free. Including Callistina."

"Don't forget Nysta. She's part of the plan."

"Yeah." Pie sighs. "Banishing her was not my best moment."

"OK. I can get on board with this. I'm not sure what Tomas is doing, but we don't need him. I'm pretty sure we can wrap this shit up in like thirty minutes. And you are not having Tarq's baby."

Pie's face screws up like she's confused. "I'm not?"

"No, Pie! If you're having someone's baby, it's going to be *my* baby!"

Pie swoons a little. And I feel better that I can still make her do that, even though she's been love-spelled.

"I'm sure, once we take Tarq back to Eros, we'll have another, better plan in place so we can just… win." I shrug. Like this going to be easy.

Pie is not convinced. "What kind of plan? Because the way I see it, the next year of my life involves having Tarq's baby."

"I will destroy the world before I let you have Tarq's baby."

Pie swoons again. She still loves me. I can tell. So even if the eros did love-spell her to Tarq, she's not really on board.

She isn't.

"But what if you have to fight Tarq to make him come with you? Won't that get messy?"

I'm going to pretend I didn't hear the worry in her voice.

Because that worry isn't about me. And it's my fault, I planted the seed. So I'm going to deal with this new twist like a mature adult. "It won't come to that. I'm just going to lure him here using Nysta. Even if he did love-spell you, he didn't love-spell Tarq. He's still in love with Nysta."

"Ooooh. That's a little diabolical. And there is no love spell!"

There absolutely is a love spell, but I let it go. We'll deal with that later.

"OK." Pie blows out a breath. "Now that we've got a plan, we should... just... go, right?"

Her hesitation makes me grin. "You're having second thoughts. You want to come with me, don't you?"

"I am, and I do. But I'm not going with you. I'm just..." But she doesn't finish her thought.

"You're just what?"

"A little bit worried that I'll never see you again."

And she really does look worried. So far, Pie Vita has handled this particular challenge with grace and courage. And now she's second-guessing herself. I take both her hands in mine, then lace our fingers together. "Do you know what I was doing right before the whole sanctuary went to shit?"

She pouts her lips a little. "What?"

"I was making you a ring. Actually, I already made it."

"You did?"

"I did."

"Let me see it!"

"Absolutely not. It's a surprise. But I wasn't done with it. Not completely. Because I was writing a spelling to make an inscription."

"Tell me."

"No, I can't tell you. It's for the wedding."

"Wedding?"

"Oh, fuck yeah, Pie Vita. You see, this is why you don't have to worry about us going two separate ways right now.

This is why you don't have to worry about the love spell, either. Because I'm gonna marry you. You will not fall in love with Tarq and you will not have his baby. And there isn't a chance in hell that you never see me again. You're gonna see me again, every day, for the rest of your life—and beyond."

"Beyond, huh? That must be some spell. But where will we have the wedding? Here?"

"It doesn't matter where, Pie."

"But I want to envision it. And what about my dress? What if Eyebrows really does hate me and won't make me a dress?"

"Please." I scoff at her. "After you become the fairytale hero and save *everyone*? You're gonna be the toast of the tombs. Our wedding is going to be spectacular. And you know what?"

"What?"

"I'm glad you're saving everyone. Because then they'll all be able to come to the wedding and watch me proclaim my love for you, and kiss you, and make you all the promises that I will absolutely keep. And they'll bring gifts. They'll probably get drunk and start having sex on the dancefloor, but we'll be drunk too, so will we care?"

"Fuck no!"

"Fuck no." I place my hand on her cheek and smile. "Thirty minutes. OK?"

She nods. "OK."

"And don't take any shit down there in the Bottoms. If anyone fucks with you, spell them into oblivion."

She places her hand over mine and sighs. "I will."

"Thirty minutes."

"Thirty minutes."

I kiss her.

And then we go to our doors, stand in front of them, take one last look at each other, and walk through.

*J*ust like the first time when I came up from the Bottoms and got a weird sense of out-of-place-ness, I get that same feeling going back down. And it's something very different than when I walk through any other door.

Of course, it's still Pell's tomb. It's just... not Pell's tomb, too.

The colors are different, for one. It's murky here. Not like I'm standing in the shade, but more like the sun hasn't come up yet. And it's cold.

Was it cold last time?

I don't remember. I have tried to block that day from my memory, and I did a pretty good job. It's amazing how you can just force yourself to forget you enslaved your sister.

I sigh as I make my way through the unfamiliar shadow forest that lives in the shadow tomb. And when I get to the stoa, there is even a shadow statue of Pell that I hadn't paid attention to before.

And you know what's funny? Well, actually, it's creepy. This one looks just like my Pell. It's not some Egyptian copy from antiquity. It's *him*.

This is a very bad sign and little ideas are starting to form in my head. Even though I do my best to push them all back down, there they are.

There has to be a reason why the statue of Pell in the shadow world of the Bottoms is the one you know and love. There has to be a reason for this.

It's logic.

But I'm in a magical copy of Saint Mark's Sanctuary filled with tombs and prisoners, so perhaps, just this one time, I don't have to follow the logic.

That's what I'm going with when I step out of the tomb.

And realistically, it shouldn't work. I should be thinking very hard about that statue of Pell. But my brain just kinda stops working when I take in the tombs.

Well, lack of tombs. Because they're gone. Not *gone* gone. But… a disaster. It's a fuckin' disaster. Everything has crumbled. Not a single tomb is left—

Oh, but I'm wrong.

There *is* one.

The black one with the gold dome roof. It looks just as new now as the day it got here. There's not even snow on the dome.

And it's freezing. Snowing, actually.

It doesn't snow inside the walls of Saint Mark's. It's been a perfect, late-spring afternoon temperature ever since I first walked through the front gate.

One word begins running races through my mind on repeat.

No. No, no. no.

And then one name, out loud. *"Callistina!"*

I look around, my heart beating—thumping—inside my chest. And then I scream it. "Callistina!" I pause to listen like… maybe she's still here. Among the snow drifts, and debris, and ruins. "Callistina!" I yell it again.

Because it can't end this way. It *cannot* end this way. Not after I met her. Not after I saw her as a teenager. As an older sister. Not after I learned all the things that matter and make a difference.

And I get it. That supportive older sister was not who she

was when I sent her down here. And even back then, she was, quite frankly, selling me into an arranged marriage that would've ended with a godling baby that would've been used for magical purposes. But it's not like Callistina was in control of any of that.

She wasn't anyone special that day. Just another older sister.

She wasn't anyone special until I disappeared.

But to be fair, when we finally did meet again, I wasn't the baby sister who got yanked through a magical door nineteen years ago, either. And what was she supposed to think all these years? I was taken by the eros. I skipped storylines. What happened to me that day changed the course of worlds, and gods, and monsters, and... well, everything.

And none of it was my fault, but none of it was her fault, either.

I'm the one who spit out clues at the last minute. I'm the one who told her about Pia, and the curse, and the bag of rings. All she did was use the information I gave her.

If I was the one left behind, wouldn't I have done the same thing too?

Wouldn't I have spent all the days that came after trying to figure out what the fuck just happened?

They must've substituted Callistina for me. They must've sent her to Vinca. To be with Tarq. To maybe have his baby too. I don't know for sure. Perhaps they did have a baby. But if they did, it wasn't the godling they were planning. Because if it was, they wouldn't need me, would they?

There is a crumbled pedestal that once held a statue of some prisoner monster that is mostly standing. I pick my way through the snow, careful, even though I have hooves, and then climb on top of it to get a better look.

The wind is cold and bitter. And this is when I notice that I'm wearing the slutty schoolgirl outfit, even though I'm still in my monster form. That's kinda weird, but even so I am

JA HUSS

thankful for the leather jacket as I scan the remnants of Saint Mark's. Even from up here, there's really nothing to see. It's just snowdrifts over ruins.

My gaze inevitably falls on the black tomb near the cathedral and that's when reality sinks in. Because the cathedral is in ruins too.

I look over my shoulder, jump down, run to the top of the hill. There's not even a remnant of my cottage. Not even a brick.

I want to search for Callistina. I want to pretend there's hope. But there isn't.

She's dead.

They're all dead.

"Oh, my God." My hand flies up to my mouth. "Nysta!" I look around again, feeling sick.

Because she's gone too.

And she wasn't even guilty of anything. I mean, maybe none of these monsters were guilty of anything, how the hell would I know? But Nysta! All she did was get a little bitchy with us and I sentenced her to death for it.

I want to leave. Immediately. I want to go back into the tomb, leave this shadow world behind, and just... escape. Pell was right. Tomas was right. Saving people is stupid. I can't save anyone. I'm not in charge of any of this. I'm just a frickin' girl with an imaginary talking bird who stumbled into a mental condition and never fell back out.

That's it. That's all this is. I'm just crazy.

I have to be.

Because if I'm not...

I can't even finish the thought.

And what will I tell Tarq? *Sorry I killed the love of your life?* That's gonna go over well. Especially when Pell is going to use Nysta to lure Tarq back so we can hand him over to that fucking Eros.

We're the worst.

We failed.

At everything.

There is not one good thing left about any of this and we just need to accept our defeat and slink away though a door like a bunch of fuckin' cowards and then live the rest of our lives in shame.

I take one last look at the remnants of my beautiful sanctuary and then I turn—

But as I turn, I see a figure off in the distance, near the back entrance of what's left of the cathedral.

"Nysta?" I whisper it. It doesn't really look like Nysta. But it's definitely not Callistina. No antlers. And those fuckers were spectacular.

I'm just about to call out again, louder this time, when the woman slips through the ruins of a door and goes inside.

I sigh. Now what? Follow her? Or continue on my path of shame?

Decisions, decisions. But what can I do? I glance over at the entrance to Pell's tomb, then throw up my hands and begin walking towards the cathedral.

or a moment, I just stand in place, looking around, trying to make sense of things. This door should lead to the palace bakery. At least, that's where it took us when Pie made it.

But this is not the bakery.

Hell, this isn't even a palace.

It's a ruin.

I blink, then shake my head, trying to force it all to make sense. But all I end up doing is muttering, "What the fuck is this?"

I can't even step forward across the threshold of the door because there is so much debris. I have to actually climb out, clawing my way up the side of a fallen column that is massive in scale.

When I get to the top, I stand up and just look around.

It's… a wasteland.

I don't know what Vinca looks like. I came here twice and both times I was inside of a building. But Pie did describe a river to me when I asked her about it a few weeks ago. A massive river filled with barges and houseboats that was flanked on both sides by wide walking streets.

And while there isn't a river here, there is a deep and winding dent in the ground where one might've been a long time ago.

I slowly turn in a circle, taking it all in. Not wanting to

believe my eyes, but unable to conjure up a big enough lie to convince myself that I'm not seeing what I think I'm seeing.

Vinca has been destroyed. And from the looks of it, it happened a long time ago.

I cup my hands around my mouth and with all the power of my voice, I yell, "Tarq!"

The rumble disturbs the ruins, making them shift and move. But, of course, no one answers back.

Still, I yell it again. Louder this time. With even more power. "Tarq!"

And again, the ruins shift, this time revealing the remnants of a doorway off to my right. Standing alone in the middle of a space that's almost cleared of debris.

I squint at it. Because I recognize it. It's the door to the throne room where I made Tarq the king.

The spelling comes back to me now, and I let out a breath.

I take the power of this ring. My best friend Tarq is now the king.

Even I have to admit, what a stupid fucking spell. It's got no power at all. In fact, now that I think about—and now that I understand a little more about spelling—it wasn't the spell at all that did that magic.

It was me and my voice.

I keep turning in a circle, trying to imagine what happened here.

There was a war, obviously. I've been through enough hallway war zones to recognize what I'm seeing. And that's definitely what this is.

A civil war?

Did the gods come and take the city back?

Who knows. Who cares.

The only thing that matters is that Tarq is most definitely dead and now—and I'm completely embarrassed and filled with shame just for thinking this, but it's the truth—now I have nothing to bargain with when we meet back up with the eros.

I let out a long sigh. But then again, at least there's no chance at all that Pie will be having Tarq's godling baby.

That's a bright side. A sick one, but still bright.

However, we're not done with the eros. Not even close. He's expecting me to bring him Tarq and... yeah. I got nothing.

I look down at the door I came through, and I'm just about to jump off the column and go home—thirty minutes my ass. I've been here five, and I'm done—but then I notice something else over by the lone doorway that leads to the throne room and I jump off in that direction instead.

The area I'm aiming for feels close, but even with my split hooves and spectacular jumping skills, it takes me a while to pick my way through the debris and make my way to the doorway.

It's not a magical doorway. Just some grand arch that was well made and stood while everything around it crumbled.

I understand what I'm looking at even before I slowly navigate my way across the broken tiles and reach the foot of the crumbled throne. But still, it takes me several moments to accept it.

Because I'm looking at Tarq's *head*.

A skull, actually. Nothing but a skull and a tarnished crown that has been nailed to his forehead.

I pick it up by the one remaining horn and stare at the empty holes where his eyes used to be. There is a new kind of sadness inside me. Something I don't think I've ever experienced before.

It's crushing, and painful, and punctuated with the realization that I probably did this to him with my defective spell. And worse, even if I hadn't found him this way—long dead and forgotten in a pile of war-ravaged ruins—I was going to sell him out to a forgotten god to save a version of my future that never really had a chance in the first place.

I am the biggest piece of shit ever.

I drop my arm, still holding the skull by the horn, and turn to look around one more time.

I did this.

I am responsible for this.

And the last thing that comes to mind, after I make my way back across all the debris and cross through the doorway to my tomb, is that I do not deserve a happy ending.

Back inside my tomb Pie's door is standing open, but shimmering silver. And when I look around the forest, she's not here.

A panic builds inside me and my heart thumps wildly as I run through the forest towards the entrance to my tomb, then skid to a stop when I hit the stoa. Blinking. Trying to make sense of things.

Because Saint Mark's is gone too.

Ruins.

Everything is in ruin.

I scan the remnants of tombs covered in snow, my eyes landing on the only one left standing.

That black fucker.

I stare at it for a moment, trying to figure out why it's here, and then I look down at the skull of Tarq that I'm holding in my hand.

Apis came here for Tarq.

Or no. Apis came here for me. For killing Tarq.

Probably not for killing him, no. I didn't sense that much loyalty in the bull god.

But I did sense—not a hatred. Hate is a strong word and I just don't think Apis cares enough about me to hate me—but… a contempt.

And contempt is enough.

I jump down off my tomb and I'm making my way to the

black tomb, ready to go in there and get this shit over with, but then I see Pie slipping into the remnants of the cathedral.

At least, I think it's Pie.

Who else could it be?

Then I have to make a decision. Go have this final struggle with Apis or follow Pie?

I follow Pie.

All around me is darkness. But I don't need time for my eyes to adjust before I understand what just happened. I have excellent night vision.

Everything about my dungeon is both familiar and not. I know this place. I have lived here for thousands of years. But the past few weeks have left an indelible mark on the walls, the floors, and me, of course.

So the realization that I've lost everything is immediate.

It's not the cold or the snow piled up on the floor.

It's not the debris that has rained down from the ceiling at some time during my absence.

It's not even the smell.

It's just a feeling of complete and utter emptiness.

Even though I have this excellent night vision, I stand in place in front of my door and wait for my eyes to adjust. And then I process.

The eggs are rotten and Madeline is gone. The scent of sulfur floats through the air like a rancid cloud, intolerable and disgusting.

I want to rage about this. I want to burn the world. I want to kill everyone, and everything, and then I want to kill myself.

But, of course, I will do none of these things. Because if I kill everyone, and everything, and then myself—I will be unable to get *revenge*.

So I breathe deeply through my nose instead. The Love

Doctor gave me this meditative advice when I was enjoying the radio and having tea and toast with the monsters.

This breathing exercise doesn't fix anything, of course. Nothing about what has happened can be fixed. But it does calm me down and allow me the time to internalize, and fully embrace, my evil side.

When one decides to devise a revenge scheme it is best to carefully think it through in order to get the most satisfaction. There are many things to consider.

Most important is who comes first.

See, this is where most dragons get it wrong. They do not differentiate between those who are *truly* guilty and those who were merely accomplices. They simply burn the whole damn town.

Hell, I've done that myself. I chuckle here, thinking about how immature I was just a few short weeks ago and how far I've come in that brief span of time.

I am—I let out a long breath—mature now. I think.

Yes. That's quite a nice word. I've grown into myself. Finally.

And even though there is emptiness inside me as big as the world outside my gates, I fill it up with wicked thoughts and vile endings.

There is no happy ending for me.

I knew this though, didn't I?

I understood. But it was a nice fantasy while it lasted.

Still. Reality must win out in the end. That's the only way to stay sane.

So I take a deep breath, hold it, hold it, hold it—for three counts, just as the good doctor ordered—and then I let it out and make my way to the door.

Not the magic door. I walk right past that stupid fucker. Smart Friend, my ass.

No. I walk right to the stairs, which are gone. But it's all good. I have fantastic claws. I could use the wings as well, but they're missing at the moment. And if I call them back up I might not be reasonable. So claws it is.

It takes me a while to get to the hallway, or what's left of it. But that's just fine. I spend all that time sorting through my list of suspects.

Is it Batty? Oh, he's involved, I'm sure. But did he design this unhappy ending? Very doubtful.

Same goes for the rest of the monsters we've been caretaking over these last weeks. They're probably evil enough, but not the prime suspects.

No. There is only one person to blame.

This name rolls around in my head as I try it on. And I'm just about to say it out loud and firmly cement it in place when I come up to what used to be the grand hallway and who do I see coming up the stairs?

"Tomas!" Pell rushes across the floor—well, picks his way over the debris, actually. "Are you OK?"

"Isn't that sweet of you."

"What?"

"Asking about my mental health."

He looks me up and down, a worried look on his face.

I pshaw him with a wave of my hand. "I'm fine. Just fine."

He squints his eyes at the back of the hallway where I just came from. Then he looks at me. "Is your dungeon—"

"Gone."

"Oh, Tomas, I'm sorry."

"It's fine."

"You had eggs though. I know we didn't talk about this, but Pie told me and—"

"It's. Fine."

Pell knows me. Maybe better than anyone. So he's well aware that things are not fine. "What about Madeline?"

"Gone."

"Oh, Tomas."

"It's. Fine!"

He sighs, then gives in. What else can he do? "I think I followed Pie up here. Have you seen her?"

"No. But look." I point across the hallway where the apothecary is.

And when I say where the apothecary is, I mean where the apothecary *actually* is. Because it's still standing. In fact, it's even got a door. Which is closed.

"Holy shit." Pell scratches his head. "How is that thing still standing?"

I shrug and say the obvious. Pell really is obtuse sometimes and I'm tired of letting him think he's the smart one around here. "Magic, Pell. It's magic. Perhaps we should go inside and get answers. Because I'm sure that's what's in there."

"Yeah." Pell is still squinting at the door. But then he directs that squint to me. "Tomas. If you need—"

"I do not. I am just. Fine."

"Right. Well, I'm not. Tarq is dead."

"Dead?" I don't know why this surprises me, but it does.

"Vinca is gone."

And that's when I realize he's holding something in his hand. "Is that a head?"

"Tarq's head. See the horn?"

"Did they nail that crown to his head?" I'm aghast. I mean, dragons are awful and we do terrible things. But nailing a crown to a head? That feels quite over the top.

"Yeah." Pell sighs again, this time with much more weariness. "Everything is fucked up."

"You can say that again."

"There's no happy ending for me."

"Oh, I'm glad you said that."

"What?"

"Because I feel the same way!"

"Yeah... OK."

I'm confusing the poor simpleton. He's not processing the

dichotomy between my glee and my words, because they contradict. So I tuck my issues away and focus on my only true friends in this entire life. "Let's find Pie."

Pell presses his lips together and nods. "Yeah. Let's go find Pie."

It feels like it takes forever for me to make my way through, and over, all the ruins of Saint Mark's before I finally step through what used to be the door to the cathedral. There's not much difference between inside and out, but the one thing that really attracts my attention is that the extra stairwells are missing.

Not crumbled, like the real stairway. But missing.

It feels like a loss. Not that the hallways ever really participated in what's been going on here—before today, of course. Is it still today?—but they always felt like an option and now that's been taken away.

Maybe someday, if I live through the next twenty-four hours, I will have time to dwell on this and fully appreciate what they offered and what I have lost, but right now I'm just trying to figure out what the fuck is going on so I push all those thoughts away and concentrate on climbing up the remnants of seventeen bajillion steps.

I'm about halfway up when I have to abandon the stairs and start climbing over massive pieces of marble that used to be walls. But finally, I make it to the top.

I don't know what I was expecting, but whatever it was, the top falls short.

There is nothing left of the grand front entrance. Like... nothing. I can see the gate out front from the top of the stairs —which, by the way, and not that it matters, isn't even closed.

Hell, I can even see the road. There are tire tracks in the snow that alert me to the fact that even though my monster world has just fallen apart, people are out there. Living their lives. Driving their cars down this road. Going out for coffee or dinner—I have no idea what day it is, let alone what time.

The tire tracks should comfort me. It should be a relief that Pennsylvania still exists. That the world is still there.

But it doesn't.

Because this isn't even the end. The breaking of the curse and the crumbling of Saint Mark's Sanctuary is just the *beginning* of the end. Who the hell knows what's gonna happen next.

I blow out a breath and then notice two things on opposite ends of what used to be the grand entrance hall. The greenhouse on my left and the apothecary on my right. Both of which are mostly still intact.

OK, then.

Chances are high that the woman I was following went into one of these two places. I choose the apothecary, since it's closer, and start picking my way through the debris towards the massive closed door. When I get there, I don't know why exactly, but I glance up. At the curse over the doorway.

Which is gone. Because so is the curse.

And again, I have a feeling of loss.

I open the door. It creaks loudly, so the woman bent over a desk on the other end of the room should look up and notice me, but she doesn't.

She is not one of our wood nymphs, of this I'm sure. I don't know what exactly gives it away because I'm no expert in wood nymphs, but I am certain she is not wood nymph.

Her clothes, for one. She's wearing a long dress made of pale blue... cotton, maybe. Very old-fashioned style with a square neckline, showing just the beginnings of shoulder and not even a hint of cleavage, and dressed up with some embroidery and lace that is most definitely not cheap and tacky like the synthetic shit they make these days.

It's not a sexy dress. Not cut to draw the eye to her feminine assets, which are clear. But it is a pretty dress.

And she is pretty too. She's looking down, so I can't see her full face, but her hands are slight and dainty as an ink pen floats across the empty handmade pages of an open book. Her long blonde hair looks soft and freshly brushed. It's pulled out of her eyes in a way that makes it look like a curtain pulled away from a window and it's dressed up with a crown of spring flowers, small and delicate, like she just picked them off the hillside out back. She's wearing silver bracelets that clink, and around her neck hangs a large red gemstone that looks suspiciously like the ones I made manifest in Tomas's dungeon.

"Hello?" I say this, but I already know she's not real.

Well, probably *is* real, but we are not existing on the same plane, or whatever. In other words, I think she's a ghost.

Which is lovely. Not a single ghost in my story so far, but why not, right? Why not throw one in at the end? What the hell.

I don't bother saying anything else, just walk over to her so I can try to get a peek at her book.

She doesn't look up, but she does speak. "I've been waiting for you."

"What? You can see me?"

"It feels like a very long time, too." Then she blows on the inky words she just wrote on the page and gets up. I take a step back when she turns my direction, but there's no need to worry. She walks right through me. Goosebumps burst out over my skin and I turn to watch her walk over to the bookshelves.

She points up at the books. "I wrote them for you." She turns back to face me, but her pale blue eyes search the room like I'm invisible. She knows I'm here, but she can't see me. She can only feel me. "And Pell."

"You know Pell?" My question sounds overly loud in contrast with her quietness. "Do you know what's going on? What I should do next?"

I don't think she can hear me. She gives no indication that my words reached her ears. She just climbs up the ladder and starts pulling books off shelves.

Once she has an armful, she comes back down and places them on the nearest stone bench. Lays them out, face up, side by side, so I can see the titles.

How to Kill Gods

How to Break Curses

How to Start Over

How to End an Era

How to, How to, How to...

They are all about endings. Which is probably going to be helpful. But what the fuck? Were these books here the whole time?

"I wrote them for you, but you never even looked."

I guess she's a mind-reader as well as a ghost.

"And Pell." She makes a face, but it's a face of... fond remembrance.

Which worries me for a moment. Who *is* this woman? Why is she here? How does she know Pell? Is she in love with him? Was he ever in love with her? What is her *name*?

She smiles in a random direction and folds her hands in front of her like a... like a graceful princess or something. "I am Pressia. You've been using my book *Soaps, Balms, and Tonics for the Magical Nymph* to brighten your life."

"Ohhhh." Yeah. My eyes dart over to the bench I was using to make that stuff last week, but this isn't my apothecary. It's *hers*. She lives here, I think. Inside Saint Mark's. And I also think she's been here a very long time.

Alone.

"It's nice to meet you, Pie. I've been waiting for this day for thousands of years." She chuckles to herself, like she's having another memory. "When the dragon came, at first I thought he was going to hurt me. But then I saw his door-knob." She points to the red gemstone hanging from her neck. "I already had one, of course. It was a gift to me from my alchemist, Lyrica, when I was born. The dragon gave me your name. And, well, after that it was easy to follow you through time. I escaped through the door he left and…" She frowns. Like this is not a fond memory. "Of course, I knew the future. I'm an oracle, after all. But I also knew there was going to be a lot of time between then and now and I knew I would have to spend it alone. So I just wrote down everything I saw, trying to make it easier on you. And Pell, of course. We only ever met for a few minutes, but he was always part of my future. Even if we never meet again."

I look down at the books on the bench, then up at the bookshelves. The amount of time she's been here is incomprehensible to me. How is she even sane?

There is something very sad about her too. It's not just the idea of this sweet thing being a prisoner of the Saint Mark's curse, it's something else. Like she had all these years but never really lived.

Kind of like Pell. But not like Pell at all. He had caretakers. And Tomas.

She had no one.

Nothing but her knowledge of the future and the books she wrote it down in.

The woman—who comes off as very young for being so old—swallows hard. Like she's trying to repress something. Then she looks at the door I just came through and smiles. A tear falls down her cheek.

I look too, and that's when Pell walks in. "Pie! What happened?" He looks around. "Where's Nysta?"

I look back at Pressia, but she's gone. Then I look back at Pell just as Tomas walks in to stand next to him.

"Pie?" Pell says, coming over to me. "What's wrong? You look like you've seen a ghost."

I snort-laugh. "Well…" But I don't have the words right now. So I just sigh, then walk over to the couch on the side of the room and sit down. I stare at my feet for a moment, trying to process everything that has happened to me today.

"Pie?" Tomas comes over to the couch and sits down on one side of me. "Are you all right?"

Pell sits down on the other side of me. "What happened?"

I take a breath and then the words all spill out. "I met Pressia." I wave at the room. "She was just here."

"Where?" Both Tomas and Pell say this at the same time. And even though it's just a single word, the eagerness in their tone is evident.

"She was a ghost. She couldn't see or hear me, but I could see and hear her. She was sad, you guys."

"Oh, the poor thing." Tomas utterly deflates.

"That sucks," Pell says. "I wanted to save her, but I was drugged. And then…"

"It's OK," Tomas says. "I gave her a door. My door." He nudges me with his shoulder. "Your door, actually."

"Well." I snort-laugh again. "I'm pretty sure it's always been her door. I'm pretty sure this place actually belongs to her."

All three of us look around the apothecary and then silently nod our heads in agreement.

Pell sighs. "She made the curse."

"I think we all made the curse," Tomas adds.

And I think he's right.

I haven't gotten Pell's story yet. And he hasn't gotten mine. And maybe we'll never talk about it again, but we don't need to.

They fucked with us.

Maybe Tomas too.

These damn gods ruined our lives. And Pressia's as well. She had to spend her entire existence here, alone, and I'm so fucking over this.

I stand up, plant my hands on my hips, and look straight at Pell. "OK. Let's do this. Let's get that fucking Eros, save my Jacqueline, and the eggs, and Madeline, and you know what?" I point at Pell, furious. "We're not giving him Tarq, either. Eros gets *nothing*! These stupid gods are the real monsters, and they get nothing!"

I expect a little rah-rah from my teammates. This was a pep talk, after all. But they both just stare at me, frowning.

"What? Why are you both looking at me that way?"

"My eggs are dead."

My mouth drops open as I stare at Tomas. "What?"

"And so is Tarq."

I look over at Pell. "What? But… he can't be *dead*! He's how we get out of this!"

"I thought you just said we weren't going to give him Tarq?" Tomas looks at Pell, confused. "Didn't she just say that?"

"Tomas," Pell growls.

"What? I'm going for clarity here. Madeline is missing, my dungeon is in ruins, my eggs are dead, and the curse is broken! My entire world has fallen apart!"

Pell narrows his eyes at him. "Everyone's world has fallen apart. Vinca is in ruins too. Did you forget?" And that's when I notice he's holding a skull with a single horn and crown nailed to the forehead.

"Oh, God." I feel nauseated. "Is that—"

Pell nods. "Yep. This is all that's left of Tarq." He looks around the room. "Where is Nysta? I should be the one to tell her."

"Welll…" I sigh and sit back down between them, then flop all the way back into the cushions. "She's dead too. I think. I didn't find a skull. I didn't find anything, actually. The Bottoms was empty. They were all gone."

"All of them?" Tomas turns to look at me. "But they were *prisoners*."

"Well, not anymore, apparently."

Pell squints at Tomas. "This is all your fault."

"My fault? That makes no sense at all. I'm the victim here!"

"And Callistina." I start to sniffle. "And... I know I hated her, and put her in prison with a Book of Debt, and she killed my Pia—but she did it to break my curse!" I look at Pell, pleading with him to understand. "I was cursed! The god Ptah gave me a bag of rings and—"

"Wait." Pell puts up a hand. "Did you just say Ptah?"

"Yeah." I sniffle again. "Apparently, I'm a lion from the House of Fire, or some shit like that. And I really was supposed to marry Tarq. He was there. We were gonna have a godling."

"Huh." Pell takes a moment to appear thoughtful. "Interesting. I was supposed to marry Pressia and we were supposed to have a godling too. But then... the eros pulled you through a door and you disappeared. And all the plans were ruined."

"Yeah." I look at him. "How do you know that?"

"That fucking Apis bull."

"Who?" Tomas and I say this at the same time.

"The black tomb. Which is still standing, did you see that?"

I nod. "What's an Apis bull?"

"Not a what. A who. A powerful, powerful god. He's..." Pell pauses to smile.

"What?" Tomas is anxious. "He's what?"

"He's Tarq's brother. And you know what that means?"

I look at Pell dumbly. "No. I have no clue."

"It means..." He smiles. It's a weird smile. Almost devious.

Which is really not a good look on shaggy Pell. "It means we can still save everyone."

"How the hell will we do that? Even if I can find Madeline, my eggs are dead!"

"Well, we probably can't save them. I'm sorry about that, Tomas. I really am. But we could substitute Apis for Tarq, and then go to the eros, and... fix this!"

"Let me get this straight." Tomas's face goes serious. "You want us to go into that black tomb—the only one left standing after a disaster that ruined everything else—find the god who lives in there, magically subdue him, then wrestle him to town and hand him over as a substitute so Pie can have a baby with him?"

I make a face. "I'm really not on board with this."

Pell sighs. "OK. Fine. It's a stupid idea. I'm open to suggestions. If anyone else has a plan for winning, let's hear it."

"Winning!" Tomas stands up and paces the room. "Winning, you say?" He stops in front of Pell. "We lost, friend. We lost everything. We're not winning! There is no winning!"

I let out a long, tired breath and look up at Pell. "Listen, I hate to admit this, but he's right. We lost, Pell. We did everything wrong. Pressia wrote us books telling us how to win and we didn't even look through the fucking bookshelf! And now everyone is dead. Nysta, and Callistina, and Madeline, and Tarq, and my girlfriends in Vinca, and the monsters, and the prisoners. And probably Jacqueline and her stolen kids too! Everyone. And it's all our fault. We suck at saving the world. That's all there is to it."

Tomas is walking around the room again.

Pell objects to my summary. "Maybe they're not dead? Maybe they're just—"

"Stuck in a curse?"

"Pie. I'm not saying we didn't make mistakes—"

"Make *mistakes*? We fucked everything up! I killed people, Pell!"

"You didn't kill anyone."

"Hey," Tomas calls from the other side of the room. "There's a book here."

"I did! I sent Callistina into debt and I put Nysta in the Bottoms just for asking about her own future! And now, they're both dead."

"Then maybe we should go back to my plan. You're the one who wanted to save everyone."

"Your plan?" I scoff.

"Helloooo!" Tomas walks back over to us holding an open book. "Did you hear me? I said there's a book here. What is this book, Pie? I can't read these letters."

"Oh, my God! I was just bitching about how we didn't look through the books, and they're literally in the room with us! Am I just stupid?"

Pell points at me. "Cute."

"Listen, kids. This is not the time for this. Read the fucking book, Pie!"

Tomas drops the book in my lap and I stare down at Pressia's flowing handwriting. "It's a spelling." I look back up at Pell. "Dare I read it? Or will it just make things worse?"

"Worse?" Tomas yells. "How could things get worse?"

Pell sighs. "He's right. Just read it."

I let out a long breath, then read the spell:

"I STOLE THESE SPELLS. They were not mine.
  I took them through the sands of time.
  I hid them well, I hid them true,
  I saved them for the three of you.

USE them now or use them then,

Be careful though, they bring the end.
Words will make the magic flower,
But people give the spells their power.

JUST LIKE MONEY, there is supply,
But don't be fooled, the cost is high.
I put you here to fix the past,
But every choice will make it crash.

STILL A CHOICE IT IS, you see,
To move forward or let it be.
This or that, it's up to you,
But in the end, you'll own that too.

YOU CANNOT AVOID the road ahead.
Meet it well or with dread.
Waste no time in changing minds,
They cannot see when they are blind.

I WISH YOU WELL. I'll see you when
You find the final happy end.
It may take years, it may take lives,
But even so, you will arrive."

THERE IS a prolonged silence at the end of the spelling. Then Pell says, "What's it mean?"

"It's very long." Tomas is walking around the room, looking at the various books Pressia left on the benches.

"Which means it's complicated," I say.

Pell sits down next to me and sinks back into the cushions. His hand automatically rests on my leg and I lean into him as he sighs. "I'm so fucking tired of riddles."

"'I stole these spells. They were not mine. I took them through the sands of time. I hid them well, I hid them true, I saved them for the three of you.'" Tomas holds up another book. "Look what I found."

"What is it?" Pell is very growly now.

"It's Tarq's book of spells."

"The one from Ostanes?" There is a lift in my voice. It's a lift of hope.

Tomas brings the book over to me and I sit up on the couch to take it and place it in my lap. "Find something to fix this, Pie. That's what this book is for, right? It's got all the magic and all the answers, doesn't it?"

My eyes drift down to my lap. Yet another book we never even looked at. Things were so weird after the wood nymphs came. Things were normal, but they weren't. And I didn't want to spend another moment thinking about anything more magical than spelling up shampoo that smelled like flowers and making love and fireflies with Pell in the forest.

I often questioned Pell about his deliberate forgetting.

Maybe it wasn't so deliberate.

Or maybe it wasn't forgetting? Maybe it was just lack of interest?

"Well? Are you going to read it?"

I look up at Pell and nod. "I figure we should probably read all of them before we make any more stupid decisions." Then I open the book and read the first page. "'How to Kill Gods.'" I glance at the recipe for this spelling and frown.

"Why are you frowning?" Pell asks.

"Because it says… bloodhorn and dragon scale." I look up at Pell. "That's the same shit for walking through doors."

"And banishing," Pell adds.

I make a face. "Yeah."

Tomas taps the book. "What's the next one say?"

I flip the page. "'How to Break Curses.'" Then I scoff. "Bloodhorn and dragon scale." I flip the page again. "'How to Start Over.' Bloodhorn and dragon scale." Flip another. "'How to End an Era—'"

"Let me guess," Pell growls. "Bloodhorn and dragon scale."

I look up at him. "What's it mean?"

"Oh, for fuck's sake." Tomas lets out a long breath and resumes pacing the apothecary. "It means it's all worthless, that's what it means."

"No." Pell is shaking his head. "It's not worthless. We used this spelling twice and it worked both times. It's Pie."

"What's Pie?" I ask.

"The magic. You're the difference in the spells. You. Your words."

"Hmm." Tomas considers this. "You could be right."

"So we can... just... do anything? As long as we have these three things? I'm not so sure. Pressia's riddle was pretty specific. We lost."

"It doesn't say that." It's so unlike Pell to be such an optimist. But I won't complain.

"Listen, Pressia says she stole the spells. Look, there are no words. There's no spelling, only ingredients. She. Stole. *The spells.*"

"But she also said she saved them for *us*," Tomas offers.

"Yeah. But then she says, 'They bring the end.' That's all that's gonna happen here, guys. It's over. She made it very clear. 'The cost is high.' 'Make it crash.' No matter what we do, we lose."

"So what's the point of doing anything?" Tomas asks.

I just shrug. "There is no point."

"*Fix the past.*"

"What?" Tomas looks at me. "What are you blabbering on about?"

"That's what she said. 'I put you here to fix the past, but every choice will make it crash.' That's why we're losing. We're supposed to ruin it, you guys. That's our fate."

Tomas straightens up and a little smoke comes off his body. "That's fucking stupid. I'm tired of losing! What's the point of losing? No one wants to lose!"

Pie says, "You're looking at it the wrong way, Tomas."

"Am I?" He's worked up. His tone is... slightly threatening, which is out of character when he's talking to Pie. "Am I getting worked up?"

"Just listen," she says, putting up a hand. "A hero has to make a sacrifice."

"I'm not a hero! I'm the antithesis of a hero! I'm just a fuckin' dragon who wants a family!"

"Well, I'm sorry to break it to you"—and now Pie is getting heated too—"but you *are* the fuckin' hero. Whether you want to be or not. Because you're in the room, and you're part of the spell, and... and... that's enough. OK? That's enough to secure your place in history as the fuckin' hero!"

Tomas leans back a little, stunned by Pie's outrage. Then he sighs and pulls himself up to sit on the closest alchemy bench. "I don't want to do this anymore."

"None of us do, Tomas." My voice is surprisingly gentle. He's been through a lot. And while we've all had a tragic day, he lost the only thing he ever wanted. A family. And meanwhile, Pie and I still have each other. "And maybe we're just destined to lose, but what else is there to do but go face the eros and finish it?"

"What are we gonna do?" Tomas asks. "Kill him?"

"That's one option, I guess."

"No," Pie says. She has picked up the first book of Pressia's and has paged forward. "It's not. Look, there was more. We only read the end of the spelling. There was another page before it. There's so much more, you guys. Listen."

"I WAS HERE but now I'm gone.
    Because, my friend, I don't belong.
    I walk the world on borrowed time,
    Out of place and out of line."

IF MY WARNING shall find you,
    Then you are off the timeline too.
    No horn, or hoof, or magic spell
    Will save the life of the monster Pell.

NO CAKES, or cookies, only Pie.
    Moths and fireflies in the sky.
    You must go back, you must relive,
    Accept, and honor, and forgive.

GO BACK in time and make it true,
    Take the monsters with you too.
    Then you will see it's not so bad,

Goodbyes don't have to be so sad.

REAL FATE IS NOT by chance.
    Not a product of circumstance.
    You must choose, you must decide,
    But peace will come when you abide.

TO BE SURE, it won't be easy.
    Do not convince, do not bully.
    For this decision must be made,
    Freely and never swayed."

"ANOTHER LONG ONE." I'm so tired of the riddles.

"Yeah," Pie agrees. "But they mostly say the same thing. So at least they're not complicated."

"Go back," I say. "We have to go back."

"And we have to offer the monsters the same chance."

"What monsters?" Tomas is still a little hysterical. "They're gone!"

"Maybe the eros?" Pie offers. "If he's all that's left? Maybe we just need to make him an offer?"

"And then what?" Tomas shrieks. "We all die? I didn't even get a chance to live yet! This is a stupid curse! I hate this curse!"

"Calm down, OK?" I'm growling now because Tomas is acting like a child. "Didn't you hear the poem? No one is gonna force you to do shit. It's all by choice."

Tomas just stands there in the middle of the apothecary, breathing hard. He looks like he might burst into flames any moment. But then he wilts a little. "We're going to lose, you guys. We're going to lose everything."

I walk over to him and place a hand on his shoulder.

"We've already lost, Tomas. It's already gone. The only choice we're making is how we meet our fate."

"What choices?" Pie asks. "I didn't hear any choices."

"The choices were implied. We could use our doors and go somewhere else."

"Run away?" Pie asks.

I shrug. "I'm not saying it's a good choice, I'm just saying it's an option. Another option is to fight some war."

"What are we fighting for?" Tomas asks.

I throw up my hands. "I don't have all the answers."

"If that's the Pie-has-a-baby-with-a-bull plan, I'm voting no."

"For the record"—I hold up a finger—"I'm voting no as well. And then a third choice is to go to Eros and offer him… well, I'm not sure it's salvation, but I'm also not sure it's not. So. That. We'll offer him that."

"And if he says no?" Pie asks.

"I'm a hundred percent sure he's going to say no."

"Then he'll try to kill us," Tomas says. "Or take Pie prisoner, or shoot us with a love arrow, or any number of horrible things."

"Yep. He could do all that," I agree. "But I don't think that's how it's gonna go. I think the monsters might not be dead. I think they might be in Granite Springs."

"You mean Savage Falls," Pie says.

"Right."

"Wait." Tomas comes over to me. "You think they all went to Savage Falls?"

"I don't know for sure, but the poem was pretty specific. 'Take the monsters with you too.' They have to be somewhere around here. And we already know they're not in the Bottoms."

Pie nods in agreement. "And they were pretty eager to get to town this morning, remember?"

"Oh!" Tomas looks like he just fell in love all over again.

"Oh! You're right, Pie! They are in Savage Falls! Let's go! I choose number three! All in favor, raise your hands. The motion passes, it is done!"

And then he just... runs out of the room.

Pie and I look at each other, unable to stop the smiles. "It's nice to see Tomas happy," I say.

"Isn't it though?" Pie agrees. "You know, I never used to be able to imagine him as some fire-breathing dragon, even though I've seen it with my own eyes. But losing those eggs... I dunno, Pell. It changed him, I think."

It has. But I don't agree with her out loud. Tomas has always been dangerous. He's just been resigned to his fate. No real opinions about anything, actually. But now he has hope. And hope really does change a man. Even a dragon man. When a man has hope, he also has opinions. He's got skin in the game, as they say.

"OK," Pie says. "So we're going to Savage Falls, we're gonna make an offer of salvation to Eros, offer to send the monsters back in time, then come back here and... what happens after that?"

"The doors? It's the only thing I can think of."

"We send them through the doors." Pie considers this and sighs. "Wherever they want to go?"

"Why not?"

"That's a pretty good offer, I think. They were all bitching about going home this morning. I think we'll have takers. But what about us? Is this the end of us, Pell? Pressia's poem—"

"I heard that part too."

"'No horn, or hoof, or magic spell will save the life of the monster Pell.'"

"Yep. That's what it said."

"So..."

I just stare at her. She's so... beautiful, and good, and sweet, and I love her. So much. And actually, I would not

407

choose number three. I would choose number one. Run away and save ourselves.

But there isn't a chance in hell that Pie Vita would choose to run.

Not a chance in hell.

I take her hand and twine my fingers into hers. "We'll walk through that door when we get there."

This is not a satisfactory answer. Not in the least. But neither of us knows what comes after. We could guess and get ourselves all worked up over it. Or... we can just do what I said.

Forget about it for now.

There's no point in worrying because none of this is really a choice.

It's all written down in a book somewhere.

But not a fairy tale like Tomas said.

Because there isn't going to be a happily ever after for us.

There just isn't.

IT TAKES A PRETTY **good** length of time for Pie and me to make our way back down the crumbling stairs and out into the back of the cathedral. Tomas is at the top of the hill standing on the remnants of a tomb and looking down towards the lake.

He looks over his shoulder at us, snow falling onto his shoulders and hair, his ammolite scales glinting on his legs as they catch the setting sun. He's shirtless, like he always has been inside the walls of the sanctuary, but for some reason it looks out of place now. Probably the snow.

Pie suddenly stops walking, pulling on my arm to stop too. "Oh, my God."

"What?"

"Something just occurred to me. There are no walls, Pell. How will the... gods, or whoever's in charge of whatever is happening here, know that we're supposed to change into human form? Am I going into town like this? Are *we* going into town like this?" She's panning her hand down her body, indicating her monster form.

"I hadn't thought of that." But my response is really just... indifference. "Who cares. This is who we are. And it's not like Savage Falls is some normal place, right? It's part of the magic."

Neither of us understands this magic. Perhaps Tomas does. He's been around longer and every now and then I get the feeling he knows a lot more than I do. But really, it's the end now. Who cares?

"Hmm. I guess that's true. But if Jacqueline is there, what will she think of me?"

"Will you having hooves and horns change her feelings about you?"

Pie shrugs with her hands. "I feel that it might."

"Then she is stupid and not worth your time."

"I do understand where you're coming from. I get the whole this-is-me thing. But..." She sighs. "She's my only friend from my human life. I would like to keep her."

"If she's your friend, she won't care what you look like, Pie. And anyway, you look fucking amazing."

Pie lifts her shoulders up and grins. "Thanks. And for the record, so do you."

"Hey!" Tomas is calling for us from the top of his ruin. "The truck is gone, Pell! It's gone! You were right! They left!"

I picture that trip into town and just shake my head as I image hordes of monsters and wood nymphs cramming themselves onto the back of that flatbed. They were probably piled on top of each other. Sitting on the roof of the cab, hanging off the sides. I really hope the route to town is cloaked by foggy magic because if anyone saw that, it would be a whole new nightmare.

"What about the Jeep?" Pie calls back to Tomas.

"Still here!" Tomas jumps down and then he disappears over the top of the hill.

"That's great!" Pie is pulling on my arm. "Maybe my Jeep is a piece of shit, but it's *my* piece of shit."

"And walking nineteen miles into town just to make an offer to a bunch of asshole monsters really would've sucked."

She huffs a little air. "So bad."

We carefully make our way down the hill and across all the ruined tombs, then spill out into the parking lot where Tomas is waiting.

He's standing in front of the Jeep, practically bouncing up and down with anticipation. "I'll drive."

"You will not," Pie says.

"Shit. Where are the keys?" I ask.

"Only the gods know the answer to that question, Pell." Pie pats my chest. "But don't worry." She goes around the Jeep to the passenger side, opens the glove box, and pulls out a screwdriver, a wire stripper, and a roll of electrical tape. "Hotwiring is a skill every girl should know. This car didn't even come with keys. It took me six months to save up for a new ignition. But it runs and it was only fifteen hundred bucks, so beggars can't be choosers."

Pie grins as she jumps into the driver's seat, gets her horns stuck in the headliner for a moment—making it rip— then adjusts her position, pries the panels off the steering column, and proceeds to strip wires. The lights come on and a moment later, the engine sputters to life. She smiles at us.

"Wow," Tomas breathes. "That's hot, Pie."

I have to agree.

"Get in, boys," Pie says. "Let's get this over with."

I kinda wanted to drive, but I feel this is a good time to just do as I'm told. So I flip the seat up so Tomas can get in the back, toss Tarq's skull in next to him, then get in.

Tomas leans forward, his head between our shoulders. "Please, please, please," he mutters under his breath. "Please let Madeline be in town."

"She will be," Pie assures him. Then she backs up, making the Jeep stall. "Ooops." She chuckles. "I'm not used to driving with hooves. It feels weird."

Without missing another beat, she starts the car again.

And then we're on our way to confront the ancient god.

*THERE IS **no fog*** for most of the drive. We pass a few cars on the quiet country roads. Thankfully, the windows are all steamed up because of Tomas, but he's like a little heater. Which is great, because being shirtless in winter sucks and the Jeep's heater blows cold air for a good fifteen minutes.

But the fog appears the closer we get to town and by the time we get to the city limits, it's so thick we almost miss the sign that says 'Welcome to Savage Falls.'

We are quiet now. Reality is setting in. It's one thing to discuss confronting the god Eros and quite another to actually do that. Pie slows the Jeep to a crawl as we enter town, barely able to see a few feet in front of us, but then the fog clears and the music hits us.

It's thumping and loud, blaring the way it was when we came home from getting hay this morning. It's hard to believe that was this morning.

"Well, I guess it's safe to say they weren't choked up about losing their sanctuary," Tomas says.

Pie has to slam on the brakes when a wood nymph rushes out into the street, laughing and squealing as a naked satyr chases her into the candle shop. Pie blows out a breath as our eyes meet.

"The bar." I point up ahead. "That's where he'll be."

Pie nods and inches forward, trying not to hit any more wood nymphs or satyrs as crowds of them wander into the road, completely ignoring the fact that a vehicle is trying to pass through them.

"Does anyone see Madeline?" Tomas asks.

"I'm looking," Pie says. "But not yet."

I'm looking too, but not for Madeline. I'm noticing that I don't recognize a lot of these monsters. "Who's that guy?" I point to a very big dude. "He looks familiar, but—Oh, shit."

"What?" Pie asks.

"He's a statue. The statues, Pie. They're here."

"The Bottoms?" She's looking around like she's searching for someone. "Do you see Nysta? Or Callistina?"

"No," Tomas replies. "I don't even see Batty. Where are all our friends?"

Then we're pulling up in front of the bar.

We know where our 'friends' are. They're in the bar with the devil.

Tomas hits the back of my seat. "Let me out. I'm going to the feed store to look for Madeline."

"You're not coming in?" Pie asks. "I thought we were going to do this together?"

"I will. I'll be there. I just need to check on Madeline first. I promise, I'll be there."

I open the door of the Jeep and before my hooves are even on the ground, Tomas is pushing on the seat. A moment later, he's out and jogging towards the feed store. I reach back in the Jeep and grab Tarq's skull.

Pie gets out too, the wind making her hair wave around her face. She tugs her leather jacket closed, shivering. "He's not coming back, is he?"

"He will," I say. Because that's what she wants to hear. But I can't help but feel that it's a lie.

Pie sighs. "Choices, right?"

I shrug. "If he wants to stay here and not go back, then what can we do?"

"'To be sure, it won't be easy. Do not convince, do not bully. For this decision must be made, freely and never swayed."

I nod and walk around the car to her. "Yeah. That." Then offer her my hand.

She laces her fingers into mine and turns to the door of the bar, then looks up at the Savage Saints sign, the red neon blinking across her face and making her glow a little. "Welp. I'm ready. Let's do this."

We walk to the door and the moment I pull it open—even before our hooves cross the threshold—I know this was a mistake.

That song is playing. The 'Ball and Chain' one. But for a moment, it's not scary. For a moment I'm at the prom again, dancing with Pell, making memories in the photobooth, smiling and laughing like it's all gonna be OK.

But then I'm back. Right here. And I instantly understand that there's no way in hell this is going to work.

Because these people do not want salvation.

The place we step into is not the bar Pell and I visited what seems like a lifetime ago. Not the place where we drank good whiskey and had sex in the office. It's... it's... Vegas. Like... I'm talking everything you can imagine happening there is happening *here*.

Sex? Yeah. Everywhere I look there are wood nymphs in the laps of satyrs, gyrating and moaning.

Gambling? There are slot machines, and spinning wheels, and card games going on all around us. Monsters I don't recognize—probably because they were statues the last time I passed by them—are yelling and fist-pumping as they throw money around. Not dollars, either. It's some other kind of money. Red and black. Like everything is paid for in sins.

Strippers? Oh, not just strippers—wood nymphs who slither around a pole to the beat of the thumping music—but naked barmaids, too. Who carry trays of flaming shots and bend over to get their asses slapped by 'customers.'

"Well." Pell is pointing to the stage. "We found Nysta."

"Oh, shit." She's one of the strippers slithering around the pole. I didn't recognize her at first because she's wearing fake horns and claws and a black leather bikini with silver spikes sticking out of it in very strategic places. Initially, I'm a little grossed out, but then I'm relieved. "At least I didn't kill her."

Suddenly the music stops.

Everyone looks around, wondering what the fuck. The strippers stop, the gamblers complain, but the sex keeps going so that there's nothing but the grunting sound of satyrs and wood nymphs filling the void.

Until *he* speaks. "Well. Well. Well." We all turn to look at the far end of the inordinately large bar. It was not this big when we were in here last, so there is a *lot* of magic going on here. Eros is sitting on a throne made of something black and shiny that looks like stone. Maybe obsidian or onyx. His bat wings flank his bare, powerful shoulders. The leather pants are still there, but he's shirtless now, his muscular chest covered in tattoos that from this distance look like the roots of trees. His crossbow is propped up on his knee and there is a woman at his feet, kind of draped over his lap.

Not just any woman, either. But—

"*Jacqueline!*" I start to rush forward. My only goal is to get to her, but Pell pulls me back. His grip is tight at first, but he quickly loosens it when I don't fight him.

"Finally," Eros says. He pushes Jacqueline off him so he can stand. She looks up at him with adoration. Like he's her god.

And I know what's happening here. Maybe he can't hit Jacqueline with his arrow and make her fall in love with him, but he doesn't have to. He's an eros.

The Eros.

Everyone loves him. They can't help it. It's magic, or maybe even science. The Law of Attraction.

And even as I think these thoughts, I start to get a warm feeling in my gut. Like maybe I love him too.

But in the next moment, Pell squeezes my hand. Like he knows Eros is affecting me and he's reminding me of who I belong to.

I squeeze his hand back and rein in the desire to be close to the demon-looking god standing in front of his throne.

Eros frowns. "Where is Tarq!" He howls this. Like *thunders* it through the room. It shakes the chandeliers above our heads and rumbles the floor. People scatter to the edges, pressing against walls, covering their heads and ducking. Even the satyrs having sex stand up, holding onto the asses of their nymphs, and carry them to a safer location.

Pell takes a breath. "He's dead."

Eros laughs. A loud, bellowing laugh.

But then it's interrupted by a scream that pierces our ears. "What!" Nysta is still standing on the stage in her spiked leather. Her expression is one of shocked surprise, her gaze on Pell.

Slowly that gaze changes focus until it lands on me. "You." She points at me. "You did this!"

I didn't do anything to Tarq. Literally played zero part in that whole 'king' thing. And I'm just about to say this when she leaps off the stage and comes flying at me. At first, the thought of her attacking me from clear across the room is laughable. But then I realize she's still in the air, still coming my way, like she's actually gonna make it.

I put up my arm to block her attack, and then, just as suddenly, she's pulled out of the air by her foot and slammed into the floor. She squeals again, this time in pain, and then she breaks down in tears.

It takes me a moment to work out what just happened. Eros has crossed the room. His wings are folding against his back.

I didn't even see him move.

He stares down at Nysta and growls at her, "I said you could stay if you *behaved*."

And this is the moment when I feel fear.

I mean, I've always been kind of afraid of him, but what he's shown me of himself up to this point was the cozy version of Eros. Maybe a little more intense than Russ Roth, but definitely falling short of *actual* evil.

What I'm witnessing right now—the fierce look on his face, the intent and anger in his eyes, the cut muscles of his body, and the wings, and the leather, and the magic...

Oh, fuck. I can almost *taste* his magic. It's *so* strong.

He is capable of things.

Pell pulls me closer, holding my hand tighter as Eros directs his attention to me. He pauses here, his eyes so focused on me, his leathery black wings rising up a little behind his back, his posture so... on the verge of something. Like he's got something to say, but then decides not to say it.

Instead, he lets out a breath and looks at Pell. "You had better explain."

"Tarq is dead." Pell doesn't miss a beat. "I went to Vinca, I was fully intent on betraying my friend to deliver him to you, and I found *this*." He holds up the skull by the horn, thrusting it in the direction of Eros. "The whole city is in ruins."

"Impossible. It's Vinca. It's been standing for the last twenty-five thousand years."

"Well, it's gone. Maybe there was a war—"

"There was no war!" Eros bellows this, shaking the room again.

But then Pell bellows back, "Do not use that voice on me!" And he shakes the room so hard, chandeliers fall and holes appear in the floor. People scatter and within the span of a minute, there's no one here with us. Even Nysta has the good sense to get the hell out.

During all this Pell and Eros are staring each other down. Silent.

Eros breaks the standoff first. "As I was saying, there was no war, monster. You did that by making him king." Then he turns, huffing out a breath, and walks back over to his throne to take a seat.

Surprisingly, Jacqueline is still sitting on the floor at the foot of his throne.

"Jacqueline," I whisper-yell, like no one but her can hear me, which is dumb. "Come over here, Jacqueline."

"No," Eros says. There's no rumble in this command, but Jacqueline does not move.

I don't really blame her. Even though I'm a freaking wood nymph chimera with horns and hooves and I'm standing next to a shaggy, but very imposing, satyr, she hasn't even asked about why I look this way or what happened to Pell's legs.

She hasn't asked any of this because she hasn't noticed. And she hasn't noticed because she's under his spell. And whatever power, or magic, or attraction Russ Roth had, this is a million times worse.

There isn't a chance in hell that Jacqueline is going to get up off that floor. She's going to stare up at this demon with that adoring look on her face for the rest of time. Or until Eros lets her go.

"You can have this." Pell tosses the skull and it goes skittering across the smooth tile floor, coming to a rest in the middle of the room.

Eros looks at the skull with disgust, then directs his gaze to Pell.

But before he can speak, Pell says, "We have come to make you an offer."

"*That* is your offer?" Eros' eyes light up violet for a moment, directed at me. But it's such a quick thing, and disappears so fast, I almost think I made it up. "Some remnant of the monster Tarq? I needed him alive, you fool. I needed his genetics. I have no use for his bone or horn. I need access to the gods. I want revenge, Pell. They took from me and now it is their turn. If you've come with an offer that falls short of that, forget it. I will just have to take my Pie."

How did we ever think we were going to convince this god of anything? Salvation? What a joke.

And Pell must be thinking the same thing because he pauses. In fact, the pause is long enough that Eros leans forward, opening his mouth like he's going to say more.

But then Pell blurts out, "We came to offer you a door."

Eros and I both say at the same time, "What?" But I say it in my head and Eros roars it out with a rumble. "A door, you say?"

"That's right." Pell doesn't look at me or even squeeze my hand to let me know he's got this. He just stares intently at Eros. "We've mastered the power of doors."

Eros looks at me and, yep, his eyes light up violet. "You've learned how to use the rings?"

I swallow hard, then nod. "I have. I can, I mean."

"But that's not all." Pell glances at me, but it's quick. Then he's looking at Eros again. "We've come to make a deal. In exchange for the freedom of any of the Saint Mark's monsters who want to come back with us, we will give you a door to the tomb of the Apis bull. And through this tomb is a direct line to the gods themselves. If you accept these terms—"

He's cut off by a growled whisper coming from a dark corner. "*Apisssssss.*"

All three of us turn to look in that direction. I squint into the shadows until I can make out a silhouette of antlers.

"Callistina?"

I ***burst through the feedstore*** doors, out of breath and nearly out of my mind. *Please, please, please. I'm begging you stupid gods, if you're even there. If you have any sense of fairness, you will—*

My begging ceases.

Because there she is.

"Madeline?"

The girl behind the counter is not a dragon chimera— which I actually am. Funny, since recently I've been a man on the other side of the walls. Regardless, Madeline is not like me. And neither is she a transforming dragon.

She is the human girl I met several weeks ago on my very first trip to town.

I'm just about to start demanding answers when she smiles at me. "Well, hel-looo there, handsome. Those are some legs you've got. I like the furry ones, but scales... interesting." She appraises me with her eyes, giving me a very thorough once-over, like it's the first time she's ever seen me.

"Madeline?"

She squints her eyes at me. "Have we met?"

Have we met? Is she insane?

Things are not what they appear. Or, actually, things maybe *are* what they appear, but certainly are not what I was expecting.

Could it be that Madeline has gone back in time?

Possible... possible. After all, we are crossing into worlds through doorways and using hallways to visit memories. So is it so far-fetched to assume that one could do more than visit memories? That one could actually go back in time? Isn't that the whole plan here?

I think it is possible.

And I do want to believe that this is what happened with Madeline.

However, I do not think that's whats happening here.

She is furrowing her brow at me, waiting for my answer, so I smile at her, wide and with a lot of warmth that isn't very hard to conjure up because I truly do love this girl. We've had a whirlwind romance, that's for sure, but our hearts are aligned. I can feel it.

"I'm Tomas," I say, walking to the counter and extending my hand. "I'm a dragon."

She's already grasping my hand when this last bit comes out. But then she gasps. "Oh!" It's not a shocked gasp. It's... a delighted one. "That's fascinating. I had no idea there were dragon men."

Her reaction has given me some confidence. It would be nice to be upfront with her and not have to pretend that I am something I am not, so I give it a go. "I'm not really a man. I truly am a dragon. Maybe the last in the world."

Or... maybe not.

"Really?"

"Truly."

"Do you breathe fire?"

"I can burn whole towns to crisps."

"Wow." She points at me. "But you don't really do that though, right? I mean, that's kind of like... murder. Don't you think?"

My smile is tight. Maybe honesty is overrated? "Oh, no. Dear me, no. No, no, no. I am not the town-burning type, dear Madeline." A lie. "I am the... Madeline-loving type, actually."

She giggles, then points at me again. "You're flirting with me."

"I am." I lean on the counter, flirtily smirking at her.

She blushes, then looks down at the dirty, plastic-covered pages of her hay book. "Well, sorry to disappoint you. But"—she holds up her hand, highlighting a big, fancy, diamond ring, then wiggles her fingers—"I'm already taken."

"What?" My exclamation comes out quite loud. "How is that possible? I've only been gone for half a day." Well, most of the day, actually. But still. One day and she finds another man? One who proposes marriage with a ring?

Madeline appears confused at my outburst. And of course she does. Something weird is happening here. Something with time, I think. Because half a day is simply not long enough for my dear Madeline to change back into a human and become engaged to a stranger.

An idea strikes me.

Perhaps I have been gone longer than I thought?

Or, equally possibly, perhaps we have crossed realms? Into one where all the same characters are there, but the story has changed.

Because things are not quite in line, are they?

It's all very intriguing.

"But," Madeline says, still appearing confused, but now also uncomfortable, "I really do like your legs. Those scales are beautiful."

I look down at my dragon legs, then back up at her and force my smile this time. "Thank you."

"My man has wings."

"Really?" I couldn't be less interested.

"Yep. Not the fluffy kind. You know. Like an angel." She blushes. "He's no angel."

I don't want to hear anymore about her 'man.' But I don't want to leave yet, either. I feel like I should try harder. She is my one true love. My first love, my only love. And love can't be all peaches and cream, can it? There have to be pits along the way.

Pits one shall overcome. Pits that shall be... whatever. Analogy over.

"The bat kind," Madeline continues.

My ears perk up. "Did you say bat wings?"

"Mmm-hmm." She practically moans out her affirmation. "Yeah. They're like leather. Soft and—"

"Is his name Darrel, by chance?"

And just as these words come out of my mouth, the bell over the door jingles. Madeline smiles in that direction, her whole face changing and turning into... well, adoration seems like such a strong word. But there it is.

I already know who just came in, even before I turn and look at him.

Batty stares back at me, a strange look on his face. Then he redirects his attention to Madeline and that expression turns into warmth.

"Have the two of you already met?" Madeline asks as she makes her way around the counter. "A dragon, Darrel. It's crazy, right?" She joins Batty and they slip their arms around each other like they've done it a million times before. So easy. So comfortable.

My heart begins to ache.

Then Madeline gasps and holds up her arm, pointing at a red spot. "Oh, no!" Her eyes flash to Batty's. "Oh, no! It's coming back!"

Batty looks at me when he says, "Go put some ointment on it, Maddie. I'm sure it will clear up."

Madeline nods, looking panicked now. "OK. But will you watch the store for me?"

"Sure, babe. I got this."

Madeline rushes out the back and I turn to look at Batty. "Babe? What the hell is going on here?"

"Let me tell you what's going on here, Tomas—"

"So you do remember me."

"Of course I remember you."

I point in the direction Madeline went. "Well, she didn't!"

"She didn't. Because in order to save her—to prevent her from turning into a fucking beast for the next four or five thousand years, thanks to your selfishness—I had to do some pretty complicated backtrack magic to keep her transformation in check. She has no memory of anything before six weeks ago."

"Six weeks? What are you talking about?"

"That's how long you've been gone."

"What?"

Batty sighs, relaxes a little, and his tone changes. "Look, Tomas, I know you think you're in love with her—"

"Think? I'm absolutely certain!"

"Just listen to me. I'm not trying to be a dick."

"Well, you could've fooled me."

"I'm trying to save her, Tomas. Save her from the sentence you placed on her."

"I didn't do anything! In fact, you were the one who brought her back from the dead!"

"She wasn't dead. You can't bring people back from the dead. She was in a transition. Your…" He sighs and runs his fingers through his hair. "You, Tomas. You are the problem."

"What problem? You're not making any sense! She's a dragon!"

"She's one-fifth dragon, Tomas. I've done the genealogy for Eros. He put me in charge of all the magic after the sanctuary crumbled and we escaped to Savage Falls. After you, and Pell, and Pie ruined everything and then just… disappeared." He throws up his hands. "My point is that Madeline should not be transforming. At all. She's one-fifth dragon. It's not even enough to be a chimera."

"So I just, what, made it all up?"

"No. You didn't make it up. She was turning into a

JA HUSS

dragon. But the only reason she was turning into a dragon was because of you."

"What did I have to do with it?"

"Your pheromones. They trigger this change. You can't be around her, Tomas. If you keep coming by here, she will get sick again."

"Sick?" I blink. Is he calling me sick? What I am, is that sickness?

Batty places both hands on my shoulders. "Tomas. I'm not trying to hurt you. I'm simply trying to save her. You cannot be here. You can't see her anymore. You are the trigger."

"What? But I love her!"

"If that's true—"

"What do you mean 'if?' I do! I love her. And before you fucked everything up with your sparkle sand, she loved me too!"

"Maybe that's true. But it doesn't change anything. If you love her, Tomas? Then you will leave her alone. Because if you stay here, you will ruin her."

"You shall call me queen!"

Callistina's rage rocks the room as she slinks out from the corner. She is... disturbing. Even to a monster like me. And it takes me long moments to grasp what I'm actually seeing.

Pie as well. Because her words stutter out like she's still in the middle of processing. "You... what... this..." She looks at me. "What is this?" She's pointing at Callistina.

Callistina bangs a broken broom handle on the floor like she still thinks it's her gem-topped scepter and bellows her command again. "You shall call me queen!"

Pie cowers back, almost hiding behind me. "Please tell me this is an illusion."

"It's not," I murmur under my breath. "We just wish it were."

Callistina is... not a gryphon chimera. She is still human. In every regard. But she has dressed herself up as one like a child playing in an attic on a rainy afternoon. Picking up, and putting on, old clothes and jewels. Fashioning crows from tinfoil and wire.

She is wearing an old fur coat. Spotted leopard, maybe. And it looks like it has the mange. Underneath the coat she's wearing some kind of... tunic... that may, in fact, be repurposed gold draperies. Her belt is a motorcycle chain and there is a ring of grease around her middle, like she actually ripped it off a fucking bike and didn't bother to clean it. She's not wearing any pants but the drapery tunic goes to her knees. On her feet are... I don't know. Wooden blocks? Maybe? Like she's trying to fashion hooves? But she never had hooves, she had paws. So... I'm at a loss for that.

But the icing on the cake that is Callistina are the antlers. A nice rack, too. Twenty-two points. Sloppily spray-painted gold and precariously affixed to her head with some kind of cord that is so tight under her chin, I wonder how she can breathe. They rock and jiggle when she takes a step forward.

She. Has lost. Her fucking mind.

"Oh, my God," Pie whispers. "I did this to her."

"You didn't."

"You shall—"

"Shut up, Callistina!" Eros bellows this from across the room.

Her whole demeanor changes. And when she directs her gaze to the god, I think she's crying. "He said Apis! I heard him! He said Apis!" Then she looks at Pie and wails, "I want to go home!"

Pie almost falls over. I literally have to hold her up. She's already beating herself up over casting her sister into a debt prison, and this... well, this is enough to shock her into a collapse.

"Again," Eros says. "As I was saying." He's in a bad mood now, his eyes darting to Callistina quickly, and his gaze makes her slink back into the shadows. "You ruined Vinca by making Tarq king."

"I don't understand," Pie says. "I don't understand what's happening here."

Eros softens. It's clear he does not hate Pie. Me, yes. Her... there's something going on there. Guilt, maybe? Attraction? I don't think it's actually attraction. But I do think it's fondness.

And this disturbs me. So I redirect the subject back to

Tarq. "If you knew Vinca was gone, why did you send me to get Tarq?"

Eros sneers at me. "Because, obviously, I didn't have any details." He glances down at Tarq's mangled skull, then over to Pie. His gaze locks with hers and they just stare at each other. "And now I do."

"I don't understand." I hate to admit this. It gives off a sense of weakness. But I don't have any choice. I need more information.

"I was locked out of Vinca. Not just Vinca, though. All of the realms but this one."

"Wait." Pie puts up a hand. "Hold on. Let me get this straight." Her tone has changed from confusion to... anger? "You had Lisa grab me from my world, take me to the human realm, then you disappeared, left her in charge of me, and... and you were here the *entire time*?"

Eros says nothing. He doesn't tell Pie to shut up. He just stares at her.

Guilty.

He really does feel guilty about this.

Pie scoffs. Because his silence tells her everything she needs to know. "You're a piece of work, you know that? I fucking hate you. And you know what?" She pauses, like maybe she's trying to talk herself out of what she's about to say, but it doesn't work. "The deal's off."

"Pie." I squeeze her hand.

But she pulls her hand right out of mine. "No. I'm leaving."

And then... that's what she does. She walks out.

CHAPTER THIRTY- PIE

J don't truly understand my anger right now. It doesn't make a lot of sense. This Eros guy is nothing to me. I have zero feelings for him. Why do I care if he's been in this world since he pulled me from my life and left me with Lisa?

I don't!

But I do. So much. I don't even know where to begin, there are so many feelings inside me right now. And they are all about him.

It has to be because he's an eros. That has to be it. It has to be.

It's just not. That's not what this is. And now my chest hurts, and my eyes are watering, and my breathing isn't working right, and I think I might be having a panic attack.

Over someone I hate. No. I don't even hate him! I have no feelings at all!

The door to the bar bursts open and a hoard of monsters stream through it like they can't get out of that bar fast enough. Something is happening inside. Something between Pell and Eros. Something big.

And I feel terrible about leaving, but I had to get out of there because if I didn't, I was going to burst into tears and I wasn't going to do that in front of the devil.

"Pie?"

I look up and find Tomas staring at me with a worried face.

"Are you OK?"

I want to say yes. I always say yes. I'm fine.

But I'm not.

And then I'm crying. For no reason at all, I'm crying.

Tomas folds me into a hug, holding me tight and rubbing my back as I sob and snot all over his shoulder. He doesn't even ask what's wrong. He just lets me get it out. He lets me get lost. He lets me get it under control.

He lets me pack it all back up and tuck it away.

And once that's done, I step back, wipe my eyes, and sniffle. "Thank you."

"You're welcome. What happened in there?"

I look over my shoulder at the door to the bar, sad all over again. "I don't know." I'm sniffing like crazy. "I'm not sure."

"Why are you crying?"

"I don't know that either."

Tomas nods. Like he understands. And the funny thing is, I think he does.

"Did you find Madeline?"

"I did."

"You did!" I perk up. Life is getting better. Finally, someone gets good news. "Where is she?"

"In the feed store. With... Darrel."

"Darrel?" I'm just about to ask who Darrel is when it hits me. "Oh, my God. You don't mean—"

But Tomas nods. "It seems we've been gone six weeks, and in that time, Madeline has turned back into a human."

"Really? Well, that's great. Right?"

"It's wonderful." He smiles. "It really is. There is no happiness in being a dragon."

He's still smiling on the outside as these words come out, but maybe it's me, or maybe he's showing me more of himself, but for the first time I can see all the unhappiness just below his surface.

And I think this is why I love Tomas so much.

He's the bright light in the never-ending darkness.

He's the ray of hope in the face of doubt.

He's found a way past the bad stuff but it comes with a price. And that price is hitting him on the head right now.

"What happened, Tomas?"

He shrugs and looks over his shoulder at the feed store. "She's better off without me."

"What? No! That can't be true. You're... you. You're—"

"Me." He meets my gaze and shakes his head. "I will ruin her, Pie. If she stays with me, I will ruin her. Because I'm the whole reason she's changing into a dragon. I do that to her. Just being around her is a curse. And I love her, you see. So I must walk away now. Because I don't want her to be a dragon. I don't want anyone to be a dragon. Not even me."

"Oh, Tomas." And now I'm fucking crying again. I pull him into a hug and we just hold each other like that for a good long time.

The only reason we pull apart is because the door to the bar opens and Jacqueline comes out.

She stops when she sees me, her face all crinkled up in confusion. She looks me up and down, like she's seeing me for the first time. Like she didn't even know who I was inside the bar. Like she was under some kind of spell, and now she's not. "Pie?"

I put on my happy face. Because that's what I do. "Surprise!"

Jacqueline looks around the town. There are hundreds, maybe even thousands of monsters here. All the prisoners—I don't even know what that number is. Plus the fifty we brought back. Forty-nine, actually, since Frecks is dead. And the nymphs. This is when I notice Nysta standing across the street, glaring at me.

I want to tell her I'm sorry, but Jacqueline starts talking. "You're one of them."

It's not a question. I take my gaze off of Nysta and look Jacqueline in the eyes. "I am. Not this, though. Actually, I'm not sure what kind of monster I am. I just know I'm not like you."

"What?" Jacqueline is incredulous. "Not like me? Sister from another mister. Come on. We're peas in a pod, Pie."

I smile, then laugh at that old saying. But even as I'm laughing, I'm thinking of Eros. He's not my father. He's just some jerk of a god who kidnapped me for nefarious purposes and then abandoned me with a trashy woman who maybe even did her best, but still fucked everything up. "I don't know what to say to you."

Jacqueline's smile falters. "I don't know what to say to you, either. I feel like I just walked out of a cloud."

"I think Eros shot you with an arrow, or something."

She makes a face and looks at the door to the bar. "Is that what he did?"

"I don't know for sure. But you looked pretty out of it when you were in there with him."

"You were in there?"

I nod.

She winces. "This place is weird." Then she gets a look of panic on her face. "Oh, shit!" She puts her fingers on her tongue and whistles. Loud. The way people do in movies. She once spent an entire week trying to teach me that trick. I never really got the hang of it.

Then the door to the diner opens and the teenage boy who was helping her change the tire comes out, holding it open for the other kids. Jacqueline rushes down the street to meet them and they hug. And I'm jealous. Of her and them. Because if one gets to choose a mom, you could do a lot worse than Jacqueline Larue. She might be a little crazy, but she is loyal. Like a lioness. And she will fight to the death for you.

"Well," Tomas says, sighing. I think he's envious of that little family reunion going on as well. "What's the plan?"

"The plan?" I shrug. "Pell offered Eros a door and a ring. But I told him the deal was off, so... I don't know. Are you coming home with us?"

"Dear girl, where else would I go?"

"I still think we should go through with it. Regardless of what kind of deal is being brokered inside."

"Little Pressia. The oracle. You would've liked her, Pie."

"I think you're right."

"Well, let's put out the offer and round up the takers."

Tomas turns, and with a single word—"Listen"—the whole town stops. I'm talking silence. Like the fucking satyrs and wood nymphs actually pause. Even Jacqueline turns around to watch Tomas.

"Damn, Tomas, I didn't know you had a voice like that."

"I don't like to use it. It's magic, you know. Bad vibes all around. But I would like to end this now. And, well, nothing really matters anymore, so who cares."

I hate seeing him like this.

"My good monsters," Tomas says, "and lovely wood nymphs. We have an offer for you..."

As he's explaining the details of the doors, Jacqueline comes over to me with her stolen kids. "Does the offer pertain to us?"

"I don't think you want to do that, Jacqueline."

"Why not?"

"The doors, they don't lead here. To this world, I mean. I'm sure there's a way to get here, from there, using like... bus transfers—which are hallways in our world. But the truth is, even if I knew how to do that, I can't go with you." I frown. Deeply. "I won't be with you."

"I don't want to go."

"You don't?"

"No." She shoos the kids away, telling them to go find a

spot in the truck with the monsters, who are now piling in it to go back to Saint Mark's. Reluctantly, they do this. And then Jacqueline turns back to me. "I just want the kids to go."

"It's not the same world, Jacqs."

She smiles at the old nickname. "They don't want this world. They don't belong in this world, either. They need a little magic, Pie. A lot, actually. You know what I mean?"

Sadly, I do know what she means.

Jacqueline and I have only talked about our pasts once. We were seventeen, we were drunk and pretty high, too. And we had just gotten in a fight on the street with a bunch of guys who may or may not have been planning on doing horrible things to us.

But you don't mess with Jacqueline Larue. She pulled out a knife, started flashing martial arts hands, and she only had to cut one of them to make them all go away.

We were staying in an abandoned building because our foster mom had locked us out until morning. It wasn't true winter, but it was freezing. So we were all hugged up together in a corner, sharing our coats, and body heat, and a bottle of Mad Dog.

And then she just opened her mouth and her story came pouring out.

I didn't say a single word. Not one. I hugged her and listened.

She didn't want my sympathy. Or my opinion.

And even though I couldn't give her my whole story back—because at that point, I didn't even remember most of it—I gave her the bullet points. Not including Pia. I wasn't telling anyone about Pia by this time.

So what she just told me, without telling me, is that these kids are just like us. And they need a frickin' happy ending.

I think I can do that.

Maybe my life is just fucked 'till the end.

But I think I can save these kids from the same fate.

stare at the door where Pie just disappeared while the monsters—still hiding in various places out of sight—begin to murmur.

"Enough," Eros bellows. "Monsters. Get out!"

They scurry after Pie. It takes a little while to empty the room, but eventually the last monster disappears back out to the street.

Everyone, with the exception of Jacqueline, that is.

Eros gets up from his throne, walks across the room—right past me without even making eye contact—and goes behind the bar. I turn to watch him as he grabs a bottle of Blanton's Special Edition, two glasses with ice, then comes back around the bar and settles himself at a table in front of the now-empty stage.

He points to the second glass as he pours his drink. "Come on. Let's do this deal like gentlemen. You've earned it."

"I've *earned* it?" I want to slap his fucking nose off his face. "How condescending, how—"

"Stop, Pell." Eros actually huffs. "I'm not insulting you. I'm merely pointing out that you are a godling in the presence of a god. And while you might think we're equals—and in some ways, we are—we're really not. So please. Have a fucking seat and a drink on me so we can get through these negotiations and be on our way."

I take a moment to parse all these words and here is

where I land: He's tired. As am I. And he's not losing. But I'm not losing, either. So we're at an impasse and maybe it's possible that we can come to an agreement where we both get what we want.

I walk over, sit down, and point to the glass. "Pour."

He does this. And I sip. We both sip. I really like this whiskey. Plus, it reminds me of Pie now, and our date—at another version of this very bar, in fact—when things were much simpler.

We're a few sips in when Eros finally gets to the point. "Do you know who you are?"

I look him in the eyes. "The son of Ptah."

"Your mother was Venus."

I blink at him, confused. "But—"

"That's right." Eros takes a sip of his whiskey, looking away from me. "We're half-brothers."

"But that's not possible. A godling is only half-god."

"A godling meant for *breeding*"—his gaze returns to me— "must be full-blooded. But you were not conceived, you were engineered. There was no love between Ptah and Venus because… it's just science. You were not born from her womb, you did not suckle on her breast, you were not raised as one of us."

"Because I was expendable."

Eros points at me. "That. But." Now he smiles. "You beat them all, didn't you?"

"Did I?"

"You're still here. You've never produced a godling. I think that's a win." His face darkens a little. "You know where Pressia is, don't you?"

"No. I really don't. But I do know where she *was*."

"Where?"

"In my sanctuary. On another plane, though. Some… in-between realm. I have literally not seen her since the night before the called-off wedding. But I have read her books."

"What books?" He leans forward in his chair.

"In my apothecary."

"At Saint Mark's?"

I want to lie here. I want to tell him that they're gone with the rest of it. But I don't care about the books. I'm so done with this history. "Yes. At Saint Mark's."

"Are they still there?"

"Yes."

"Can I have them?"

"What do I get?"

"What do you want?"

I think about this. I look at my drink. Take a few sips. Contemplate. Finally, I say, "I would like you to apologize to Pie."

Eros laughs. "What?"

"You heard me. I would like you to apologize to Pie. And I would like you to mean it."

He and I stare at each other. Then he says, "I'm a god, Pell. I can give you lots of things. And this is what you ask for?"

"I don't need your gifts. I can make my own fortune. But what I can't do is fix the fact that you ruined her life. That you left her with that shitty mother of hers—who abandoned her, by the way—"

"I knew that."

"If you knew that, then what the actual fuck?"

He and I have another little staring contest. But he breaks away first. Then he stares into the shadows for a good long while. I think Callistina is still lurking in there, but I'm not really sure.

He stares at the shadows so long, I start to get impatient. "You have an answer and don't want to spit these words out, or you don't have one and you would prefer to remain in denial? Which is it?"

He looks back at me. "In order to get what I wanted from

her—which is her magic, Pell. I needed her magic. In order to get that, I would've had to kill her."

"What?"

"That's how you steal magic. This is how the gods get their power."

"I thought they wanted a godling?"

"They did want that godling. She would've had that child by the time she was twelve. Then she would've been killed for her power and... well, you don't want to know the rest because it's the Cult of Saturn and—"

"Yeah." I put up a hand. "Just stop there." Saturn worship is infamous for child sacrifice.

"I was going to do that too. Not the godling, of course. I would've needed Tarq. And after my little stunt at the House of Fire, they put him in the palace at Vinca and gave him Callistina. They have produced many children—"

"I don't care about this shit."

"Well, you should. Because Pie's power is a once-in-a-life-time opportunity. You're driving the gods crazy, Pell. You know that right?"

"No."

"Saturn. How many times has he broken into your sanctuary?"

"Once."

"Once?" Eros laughs. "Who do you think all those care-takers were?"

I make a face. "All of them?"

"All of them."

"How is that possible? I thought they were all eros?"

"They were. My people, of course. But he's powerful. It's an easy thing to possess a half-breed eros. He corrupted every single one of them. Why do you think they never just... pointed to the gate and doors where your stupid curse was written?"

"Huh. Wow. But... why? Why did he go through all that? Why didn't he just kill me?"

"I'm sure he tried. Probably thousands of times. But that stupid curse of yours—probably in combination with mine, since they literally happened simultaneously—was very protective. And, of course, he was waiting for Pie to show up. He knew you and Pie were in the same world, but not the same time. So he just had to wait it out, didn't he? The time-line is super fucked up."

"Yeah, I've heard. So what?" I'm talking to him, but also Pressia. Because she practically ordered me to set this right in that spelling. And I'm not sure I need to listen to her. I'm not sure I need to listen to any of these people.

"Since your meddling caused it, you need to fix it. You and Pie, of course. You need to go back and take those monsters with you."

I already know this, of course. But now that I get a conversation with someone who is actually in the know, I feel like asking questions. "We go back, and then what happens? They just get to kill us?"

"It's your fate, isn't it?"

I shake my head.

"She's gonna die anyway, Pell. You both are. And if you get to your end by cheating...well." He throws up his hands. "Cheaters never win. Not in the end."

"I'm not cheating."

"Your whole life is one long cheat! You've spent thousands of years using the magic of that sanctuary to *cheat*."

He's right. I know he's right. But this feels like an extra loss.

"You won't have to live through it, if that's what you're worried about. It will just... be over."

I don't even have words. I just huff.

"You will say your goodbyes—you, and Pie, and that dragon of yours—and you will walk through a door, and

441

when it closes, it's done. Everything is fixed. You already know this is your path forward. You came here demanding that I allow you to take the monsters home. It's a good first step, but they're just innocent bystanders. You. Pie. The dragon. You three are the guilty parties."

"What's Tomas got to do with anything?"

Eros smiles big. "He's your real caretaker."

I will need to think about this revelation. For like… maybe a lifetime. But later. "You keep saying 'we.' But you're not going to set this right, even though it was your fault too. You did that spell when I did mine. It was you who fucked things up, not me. And you took Pie! You brought her here."

"It was us. I already said that. I asked you what you wanted and you said an apology. And for your information, I have been paying my penance for my cheat."

"How?"

"By staying here in this human realm."

"Big fucking deal."

"I can't go back, Pell. I've been banished. You've seen my bloodline. It's a mess. That poor Madeline." He shakes his head. "A rogue dragon gene. This is the end of me. I'm done. The only way to fix it was to kill Pie and take her power. And I didn't do that. I walked away from her nineteen years ago. I've been living my own version of hell for nineteen years. And she can be mad at me all she wants. I don't care."

But he pauses to sigh here, so he does care.

"I'm not her father. But…" Another pause. "But she sees me as one. She thinks of me that way. At least, in the primitive part of her brain. Lisa isn't a bad person, she was just… in love with an eros and when the love spell wore off, she realized that Pie wasn't even hers. She did the best she could. And I'm sorry about everything that happened to Pie. I really am. I stayed away as much as possible, but every now and then I would drift into her sphere, wondering if I made the wrong choice by not stealing her power. So I saw a little of what was happening, but I was powerless to change it. I would've killed her, Pell. If I had stayed, I would've killed her. And I didn't."

I get up and pace the room, sad and unsettled. "Nothing is what it seems."

"It never is, brother. I'm just going to say one more thing and then…" He throws up his hands. "That's it. The rest is all you."

"Fine. Say it."

"I don't want your door. I mean"—he laughs—"I really, *really* do want your door. But I'm not going to take it. I want those books, too. But I'm not going to make you deliver them."

"Then what do you want?"

"I want to be done. Like you."

"You want to die?"

"Oh, I've wanted to die for millennia. But it's not going to happen, is it? Gods don't die. They simply… fade. I don't know if you've noticed, but I've created my own sanctuary here in Savage Falls. And this is where I will stay. Forever. Fading away."

I'm annoyed. I have already been the cause of my best friend's death, annihilated a whole realm, and sentenced a little girl to a life of something that is beyond my comprehension. Soul-crushing loneliness, at the very least. And now I have to end myself, the love of my life, and my new best friend by sending us back in time to smooth out the bumps in the fucking timeline and he's moaning about some self-imposed imprisonment? "I've got to be honest with you, Eros. I don't feel like I'm winning here."

"Maybe you should have higher expectations of yourself?"

"Why have you been chasing us then? Why the sudden change of mind? You ordered me to bring you Tarq so you could make Pie—"

"Stop." And for the second time tonight, he uses that

voice. But he's not trying to stop me so much as stop hearing what I'm saying.

Stop hearing the truth.

Pie is his trigger. He is guilty and he knows it. She is his weakness because he is in debt to her.

And this is the moment when I believe him.

Everything he's said is true.

He just stares at me for many moments. I wait, because I don't know what else to do. Everything is falling apart. Or, in the words of Pressia, 'No horn, or hoof, or magic spell will save the life of the monster Pell.'

Finally, he says, "I have learned things. Recently. Very recently."

"What kind of things?"

"About Pie."

"Like what?"

"Like…" He sighs, then snaps his fingers. "Jacqueline!" I look over at his throne in time to see Jacqueline's head snap to attention. "Get out."

She smiles and nods as she gets to her feet, then floats her way over to the door and does as she's told.

I look back at Eros.

"Jacqueline told me…" He pauses. "I don't know how much you know…" He gives up. "I just changed my mind, that's all."

And now I want to know what Jacqueline knows. "What were you gonna say? Tell me."

"This is Pie's story. Her recent story. And it's not my place to tell you. But I will say this." His whole face softens. "Pie didn't deserve the life she had. You're right about that. Even if Jacqueline had told me nothing about the things that *really* happened to Pie while she was in the human foster system, I would still owe her that apology. And as I said, I saw a little of her life. The outlines of it. But it was Jacqueline who colored in all the shapes."

"What are you saying?"

"I'm saying…" He stares at me. "You know what I'm saying."

"No. Pie's life was bad, but it wasn't—"

"Wasn't it?"

"How could it have been? She's… delightful. People with tragic pasts don't come out the other end delightful."

His only response is a sad, sad smile.

What the hell could've happened to Pie that would alter this god's whole purpose in life once he heard about it?

"I wouldn't ask her about it, if I were you. Either she's purposefully repressed it or she's gotten past it. There is no point in making her revisit."

I can't actually talk right now. I want to call him a liar. Yes, Pie got fucked over. She got shit on. But that's all it was. Just bad luck.

Wasn't it?

"So." Eros ends my train of thought by putting a little voice in his word. "Are we in agreement? You three will return to your tomb, return the monsters who want to go home, and that will be that."

Could he be lying about everything? He could, couldn't he? Might this just be a convenient way to get rid of me? The one guy in the room who might offer up a challenge?

"What happens if we don't do it?"

Eros shrugs with his hands. "It just keeps going, I suppose. You will live, but you will be running."

"From who? You?"

"No. It took me a while, but I have made my final choice. Those gods will never let you be. You got the better of them, both of you. The war will go on. If that's the future you fancy, then by all means, stick around and fight. But you won't be able to hide behind those walls anymore. And Saturn has been practicing his magic in this human realm for thousands of years now. He *will* get you. And then what will he do?

Breed Pie? You? Use Tomas to burn the world? I couldn't imagine the guilt of living with those consequences, can you?"

We stare at each other for a moment. Man to man and eye to eye.

Maybe even… brother to brother.

"Either way, Pell, you will lose everything. The only decision you're making right now is how you want to spend your eternity. Being used by damaged gods to do horrible things? Or at peace."

He shrugs.

Then he gets up from the table, downs the rest of his whiskey, and walks out the door.

*J*acqueline is waiting for my answer. And what can I do but agree?

"OK," I say, breathing out a long breath. "But Jacqueline, you have to go with them. Who will take care of them?"

"I'll take care of them." This comes from the teenage boy. Cecil, I think his name was.

I smile at him, then grab Jacqueline by the arm and turn her away so he can't see us whisper-fight. "You can't just send a bunch of kids into the monster world with a teenager, Jacqs. That's... wrong."

"What are these worlds like?"

"Umm... I mean, they're all different, I guess. They're... I've only been two places through the doors. And both of them were kinda fucked up, to be honest."

"I know a place they can go."

Jacqueline and I both turn in the direction of the voice. It came from Cookie.

"You do?" Jacqueline says, eager.

Cookie looks at me and offers up a small smile. "I do. " Then he directs his attention back to Jacqueline. "It's where I grew up. " He glances at me again. "It's not Vinca. It's not anything special like that. It's just a little village in the countryside. But my people are there and they are good, Pie."

"You know this guy?" Jacqueline asks.

I nod. Cookie and I are staring at each other again. "He took care of me." I grin. "Thank you, Cookie. Do you want me to call you by your real name?"

"I rather like Cookie."

"The Cookie Monster. You're called the Cookie Monster?" Jacqueline laughs. Then the kids do too.

I don't think Cookie gets the joke, but he's cool with it. "If you drop us off in Vinca, it will be a long walk. But—"

"I won't have to drop you off in Vinca, Cookie. I have fifty —well, forty-five-ish doors. I think we can get everyone pretty close to the right place with that many doors."

Cookie looks at the kids. He's a little bit scary when you first meet him. He has very big monster teeth, almost like tusks, but not that pronounced. And they are sharp. He's not older, like Eyebrows. And he's not really handsome, either. He's big, and muscular, and quite hairy. His fur is a very dark mahogany brown just like his eyes, and horns, and hooves. But his skin is a little bit golden and this contrast gives off a little bit of a warm glow-y feeling. Even before pants started gaining in popularity at Saint Mark's, Cookie always wore an apron. Not the bib kind, but just one around his waist. And I always appreciated this about him.

"Thank you, by the way," I say.

"What for?"

"For taking care of me." I look at Jacqueline. "He's very good at taking care of people."

She and Cookie look at each other for a long moment. Then Jacqueline says, "They're independent. Even the little ones. They don't like to be bossed. They like to be asked. They're small, and young, but they have not been children for a while now."

Cookie offers her an understanding smile and then he offers her his hand. Jacqueline's hand is engulfed by Cookie's, completely disappearing into his palm when they shake. But again, this isn't as scary as it could be. When Cookie puts an arm around you, or shakes your hand, or hands you a sack lunch on your first day of work in a brand-new world, it comes off as... just what you needed.

When Jacqueline pulls her hand back, she nods, satisfied.

"But Jacqueline, why not go with them? Where are you gonna go if you stay here?" I ask.

"I'm going back to do my job."

"You stole children, Jacqs. You can't go back to Philly. They'll put you in jail."

"They don't even know those kids are gone, Pie. We were in a bright blue bus on the highway. No one is looking for them. Kids go missing all the time. They just stamp the word 'runaway' on the file, put it away in some storage closet, and never think of them again. I'm just getting started here. I'm—"

But she's interrupted by the opening of the bar door. I turn, expecting Pell.

Instead, I come face to face with *him*.

Cookie is already ushering the kids down the street when Eros directs his gaze to Jacqueline first. He's working some kind of magic on her. And it's right there on her face. That adoration.

Eros flicks his fingers at her. "You are... dismissed. Go away."

Then Jacqueline slowly comes back to normal, relaxes, and then blinks and shakes her head. "What?"

"You heard me," Eros growls. "Go. Away."

Jacqueline is confused, still recovering from the draw of his presence, which is in conflict with the new order to leave. So I step in by touching her arm. "Go put the kids in the truck." I glare at Eros as I say this. "We're leaving."

This new direction is enough for Jacqueline. She nods and follows the still-retreating Cookie and kids as they make their way towards the diner.

Then I take a deep breath and prepare myself for whatever comes next. I don't want to talk to Eros, I just want to walk away.

But I can't help myself. I turn and look at him, taking in his wings, and his leather clothes, and his beautiful face. A warm feeling washes over me, and I know that this is his magic. But then he swipes a hand through the air and the feeling disappears.

He clears his throat. "I would like to apologize to you."

"What?" I make a face at him.

"I'm very sorry for fucking up your life."

Is he for real?

"And..." He pauses to sigh. "And if there is anything I can do—"

"There isn't."

He presses his lips together and nods. "OK. Regardless, the offer stands."

My attention is momentarily diverted when I notice that Jacqueline has reached her kids and they are all talking excitedly. The smaller ones are completely enthralled with Cookie, almost jumping up and down with excitement. I know Jacqueline. Maybe we haven't kept in touch like we should've, but I still know her.

"Pie?"

I ignore Eros as I continue to study my friend. She's putting on the brave face. She's excited for those kids, but she's going to miss them.

I turn back to Eros. "You know what I want you to do?"

"Name it."

Wow. Pell must've done some serious negotiating in that bar. Why is this stupid god so accommodating? *Who cares, Pie? Tell him what you need.*

"I want you to..." How do I put this? Eros frowns, but I put up a hand to shut him up before he speaks. "I want you to... bless her." I nod my head in the direction of Jacqueline. "You manipulated her."

"As one does," Eros retorts.

"As one does *not*. It's… gross. The way you make people like you, it's gross. It's like you can't get anyone to like you for yourself, so you have to trick them into it. And shooting people with love arrows, that's gross too. You shot me!"

"I'm apologizing!" He's loud and getting angry.

But I don't care. "It's not enough. You're a jerk. You're a bully. And you know what? Worst of all, you're…" I narrow my eyes at him. And the last part comes out as whispered venom. "You're a coward. A deserter. You're. A. *Quitter*."

"Because I quit *you*?" He says this like… like it's just another thing 'one does.'

I don't say anything. Because he doesn't deserve this conversation with me. He hasn't earned my feelings. He hasn't earned my thoughts.

"You can hate me, Pie, if that's what you want to do."

"It is."

"Fine. Hate me. But I'm apologizing. And if you need anything, I will accommodate you."

"Why?"

He throws up his hands. "Obviously, because I'm sorry."

"But why are you sorry? Why this sudden change? You shot an arrow at me to make me fall in love with Tarq, didn't you?"

He presses his lips together again, caught. "That was before."

"Before what?"

"Do you or do you not have a request for me?"

I straighten my back, push out my chin, and growl, "I do."

"Then voice it."

"I want you to bless Jacqueline."

"Bless her how? I don't even know what that means."

"It means, if she needs help, you will be there. It means, if she's sad, you will make her happy again. It means, if she gets a flat tire in the middle of the night, you will drag your ass

451

JA HUSS

out of bed, fly to wherever she is, and fix it. You will bless her. That's what I want. You will make her life a living dream."

"No."

"Yes!"

"No! I don't even like her."

"You shot her!"

"I didn't. I didn't shoot her. It doesn't work like that for me. I can't use the arrows for my own love. It…" He pauses. Looks away. Clenches his jaw. Looks back. "It was a teeny-tiny spell. It wasn't an arrow. She is free to leave and then I am done with her."

"No. You're not. You brought her into this."

"You literally brought her into my town!"

I point my finger up at him. "I brought her to Granite Springs. You made her cross the fog into Savage Falls."

He looks away, caught.

"So I win. You will bless her."

He just huffs air and shrugs.

It's not an agreement, but whatever. I never really thought he'd agree to it. I was just giving it my best shot.

And anyway, the bar door opens and Pell walks through. He looks around, taking in the scene. I look around as well, noticing that we've got several hundred monsters and nymphs taking us up on our offer. The nymphs are already packed onto the flatbed and the rest of the monsters are lined up behind it. Gonna walk back, I guess. Pell yells, "Tomas. Let's go home." Then his gaze finds mine and he smiles, coming towards me with an open hand. I take it and we turn to walk back to the Jeep.

"What happened?" I ask.

"Nothing."

"But the door?"

"He didn't want the door."

"What did he want?"

"Nothing."

"What?" I look over my shoulder at Eros and find him staring right at me. I turn back around, unable to meet his gaze. "Why not?"

"Says he's had a change of heart."

"But—"

"Forget about him, Pie. He doesn't matter anymore."

And that's all Pell has to say about Eros.

Jacqueline and I have a tearful goodbye. She says she will be on her way out of here soon, after she packs up her things in the apartment over the diner. She blows kisses to the small kids, who are sitting in the cab with Tomas, and waves to the older ones on the flatbed with the nymphs.

On the way out of town we have to drive by the bar again. Eros is no longer standing out front, but in the shadows of the open door I think I see Callistina.

I should've offered her a chance to go back, but I couldn't even look at her. That's not my sister. Maybe she was never really my sister. Not in the affectionate sense.

So I just... let her go.

Just like Tomas let Madeline go.

We drive back to Saint Mark's, Tomas following close behind in the truck, the rest of the monsters walking. And when we get to the ruins, we lead them into the tomb and start making lists of where everyone wants to go.

This is when I notice that Nysta is not here either. And for a moment, I almost ask Pell to take me back to town so I can straighten things out with her.

But there's way too much to do and too many other people to worry about, so I just let that go too.

I didn't mean to hurt anyone. I *didn't*.

*AFTER ALMOST AN ENTIRE **day*** of sorting things out, we are finally ready to send people home. The hardest part was putting them all in groups to make it all more efficient. But the part that took the longest was me writing each spelling for each door.

There are lives at stake. So this was important and I took my time.

In the end, we use all the virgin doors but three. Pell puts on the ring, I say the spelling, and after the group walks through the door, Pell takes off the ring, hands it to Tomas, and he puts it in the new chainmail bag.

After the last group walks though, we pause and all three of us kind of monkey-walk in place. Drooping a little. Feeling sad.

Because this is it.

We don't get the happy ending. We don't even get to go home. Because we don't even have homes.

Pell puts up a finger. "I would just like to say… that none of this is our fault. Regardless of what we've done over the years, we didn't ask for this life. We just did the best we could with what we had."

Tomas nods, makes pouty lips. "Wise words, Pell. Wise words."

I don't think I quite understand what we're doing. I mean, I get it. We're walking through the doors and never coming back. It's going to be the end of us and the world we created.

But it hasn't sunk in yet. I'm just on autopilot.

However, I am anxious to get it over with. "Now what?"

"We seal up the bag. Tomas, are they all in there?"

Tomas pats the bag. "All accounted for. Except the three left and the ones already in use."

"Should we take them off and put them in the bag?" I ask, as we all three look at each other.

Pell nods. "We should seal them all up together. There's no way to seal the last three, but we need them to walk through the doors, so"—he shrugs—"that can't be helped."

We slip our rings off and drop them into the bag.

"OK," Pell says. "Now we need to seal it for real. Get ready, Tomas."

"I'm ready," Tomas says.

Pell clears his throat and starts the spell:

"RINGS AND BAGS are hard to tame.
 They must be sealed with dragon's flame.
 Blackened iron, ammolite.
 Nuts and bolts and smote and smite.

I HAVE DONE ALL the steps.
 Take these rings, remove the threat.
 God Portunus, god of keys,
 We beg you for your expertise.

CLOSE THE DOORS, seal them tight.
 Nothing there, all is right.
 Tame the rings, keep them hidden.
 Never once again be bidden."

PELL HOLDS UP THE BAG.

Tomas takes a deep breath and on the exhale, he sends out a little stream of dragon's fire, which doesn't look like fire at all, but liquid. Like water, almost, but red and orange, like it came from a lake in Hell.

The chainmail glows bright yellow in an instant, and then... it just explodes into dust, which slowly falls to the ground and disappears.

We stare at it for a few moments, then look up at each other, knowing what comes next.

"Are we ready?" Tomas asks.

"We didn't write our poem yet."

"Yeah, we need to do that," Pell says. "And we don't want to fuck it up, so a little one-stanza poem won't be enough. We should each come up with one stanza. Then we use the same spell for all of us."

"Combined magic," Tomas says. "Great idea."

"We'll need to walk through at the same time then," I say.

"Yeah." Pell nods.

Then we go silent. Blowing out air, and sighing, and even pacing a little.

Because this is really happening.

We're going to spell ourselves into death.

We're going to end it.

"We're certain this is the only way?" Tomas asks.

I look at Pell, almost pleading with him to come up with an excuse, any excuse, for why we don't need to do this.

But he nods. "Like Eros said, our end is certain. All we're doing is choosing how we get there. It's either this or go to war with the gods. Because they want our magic, you guys. And I don't want to fight anymore."

Tomas and I silently agree.

Pell says, "Pie starts the spell, I'll go second, and then Tomas, you can finish it off. Agreed?"

Again, we nod in silence.

"OK. I'm ready." I say.

Pell nods. "I've got mine too."

"Trust me," Tomas says, "I'll send us out with a bang."

Pell and I both chuckle. Then he comes over to me, kisses me. Touches my face. Strokes my hair and my cheek. Kisses me again.

But he doesn't say anything because we've said all that.

We don't need to say it.

CHAPTER THIRTY-FOUR - PELL

"The end is here, and we are set,
Take us home, remove the threat.
Mistakes erased, forgive our sins,
Let us love, and grow, and win.

One path for each to block the trail,
No more magic doors to veil.
No rings, no crowns, no authority,
A place of peace and forest trees.

Goodbye, my mates. I wish you well,
Grateful to be free from hell.
If we never meet again,
Know that we are always friends."

There's a moment when I think we're not gonna go through with it. It's a hopeful moment.

But it's not real. Because the next thing I know, I'm crossing my threshold...

CHAPTER THIRTY-FIVE - PIE

*T*here is a weird noise in my head. But I can't quite make out what it is because my head is pounding. Like someone hit me with a bat kind of pounding. That's not even an exaggeration. The pain is awful.

The noise becomes a mumble. Like sound underwater.

I listen to it, sleepily, as I try to just... drift.

Then something smacks me and the mumble becomes a voice.

"... dare you! The sacrilege! Who do you think you are?"

I try to open my eyes, but they are not cooperating. Then I get smacked again, and this time, it stings. "Oww!"

"Wake up! Get up! You do not belong here!"

"Tell me something I don't know, lady."

Whack, whack, whack.

I get slapped three more times. Despite my protest, my eyes fly open just in time to see a towering nun aiming a yardstick at me. I cover my face, roll over on the wet stones, and then scramble to my feet "What the hell!"

"Don't you cuss at me, you little Babylonian whore!"

"Wow." She takes another swing with the stick and I skirt around her and take off running.

She yells after me, but I just keep going, my heavy combat boots thunking on the pavement as I make my way over to the chapel parking lot where I left my Jeep last night.

Ah, last night. It's all coming back to me. The Halloween party, the Jell-O shots... oh, God. I can still taste those. I don't remember passing out, but… I'm easy. I go with it. At least I didn't wake up in some strange dude's bed.

Always a bright side.

The air is crisp and fall-y. And the wind is blowing red and gold leaves everywhere. Maybe Pennsylvania is not the best place to live in the world, but you gotta love it in the fall. It's all very postcard.

When I get to the Jeep, I snag the parking ticket off the windshield, get in, stuff the ticket in the glovebox, and then grab a bottle of aspirin. I fish through my trash bags in the back seat until I come up with an unopened water bottle, pop those aspirins, and then guzzle the whole thing and let out a breath.

"Well." I start the Jeep. "What will today bring?"

You just never know.

But it's almost always fun to find out.

"Oooh!" I smile. Because I suddenly remember what the plan was yesterday and why I'm out here in the middle of nowhere.

I'm heading to my BFF's house in Toledo where I will beg to sleep on her couch. It's going to be so great to see Jacqueline again.

I'm already on the road when I look down at the gas gauge. "Shit." I need some. I'm not even really sure where I'm at, but if you just drive long enough there's always a gas station. I've got almost a quarter of a tank, fifty bucks left on my credit card, and gas is only two bucks a gallon these days, so I'm not worried. I definitely have enough cash to drive straight through to Toledo.

Sure enough, just a few miles up the road, there's a highway with a gas station near the on-ramp. I'm humming a song as I pull in, pretty satisfied with my life right now. I'm on the verge of a new adventure. I can feel it. Things are gonna work out in Toledo. Even if I do have to babysit Jacqueline's kids and sleep on her couch, it's all good.

I use thirty bucks to fill the tank and then go inside the gas station to pee and wash my face. It's crowded. And people are looking at me.

This is when I realize that I'm wearing my Halloween costume. Slutty schoolgirl.

I almost snort with the irony since the college I was partying at last night was Catholic.

But I ignore all the stares and just slip into the bathroom. I pee, then wash my hands and stare at the mirror. I screw up my face, still staring at the mirror.

On most mornings, after an all-night party, I would mostly be concentrating on how shitty I look. The bags under my eyes, the pale face, the messy hair—which has leaves in it. No wonder people were staring.

But on this day I'm focused on something else. Because someone has written a poem on the mirror.

I read it out loud:

"No cakes, or cookies, only Pie.
Moths and fireflies in the sky.
You must go back, you must relive,
Accept, and honor, and forgive."

Wow. Someone had a good time last night. Then I snort and grab a paper towel.

But then… wait a minute.

I look back at the mirror and read the poem again, just as someone knocks loudly on the door. I just stare at it, confused, almost… dizzy.

I walk back over to the sink, lean my hands on it, and look at those words. Is it weird that my name is inside this poem?

It's not, right?

Just a coincidence.

More pounding on the door. And I'm just about to open my mouth and shame them for doing that when I suddenly see an eight-year-old girl in my head, standing in that grungy hallway outside the bathroom door, crossing her legs because she needs to pee so bad, she might wet herself.

I go over to the door, throw it open, and just stare down at her. "How did you get here?"

She pushes past me and then closes the door behind her, shoving me out of the way.

How did I know that?

That was weird, right?

"Anyway." I sigh, then straighten my girls out inside my red, leather bustier—"Ow." Something is poking my boob.

I reach into my bustier and find a piece of paper. I pull it out, expecting it to be someone's phone number, but I find a picture instead.

I stare at it, my head cocking to the side like a confused dog.

It's a picture of me. It's actually one of those photobooth things with a row of different poses and it's been ripped in half. Like two people wanted to keep it, and this was the answer.

I'm sitting in some man's lap and we're... wow. I click my tongue. He's super-hot and we're kinda sexy. But what the hell am I wearing?

It looks like a prom dress. A very outdated, ugly prom dress.

I look down at myself, and nope. This is not adding up.

Then I hear a song on the gas station sound system. Joan Jett's signature piece. And then, suddenly, a memory of last night flashes through my head.

Me and this guy. Dancing and kissing.

But... I glance up, scanning past a bulletin board on the opposite wall. Past the lost dogs and free kittens. Past the business cards for random services. That's not what I did last night. I wasn't wearing that dress, I didn't meet that guy.

My gaze lands on a flyer. I reach across the aisle and snatch the piece of paper off the bulletin board. It's that poem from the bathroom and it's got another verse or whatever underneath.

Waking up is never smooth.
This time you get to choose.
Which direction, you will know,
Once you forgive, and love, and grow.

"What the fuck?" I look around, wondering if someone is doing this.

Doing what, though?

I don't understand what's happening. I stick the picture of me back into my bustier, crumple up the paper from the bulletin board, and I'm walking out, ready to toss it into the trashcan, when I don't.

I keep it in my tightly-balled-up fist and get in my Jeep instead.

That's when I see the writing on the outside of my windshield.

I get back out and stand in front of my Jeep, scanning the words.

One last chance, the choice is yours.
You have your ring, you have your door.

"What?" I look down at my hand and sure enough, there's a ring on there. A ring I do not recognize. I look back up at the words on my windshield.

Leave the magic, leave the curse
Live your life, it won't get worse.
But he is waiting in a place you know,
Where moths have eyes and fireflies glow.

A horn honks and I look up at a man in a car parked behind me. "Are you done, lady? I need gas!"

"Sure." I nod and smile, then get in my Jeep and pull out of the gas station, thoroughly confused.

Someone is playing a trick on me.

That's the only answer.

The only one, Pie?

I pull over on the side of the road, needing a moment to pull myself together. What could it all mean? I should've written that first verse down because—

But then the words are spilling out of my mouth:

"No cakes, or cookies, only Pie.
Moths and fireflies in the sky.
You must go back, you must relive
Accept, and honor, and forgive."

I suddenly have an urge to make a phone call. I fish though my purse, find my phone, scroll through my contacts, and before I can even make sense of this urge, I press send.

She answers on the first ring. "Pie?"

"Mom?"

I hear a breath of relief on the other side. "I tried calling you yesterday. Halloween. You always did like Halloween."

For a moment, I am filled with rage. I don't actually have any particular fondness for Halloween. It's just another stupid fucking holiday where I was always reminded that I had no family. Oh, good old Mom is still here, obviously. But she put me in foster care when I was nine. Said I was crazy because I had an imaginary friend. Who I grew out of two years later, so way to fucking hang in there, Mom.

I want to say all that. I've said it before. I don't even know why she keeps trying. I'm not interested in having any kind of relationship with this woman.

But my head still hurts, and my mouth tastes like Jell-O shots, and I'm wearing yesterday's clothes, and someone is fucking with me using poems, so, for reasons that are mostly a mystery, I sigh and say, "I just wanted to let you know I'm OK."

And in this moment, my world goes black.

I sit in my Jeep, inside emptiness, and then, just as suddenly, there is light.

I watch it grow.

And I remember.

You must go back, you must relive. Accept, and honor, and forgive.

I don't have to go back to where it all started.

I only have to go back to the place where I was *tricked*.

And that was in that gas station when I saw that flyer.

Because I never had a real home and that's all I've ever wanted. And I don't have to love her, or spend time with her, or even have any thoughts at all about my mother.

I just need to forgive her.

Because that is the only way to start over.

So after I end the call and pull back on to the road, the choice to be cursed is all mine.

CHAPTER THIRTY-SIX - PELL

*T*here *is a moment of nothing* and then there is a moment of realizing there is nothing.

It's kind of like waking up from a deep, dreamless sleep. One moment you are still, and quiet, and part of infinity, just drifting. And in the next, you are... you. And not only are you you, but all that comes with being you.

I open my eyes and stare up at a sky the color of a bruise.

There is an ache in my heart when I see this sky. Because it is not the sky of Saint Mark's, which is always a perfect summer blue.

A red leaf blows past me. Then a gold one, and a brown one. And more and more.

I sit up, looking around.

Trees and grass. But that's it. I'm on a hillside looking down at an empty field.

A flock of geese go over me, honking about their journey. The wind blows the trees and more leaves go tumbling by.

And I'm cold. Naked. But... "At least I'm not human." I mutter this out loud because I'm the only one here and I don't want to think about that yet.

I get my hooves under me and stand up, turning slowly in a circle and then stopping when the lake comes into view.

There is no cottage. I turn the other way, find where the cathedral should be, and sigh. There is no cathedral, either. There is no wall, there are no tombs—nothing. It is just a hillside meadow surrounded by woods.

"If this is death, fuck. You."

More geese go overhead. More honking.

I have no idea what to do next. Go look for Granite Springs? Or—Savage Falls?

I'd rather be alone.

Am I in the human world?

What am I supposed to do here?

Not that there are many options. I'm fucked no matter what.

So I just turn slowly in place trying to choose a direction. It occurs to me that the meadow on this hillside is much smaller right now than it was the last time I saw it. And the reason for that is because the woods are bigger.

Wider, actually.

I squint my eyes, looking past the trees as I turn, and my gaze lands on a cabin.

My hooves are already heading in that direction when I mutter, "Please don't let there be a witch living in there."

Unless her name is Pie, of course. Who—also of course— is not a witch.

I smile as I think that last part. She was so sure she was not a witch. "Joke's on you, Pie."

But then my smile falls because I know Pie is not in there.

This is not a place for Pie because this is not a time for Pie.

She doesn't live in this 'now'. She lives at some far, far point in the future.

The cabin is crudely made of logs and looks lived-in. I'm debating whether or not I should stay, or just keep going into the woods, when I walk in and realize this is my cabin. I know this because it's not actually a cabin, it's my smithy.

All brand-new and shiny just like the day I built it.

I walk back to the door and look out one more time, kind of hoping Jonas is around. He was my caretaker when I built this place.

And I don't even care if Jonas was Saturn in disguise, I would gladly spend my purgatory years with him, possessed by a god or not.

But there is no Jonas.

So I just close the door.

THIS IS how I spend my time:

Wake up, start a fire, stoke the coals, put some iron it in, shape the iron.

Eat breakfast—I'm so sick of rabbit.

Shape more iron.

Bury the coals to keep them warm for tomorrow.

Eat dinner. I hate rabbit.

Sleep.

Eventually, I run out of iron and switch to bricks. I've never really been a mason, but how hard can it be? There's a new trading post that popped up while I wasn't looking and I put on pants for this trip—because Pie. Then I smile about that the whole time I'm negotiating with a man from Pittsburgh to deliver the bricks to my new sanctuary.

No one notices that I'm a satyr. Not because they're blind or stupid, but because I'm magic and I now know how to spell.

I build a wall. Not a huge countryside-encompassing wall, just enough to connect my two sets of gates. One set by the new dirt road in front of where the cathedral used to be, and another set down in front of the lake where I am now building a cottage.

I do not put a spell over the top of the gates, but I do make a place for one.

And once all that is done, I just… wait.

And hope.

And give up hope.

Then hope again because it's all I've got left.

She doesn't come.

Not even when the new century does.

So then I just go to sleep and stop getting up.

ere's my problem:
There is no such town as Granite Springs.
There is no such town as Savage Falls.

It's just as Jacqueline said when I found her on the side of the road. These places don't exist. Except that I know they do. I just can't see them.

I try out all kinds of spellings over the course of the day. I'm a damn good speller. All of my previous life with Pell has come back to me over the hours. I know I'm good at this. I know I can do it.

But none of them work.

I don't think I'm close enough. I need to find the road. I need to find the gates.

But instead I have to find another gas station because I've used up an entire tank of gas.

And I'm just coming out of this gas station, my credit card now maxed out, when I realize that this is the gas station that Pell and I came to after my disastrous date with Russ Roth.

I stand in front of my Jeep—mouth open, eyes looking past the highway on-ramp—and realize I know how to get home from here.

I drive past three times before I actually see them. The gates.

It's a little bit confusing because there's no Saint Mark's Sanctuary. In fact, these are not my gates. This is not my wall. There is no curse over the top. No walking gate, either.

But these are the only gates on that whole road. Of this, I'm sure. I've checked.

So even though I don't recognize any trees, I know these are my gates. And if I could just make them open, I will find him.

Even if he is nothing but bones, I don't care.

I just need to find him.

So I take a breath, call on the hallway gods for help and then tack Pressia's name on at the last moment out of desperation, and say—with sudden confidence like this is the whole point of everything—

"A horn, a hoof, an eye, a bone.

A man, a girl, a place of stone.

They fight, they fall, they rise again.

A brand-new dawn, a new domain."

It's the second curse that appeared over the doorways after I banished Saturn from the sanctuary.

But it's not a curse.

It's my answer.

And when I pull those gates open and rush through, my hooves dancing across the grass as I shout his name, I cry happy tears when he runs over the top of the hill towards me

Because he's not bones.

He's not dead.

And I'm not either.

And this *is* the whole point of everything.

EPILOGUE - TOMAS

*A*s soon as **I pass across the threshold** of my door I know where I'm going.

Home.

And when I step out into my familiar, but at the same time unrecognizable, dungeon it all becomes clear.

I smile at first, then chuckle, then guffaw as I take in my wall of doorknobs. They glow a soft pink color and they are neatly lined up in the stones. Each one has a silver tag above it. And on each of those tags are stamped places and times.

Destinations that lead to star-crossed lovers.

But the doorknobs don't simply line one wall, they are everywhere. Hundreds—no, thousands—no, tens of trillions —or even more than that, who knows.

All the places and times belong to me.

I am not the dragon of Saint Mark's—I'm the timekeeper.

Oh, the irony.

Because in this last iteration of my life I *am* the hallways.

A slow clap emanates from a dark corner. And then his eyes glow. "Well done, good sir. Well done."

"Thank you." I take a little bow. "Would you like some tea and biscuits? I'm famished."

"As you should be. Two thousand years. That was a long game, friend."

I walk over to my small kitchen, fill up the tea pot, and put it on the flame. "Indeed. It really was. Pie and Pell were

475

sweet, but a little bit slow to catch on. Still, they made it. Happy endings are my specialty."

"Your *penance*, you mean?"

"You say potato, I say tomato."

My friend chuckles and gets up, walking over to me with a little bit of hunger in his eyes. And those eyes really are something. The greenest green ever imagined. "How *do* you do it?"

Eros is quite possibly the most spectacular specimen of a god that was ever created. Even I am not immune to his charm. I would do very dirty, *dirty* things with him if I wasn't on the opposite side of the game.

But I am nothing if not in control. "One hand tied behind my back, my friend. That's how I play. I like the challenge. And still, even with no memory—even playing as a *dragon!*"—I have to pause to laugh—"I still find them all a happy ending when it's over. I am unbeatable!"

He's very close now. One hand goes to my hip, his eyes burning into mine, his chest pressing forward, as he leans in to me like we are going to kiss.

We are not going to kiss.

Though, to be honest, one day, when this is all over, I might take him up on a future provocation.

But not right now. I tap the pad of my finger gently against his chest. "You know what I find funny?"

"Tell me, you evil, evil thing." He whispers these words, his voice seductive and low.

And yes, his attraction is godlike. I pity his targets. They have no chance at all.

"That you had a direct route to Pressia and you gave it up. Pell could've taken you to her. At the very least, he could've given you the books. You don't need to seduce me to get what you truly want, Eros." I shrug my shoulders. "Well, you *didn't*. Now that I have produced *yet another* happy ending, Pell is off limits."

"I let you win."

"Did you?" These words come out as a laugh.

He places the back of his hand on my cheek, stroking my face as he looks into my eyes. "I *wanted* you to win."

"You threw a mutant dragon-girl at me, Eros. Nice play. However, I feel it went against the rules."

He *tsks* his tongue and steps back, his voice back to normal now. "Not so. Totally within the rules."

"I feel otherwise and I will be filing a complaint. If it wasn't for Darrel—"

"Fuckin' Darrel," Eros growls. "I don't like him. And now I'm stuck with him. Thanks for that, by the way."

"No one likes him. He's here for punishment because he impaled a *donkey*! Who does such a thing? That is true evil."

"And you gave him the girl?"

"I'm actually quite tired of him. This is his, what, fifth round in purgatory? He's never going to get out of my hair if I don't push him along."

Eros shakes his head, smiling. "You're going to help him win his game because you're *tired* of him? I will take that win as my own, my friend. I will fuck that little relationship up with a vengeance."

I wave a hand in the air. "Have it. I'm out."

"So you really don't have any feelings for Madeline? She's quite cute. And good, too. So sweet."

My tea kettle begins to whistle, a perfect excuse to turn away so he can't see my face.

Madeline. And those eggs.

I was dreaming of another life when we were together. One where I wasn't responsible for millions of deaths and atrocities. One where I wasn't locked in a prison of my own making. One where I got the happy ending instead of making them come true for others.

I turn the flame off, put some leaves into an infuser, and breathe in the scent of peppermint as I pour water over

477

them, finally answering his question. "None. No feelings what. So. Ever."

"Liar."

I shrug. I am the god of happy endings.

This is my eternal punishment for the life I lived in my human form.

It could be worse. I could be the god of unhappy endings. That really would be terrible.

But the catch is—there is no happy ending for me. Or Eros, for that matter. He is the god of love, yet he will never love. Not truly.

This is how punishment works. You cannot have your heart's desire.

I understand that he told Pell he had a change of heart because of how he hurt Pie. How he ruined her life. He didn't want his door, he didn't want those books—blah, blah, blah.

But that's not why he refused. Eros and Pressia have been battling for centuries. She's much, much smarter than him. And good, too. A true, pure soul. She is not a part of our punishment—she doesn't even live in purgatory. She's not in our game, either. She is the oracle of love.

She predicts the soulmates and it's Eros's job to fuck them up with those nasty arrows of his.

They are true enemies. Just like he and I.

He refused because he knows how it will end.

With heartbreak.

His heartbreak.

Pressia and I work together often, as our duties intersect in many ways as well. But we are not enemies. She often helps me achieve my goals because our goals are the same.

Eros wants her. Has always wanted her. From the moment they met, he has wanted her.

I don't think he's admitted that he loves her and she would *never* admit she had any feelings at all for him. But like it or not, they are bound to each other as opposites.

Just like he and I.

I turn to face him. "Well." I take a sip of my tea, smack my lips with delight. "Who will you go after now, hmm? Who's the next target?"

Eros directs his gaze over to my wall of doorknobs. Lets himself get caught up in their slightly pulsating glow. "You lead, I follow."

"I'm taking a small vacation."

"To do what?"

"Relax. Drink tea. Eat biscuits." *Forget Madeline, and Darrel, and the eggs, and the future I could've had if I were to ever manage to end this punishment, and get out of this place, and get my happy ending.* But I don't say that last part out loud.

Eros sighs. "Well, I'm out of here, I guess."

"You're going back to your new little town? Gonna fuck up humanity with the arrival of magic monsters?"

"Why not. Sounds fun, doesn't it?" He shoots me another one of those seductive looks. "Why don't you join me?"

I allow myself half a grin as I picture myself amongst those monsters in Savage Falls and a new life with the God of Love. One where I don't fight my punishment, but embrace it instead. Write a new story. Write a new ending, as well. Give in to all those carnal urges and just... be evil forever.

But this is mostly just his magic affecting me, so I shake myself out of it. "Maybe one day."

This widens his smile. "Well, that's a new answer." He tips an imaginary hat at me, then turns towards the stairwell that will take him up to the main part of my cathedral and calls out, "You know where to find me."

*I marry **Pie Vita*** on the top of the hill and in the middle of a field of buttercups. We've been here almost nine months and there is no end to our love.

No one officiates the ceremony. No guests come to celebrate. Though, if we wanted these things, we could have them.

There is a world out there beyond our gates, just like there always was.

I already made Pie's ring. And I still have it. I found it in the smithy a few days after Pie came back to me. I didn't even need to write an inscription, either. Because one was already on there.

A story of a monster's curse.
A Book of Debt and a spelling verse.
Blood, and horns, and doors, and trees.
Pie and Pell, forever free.

I never wrote it down because... happenings. But I did write this vow. And it's like the God of Happy Endings knew it was perfect and inscribed it onto the ring for me.

Like a gift.

Pie made me a ring too. I showed her how to use the forge. She wanted to make it very fancy, so it's gold mixed with a tiny bit of copper and silver. And then she spent days heating it up just enough to carve tiny hearts along the inside with her own inscription.

It says:
I make a promise with this ring,
You are my love, you are my king.
Forever we will be together
You are my life, you are my treasure.

THIS MORNING **I get up early** and walk the woods and the fields. It's summer again, and this makes life feel like the old days. The hot sun on my bare shoulders. The green grass under my feet. I don't usually go as far as the front gate. I prefer to stay away from the road just in case someone looks in our direction as they pass by in a car.

But today, there is a piece of paper trash flapping on the outside of the iron bars, so I go over there to release it and throw it away.

It is the front page of a newspaper and the headline makes me hold my breath. Because it says, *MONSTERS ARE REAL!* And the subtitle reads, *An entire town of magical monsters has been discovered in central Pennsylvania. World goes crazy!*

And there he is in all his glory.

A black and white photograph of beautiful Eros standing on top of a building with black wings outstretched, and holding a sign that says, *Come fall in love with us.*

I crumple the paper up in my hand. Not angry, just... not interested.

The outside world can wait.

No god or monster can make us leave
Our time is now I do believe
Forget the sins, forget the past
The happy ending is ours at last.

END OF BOOK
SHIT

Welcome to the End of Book Shit. This is the part of the book where I get to say anything I want about the story. It's never edited so if there are typos, you just need to deal.

What a ride! I'm pretty happy with this series. And a little bit surprised at how it ended up going. Some of it was planned but mostly I just let these characters do what they wanted. And for the most part, they did pretty good.

When I got to the end of Royal Beasts it became clear to me that this was Pie's story more than anyone else. I didn't plan it that way. But I like the ending. And I like where this is going next.

More about that in a bit.

Almost all of the magical stuff in these books about Pie, Pell, and Tomas just kinda came out of nowhere. And I guess if you're a die-hard paranormal reader you have certain expectations for a magical system in books. There is a 'traditional' way to do magical things. I know this. We all know this. But if I'm gonna write a book with magic in then I'm make up something new.

I don't like following the rules. I don't want to write 'on trope', and I don't want to worry about expectations. That's the best part of writing fiction—I get to make it all up.

This is one reason why I love science fiction. There are die-hard SF readers out there too and they are always going on and on about the fucking 'science' in science fiction. Which I can understand. Being trained as a scientist myself I feel like it's important to follow some logical pathway when y you're inventing technology.

But the science is always changing. So a good SF author will think up 'new science' and then come up with a way to make the reader believe it to be possible. That's what I do. I know there are a ton of hard science fiction books out there that go over every detail on how the fucking space travel works (or doesn't) but I can't be bothered with technical details after a certain point. Just give me enough to believe you, author. Right? That's all I need to be a happy reader.

That's how I look at the magic too. It's easier with magic. Although there are a hundred years of previous magical books out there that came before me and—as I have stated—that comes with a certain amount of expectations, I don't want to rehash someone else's magical system, ya know?

How boring.

And again—I'm sure this pisses off some readers.

Don't care.

They can write their own magical book and follow all the rules to their heart's content as far as I'm concerned. This story here is mine and that means I can do it any way I want.

:)

And I kinda love the magic of doors and hallways.

How cool, right? How cool to have a door to another place that you can just step through. It's a little bit Lion, Witch, and Wardrobe. Which I did read as a kid—though I can't remember most of it—but it wasn't an inspiration for this series at all. I just know that everyone loves a fresh start.

Everyone, at some point or another, wants a do-over.

And here's the really important thing—and the reason why we all loved that stinking wardrobe and the hallways and doors in Monsters—we all want that do-over to be instant.

A real 13-Going-on-30 moment, if you will.

One moment we're in our old boring life and poof. The next, we're opening a door and stumbling to our new grand adventure.

Doorways do this.

I think that's why people liked this story. Book one only had hallways and I was pretty surprised to learn that readers loved that idea. I didn't plan those hallways at all. Just a moment of inspiration. But it went over well.

And there was a promise of doorways at the end when Pie was able to enter a whole new world via the tombs.

That was fun in book two. I like going to that new world.

But when I went to start Royal Beasts I knew one thing – that new world was not my story. I know people wanted to go back there. And I also know I left you hanging in this series about what really happened there—but Vinca was not my story.

I'm gonna go back there, but I didn't want to go back there at ALL in this book. I only went back long enough to erase it from the ending. lol I totally did that on purpose.

There's too much there. Way too much to wrap up in a book 3 about Pie, Pell, and Tomas. Because Vinca is about Tarq, and Eros, and Pressia, and Callistina. They need their own story. And they're gonna get one.

The spin-off series is called Savage Falls and book one is called The Savage Rage of Fallen Gods. It will release in the summer of 2023 and then all these characters, and the world of Vinca, will get the story they deserve.

Oh, and Tomas will be there too, of course. His story is far from over.

So if that was pissing you off at the end, there. I just let you in on what comes next. Stay for the ride or get off now, it's up to you. But Vinca was not my story in Monsters.

Pie was my story.

Pell too. And Tomas.

But Monsters was really about Pie and Pie wants nothing to do with Vinca. I wasn't gonna make her go back there. Someone complained in a review for Saints that Pie was focused on stupid stuff while she was in Vinca. But that reader missed the whole Pie story in my opinion.

Pie didn't want to be there. She said it so many times. She did *not* want to be there.

Why should she care about that place when all she wanted to do was go home?

HOME was the point of Pie's story.

And home was Pell and the sanctuary.

It was never Vinca.

Anyway. Back to the doors.

This is gonna get a little esoteric, but what the hell? I like esoteric.

We all want a door. Wouldn't it be nice to have a key to a fresh start and to be able to open that door any time we want?

Well, the truth is, we do have doors. And keys.

It's just that they're not literal things like they are in my fictional story.

You need to make a key before you can use a door.

Here's how you make a key:

You have a goal.

You make a step-by-step plan to achieve that goal.

You follow all the steps.

And at the last step you have a key.

Now, finding a door to use your key can be both easy and hard. It depends on if you're looking for a door or you're going to make your own.

Sometimes just having a key is enough.

You can put out feelers—"Hello? I have a key! Does anyone have a door for me?"

And maybe 50% of the time someone *will* have a door for you. This is good! You made a key and just by having that key you got offered a free door!

Problem is, it's not *your* door, it's theirs. So wherever that door takes you, you're still kinda stuck. Probably a better kind of stuck than when you had no key, but it's not your dream destination.

That's one way.

Or you can just find your own door that fits your key. This one involves a lot of risk. Lots of failure too. Because if finding doors was easy, everyone would have one.

There's two ways to find a door of your very own:

One. Push your key into every door you pass and cross your fingers that it fits.

It's gonna take a lot of doors. Lots of failure this way, but eventually, the odds are fairly good that your key is gonna find a door.

It might be a little lose in the lock, but the door opens, and it goes somewhere pretty close to the place you imagined, so who cares?

OR. Two. You can plan a door that fits your key perfectly.

People who plan and create their own keys and doors more often than not end up where they want to go. The destination might still be a little... not quite what they were expecting, but they created this destination all by themselves. It's kind of like a dream. It's their magical destination.

Did I lose you yet?

The point is—doors are real. They're everywhere. They're invisible to you now because you don't have a key.

Your key is different than anyone else's.

There is no way to *find* a key. There isn't.

You can be born with a key. That's called TALENT.

Or you can make a key. That's called TRAINING or EXPERIENCE.

If someone gives you their door so you can use your key, that's call A JOB OFFER.

If you find your own door through trial and error that's called PERSEVERANCE.

If you make your own door that's called HARD WORK.

If you can get both a key and a door (Talent, training, experience, perseverance, and hard work) regardless of how you got them, they will take you new places.

And the whole point is that DOORS ARE REAL. And everyone can use them if they get a key.

Every once in a whole some people stumble into keys and doors left unattended. This is called an ACCIDENT. :) Accidents are cool. And they can for sure look a lot like a key and door you made yourself, but they're not the same thing.

Still, if you stumble into an accident, ride that fucker until it throws you off. In fact, while you're riding that ACCIDENT, make sure you're using it to get TRAINING AND EXPERIENCE. So that once the ride is over you can still get a JOB OFFER, or make a new door through PERSEVERANCE and HARD WORK.

And now you know what this book is about…

Pie found a key and a door by accident.

This led to a job offer.

Which led to training and experience.

Which led to brand new doors.

It really is as simple as that.

I hope you enjoyed this story and I hope you stick around for the other side. The Savage Rage of Fallen Gods will be a love story staring Eros, Tomas, Pressia, Callistina, Tarq, Madeline, Batty, Nysta, and Jacqueline. (With guest appearances from Pie and Pell).

Thank you for reading, thank you for reviewing, and I'll see you in the next book.

Julie
    JA Huss
    November 3, 2022

ABOUT THE AUTHOR

JA Huss is a New York Times Bestselling author and has been on the USA Today Bestseller's list 21 times. She writes characters with heart, plots with twists, and perfect endings.

Her books have sold millions of copies all over the world. Her book, Eighteen, was nominated for a Voice Arts Award and an Audie Award in 2016 and 2017 respectively. Her audiobook, Mr. Perfect, was nominated for a Voice Arts Award in 2017. Her audiobook, Taking Turns, was nominated for an Audie Award in 2018. Her book, Total Exposure, was nominated for a RITA Award in 2019.

She writes Sci-Fi Romance and Paranormal Romance under the name KC Cross.

www.ingramcontent.com/pod-product-compliance
Lightning Source LLC
Chambersburg PA
CBHW060241030726
47493CB00024B/1450